Really, Your Highness!

Really, Your Highness!

OTHER LOTUS TITLES

AMRITA PRITAM	*The Other Dimension*
ANIL K. JAGGIA SAURABH SHUKLA	*IC 814: Hijacked! The Inside Story*
ARJAN SINGH	*Arjan Singh's TigerBook*
DHANANJAYA SINGH	*The House of Marwar*
E. JAIWANT PAUL	*'By My Sword and Shield'*
E. JAIWANT PAUL	*Rani of Jhansi: Lakshmi Bai*
GANESH SAILI	*Glorious Garhwal*
GERALDINE FORBES (ed.)	*The Memoirs of Dr. Haimabati Sen*
INDIRA MENON	*The Madras Quartet*
IRADJ AMINI	*Koh-i-noor*
J.C. WADHAWAN	*Manto Naama*
JOHN LALL	*Begam Samru*
JYOTI JAFA	*Nurjahan*
KHUSHWANT SINGH	*Kipling's India*
KANWALBIR PUSHPENDRA SINGH	*The Ruse*
K.M. GEORGE	*The Best of Thakazhi Sivasankara Pillai*
LAKSHMI SUBRAMANIAN	*Medieval Seafarers*
LALI CHATTERJEE	*Muonic Rhapsody and Other Encounters*
MAGGI LIDCHI-GRASSI	*The Great Golden Legend of the Mahabharta*
MANOHAR MALGONKAR	*Dropping Names*
MAURA MOYNIHAN	*Masterji and Other Stories*
MUSHIRUL HASAN	*India Partitioned. 2 vols*
MUSHIRUL HASAN	*Knowledge Power and Politics*
NAMITA GOKHALE	*Mountain Echoes*
NINA EPTON	*Mumtaz Mahal: Beloved Empress*
P. LAL	*The Bhagavad Gita*
ROMESH BHANDARI	*Goa*
RUSKIN BOND	*Ruskin Bond's Green Book*
SAVITA DEVI	*Maa . . . Siddheshwari*
SHOVANA NARAYAN	*Rhythmic Echoes and Reflections: Kathak*
SUDHIR KAKAR (ed.)	*Indian Love Stories*
VIBHUTI NARAIN RAI	*Curfew in the City*
V.S. NARAVANE	*Best Stories from the Indian Classics*
V.S. NARAVANE (ed.)	*Devdas and Other Stories by Sarat Chandra*

FORTHCOMING TITLES

CLAUDIA PRECKEL	*Begums of Bhopal*
DHANALAKSHMI FORDYCE	*Purna Ghata*
E. JAIWANT PAUL	*Baji Rao, The Warrior Peshwa*
RALPH RUSSELL	*The Famous Ghalib*
V.G. KIERNAN	*Poems by Faiz*

Really, Your Highness!

Jyoti Jafa

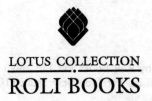

LOTUS COLLECTION
ROLI BOOKS

Lotus Collection

This edition first published 2000
The Lotus Collection
An imprint of
Roli Books Pvt Ltd
M-75, G.K. II Market
New Delhi 110 048
Phones: 6442271, 6462782, 6460886
Fax: 6467185, 6213978
E-mail: roli@vsnl.com
Website: rolibooks.com
Also at
Varanasi, Agra, Jaipur and The Netherlands

ISBN: 81-7436-099-9
████

Typeset in Galliard by Roli Books Pvt Ltd and
printed at Pritha Offsets Pvt Ltd, New Delhi-110 028

Contents

Dedication		vi
Acknowledgements		vii
Historical Note		9
1	The Resident Rolls in	11
2	Tit for Tat	57
3	Elephants Ahoy!	103
4	The Prince of Wales in Princely India	135
5	Horsing Around	169
6	The Viceroy's Visit	205
7	London Escapades	239
8	Maharajahs in Europe	265
9	Paid Back in His Own Coin	293
10	The Jinxed Bride	325
11	Heir(ring) On . . .	347
12	Camels to the Fore	381
13	Merger Muddles	401
	Glossary	429

DEDICATION

To the memory of my Rathor ancestors, who
created such splendour in the sands of that
vast wasteland called Marwar. And to those heir
to their Nutty credo:

Raghu kul reeti sada chali ayi,
Pran jayi par vachan na jayi

+

Ateethi Devo Bhava!

————◆————

Acknowledgements

My heartfelt gratitude to my publisher, Pramod Kapoor, for his extraordinary patience for a deadline which kept stretching—indefinitely!

And to T.S. Narasimhan, the famous producer of R.K. Narayan's *Malgudi Days*, for making me conceptualise this project—in Moscow of all places. At the height of Andropov's Commie regime he told me to forget journalism and focus on fiction connected with the funny side of life with 'all those Maharajahs, because even the KGB knows that your frame of reference is princely India'.

My thanks to Anta and Maharanisa (Dr Karni Singhji, Maharajah of Bikaner; and Maharani Sushila Kumariji, Princess of Dungarpur) for the Lalgadh years, which made me a bonafide member of their privileged princely world.

Very special thanks to Kotah Bhuwasa (Princess Shiv Kanwar of Bikaner and Maharani of Kotah) for her exemplary graciousness and superb hospitality. The seniormost member of the houses of Bikaner and Kotah from which I too am directly descended, she has been incredibly informative about the magical world reflected in *Really, Your Highness!*

And to Jaipur Mamisa (Maharani Gayatri Devi of Jaipur and Princess Ayesha of Cooch Behar), with whom I was privileged to interact while collecting stories for this novel. This inspiring international celebrity, educationist, author and activist spent hours with me over the years discussing the plot and characters, giving unstintingly of her time to vet the first few drafts, sharing many delightful memories, and often exposing the really funny side of our sedatest connections.

My thanks also to 'Jyoti Sankhu's so irreverent!' Baapji Jodhpur (Maharajah Gaj Singhji of Marwar) who understood, after an initial hesitation, that the endearing traits of our common ancestors would also be dished up alongside their renowned historical howlers. So, Your Highness, many thanks for laying on all the *bandobast*, and for encouraging old-timers like the polo ace Maharaj Prem Singhji of Jodhpur, Colonel Mohan Singhji Bhati and Thakur Karan Singhji to share their most disreputable stories with me.

Last but not least, many thanks to all my friends and relations who happily shared anecdotes about the attitudes of these royal Rajputs and the culture of feudal Rajasthan circa 1937-47 which sustain this light-hearted novel. Among these, my special appreciation for Princess Kitten Bundi (Yuvrani of Alwar); Bubbles Dada and Joe Dada (HH Jaipur and Maharaj Jai Singhji); Maharajah Kirit Tripura and Maharani Vibhu Devi; Princess Bhawana Panna; Kamla Jija, (Rani Saab Ramkote); Devinder Dadabhai and Jeetu Bhabisa (Rao Saab and Rani Saab Koodsu); Pittu Singh; Kr. Maan Singhji Loadsar; Zorji and Gomji Mama (Lt. General Zorawar Singhji and Colonel Govind Singhji of Khatipura); Krishna Bagsuri and Lt. General Ajay Kunhari, Wazir Khan of Tonk; Uncle Bijay and Baby Aunty; Monty and Meera; Mohini Padrona; Margaret Barwara; Rawatsar Aunty (Rani Laxmi Kumari Chundawat) and Raja Saab Klaswala.

Historical Note

India's last Maharajahs were people caught between two worlds—the ancient feudal one at home, and a modern Europe riven by conflicting imperialistic aims and political ideologies. This helped create an anti-colonial Indian leadership addicted to Western-style parliamentary democracy. And socialism. The Indian Princely States, ruled by autocrats, continued to exist with astonishingly little change into the middle of the twentieth century, specially in Rajputana (modern Rajasthan), where even today visitors can drift back into the past, surrounded by fairytale forts and palaces once peopled by romantic Rajputs with Quixotic ideas of honour, pride and courage.

In 1858, the British Crown swore to uphold the rights and privileges of the Indian princes. With Queen Victoria as their imperial godmother, they began enjoying intimate friendships with the British Royal family, and became members of the Viceroy's Council which effectively ruled the Indian subcontinent.

Yet, the British Raj kept intervention and involvement in the Princely States to the minimum necessary for sustaining its economic and political objectives. This created a perfectly ridiculous imbalance of power. Although the Maharajahs were forced to abdicate all responsibility in military and diplomatic affairs to the British—especially after what they called the 1857 Mutiny, and the natives termed the War of Independence—they remained sovereign within their own States. The larger States had accredited English Residents representing the British Crown, while Political Agents were responsible for maintaining relations within a group of States.

Although relations between the Maharajahs and the Crown Agents were usually strained, mutual trust, and even friendship, did develop sometimes. Often isolated and lonely because they remained aloof from the Indians, British officers happily socialised with the princely class. Any claims of White Caucasian Supremacy sounded ludicrous to an ancient ruling class confidently tracing its descent back to the Sun and the Moon, or to Aryan heroes who were so obviously certifiable divine incarnations!

The bizarre fads, fancies, and questionable morals of a few Indian Maharajahs—combined with their fabulous wealth, enviable lifestyle, and formidable power—made them objects of public curiosity and sycophancy. Indulged from birth, conditioned by heredity and environment to have every whim fulfilled, most Maharajahs pursued pleasure single-mindedly. But there were enough enlightened despots who took their patriarchal feudal duties seriously, and enthusiastically set about modernising their states.

British officials often found themselves tossed willy-nilly into this crazy Wodehousean world, where anything could happen, and everything was open to two distinctly different interpretations. It was obligatory for every Maharajah to engage in a constant game of one-upmanship with his brother princes. There were also historic rivalries between different States, intrigues within princely families over matrimonial alliances and succession to the throne. The world of the Indian Maharajahs, with all its splendour and colour, amused foreigners and natives alike, though, naturally, for different reasons.

Really, Your Highness! tells the story of three Princely States—Chattargadh, Pisshengunj, and Fateypur—linked by centuries of kinship and conflict. Into this they drag British Viceroys, Residents, Military Secretaries, Memsahebs and visiting Royalty. The utterly different Rajput and English frames of reference, attitudes, upbringing, and conduct in the council chamber, sports field, battlefield, and the world at large result inevitably in muddles and misunderstandings.

These are the cornerstones of this book.

The Resident Rolls in   1

The combined cacophony of competing kettledrums, bugle fanfare, war horns, sentries presenting arms and Charan bards eulogising his warrior ancestors, was just another of those daily routines for Maharajah Jai Singh of Chattargadh. But it imposed an endurance test on his normally easy-going Military Secretary, Colonel Claude-Poole, every time the latter accompanied the Maharajah out of the charming sandstone palace he had enjoyed designing just to prove his aesthetic-cum-engineering skills to a sceptical prince, who liked dispensing commissions but was perennially short of cash. Above its impressive Bengal arch pavilions, domes and double marble *jharokha* windows, fluttered the 1400-year-old saffron and crimson Rathor standard, smartened up with a coat of arms created by the Royal College of Heralds in London.

As the well-known green Shooting Chevy passed through Chattargadh, a colourful Rajasthani town dominated by a magnificent medieval fort, children on the roadside ran to greet their Maharajah. He smiled, waved at them, and stopped the car several times as people passing by on cycles, tongas, cars or motorcycles dismounted as a mark of respect. People on foot immediately gathered round, folding their hands and shouting greetings in the local dialect: '*Khamma*, Baapji!' or '*Raj amar ho Jai Singh koh!*' Women in bright veils, silver jewellery, and ivory-and-glass bangles leaned out of windows and balconies lining the narrow bazaar lanes, calling out to sisters and mothers-in-law: '*Dekkho, dekkho*, Rajaji!' To them he folded his hands politely in greeting. Riders on camels and horses conceded right of way, while bullock carts creaked to a stop, and the Maharajah's ADC (aide-de-camp), Zorji, urged their driver to keep as many donkeys as he possibly could on the left, because it brought good luck.

If driving off the road to honour an old superstition could change their luck, Jai Singh would have gladly instructed good old Dhonkalji to do so. But only a modern canal system capable of providing adequate drinking water and irrigation facilities to his people could turn the veritable tide of bad luck that had ruined all his efforts at nurturing a windswept desert into the most enviably prosperous princely state in India. Only his daft ancestors could have abandoned their wealthy Kanauj kingdom, with its fertile wheat fields, mango orchards and rose gardens to the tiny Turko-Afghan army of Mohammed Ghori in 1194, to conquer and colonise this vast wasteland called Marwar. And take great pride in such a silly swap.

'Really, Your Highness, it's about time the Maharajah of Pisshengunj conceded our reasonable request for water-sharing.'

'Colonel Claude-Poole, have you ever seen Nutty being reasonable?' demanded Jai Singh.

Colonel CP smiled. 'Then I suppose we'll have to mobilise support through the Viceroy.'

'If it wasn't for His interfering Excellency and the British Government, I would have sorted Nutty out long ago, and built my canal,' Jai Singh retorted with a martial spark in his splendid black eyes.

'Perhaps, Your Highness. But let's look at the bright side. One day, Pisshengunj will revert to the Chattargadh branch of the Rathor dynasty . . . .'

'Only if Nutty continues to remain childless and the British honour our ancient adoption customs. But by then it will be too late. We need water now!'

The Maharajah and his Military Secretary-cum-Chief Engineer continued studying the chart and canal blueprint as they drove along the narrow metalled road that connected the state capital to several *thikanas* (districts) and villages. Sand dunes rose in shimmering mounds under a hot sun even though summer had scarcely begun. Goats nibbling on thorn bushes, and a few thatched huts surrounded by low mud walls decorated with ochre and white geometric designs, broke the stark monotony of that inhospitable land.

Colonel CP kept his handiwork from being blown out of the window as the Maharajah spoke eloquently about introducing cash crops like sugarcane, cotton and citrus fruits to Chattargadh. Both wore well-tailored, comfortable khakis without any rank insignia. But the similarity ended there. While the Maharajah ignored his ADC except for instructing him to stop at the Jobner lake for lunch (even if it was almost dry), the Englishman couldn't help feeling irked by Zorji's constant turning and peering back.

Questioned, Zorji in turn very politely asked: 'Then who will strain his neck keeping an eye on the follow car? Durbar or his Mil-tree Shakey-tree?'

CP made a point of pointing to the rear view mirrors, suggesting that that's what they were there for.

But the ADC had the last word. 'Kernull Saab's *bilayati* eyes might penetrate through desert dust, but my poor Rajput hawk eyes cannot.'

Scattered among the ancient Jobner township, visible through the afternoon haze, stood small canopied *chattris*, and lavishly carved Jain temples built in more prosperous times, when Chattargadh derived rich revenues from the trade caravans passing between north-west India and Arabia, Persia and Egypt. Wealthy Marwari and Jain merchants had confidently parked their families and fortunes under the dual protection of their upright Rathor rulers and their impenetrable desert, amassing and repatriating more and more wealth home as India rapidly industrialised under the British. Jai Singh couldn't help reflecting that it was all very well for Congresswallahs to moan and groan about the threat to cottage industries and *swadeshi* handicrafts, but any responsible ruler could see that only cheap mass-produced items could satisfy this country's growing mass consumption.

It was nearly teatime before they spotted the blobs of green on the horizon which signalled that they were about to reach Koodsu, the *thikana* located 69 miles from Chattargadh, and just 16 from the river in Pisshengunj. The Maharajah had summoned all the local chiefs, *choudhries*, *tehsildars*, and *patwaris* there to hear his plans, and submit their suggestions before actual work on his pet scheme could begin.

As was his unvarying custom every evening, Maharajah Natwar Singh of Pisshengunj, Nutty to family and friends, stood on the marble terrace overlooking the Guptaganga river, tossing cream cracker biscuits to his highly pedigreed collection of prizewinning dogs. The sun was setting in a burst of bright pink and gold over an interesting landscape which included well-tended green fields, gardens, and flat-roofed houses surrounded by low hills.

He fondled a sprightly Springer Spaniel, examined an Irish Setter's ears, and scolded a dog handler holding two Dachshunds on leashes. 'Otto and Hilda have not been getting their Vitamin E! I can tell from their not-shining coats.'

The old dog handler folded his hands. '*Hajoor*, these dogs get better care than the children of English Lat Sahebs.'

Nutty's favourite Pomeranian was wheeled up to him in a beautiful pram displaying a MADE IN ENGLAND label. The Maharajah picked her up, kissed her on the nose, making soft koochie-koo sounds and fondling the aging animal as though she were a beloved child. A retainer, wearing the green and brown Pisshengunj livery, rushed up to present his ruler with a feeding bottle, also stamped MADE IN ENGLAND. The Maharajah sat down on the canopied, chintz-upholstered, wrought iron garden swing kept for his exclusive use, and started feeding Pom Pom. He also nodded to his two ADCs, Kalu Singh and Bhoor Singh, who promptly sat down facing him on cane chairs. A butler handed them cups of tea.

Nutty's Prime Minister, Baron Tikemoffsky, walked towards the Maharajah along the flagged garden path lined with porcelain pisspots full of colourful flowering plants, ferns, succulents, and cacti. Two little boys in white shorts, shirts, and red turbans, shooing peacocks off the flower bed, chanted 'Aloo Tikky!' behind his ramrod straight back. He ignored the cheeky blighters (obviously recent recruits from the palace garden Superintendent's home village) even though he longed to whack them with his sapphire-topped ivory swagger stick.

After giving specific instructions to his kennel Headman, Nutty turned towards his Dewan (Prime Minister). 'Well, Tikky, where is she?'

Bowing and clicking his heels in greeting as he'd been trained to do at the Tsarist Court before Bolshie behaviour became de rigueur for surviving in his beloved country, Tikky replied, 'I regret informing Your Highness that my mission was rather unsuccessful.'

Annoyance radiated from the Maharajah's rotund, fair face. 'Do you wish to be known as the most inefficient Dewan or Prime Minister in all the Indian states put together, like Humpty Dumpty? I did not send you off empty-handed to Chattargadh, y'know.'

'Really, Your Highness, it's my duty to advise you that your offer of a huge bride price was quite counter-productive. Strong-arm tactics will get us nowhere. We must negotiate an alliance with Maharajah Jai Singh.'

Rudely keeping his Dewan standing, Nutty confided to his ADCs: 'Listen to this new nonsense, Bhoorji, Kalu Singhji! In 15 years of eating Pisshengunj salt, Baron Tikemoffsky hasn't bothered to learn our history. But I can give him whole chapters and verses on the Russian Revolution. Do you think I'll go begging to Chattargadh, which holds a grudge against my branch of the family tree?'

Kalu Singh and Bhoor Singh nodded their sycophantic heads, and made some snide remarks about White Russians and European adventurers, who never got their facts on India right.

Taking a chair, Tikky countered, 'I have some news which will help Your Highness achieve your heart's desire. Chattargadh is facing a severe drought, and . . . .'

'That's not news, Baron Saab,' Thakur Kalu Singh interrupted. 'Chattargadh's permanent condition happens to be drafty!'

Nutty took malicious delight in counting off the exact days and years in living memory when rain had actually fallen on his neighbouring state, and his cronies guffawed.

'As I was saying, Your Highness, being their nearest riparian state is our trump card. And a visit to the shrine of your common family goddess is overdue.'

Nutty caught the drift of his Prime Minister's Machiavellian mind. 'Marvellous, Tikky! You're worth your weight in gold. And once this matter is settled to my satisfaction, you shall have it. The word of a Rajput who's a Maharajah on it. *Raghu kul reeti sada chali ayi, pran jayi par vachan na jayi!* But insist on a pukka 19-gun salute this time.'

'Hukum, Anta!' advised Thakur Bhoor Singh. 'It's a question of our prestige. We may be the junior branch, but we are certainly entitled to more big bangs than Chattargadh Durbar.'

On April Fool's Day, 1938, Nutty arrived at the Chattargadh Palace in an open carriage drawn by two showy white horses and accompanied by an enormous St. Bernard who occupied the entire front seat. Jai Singh's only son and heir, Robin, escorted them. The Pisshengunj party followed in another carriage.

The Maharajah of Chattargadh stood ready to receive his guests on the steps of the main portico with his little grandson Pat, Colonel CP, his ADCs, Zorji and Ganpat Singh, and some *Sardars* and *Rajvis*, who greeted Nutty with folded hands and loud cries of '*Khamma*, Baapji!'

Robin jumped out even before the carriage halted. Kettledrums boomed, bugles blew, and the palace *dholidamamis* broke into song, welcoming their Maharajah's kinsman who sat tight, returning their *Mujras* no doubt, but concentrating more on counting off the gun salutes he demanded before he set foot in his cousin's home. However, at the first sound of cannon fire, his carriage horses started bucking like circus ponies, and kicked the buggy. The stunned Pisshengunj Maharajah found himself tossed up and down by the wild pair that the coachman seemed unable to control. The St. Bernard added to the dreadful din, barking loudly, and pawing his master. Nutty's turban may have slipped over his face and covered his eyes, but he could still hear the Chattargadh princes and chiefs laughing at his plight even as the crazed horses continued to rear and kick till all the 19 gun salutes had finally sounded.

Jai Singh embraced a dishevelled and murderously peeved Nutty. 'Satisfied, Nutty? You can't say we stinted on giving you the welcome you deserved, with a pukka 19-gun salute.'

'You did that purposely!' fumed Nutty.

'Even horses jump for joy when you're around, dear Uncle Nutty,' insisted Robin with a roguish grin.

Adding fuel to the fire, a group of fat and ageing *purohitayans* (Brahmin women) decked in *zari lehnga-odhnas*, huge red *bindis* and all other auspicious ornaments—who stood holding coconut-stuffed *kumbha kalash* and silver *puja thaals*—began chanting to ward the evil eye off their dear younger brother, Maharajah Nut-Bolt Singhji of Pisshengunj.

Colonel CP realised how well founded his apprehensions had been as the Chattargadh and Pisshengunj Maharajahs sat sniping at each other around the conference table in Jai Singh's study. Preferring pranks to serious negotiations seemed to be another ingrained Rathor trait that was so counter-productive. Even their respective Dewans, Tikky and Raj Kumar Kishen, were disagreeing, and the scheme over which they, and their respective Maharajahs, had laboured so long, was forgotten.

Curbing his impatience, Colonel CP repeated the entire exercise of showing HH Pisshengunj (on the detailed Survey of India map spread before them) exactly which areas the C-P canal—named after the two states, as he was quick to explain—would irrigate. But Nutty continued to distract him by fondling the St. Bernard, fiddling with his *pan* box, and calling for his own special spittoon. He didn't want anyone getting hold of parts of himself for performing any *totka* (black magic). Neither did he want anyone else to make the gesture of offering deadly, spasm-inducing, tobacco-stuffed *pan* to his cousins, and the two Europeans.

'Reverse names. Pisshengunj has to come first,' insisted Nutty.

'Certainly,' conceded Jai Singh.

'Hmm. But let's not beat about the bush all over the countryside, my dear Bhai. Because *you* need water for your people. I don't. I just want to fix those foreigners who questioned my Sunny's pedigree in London through you!'

Striving to keep a straight face, Jai Singh said, 'The British can be so dogmatic at times. Nutty, why don't you persuade the Duchess of Dalmatia to cross your stock with hers?'

'She's more than willing. But some stupid organisation . . . what organisation, Tikky?'

'The Royal Society for Prevention of Cruelty to Animals, Your Highness.'

'Butted in,' continued Nutty. 'Some guttersnipes wrote tommy-rot about my shooting dogs who don't win Blue Ribbons at Crufts or the Calcutta Kennel Club. All lies, Colonel Clod-Pole, as I'm sure any fool can tell His Majesty's Government after seeing me in my dotage with my dogs! But what am I to do?'

'Really, Your Highness, a letter to *The London Times* should do the trick,' said the Englishman, turning a chuckle into a cough.

'How doggedly the British press pursues scandal,' added Jai Singh. 'But coming back to the issues you've raised, I'm ready to transfer those five villages, which have been a bone of contention between the two branches of our family for generations.'

But Nutty shook his whole body from side to side, almost upsetting his straight-backed leather chair. 'That's not enough, Bhai. You're forgetting that Pisshengunj is your Upper Volta state!'

Jai Singh's thick black eyebrows shot up as he and Colonel CP exchanged amused looks. Kishen was thoroughly foxed by his 'Nutty' cousin's latest claim.

Suppressing a smile, Tikky amended: 'Upper riparian state, Your Highness.'

'Call it anything you like, as long as my dear brother Maharajah Jai Singhji of Chattargadh understands that this time, I've got the upper hand.'

Jai Singh joined his wife, Maharani Padmini, on the comfortably sprung sofa as soon as the maids cleared away the huge silver dinner *thaals*, water tumblers, and starched white napkins from the adjoining dining room. The Maharani poured some Cointreau into two crystal liqueur glasses from the stylish art deco trolley before her, added crushed ice, and handed one to her husband. Toasting each other, they smiled and sipped the soothing cool drink—as usual, in total harmony with each other.

Padmini looked graceful in a French chiffon sari draped round her head. Perfectly matching pink glass bangles, ruby earrings, ring, simple gold chain, and the obligatory diamond nose pin and gold anklets enhanced her classic beauty. The Maharajah relaxed in a spotless white, superfine, Afghan-style kurta and comfortable baggy pyjamas. The noisy desert cooler fixed outside the Maharani's suite made it difficult to hear the loud Latin tango records their daughter Kitten insisted on playing. She had also switched on all the wall sconces and chandeliers, making the room much too bright. But then, repose was impossible with Kitten around.

The spacious drawing room was decorated with lovely locally woven silk rugs, similar floral-patterned damask curtains, a gilt-framed overmantle mirror reflecting the rococo clock, enamelled silver birds, rose quartz, jade, ivory and porcelain figures collected over the years. A group of excellent Rajput and Mughal miniatures adorned one wall. The Maharani's own almost professional paintings of famous Indian forts and European gardens hung opposite. She had also done the very lifelike portrait of her husband on horseback above her neatly organised writing table. The table itself was stashed with the Indian, British and American magazines she enjoyed reading. Two crystal bowls filled with fragrant roses and jasmines floating in water, heavy cut-glass ashtrays, a pair of classic Chinese cloisonné lamps, and family photographs in crested silver frames were arranged on various marble and glass-topped tables. In the photographs, the fierce faces belonged to her dauntless Sisodia clan; the fashionable dressy ones were her husband's dopey-eyed Rathor relations renowned for the Three Rs— riding, romance, and recklessness.

Kitten stood before the brand new radiogram, choosing and discarding from the stack of 78 RPMs collected on trips to Bombay, Calcutta, Delhi, and Bangalore. Restlessly flipping back her thick, unruly, shoulder-length black hair from her face, she turned around, enjoying the feel of cool marble against her bare feet. Her puff-sleeved crêpe de Chine blouse was neatly tucked into fashionable dark blue slacks.

'Thank God, we're rid of that Nutty character. Imagine a chap like him holding me to ransom.'

'Come on, Data Hukum. What's a dog between sister-states?' teased Kitten, with her usual irreverence.

'Everything!' exploded Jai Singh.

Trying to avert another argument between her equally hot-headed and opinionated husband and child, the Maharani said: 'You're taking this thing too seriously, *Hajoor* (Sir). If you could give ten of your best polo ponies to your sister's husband, why can't you part with one St. Bernard?'

'Because there's a world of difference between Sir Pratab Singh of Fateypur and Nutty Pisshengunj, darling.'

'Did you offer him those villages?' his wife asked.

'Oh, yes. But Dog-Along Cassidy has a bee in his bonnet!' swore the exasperated Maharajah.

Everyone laughed. 'And a chip on his shoulder,' added Kitten.

The proud mother of two carefully-nurtured children, who had survived out of the four she had borne, Padmini was inclined to be compassionate.

'It's really quite sad. Three wives, and no heir yet. So one day, I suppose, Pisshengunj has to revert to the parent state . . . .'

'In the year 2000!' scoffed Kitten, with a tilt of her perfectly pointed chin. 'His Nutty Highness is just the sort of chap who lives to be a 120!'

Managing to light a cigarette with his monogrammed Cartier lighter despite the constant draught from all the fans, Jai Singh mused: 'If we had a sympathetic Resident, he could take this matter up with the British government.'

'What a pity you dismissed Sir Henry Higgins, *Hajoor*.'

'But, darling, Sir Henry was getting too big for his boots,' explained the Maharajah.

'Specially when he refused to believe that you could make any fool your prime minister, and still run one of the best states in India!' added Kitten, with a comic roll of her enormous long-lashed black eyes.

'Kitten, that's not a very flattering description of your Uncle Kishen,' said Jai Singh, unable to hide his amusement.

'Who's the perfect foil to your one-upmanship show?' retorted his shockingly forthright 16-year-old daughter.

'Kitten!' cried her mother.

But Kitten continued unabashed, 'Or was it because Sir Henry discovered our best-kept state secret? C-R-O . . . .'

Just then, Maharajah Jai Singh started sneezing. It triggered Kitten's loud unladylike laughter.

Hastening to fetch a box of super-soft Kleenex tissues for her allergy-prone husband, Padmini protested: 'Now look what you've done, Kitten.'

The usual racial assortment of dark, fair and pale white-skinned people hurried up and down the crowded Delhi Railway Station. Red-shirted and turbaned coolies in frayed dhotis or pyjamas carried heavy trunks, bulging holdalls, and bundles tied with string or rope. Food, fruit, and tea vendors pushed their carts along Platform 9. Shunting trains, whistling engines, birds nesting under the sloping railway sheds, and unruly children added to the frightful din. The children demanded balloons, toys, and food from harassed mothers whose main concern seemed to be to keep their faces covered as they followed their husbands trying to find the right compartment. Boys peddling bottled lemonade, raspberry, and Vimto did brisker business than the boys selling magazines and books. The latter had to keep looking for educated buyers inclined to spend money.

Gerald Redverse threw down his much-worn sola topi on the lower berth of the special first class compartment reserved for him, and pushed his damp blond hair off his broad sweating brow. His long-time Gurkha orderly, Thapa, placed the wicker picnic basket, thermos water flask, ice box, and bulging book bag on the flap table. He switched on all the fans and lights, dusted one of the two overstuffed leather armchairs for his master, and got off after making sure that the coolies had satisfactorily arranged all the luggage necessary to ensure his Saheb's comfort on the long 12-hour train journey.

Hearing the guard blow his whistle, Redverse bent to bolt the door.

But it was pushed open, and Colonel CP climbed into the coupé.

'Holy Maa Kali! Reverse Gear, or I'm hallucinating! Travelling on the astral plane from Bhutan, old chap?'

Smiling as they shook hands, he replied, 'In the flesh, CP. Palace politics made Bhutan rather a hot spot, you know.'

They laughed, and sat down facing each other on the armchairs. Both looked amazingly fit, considering the enervating summer heat and the hectic nature of their respective jobs. Gerald noted that CP was still waging a losing battle with his copper-coloured hair, which always covered his head in a mass of corkscrew curls no matter how short he cropped it. This had earned him the childhood sobriquet of Curly Pate Claude-Poole. It hadn't deterred him from cultivating a ludicrous handlebar moustache, which did nothing to enhance his military image.

No one ever got completely out of touch when abroad because the British empire in Asia was really rather small. Everyone who mattered moved around in the same tight-knit circle, often bumping into each other in the same city, hill station, club, army mess, princely palace, or shikar camp from season to season. However, though special chums since boyhood, these two had a lot of catching up to do.

'I've fallen into your bad company only because that bamboo bridge arranged for me by the Queen Mother's brother failed to finish me off.'

'Welcome to the Political Service, the last resort of officers who don't work,' said the Colonel.

'And soldiers who don't fight,' retorted Redverse.

Accepting a cigarette from the tin offered by his protesting friend, he continued: 'How're things with you, CP?'

'Static. Still fancy free, without a worry in the world. But tell me, where's Dorothy Memsaheb?' asked the confirmed bachelor who enjoyed brief flirtations, but never intended getting shackled by marriage.

'In England, helping the twins to settle down at prep school.'

Distorting his pleasant sunburnt face, CP protested. 'Someone should spread the word around that there's nothing more unsettling than a mother camping in the neighbourhood! Remember your Aunt Sissy haunting the old school grounds to pamper her repulsive brat?'

Clear blue eyes twinkling at the recollection of shared school days, Gerald said, 'That repulsive brat has turned into an establishment pillar, proficient in five languages apart from German, French, and English!'

This sally drew a chuckle, and other damaging reminiscences about persons now scattered in places spread over every continent, including Hollywood. Before the metre gauge train stopped at Rewari Junction (where the railway dining car attendants would serve the five-course dinner recommended by his companion), Redverse asked the question uppermost in his mind.

'CP, how long have you been military secretary to HH Chattargadh?'

'Long enough to brief you.'

'All right. Why was my predecessor Henry Higgins kicked out so unceremoniously?'

'Because of his loud mouth. You know Sir Henry. For a Maharajah, Jai Singh's pretty decent. There's the occasional— you know—row. But I'm sure that a chap with your polo handicap can handle him.'

Colonel CP spotted Jai Singh the minute they got off the train at Chattargadh. Effortlessly exuding his usual charisma, the Maharajah stood talking with the Station Master. All normal business on the neat little kiosked and sandstone-pillared arrival platform was suspended as travellers, coolies, vendors, veiled women, and several eager children gathered in a respectful circle, waited for a chance to touch their ruler's feet, or even speak to him.

'I can hardly believe this, Reverse Gear. The Maharajah has come to receive you himself . . . and along with his Dewan!'

Flattered, but refusing to react—because this was not part of the drill except for visiting royalty and viceroys— Gerald Redverse followed Colonel CP through the crowd, trying not to trip over the luggage and hand carts left unattended in all the excitement. Raj Kumar Kishen Singh asked the ADC on duty to clear the way when he saw the Military Secretary approaching with another foreigner.

As he was in uniform, Colonel CP saluted, and formally announced: 'Your Highness, may I present Reverse Gear, the new Agent . . . .'

Jai Singh responded with an affable smile and a handshake. 'How typically British, and so appropriate too. Welcome to Chattargadh, my dear young man. I'm so impressed with your Company's efficiency.'

'Indeed, Your Highness. The old John Company usually does its best for the Princely States,' Redverse assured him.

Still radiating regal courtesy, the Maharajah corrected: 'You mean the Rolls Royce Company.'

Gerald's patrician reserve vanished as he laughed. 'Ha ha ha ha! That's a good one, Your Highness. But Rolls Royce is still in private hands. Though one never knows what a Labour government might do.'

Stroking his impressive, perfectly groomed moustache, Jai Singh said, 'Unh-humm. But my agreement is with Rolls Royce, and I'm not accepting anything else, agent or no agent.'

Gerald Redverse drew himself up with dignity, matching the Maharajah in height while abandoning hope of bridging the generation gap CP had warned him about. 'Really, Your Highness, I fail to understand this volte-face. The agreement was signed by the Political Secretary and your Dewan, Raj Kumar Kishen Singh . . . .'

'My crazy cousin!' interjected the Maharajah. 'Kishen, how many times have I told you not to do things behind my back?'

This prince, bearing a marked family resemblance to his father's elder brother's son who had became Maharajah whether he deserved to or not, immediately lodged an indignant public protest. He translated everything said in English into Marwari for the benefit of those who hadn't yet realised that someone had blundered. 'Your Highness knows I'm a straightforward on-your-face man. And I was against this whole unnecessary expenditure from the very beginning.'

Thoroughly put off, Gerald Redverse protested with an

ironic bow: 'It's high time everyone realised that this unnecessary expenditure happens to be the Viceroy's choice.'

'We've got very similar tastes,' acknowledged the Maharajah tactfully.

But R.K. Kishen was still belligerent. 'Yes, we know that great men think alike. And fools seldom differ.'

Completely foxed by this strange reverse his friend seemed to be suffering, Colonel CP wondered how soon they could get away from this exposed public arena, and tackle the Maharajah in private.

As though reading his mind, Jai Singh said, 'Shall we get on with the inspection?'

'That's very kind of you, Sir. I too would like to see the Residency right away.'

'The Residency?' frowned the Maharajah. 'What for? The new chap hasn't even arrived yet. I'm talking about inspecting my first Rolls Royce, for which your Company has already been paid. In pounds sterling, let me add.'

Suddenly, the whole mystery cleared; the two Englishmen were torn between vexation and amusement. The Maharajah had got it completely wrong.

Before any more misunderstandings could arise, Colonel CP hastened to complete the introduction gone awry. 'Really, Your Highness, there's some confusion here. This is Reverse Gear—I beg your pardon—the Hon'ble Gerald Redverse, ICS, Agent to the Crown of England, and Chattargadh's new British Resident.'

The Maharajah laughed heartily. 'Oh, I see. But when you said Reverse Gear, it was but natural that I got my agents muddled. How d'you do, Mr Redverse. I wish you'd sent me a telegram, then we would have made full *bandobast* for your proper reception.'

'Really, Your Highness, that wouldn't have broken the ice as quickly,' responded the Resident, his upper lip not quite so stiff as it had been earlier.

Why hadn't the Colonel Saab blown his horn, wondered Bhoot Nath, the sleek, well-fed Residency chowkidar enjoying his first morning *chillum* under the deep shade of the huge banyan tree dominating the neglected garden. Parrots, crows, mynas, and squirrels were busy feeding off its big berries, while several sparrows and doves pecked around the practically dry lawn. Rising quickly from his resting place he hurried towards the porch where the Maharajah Saab Bahadur's Military Secretary and a strange *angrez* were just stepping out of the grey Rover.

Raising his folded hands, Bhoot Nath greeted them. 'Salaam, Kurnul Saab! Hukkam, *Hajoor*?'

Colonel CP nodded in return. 'Salaam, chowkidar. *Sab theek-thak hai* (Is all well)? This is the new Resident Saheb.'

The chowkidar's face lit up with a broad smile. 'Happy to have you back, Saab, even if you feel strange thinking its a new place. Your whole staff will be very glad to see you filling up this huge empty house!'

'Thank you, chowkidar. What's your name?'

'Bhoot Nath, *Hajoor*. I have been with the Rejdunt Saab Bahadur ever since the begging.'

'Good. That's my orderly, Thapa, who has also been with me ever since I came to India. Just show him where to put my stuff, will you.'

Dozens of pigeons flew off with loud, fluttering wings while the two servants and the Colonel's driver unloaded the luggage, and began carrying it into the house. Two peacocks peered at Gerald Redverse as he stood back from the verandah steps, examining the squat sandstone building speculatively. 'A bit dreary, wouldn't you say?'

CP made a face. 'You obviously weren't expected, old chap. You can still change your mind and make yourself comfortable in my less pretentious bungalow till you get this place organised.'

The Resident declined quickly. 'Don't go offering me

temptation, CP. Because we both know that the Maharajah won't take me seriously after what happened this morning if I don't get the Residency functioning immediately.'

'Ahh hmm. I don't want to know what you did to make yourself totally dispensable to the Bhutanese royal family, but the only way to survive here is by remembering that the Rajputs put "*ad absurdum*" above everything!' warned CP.

Observing that unless CP wanted his old nickname revealed, he would be very much obliged in future if the Maharajah's Military Secretary took greater pains while introducing the new Resident to chaps who interpreted everything literally, Gerald Redverse followed Colonel Claude-Poole through the verandah into an empty bedroom. Both were keen to wash their dusty, travel-stained hands before ordering breakfast. The bathroom door stood open, and a peculiar musty smell hung in the air. But he couldn't fault the tasteful double frieze of patterned Victorian tiles, modern bathroom fittings, well-lit mirror, and white painted, marble-topped toilet table. Redverse strolled over to the large, old-fashioned sunken marble bathtub in which four adults could comfortably bathe together.

Leaning over to try the taps marked Hot and Cold, he said, 'Not bad, after all your austerity guff.'

However, it all changed immediately after.

CP was surprised to see his normally unflappable chum Reverse Gear suddenly recoil in revulsion at that very moment. 'Take a look at this revolting mess, CP!'

Colonel Claude-Poole leaned over and saw that the bathtub was full of baby crocodiles. Some were in the water, some lying on the low step leading down into the round bath. He gave a most unsoldierly shudder. 'By Jove, this takes the cake. Anything's possible in India as we both know, but crocodiles in the bathtub are too dreadful to be merely bizarre!'

Redverse heaved an exasperated sigh. 'Looks like another conspiracy to drive me out of this state too . . . .'

'What d'you mean?' demanded CP.

'Remember what I told you about all that hoo-hah in Bhutan over the regency? When the Queen Mother's brother arranged a bridge for me at the height of the monsoon? And if it hadn't been for a friendly Lama's warning, I would undoubtedly have drowned in the Teesta while driving down to Darjeeling. But who could have a grudge against me here? I've barely arrived. Unless its one of *your* ludicrous pranks.'

'Good heavens, Reverse Gear, you can't mean that! I had no idea that you were being sent out as Resident to this place,' the officer protested. 'Look, let's ask the chowkidar. He's bound to know, because in India servants know everything before anybody, even the military intelligence.'

The Resident clapped his hands, calling out loudly to summon the chowkidar. 'Bhoot Nath! *Idhar aah-woh*, please.'

The chowkidar soon popped his head through the bathroom door. 'Anything urgent, Sarkar? I'm making tea for *Saab-log phatafatt* with my own milk, but I can also produce lemon sleighs.'

His mutilation of the King's English was no longer funny. Quelling him with a gunmetal glance, Colonel CP demanded, 'Chowkidar, who put these crocodiles in the Resident Saheb Bahadur's bathtub?'

Bhoot Nath made a typical nonchalant hand gesture. 'The Rej'dunt Saab, Saar.'

'What nonsense,' scoffed Gerald.

The chowkidar gave him an indulgent, patronising 'what-do-you-know' smile. 'It was his number one hobby, Saar. He had a very good crocodile-farming scheme to make Chattargadh richest again . . . . But for some reason, Baapji, you know—our Maharajah Saab Bahadur—hates crocodiles. Memsaab also very angry. Sweepers fled away, pretending they're scared. But Sir Enree Igginz told trusted Bhoot Nath, "Don't let anyone touch them . . . ."'

Torn between relief and revulsion, Redverse said, 'I should hope not. Just get rid of them, will you.'

'But why, *Hajoor?*' the chowkidar asked. 'They won't disturb you. This is only number one guest bathroom, and Rej'dunt Saab-Memsaab *log* have separate bedrooms AND separate *tub-shub*. Sir Enree Igginz dreams of great big crocodile skin suitcase and shoe *bijnish* to beat Africa and America right here from Chattargadh . . . .'

Gerald quietly but firmly repeated his order to have the reptiles removed from the Residency.

'*Joh hukam, Hajoor.* But how?' countered Bhoot Nath.

The new Resident shrugged. 'Just throw them into the nearest river.'

The chowkidar and Colonel CP exchanged looks. 'But that's in Pisshengunj, my dear chap, which happens to be our hostile neighbouring state,' the latter protested.

'Surely you can think of something, CP. They'll be just as happy in some local lake.'

Before the Englishman could answer, Bhoot Nath explained, 'All the lakes in Chattargadh have gone nearly dry, *Hajoor.* And that is why we have got you here, even though Baapji—our Maharajah Saab Bahadur—can make any fool his Prime Minister, and run the best state in the whole country without any Rej'dunts, just like his father and grandfather!'

Goaded into clutching his thick blond hair, Gerald Redverse swore that he'd had just about enough of this silly surrealistic nonsense. A chowkidar who not only understood but spoke the King's English—planted here no doubt to spy for the Maharajah—was bad enough. And now this. Both were aggravations he didn't need.

Trying to pacify him, his steadfast old school ally promised: 'Tell you what, Reverse Gear. Let the army handle this. My chaps will remove these crocs in a water tanker, and dump them in the nearest body of water without anyone, including the Maharajah, being any the wiser.'

Unaware that his official reception at the palace had been delayed for four days by arguing astrologers, Gerald Redverse couldn't help wondering why it was so vital for him to be ushered into the Chattargadh Dewan's office at precisely a quarter past twelve. Unless one went up to the hills, didn't everyone in India knock off for lunch and long siestas throughout the long summer?

The Maharajah's ADC, Ganpat Singh, hovered around while two turbaned and liveried *chobdars* held the double gauze doors open for the Resident. A welcome draught of cool *khus*-scented air blew over the Englishman as he walked into the spacious, carpeted room, with the usual maps, bookshelves, shikar trophies and polo team photographs on the walls.

Suddenly, a file fell at Redverse's feet with a dull thud, forcing him to halt. He glanced down, and saw a narrow strip of red felt laid down over the carpet from the door to the desk where the Maharajah's cousin-cum-Dewan, Raj Kumar Kishen Singh sat. His eyes were shut tight and several neatly stacked files lay before him. With the single-minded concentration usually exhibited only around casino and bridge tables, the prince was tossing file after file over the desk. Two *mehakma khaas* Babus, sitting at two small tables, kept calling the score as each file fell on one side or the other of the red strip. Two brocade-belted *chaprasis* wearing narrow felt caps, kept picking and presenting the files to the babus, who stamped them with the Dewan's state seal, as they kept tally. 'Approved!'. . . 'Rejected!'. . . 'Rejected!'. . . 'Approved!'. . . 'Rejected!'

Baffled and intrigued, Redverse stood watching this

strange procedure for a while before speaking. 'Good morning, Raj Kumar Saheb. Or good afternoon, actually.'

Kishen Singh opened his big brown eyes and instantly rose to greet his guest, smiling affably. 'Ah, Reverse Gear Saab. How d'you do? You don't mind if I clear up these pending files before joining HH for lunch?'

Sitting down on the indicated leather-covered swivel chair identical to the one often used by the Dewan for stick-and-ball practice, the Resident responded, 'Please do carry on, Raj Kumar Saheb. Forgive my curiosity, but don't you read the files before they are stamped and returned to the departments or persons concerned?'

Kishen gave the Englishman a triumphant smile full of tolerance. 'No need to read what trained department personnel have already vetted. Plus, I have my own foolproof system of cutting out red tape, and preventing favouritism. Impartial, efficient and quick, just like your British system.'

Redverse couldn't help chuckling at his host's notions of parity.

Apprehensive at first about having to cope with the pungent, over-spiced Rajput kebabs and curries he'd been cautioned about, Redeverse was relieved to find himself sitting down to an excellent Anglo-Indian meal consisting of fresh tomato soup followed by fried fish with tartar sauce, partridges grilled to perfection, ribbon potatoes, creamed spinach, dinner rolls and brown bread with curls of salted butter, and a feather light but creamy lemon soufflé almost as good as the ones you got at the London Savoy. He didn't know that the Savoy had lost one of its pastry cooks. Or that this menu had not been planned out of any consideration for his English digestive sensibilities. It was dictated by HH Chattargadh's horsy habits. Whereas every Princely State Gerald had ever visited stuck to soporific *ghee*-rich Indian midday meals and light

Continental dinners, Jai Singh had discovered the advantages of gastronomical self-discipline on the polo and hunting fields of England as a Sandhurst cadet.

The Maharajah, the Resident, Colonel CP, and R.K. Kishen sat discussing the canal scheme over demitasse cups of strong South Indian coffee and a choice of liqueurs served by the efficient Goan-Portuguese butler who had been running the Chattargadh palace pantry for nearly 19 years.

'Really, Your Highness, the scheme itself seems sound. But you know the official attitude to deficit financing,' said the Resident, regretfully aware that His Majesty's government expected the Crown's Agents to play the devil's advocate.

Jai Singh confidently countered, 'Raising funds will be no problem, Mr Redverse.'

'Indeed, Your Highness? But His Majesty's Government expects all the Princely States, without exception, to base their annual expenditure on existing revenues, rather than increase their taxes to offset mounting expenses. This is so even for public welfare schemes.'

The Maharajah looked at the Resident seated across him at the round table he preferred for small gatherings involving not protocol but politics. 'Mr Redverse, preconceptions to the contrary, I have no intention of extorting money from my famine-stricken people. I've raised a personal loan for this canal.'

Puzzled, Colonel CP asked the Dewan, 'But Raj Kumar Saheb, the British bankers had refused to consider our proposal despite all our efforts when we were in London.'

Receiving a nod from Jai Singh, Kishen couldn't help gloating over the coup his cousin had pulled off single-handedly. 'Yes, but the German ones didn't, Colonel Cloud-Pull!'

The Englishmen congratulated the Maharajah, and toasted the venture. Jai Singh responded by mentioning that there still remained one horrible hurdle that all his efforts at appeasement had not budged.

'And, specifically, what might that be, Your Highness?' enquired Gerald.

'That dog in the manger!' retorted Jai Singh.

Still none the wiser despite this vehement statement, the Resident gave CP a puzzled glance. 'I'm afraid I haven't been here long enough to follow all the subtle nuances of affairs pertaining to Your Highness' kingdom.'

Compressing his generous, full mouth, Jai Singh exploded, 'Who else but my blasted neighbour, Nutty Pisshengunj. He wants a matrimonial alliance if you please, before he'll let us dig an inch.'

Now truly puzzled, Redverse frowned. 'But I was under the impression that HH Pisshengunj was childless.'

Jai Singh pushed back his chair with a dismissive gesture. 'Huh. Our children couldn't get married even if he had any. I'm ashamed to admit it, but Nutty's an off-shoot of the Chattargadh Rathor dynasty. And for genetic reasons, we have always tabooed all marriages within the father's clan, and avoided matrimonial alliances even with the mother's clan, seeking partners from as far off as possible. That's why the Rajputs have remained so strong and sane. In fact my own mother was from Mysore . . . . But let us stop digressing. The hurdle obstructing the prosperity of this 33,000-square-mile state of 3,21,000 people—according to our latest census report—is one mad man's determination to cross our St. Bernards!'

Jai Singh was exaggerating. Everyone knew Chattargadh had never been dependent on agricultural or land revenue. It had rich copper, gypsum and lead mines; sandstone, marble, and granite quarries; and flourishing carpet and wool-weaving industries supplied by home-grown camels and merino sheep—which he also exported to Australia and the Arab countries. There were also the profits from the

State railways. Because of its location, all south and west-
bound trains from British-administered or native northern
states had to pass through Chattargadh.

Gerald relaxed. 'Really, Your Highness. Then it's simply
a matter of sending the St. Bernard to stand stud in
Pisshengunj with a reliable handler or two . . . .'

'But Nutty has that advantage because we've only got
the bitch', R.K. Kishen hastened to clarify, not wanting the
Resident to form any false impressions.

'Indeed, Raj Kumar Saheb,' said Redverse, suppressing a
strong desire to laugh. 'That simplifies things, in my opinion.'

'I wish to God it was as simple as you think, Reverse
Gear Saab,' interrupted Kishen. 'But Maharajah Nut-Bolt
Singhji wants nothing less than a proper wedding!'

The Resident couldn't help chuckling at this revelation
while the others applied their minds to circumventing His
Nutty Highness.

The notion of roping in the Resident on his side induced
Maharajah Jai Singh to take him along on his very next tour
of Chattargadh's remoter backward areas. Unconnected to
the outside world by rail or road, they could only be
traversed by camels and sturdy Marwari or Kathiawari
horses.

As they rode along followed by the two ADCs, Zorji and
Ganpat Singh, the Maharajah made a sweeping gesture over
the dry, parched fields surrounded by sand dunes. He bade
Redverse to figure out for himself what prosperity and
employment opportunities the world's longest concrete-
lined canal would soon provide to this sandy wasteland.
Gerald listened attentively as Jai Singh held forth on the
need for hiring donkeys and camels to transport equipment
and materials, and for seducing a couple of qualified
engineers with work experience in the Punjab to help
Colonel Claude-Poole.

The Englishman found it difficult to cope simultaneously with Maharajah Jai Singh's grandiose plans, his restive mare—who kept trying to break into a run over the long stretch of open ground—and the swirling dust thrown up by four pairs of hooves. He couldn't help coughing, pulling his handkerchief out of the pocket of his breeches, and apologising as he wiped his gritty mouth.

Perceiving his companion's discomfort, Jai Singh slowed his own horse to a walk. 'I'm really sorry to drag you through the desert before you've become acclimatised, Mr Redverse. The dust won't bother you if you cover your face like this. And don't worry. My horses are trained to stand still if the reins are knotted and dropped over their necks.'

Still holding the double reins in his left hand, the Maharajah covered his entire lower face with the loose end of his bright orange turban sitting comfortably over his high bridged nose. He tucked it firmly over his left ear in one smooth action.

'An excellent suggestion, Your Highness,' said Redverse who also knotted his reins, untied the scarf he'd fortunately worn to prevent sunburn, and covered his face, cowboy fashion.

Leaning forward in the saddle, the Maharajah took great pleasure in galloping through the soft sandy ground so excellent for horse and rider. He was followed closely by his three companions. They soon rode parallel into one of those sacred groves which seem to exist around every Rajasthani temple and village. Birds flew up as they thundered past.

Suddenly, Jai Singh was forced to rein in hard. Signalling with one hand, he pointed to a statuesque young girl wearing a colourful mirror-work *ghaghra-choli* who had, with clinking bangles and anklets, bounced out of the grove. She was carrying a bleating goat kid in her arms. He immediately noticed how pretty she was, and how much jewellery she wore from head to foot, even as he soothed his snorting grey gelding.

'A good-looking girl, and loaded with jewellery to tempt all the dacoits in the area!' said Jai Singh, with his usual bonhomie.

He knew she was a Bishnoi Jat girl from her belligerent reaction to his harmless remark. '*Hat chaal re Ram-marya*! You think this is Pisshengunj, *Daakira* (devil)? We don't have dacoits in Chattargadh *riyasat* (kingdom)! Run away immediately or I'll make my Maharajah—you've heard of Jai Singh Baapji—flay you alive!'

The appalled ADCs tried to uncover their faces, protesting loudly; but their ruler signalled them to be quiet. Instead, he loudly blessed the girl who strode off towards the nearby village in high dudgeon, hurling curses in Marwari (which Redverse, after nearly 15 years in India, understood almost completely) over her shoulder at the four horsemen.

'Really, Your Highness, that was the most magnificent vote of confidence any Maharajah could ever receive!' remarked the Resident, suddenly seeing Jai Singh in a completely new light.

Jai Singh quipped: 'It's called feudalism in action, Rajput style!'

They both burst out laughing.

Thanks to a technology transfer from Australia just after the Great War, there was not a single Princely State in Rajputana without deep-bore artesian wells. They made it possible for their Maharajahs to provide running water to (at least) the capital cities of their states. They also made it possible to maintain the gardens, lawns, fountains, and lily pools without which no self-respecting ruler had yet built a palace, fort, or public monument.

Jai Singh had chosen to locate the new Chattargadh palace in his Gujarati grandmother's large pleasure park. Besides standing well beyond the expanding old city's municipal limits, it had the added advantage of having mature well-established fruit and shade-giving trees, existing lawns, fountains, and lily pools. These had been divided into three gardens, called the *Hajoor, Zenana,* and Croquet Bagh, which provided separate secluded space for the fitness and leisure activities of the male and female members of Chattargadh's ruling house.

A gardener swept up the leaves in the lawn adjoining the main porch visible from the ADC Room. A turbaned retainer arranged the croquet balls and mallets neatly next to their sturdy, varnished wooden box a few feet away from the first hoop, placed in readiness for Baapji's family members, ADCs, or any of their guests who might wish to play.

The Maharajah's grandson, Pat, sat on the low marble parapet surrounding the rectangular lily pool reflecting the burnished sunset sky, the main wing of their sandstone home, and the two tall trees nearby. A few silver and orange goldfish and tadpoles darted among the water lilies. There were other darker shapes too among the large waxy leaves which intrigued Pat. He continued breaking off small pieces of bread from the Beatrice Potter rabbit motif plate full of sandwiches on his lap, and threw them in the water. He was completely indifferent to the shrill kites, crows, and eagles swooping down over the water, trying to grab this treat for themselves. His personal attendant, Heerji, had marched off as usual to the big kitchen to procure a bowl of roasted *channa-chawal* (chick peas and puffed rice) which he said was the right food for fish-folk. There were plenty of other hungry boys who loved *double-roti* (bread).

Softly calling 'Macchi aa, aa, aa,' Pat leaned over the water holding a sandwich in one hand, and kneeling on his bare knees. His sensible elastic-waisted shorts were already damp and mud-stained. A great glob of buttery tomato juice streaked over the Mickey Mouse embroidered pocket of his fresh cambric shirt just as a monstrous scaly thing suddenly startled him by leaping out of the water and grabbing the bread right out of his hand. He saw, then, that there were more of them. They even had sharp pointy teeth. Puzzled, scared, and curious all at once, Pat jumped up, scattering the sandwiches as he dashed off towards the ADC Room for safety. Pat had not recognised them, but they were crocodiles, and soon two baby ones managed to leap out of the water, immediately slithering up to devour the food before them.

Despite constantly being told that the brave Ranbanka Rathors feared nothing and no one, Pat was greatly relieved to see the two Englishmen strolling towards him in their white shorts and open-collared shirts, and carrying their expensive Slazinger tennis racquets. Despite his inborn reluctance to let grown-ups touch him (for he was no longer a baby), he tugged at Colonel CP's hand. Pointing over his shoulder with his chin, he said, 'Crokkys, Colonel CP!'

The Maharajah's Military Secretary ruffled the boy's hair, saying: 'Not now, Pat old chap. After tennis, perhaps, if there's still enough sunlight left to play croquet!'

Pat immediately launched into an incoherent tale, switching so rapidly between English, Marwari, and Hindustani that the two Englishmen couldn't make any sense of his words. Redverse was reminded of how his own sons demanded attention by embellishing everyday events with awesome gory details. However, as he stood smiling down at the young prince from his superior height, he suddenly spotted familiar reptilian shapes scrambling over the grass towards them, following the bread trail left by Pat.

At that very moment, Maharajah Jai Singh also came down the broad palace steps towards them, accompanied by R.K. Kishen. As soon as he saw his garden swarming with crocodiles apparently chasing his grandson, he stopped—shocked, stunned, and outraged! But, before he could do anything or issue commands, a colossal sneezing fit seized him. He doubled up helplessly, able to pull out his pocket handkerchief to blow his nose just in time.

Luckily, at that moment, the car in which Princess Kitten and her cousin-cum-companion Ratna took their daily evening drive with their governess, Mrs Rawlins, drove into the porch. Kitten quickly jumped out. She knew intuitively that something bad was happening. Grasping the situation immediately, she dashed up to the Resident, grabbed the tennis racquet out of his hand, and made a determined swipe at the nasty crocodiles to which she knew her father was hopelessly allergic.

'Careful, everybody!' she ordered, taking charge as usual. 'Sister Rawlins, please take Pat away, and give HH his allergy pills. Don't just stand there, Colonel CP, but use your deadly smashing strokes! Uncle Kishen, can the *malis* throw the tennis net over these crocodiles, and have them removed from this palace?'

Later, safely ensconced in the drawing room with no chance of the tennis game which they had all looked forward to, Colonel CP repeatedly wished he had understood that Pat was not referring to croquet, but crocodiles. Even though Mrs Rawlins had quickly located his medication and inhaler, Jai Singh was still continuing to sneeze, and wipe watery eyes.

'This is Nutty's doing! He's the only outsider who knows that I have this terrible weakness,' he fumed. 'And I know he wants to destroy the Chattargadh family, root and branch, because he and I both have our own sources of information inside the enemy camp. My only grandson could have been killed because everyone knows he feeds the goldfish, or sails paper boats almost every day in that lily pool.'

The moment they were alone in the palace car, Gerald Redverse gave his old friend a hard look. 'CP, where did you tell your chaps to dump those crocodiles from my bathtub?'

Colonel Claude-Poole sighed, slightly shamefaced. 'Err, in the nearest body of water, what else? Soldiers tend to take orders so literally, you know!'

'And, it had to be this infernal ornamental pond! Now thanks to you, I'll be caught in a totally unnecessary quarrel between these two Maharajahs who seem to hate each other.'

Well aware that in his position there was no such thing as perfect privacy, Maharajah Jai Singh still wished that whoever was knocking so insistently on the door of his study would understand that he sat up late at night *only* when some urgent documents and private letters demanded his attention, or, when he was engaged in what his perceptive wife provocatively referred to as 'flirtation by post!' Tonight, he had no intention of curtailing a thoroughly enjoyable exchange of letters between himself and the Queen of England. Correspondence with her had begun immediately after the Great War when, much to his disgust and disappointment, he had been too young to serve in any capacity, except as an honorary ADC to His Majesty the King Emperor while doing the obligatory Sandhurst course. The communication begun then had evolved into an intimate personal dialogue, which had intensified after his stay at Windsor during the Hurlingham Cup finals and Ascot week.

For once, everyone, including His Majesty, the Prime Minister, the Secretary of State for India, the Viceroy and Fleet Street had agreed that they were so alike. Their regal bonhomie, their effortless ability to enslave people, their single-minded pursuit of excellence and equal rights, their empathy for horses and underdogs, were points most in common between the British Queen and the Indian Maharajah. There was a simple explanation for this astounding phenomenon, as their mothers well knew. They were born on the same day of the same year, at the same time—given the time difference between England and India—on the cusp of Leo and Virgo, and so were bound to share the same traits. Like Siamese twins. Even their profiles matched, minus of course, the Maharajah's impressive moustache and Her Majesty's beautiful blond hair.

Although no Rajput Maharajah ever displayed photographs or paintings of his own wives even in his bedroom or study, a flattering formal portrait of the Queen (fondly inscribed to him) stood on the tall mahogany bureau-bookshelf in Jai Singh's study. It shared pride of place with a portrait of his father, the former Chattargadh ruler, and one of the Mysore Maharajah, his maternal uncle. He had the highest regard for the latter, from whom he had learnt as much about progress and reforms in the Indian context as he had from his polo-playing tours of Europe and both the Americas. Or, indeed, from his African safaris which had yielded some of the magnificent trophies that hung on the walls of his study. In fact, he rather liked the way they interspersed with historic maps, lithographs, ivory miniatures and a huge jewel-toned lacquer work camel-hide painting for which Chattargadh was famous.

The knock on the door was getting bolder. Putting down his thick-nibbed Mont Blanc pen mid-sentence, he called, 'Come in.'

Not by a flicker of his eyelashes did Jai Singh betray his surprise at seeing both his children walking into his study so late at night. It was well past nine o'clock. Robin could usually be relied upon to spend those evenings when his cronies failed to show up for billiards or chess, entertaining his pregnant wife. The latter deserved special care because she was always so modest, respectful and poised, besides being as fragile and as pretty as most hill princesses. As for Kitten, she had no business being downstairs at this hour on any pretext whatsoever. He would have to speak to her mother and the governess about instilling respect for the traditional conventions of royalty into Kitten. Her cousin Ratna, daughter of Padmini's younger sister, who also attended the same convent as Kitten, would never have done anything like this. But then, the two girls were so different. And, it was useless to expect Ratna to control Kitten—or even influence her—once she had decided on some madcap venture.

'Sorry to disturb you, Data Hukum, but we've just thought of an excellent scheme for fixing Uncle Nutty,' began Robin.

'Indeed, Maharaj Kumar Saab?' interposed Jai Singh with frigid politeness. 'Your last brainwave cost me two extra villages with a revenue of six lakhs from their copper mines. And, what is Chattargadh Baiji Lal doing here at this time of night?'

Brother and sister looked at each other. The 26-year-old Robin's face was a bit apprehensive. But the much younger Kitten's look was roguish. Their father, Maharajah Jai Singh, was undoubtedly progressive by many standards, but there were certain customs and taboos that even he expected the female members of his family to observe. Princesses in Rajput society stayed upstairs in the, zenana, and only went out for fresh air and exercise with their governesses, or when they were properly escorted, and chaperoned, by a blood relation. But Kitten had a knack for getting around her father, often stymying his objections with the perfect retort.

'Really, Your Highness, I'm actually trying to help. And you may set your mind at rest about my being adequately chaperoned! In fact, I consider your simultaneous presence here with Big Brother enough to deter even the demons from hell, though why we have all these absolutely antiquated medieval notions of bondage disguised as chivalry, I fail to understand!'

Jai Singh couldn't help laughing at his daughter's deliberately flippant words. 'All right, sweetheart. Sit down, both of you. Now tell me what you want.'

'Saving this state from going to the dogs can be turned into child's play if you listen to us, Data Hukum,' said Kitten, linking arms with her brother. '*Bhanwar ree barasganth pur aap Nutty Kaka ney bhi yaad farmavjoh tamassah vastey* (You can invite Nutty Uncle for your grandson's birthday celebrations and have fun)!'

Eyeing his daughter with new respect, the Maharajah wondered why this excellent solution hadn't occurred to him. 'Good God, Kitten! Do you mean what I think you mean?'

Kitten nodded with a huge grin.

Patting his sister patronisingly, Robin conceded: 'Miss Sticking Plaster does get some bright ideas—occasionally!'

'Wonderful!' exclaimed the Maharajah. 'Now we'll get our canal, teach Nutty a lesson, and keep our *izzat* (honour) intact!'

The following Tuesday, Raj Kumar Kishen Singhji sat watching the rain in Pisshengunj from the pleasantly cool palace pavilion overlooking the riverside garden, nourishing vengeful thoughts against Nutty. Quite oblivious of them, Nutty kept spouting utterly irrelevant Sanskrit verses. '*Mangal Mukhi, Sada Sukhi* (Work begun on Tuesday always gives joy)!'

Kishen Singhji's mind was still on his conversations with his elder cousin, the Maharajah. He had pointed out emphatically that the only wedding he looked forward to and was prepared to promote, organise, and slave over even with his last breath, was Kitten's. But his words had had no effect, because Maharajah Jai Singh had countered by pleading that this bloody dog business had to be conducted with proper protocol if they were to be successful in throwing mud in Maharajah Nut-Bolt Singhji's eyes.

Loyalty, plus that irrepressible Rajput penchant for practical jokes, had enabled Kishen to put aside his personal animosity, and present the silver-gilt encased birthday invitation scroll, beautifully hand painted with pure saffron on pale pink silk, to HH Pisshengunj. Standing up to receive it according to the time-honoured custom, Nutty promised to be present on Pat's fourth birthday with the best gifts ever for his grand nephew. He passed on the heavy metal cylinder to his Dewan, Tikky, and everyone sat down.

The heavy downpour had stopped, and handlers started bringing the usual assortment of his dogs to the Maharajah for the daily inspection. Kishen tried to prevent a large, over-friendly Golden Retriever from planting muddy forepaws on his pure white sharkskin *achkan* and ruining it forever. Tikky pushed away a slobbering Doberman who seemed determined to lick the fixer off his beautifully brushed, brown beard.

After rewarding each and every one of his 99 pampered and pedigreed dogs with their mid-morning snack of one or two cream cracker biscuits—the number being decided strictly according to size and weight—Nutty held a discussion with his head kennel keeper, Gordhan, about which dog they could safely send upstairs as a gift to Their Highnesses the Maharani Sahebas, so that the auspicious number, 99, could still be maintained after the *Barat* returned from Chattargadh with Sunny's bride, Bunny.

That important matter settled, Nutty turned towards Kishen. 'I hesitate to mention this, Kishen. But last time I couldn't sleep properly in Chattargadh, because my vital essence kept leaking out uselessly instead of heading straight for reunion with that great ocean of Bliss .... Please tell Bada Bhai, my Guru Maharaj says that one must sleep in a pitch dark room . . . as black as possible . . . for receiving *shakti paat* or beneficial vibrations from *antariksha*—you know, outer space, and retaining the pure astral energy one has earned through the mineral, plant, animal, and human kingdoms God has created for our entertainment and His liberation!'

With a broad grin, Kishen pointed out that it was actually the other way around.

'Normally, I'm a modest sort of man who's ever willing to learn from others. But there is nothing anyone can teach me about four things—polo, shikar, dogs, and spiritualism—that I don't already know!' Nutty retorted. 'So let's stick to relevant things like proper Rajput hospitality.'

'Certainly, Chota Bhai. We'll guarantee you a total blackout if that's what your Guru Maharaj wants,' the junior prince promised.

Nodding graciously, Nutty continued: 'And one more thing. Please note it down so you won't forget . . . .'

Baron Tikemoffsky leaned closer to the Maharajah, and murmured softly, 'Really, Your Highness! He can't. Can barely sign his own name!'

In a loud, jovial tone, Nutty demanded, 'You mean Raj Kumar Kishen Singhji Bahadur, Dewan of ultra-progressive Chattargadh, is actually illiterate?'

Shaking his head in embarrassment, Tikky mouthed the word 'Dyslexic.'

'Oh, diabetic?' repeated the Maharajah.

Afraid that the notoriously short-tempered Chattargadh prince might take offence, walk off in a huff, and sabotage weeks of careful labour to ensure HH Pisshengunj's continuing good humour (and rich rewards for himself if the dog alliance was successfully concluded), Tikky explained again.

'*Jai, Jai, Siya* Ram! Sounds like a dreadful disease. Not contagious, I hope . . . .'

His candid eyes twinkling, Kishen swore that he didn't consider being dyslexic a handicap. In fact, it was quite to the contrary because it set him free, unlike all those poor babus and bookworms who remained chained to files and piles of printed matter.

'That's all very well,' cried Nutty. 'But you must promise to make certain, Kishen, that no untouchable shadow falls on top of me when I'm HH Chattargadh's guest!'

Grinning, Kishen countered: 'Really, Your Highness! Aren't shadows, being shadows, always untouchable?'

Shuddering expressively, Nutty said that he would never forgive them for polluting him in Chattargadh. 'And kindly remember that I'm also allergic to unlucky faces. Have you noticed how your day gets ruined completely if you come across certain faces, specially early in the morning when you get up, or before eating anything!'

Kishen Singh assured the Maharajah that everything would be arranged to his satisfaction.

Though it was customary to leave household matters to the ADCs, Robin couldn't help wondering why several *farrashes* were busy removing furniture, curtains, and carpets from the best guest suite precisely on the day His Nutty Highness, the most demanding and embarrassingly critical visitor, was expected to stay there. A healthy regard for his father's displeasure if this opportunity was ruined—plus curiosity—compelled him take a look.

The minute he walked in through the glazed double doors, the startling transformation of the guest suite stunned Robin. His Uncle Kishen was supervising servants busy hanging black velvet curtains over every window. The bed and walls were already covered with black silk; and a new carpet, also black, had turned a perfectly cheerful room into a dismally dark place.

Robin clasped his brow with a dismayed groan. 'Good lord, Uncle Kishen. This place looks like some weird tantric sorcerer's cell!'

'Glad you think so,' his uncle responded. 'Because Maharajah Nut-Bolt Singhji was very precise about his requirements. In fact, I made his Dewan write them down, and got them initialled by Nutty!'

Enjoying the absurdity of the notion of fixing responsibility, Robin began to laugh. His uncle readily joined him. Noticing their white bush-shirt-and-pants clad figures reflected in the tall gilt-framed over-mantle mirror, R.K. Kishen summoned one of the turbaned retainers who was filling the silver cigarette box. 'Roopji, didn't I tell you to remove every single mirror from this room? *Arrey bhai, thhey samjhoh keu koni* (Look here, why don't you chaps understand)? Pisshengunj Durbar must be saved from unlucky faces!'

Grinning broadly, Roopji, the head *farrash*, responded with folded hands, '*Joh hukum*, Rajkumar Saa! But I'll have to call the carpenters. *Aur jimmeywari sab aap ki hai joh Baapji samney peshi hogi toh* (You'll take responsibility if the Maharajah summons me regarding this)!'

It was plain to Robin that his mother had taken special care over the decorations for Pat's birthday lunch. The marble courtyard was painted with perfect roundels and pentagons surrounding lucky signs, all of which would be swabbed off the next day. Fragrant flower garlands and strands of auspicious mango leaves hung over all the *zenana* doors, and huge silver *kumbha kalash* pots stuffed with coconuts, brightly coloured marigolds and cannas, sprigs of grass and leaves, stood in the verandah flanking the arched doorway leading to his wife Wendy's apartment. The traditional birthday *havan* and horoscope-reading had already been performed at the ancestral family shrine in the Fort at the auspicious hour. Food, clothing, and scholarships had been distributed to Brahmins, and the poor and needy. All cousins, distant relations, and retainers had come to wish the Maharajah's grandson, Bhanwar Prithviraj Singh or Pat, a happy long life, and to congratulate his grandparents and parents. The males, except for very close family members like R.K. Kishen, had been up to the *zenani dyodhi*, offering *mujra* to the Maharaniji Saheba and the Yuvraniji Saheba through the *durbariji* on duty. They had received *attar*, *pan* and *supari* from the *rawla* (royal ladies' court) along with *aasish* (blessings) through their respective *badarans* (chief maids). All the male retainers had received the customary new turbans, liveries and uniforms, along with cash presents, each according to his function and seniority. All the maidservants were dressed in new satin *zari-gota ghaghras* and *mulmul odhnas*, and wore the gold and silver jewellery each had collected over the years through faithful service to their queens and princesses.

The minute Robin entered his mother's *rawla*, the *dholans* (female drummers), sitting in a carpeted corner of the marble courtyard, struck their elongated drums and rattled their tambourines and cymbals. While one of them began playing the harmonium, they all broke into a joyful Marwari song. Their bangles and anklets tinkling musically, several young dancing girls surrounded the good-looking prince, twirling and dipping in rhythm, but barring his path till he dug into his white *bandhgala* (closed collar) Jodhpuri jacket, and drew out a brocade bag holding just the precise number of silver coins given to these performers on such occasions. He exchanged a few jokes with some of the older women who had known him from infancy before walking up to touch his mother's feet on this auspicious day. She responded by putting the blood red *kesar-kasturi* tilak, plus a few grains of rice, on his forehead from the *puja thaal*, murmuring a Sanskrit mantra.

His mother and his wife were both wearing the special yellow and red *ladoobhat bandhni poshaks* (dress) reserved for the mothers of sons; while Kitten and Ratna, who had skipped school, were clad in shades of pink. They too kept their heads covered, and, except for the married women's ivory bangles and large nose rings, wore all the appropriate jewellery.

Padmini couldn't help wishing that her husband had returned in time for this special family get-together. Though birthdays were usually celebrated with great gusto in all royal houses, Chattargadh was one of the few Princely Indian States which had three generations of male members in the direct line of succession not only alive at the same time, but also living together in such harmony. She liked observing time-honoured customs which encouraged sharing on these special occasions, and instead of using the dining table, she had insisted they be seated in an informal circle on velvet *gadi masands*, before square silver gilt *bajots*.

Three silver *thaals*—full of bowls and platters containing a variety of meat and vegetable curries, *dahibadas*, a special saffron-scented sweet raisin and nut *pullav*, fried *pooris*, *paapads*, chutney, salads, and pickles—lay between Robin and his pregnant wife, Kitten and Ratna, and the Maharani who shared hers with Pat. Not used to such spicy food, Pat kept taking sips of iced water out of his own silver tumbler, embossed with birds and deer. Ordinarily, Sister Rawlins gave him boring soup-stew-macaroni-cheese. And bread or thin chapattis soaked in *dal*. Even the puddings were the predictable custard-jelly-vermicelli-sago muck. But today they would get his favourite pink strawberry ice cream.

Robin regaled his family with what he had just seen downstairs, adding: 'And Uncle Kishen sends you his apologies, Mama Hukum, for skipping lunch today because he has too many loose ends to tie up before our guest of honour arrives!'

Padmini gave her daughter-in-law a teasing smile. 'That's just his polite way of ensuring that Wendy can be at ease without either of her fathers-in-law around to make her more retiring than usual.'

'What about his daughter?' asked Robin.

'Sita has the measles,' the Maharani explained. 'So she's being kept in quarantine by her husband, who's a doctor after all.'

Telling Ratna to go ahead and enjoy the marrow bone without holding back so politely, Kitten turned to her brother. 'No mirrors?'

'Not one!' laughed Robin. 'You know Uncle Kishen! He swears that it's his humble duty to make sure that Maharajah Nut-Bolt Singhji gets everything he asks for, including the Black Hole of Calcutta for his spiritual enlightenment, because he wouldn't like Chattargadh to be backward in providing perfect Rajput hospitality. *Ateethi Devo Bhava* (Guests are gods!)!'

This made everyone laugh, and Ratna asked her aunt if they could go downstairs just to take a look before this most ungodly guest arrived.

'We'll all go, including Wendy,' said the Maharani. But torn between amusement and anxiety, she couldn't help asking her son: 'Isn't Raj Kumar Saab taking this joke too far? What will *Hajoor* say?'

Robin said cheerfully, 'You mustn't tell him, Mama. Then he can honestly swear he knows nothing, just in case Nutty Kaka starts cribbing.'

'Which he will. But dear Father won't be back from Bombay until His Nutty Highness has got the full black-eye treatment!' grinned Kitten, glancing at her wrist watch.

Pat looked his grandmother in the eye as she helped him wipe his fingers after he'd used the finger bowl. 'I don't mind his being late, though he promised to be back yesterday, Dadisa Hukum. But if it's *my* birthday, then why should I give away one of my best presents to Nutty Dada, who's a silly old chap?'

'You mustn't call him silly,' admonished his mother.

'But everyone does,' retorted Pat. 'Even Colonel CP and the Resident. Plus the Viceroy.'

'And the Kings of England, Egypt, Spain, Yugoslavia, Denmark *and* Greece!' added Kitten.

'See! So why does he get a gift stolen from me for nothing?'

Maharani Padmini hugged Pat. 'For the good of our State, and all our people who need drinking water. And to help Grandfather, who's promised you a big polo pony if you let HH Pisshengunj have this dog.'

Watching his mutinous expression, Kitten hastened to explain. 'It's really a game called Tit for Tat we're all playing with Nutty Uncle, Pat. And this time you'll score the winning goal. Ah, here comes the ice cream.'

The State band struck up a merry march as soon as the procession of motor cars full of dogs entered the palace. Nutty sat in the leading Rolls alongside his beautifully groomed and jewelled St. Bernard, Sunny. His Dewan and ADCs followed in smaller cars with the other dogs and their handlers, all of whom had come from Pisshengunj for this dog-alliance. All the children invited to Pat's birthday bash, including the five Europeans, stopped playing the party game supervised by Kitten and Ratna, and rushed across the lawn. Many of them were laughing. Some of the bigger boys and girls swore that this was going to be even more fun than their last Christmas party with the Maharajah.

Jai Singh deliberately kept chatting with the Resident and his Military Secretary, standing by the long damask-draped table decorated with colourful crêpe streamers, crackers, paper hats, and small floral arrangements, where the birthday cake and treats would soon be served. Mrs Rawlins was holding last minute consultations with the butler about avoiding serving fizzy drinks with too much cake and ice cream. He, however, kept shaking his bare head, insisting that His Highness hated stinginess even if it meant that the children overate with disastrous consequences.

'But he's not a trained nurse,' snapped the governess.

The butler only beamed. 'Come on, Sister Saab, enjoy the fun like everybody else.'

Pat began the ceremonies by promptly garlanding the enormous brown and white dog held on a ruby-and-diamond-studded leash by Nutty, who was fully togged out in ceremonial regalia, with jewelled turban, brocade *achkan*, strands of pearls round his neck, and a broad gold anklet on his right leg. Nutty's Dewan and ADCs were also formally dressed. However, except for Pat, the Chattargadh people wore simple white cotton *bandhgala* jackets with enamelled buttons over perfectly creased white trousers and casual loafers. Grinning merrily, R.K. Kishen, Zorji and Ganpat Singh garlanded their Pisshengunj counterparts, while Ratna and Kitten sprinkled them with rose water.

By this time, the excited dog had stopped barking, and had rolled over to get his stomach tickled, quite oblivious to his master's command to behave and not get his coat all muddy.

Kitten reminded her nephew to garland the bridegroom's father quickly so that they could get on with the fun.

'I can't unless he bends down,' protested Pat.

At this Jai Singh couldn't help chuckling. He exchanged a triumphant look with his daughter who had come up with this brilliant idea of bringing Nutty down to such a childish level. Followed by the two Englishmen, he joined Nutty and the others, walking towards the temporary *pandal* (pavilion) made of banana trunks and leaves, marigold garlands, and decorated earthen pots full of coconuts. Amusedly Gerald Redverse watched one of the small boys, identified as a Brahmin by birth, preparing to light the sacred fire, and start the *havan* round which the much-discussed dog wedding would be solemnised. As he watched Pat talk soothingly to his own suitably adorned dog (which had only been brought into the garden at the last minute, but was already barking and baring her teeth in fearsome growls in an effort to defend her turf),

Redverse couldn't help wondering whether he would be able to get through this mad birthday party without cracking up and seriously compromising the dignity of his post.

Colonel CP confided to him in an aside that he had recommended the use of tranquillisers. Obviously pills weren't quite as effective as stun darts. They were both truly thankful when the bizarre ceremony was over, and the two snarling St. Bernards had been taken off in different directions for their evening exercise. The children returned noisily to enjoying their own party, exchanging hats and pulling crackers with one another.

Noticing the plaster patches on Nutty's face as they stood drinking tea, Jai Singh inquired solicitously, 'What happened, Nutty? Shall I ask our doctor to take a look at you?'

'Thank you, Bhai. But I always carry my own doctor around, and don't need yours,' said Nutty. 'But really, Your Highness, you should think about installing mirrors for your guests, at least in the bathrooms.'

The Maharajah was puzzled, but only for a moment. 'Kishen Singhji Maharaj?'

Robin added, 'Why didn't you tell me immediately, Nutty Kaka? Someone must have broken the mirrors during the hectic rush to prepare your suite exactly to your specifications.'

'What, all of them?' scoffed Nutty. 'This is not the first time I've stayed here, Robin. And let me tell you, I wouldn't tolerate such a clumsy, irresponsible staff in Pisshengunj. Not for a moment. Because broken mirrors bring bad luck.'

Turning to CP, the Resident asked: 'What's this mirror business about?'

The Colonel made an expressive face. 'Settling old scores. Let's stay out of this.'

By now Kitten and Ratna had finished serving the children, and had strolled over to join the grown-ups. In their very different ways, both looked perfectly lovely in their traditional *poshaks* and diamond-studded *rakhris*. They were careful not to let their gossamer georgette *odhnas* slide off their heads or get tangled in the shrubs. They were just in time to see the Resident choking on his sandwich as Kishen Singh protested.

'Really, Your Highness, our staff is not to blame. I had the mirrors removed because Pisshengunj Durbar had given me very specific instructions about not letting him come face to face with any unlucky person. So what else could I do?'

And when, to prove his point, he pulled out a crested note bearing the Pisshengunj Maharajah's seal and signature, everyone burst out laughing.

Tit for Tat   2

Even though he had a perfectly understandable aversion to getting involved in local problems, the Resident sat listening patiently to Rao Saheb Koodsu's complaints. Ceiling fans whirred overhead, though the long hot summer was over. The Indian polo season was about to begin with the advent of October. In fact, Gerald Redverse, kitted out in spurred knee-length riding boots, white Jodhpurs with pressure pads, and a collarless red polo shirt, wondered why his garrulous visitor, a veteran of the game with an enviably high handicap, was not already on the ground.

Without pausing for the Resident's bearer, Thapa, to leave the drawing room after serving them iced *nimboo pani* (fresh lemonade) in tall frosted glasses, Rao Saheb Koodsu continued: 'Resident Saab, this *julam* . . . how you say, injustice, has got to stop. Chattargadh has nine Raos— hereditary chiefs—who would be Dukes in England, *maha-queers* in France . . . .'

Suddenly distracted by the sound of a car driving up to the Residency and someone repeatedly blowing the horn, the Rajput nobleman stopped talking.

The gauze screen door shut with a bang as Colonel Claude-Poole strode into the room, impatiently swinging his riding crop. 'I say, Reverse Gear! Can't keep the Maharajah waiting, old chap. He's always so damned punctual, y'know.'

Carefully putting down his wife's cherished glass on the carved rosewood centre table, Redverse rose to receive his friend. CP noticed the muscular greying man, previously hidden from view by the high-backed wing chair in which he sat. 'Ah, *Khamaghani*, Rao Saheb. Sorry to barge in on your private meeting with the Resident, but . . . .'

'But nothing, Kurnel Saab,' retorted Koodsu, also rising. 'Residents are not sent here at great expense to His Majesty's Government to exorcise maharajahs on polo grounds! I have urgently come to tell him about the terrible problems faced by self-respecting persons like myself, who would be holdall-goes in Spain. But our Maharajah cares two hoots about losing them! Count, if you please . . . .'

Aware that Reverse Gear was trying not to laugh, Colonel CP widened his eyes in wonder, playing along. 'Holdalls, Rao Saheb?'

'I think Koodsu Rao Saheb means hidalgos, CP.'

'Exactly!' continued Koodsu. 'First there are nine total. But one you can forget about, because now he's a bigger shot. I don't know how your feudal system works. But here in Rajputana, we aristocrats are the ruler's kinsmen. Co-conquerors and *sirayti* . . . how you say, shareholders in this State. We are not beggars, living on lands gifted to us by this Maharajah. I may not be a Rathor, but who gave them horses when they were walking barefoot in the desert after being driven out of Kanauj? My forefathers. For which they were given a *jagir*. But we Shyanis have served this State well. And now I'm being thrown out for no reason, and my estates are being grabbed by the Maharajah. That is *julam, ghor julam*, Resident Saàb. And you must stop it.'

'I understand your feelings, Rao Saheb. But we have strict instructions from His Majesty's Government not to interfere in the internal affairs of any Princely State. And the Maharajah can take away what he has given,' replied the Resident.

'No, he cannot!' retorted the Rao Saheb of Koodsu. Emphatically thumping the centre table, and making Gerald Redverse wince as the fragile crystal and porcelain ornaments danced up and down, he demanded: 'Suppose you present me this table? Will you take it back?'

Stumped for an answer, Gerald prevaricated. 'Well, I could ask you for it . . . .'

Eloquently snapping his fingers, the Rajput chief continued, 'Yes, Resident Saab. But would you send *sipahis* (soldiers) to snatch it back by force?'

Truly on the horns of a dilemma, the Resident shrugged.

Pointedly tapping his watch, CP intervened. 'Sorry, Rao Saheb, but I really must drag the Resident away.'

Walking his unhappy visitor to his chauffeur-driven Morris Minor and shaking hands, Redverse said, 'Goodbye, Rao Saheb. Actually, it might be a good idea to discuss this matter with the Chattargadh Dewan, Raj Kumar Kishen Singhji. I'll also have a word with him.'

Koodsu Rao Saheb gave a derisive snort. 'Hhrummph. That duffer will misguide you completely. This whole *gadbad ghotala* (troublesome nonsense) is all because of him and his family pressures. You are still new, Resident Saab. But very soon you will learn that in Chattargadh, the Maharajah is God, and Raj Kumar Saab is his ever-ready rubber stamp! Ask any child.'

Even though it was the first practice match umpired by two professionals well known in Calcutta polo circles, the Maharajah was in good form. No matter which pony he drew, Jai Singh instantly established a mystical rapport with his horse. After a hard-fought Hurlingham Championship Cup final which the Indian team captained by him had won, one of his renowned German rivals had quipped that Chattargadh and his mounts were telepathic. Jai Singh's courteous yet tongue-in-cheek response giving credit to team work plus his priceless pot-pourri of Scythian-Parthian-Dravidian-Hun cum Aryan genes had been cited by several sports correspondents. It had caused approval and censure in almost equal measure within Raj and Rajwara circles.

An ancient war game (which trained both mounts and riders to moving fast among other horses, and to instant turning and checking at top speed), polo had flourished in India since Mughal times. The desert States of Jodhpur and Chattargadh had specialised in breeding and training compact crossbred Marwari and Arab ponies, which knew the game almost from the moment of foaling because they came from a long line of polo-playing ponies.

The Maharajah's team wore collarless red T-shirts, and his cousin, Kishen, captained those in blue. They were as evenly matched as the handicapping system permitted, with Jai Singh and Kishen at No. 4, because they were the longest hitters and the most experienced players. The Resident and the Military Secretary played at No. 3, both very well mounted on fast, agile ponies. They rode up and down the length of the 300-yard-long boarded ground without crossing the line of the ball or cutting across another pony's path so as to avoid committing fouls. Zorji and Ganpat Singhji were at No. 2, while Robin and his equally dashing (though much younger) cousin, Arjun, as forwards stayed up to cover each other. All wore hard helmets, leather knee pads over handmade riding boots, and held their polo sticks with practised ease in order to avoid tripping or hurting any horse or player.

By the third *chukker* (round), the Blues were leading by one goal. Robin was forced to ride off the ground to change his polo stick, as its head had broken. This gave

Redverse the marvellous opportunity to feed the ball with a good clear hit to the Maharajah, who immediately galloped off to score another goal. By the time the final bugle blew after another seven and a half minutes of hard riding and clever positioning, the Maharajah and the Resident were smiling and congratulating each other even as the regular spectators clapped and commented.

Syces sprang forward as the teams dismounted, rewarding and patting their snorting and blowing foam-flecked mounts. Jai Singh and Kishen ran their experienced eyes over their entire strings, checking each gartered leg, each hoof and hock, ensuring that no horse was cut or bruised. CP's roan mare kept trying to chew off her martingale, and the rather large chestnut Robin had ridden in the final *chukker* had a bruise on her nearside rump due to excessively rough riding by Arjun, who in Robin's eyes, had taken unseemly advantage of his special status as the Maharajah's nephew and guest. But otherwise, the ponies were in good shape, and the vet could stand down.

Exhilarated though sweaty after a game that had opened up, Jai Singh sat chatting affably with the chiefs and officials on the Polo Club verandah as turbaned bearers served them chilled beer and iced lemonade. Cane chairs and *modas* were grouped around a tea trolley. While everyone's attention was on other things, Pat dashed off with the bowl of sugar cubes.

Robin, who never, out of deference, smoked in his father's presence, couldn't help enviously inhaling the nicotine from Colonel Claude-Poole's 555 State Express cigarette, his own brand. 'We may both be four handicap players, but everyone knows we're not here to win a game. We just play to give His Highness some exercise! And the best ponies automatically go to his team . . . .'

'Robin, you know your father's very fair when it comes to mounting us. He makes each one of us pick slips out of a hat, with the pony's name and colour written on it. And with two new players—Reverse Gear and Arjun—on the Maharajah's team today, I'd say that we had a slight advantage, wouldn't you?' countered the Colonel.

Redverse joined Kishen Singh next to some dusty potted palms. 'I had an interesting visitor this afternoon, Raj Kumar Saheb. He seems a bit worked up about HH resuming his *jagir* (estate).'

The prince peered at the Resident through the green Ray Bans he had put on immediately after dismounting. 'Shall I tell you the real reason for this *tamasha*? Typical Rajput mentality of this senile chap! The bloody fool is forcing his one and only son, Dumpy . . . yes, yes, our palace doctor, and Robin's childhood friend . . . to remarry for begetting heirs. So far his wife has only produced four daughters in five years. But Dumpy is very modern and really fond of his wife, who happens to be my daughter.'

'And the Maharajah's niece,' concluded Gerald.

'Whose mother died in childhood. But did *I* hasten to remarry just for the sake of giving my helpless child a stepmother? Our old governess, Nanny Ashley, was good enough. And there was my sister-in-law, the Maharani, who insisted on keeping Sita in the palace even after Kitten was born. This left me totally free to serve my brother the Maharajah, and our people.'

As Colonel CP and Robin strolled over to join the Resident, the Maharajah inquired: 'Robin, where's Pat?'

'Really, Your Highness, I'm not your grandson's nanny!' Robin retorted, still peevish after having failed to win the game.

Redverse stored up all the unsolicited information poured into his willing ears by Robin and his uncle Kishen. He had lived in India long enough to know that there was no such thing as having cousins in the European sense here. The Rajputs, especially, took blood ties and clan kinship very seriously.

The prince confided that Koodsu Rao Saheb was making life miserable for his son and daughter-in-law. However, since the law of the land was on their side, there was nothing much he could do. Of course, they were very happy to hear that the Resident had refused to get involved.

Robin, who was hungry after all that hard riding, signalled to one of the waiters, who immediately fetched plates piled with sandwiches and potato chips for them as they sat around the tea trolley. 'They've forgotten the sugar again,' noted Kishen. 'Robin, could you please ring the bell?'

'No need, Mamosa Hukum. I've just retrieved it from the horses,' laughed Arjun, only son of Jai Singh's sister, Diamond, and Sir Pratab Singh of Fateypur.

Telling Arjun to stop interrupting, Robin continued: 'One day both of them landed up to see me at the same time. They had a ridiculous slanging match. You should have heard Dumpy telling his father the facts of life! According to our Doctor Saab, it's the father—not the mother—who determines the child's sex!'

'I didn't know that,' said CP, consuming his third cheese and chutney sandwich.

'Bachelors don't need to know these things, CP, because we all know that they're never responsible.' Everyone chuckled at this sweeping indictment from the Resident.

Stirring his tea, Robin stated, 'But the father's always responsible, Mr Redverse, as Dumpy proved by showing us medical reports, statistics, and that Irish chappie's Nobel prize-winning theory.'

Impressed, the Resident asked, 'What was his father's reaction, Robin?'

Robin pursed his lips. 'Absolutely unbelievable. Koodsu Rao Saab, who's at least 58 years old, says that if his spineless son can't produce an heir to ensure the succession to their 456-year-old *jagir*, then *he'll* get a new wife, and have some more sons!'

'And now we hear that he's engaged to a 16-year-old girl,' added Arjun.

'Who'll become Dumpy's stepmother, and my 22-year-old sister Sita's mother-in-law!' concluded Robin.

'How on earth could the girl's parents agree to such an alliance?' demanded the Resident.

Colonel CP surprised his friend by revealing that the girl was an orphan. 'And her relations are only too happy to get her off their hands without having to provide a huge dowry.'

'Grossly medieval, don't you think?' said Redverse.

'Oh no, we're not,' protested Kishen. 'Because the day our Maharajah found out when Koodsu Rani Saab came to tell our Maharani Sahebah, his *jagir* got confiscated. And he went crying to you!'

'You see, we DO march with the times. There's a league and a law against polygamy in our State!' announced Robin, his good humour restored.

Thousands of people crowded the great courtyard of the 600-year-old Chattargadh Fort, to participate in the colourful annual Dussehra Durbar pageant usually held with great pomp and ceremony in every Hindu State in the country. On a flagstone terrace adjoining the great Chattar Mahal courtyard (where armies had mustered in the good old days, and where all processions and festivals still began), bards and musicians sat on striped dhurries, singing the saga of Lord Rama's victory over Ravana, King of Sri Lanka, and the rescue of Rama's abducted wife, Princess Sita.

After having kept the entire nine-day Navratri fast along with his wife, performed the traditional *havan* and *shastra puja* on the tenth day or Vijay Dashmi, and sacrificed a goat with a single sword stroke to the Rathor family goddess Mahishasura Mardini Nagnechya Mata, or Chamunda Devi in front of his kinsmen, high priests, and other subjects, Jai

Singh had bathed and changed from his blood-speckled russet dhoti-kurta into a spotless white *achkan-birjees*. This was offset by his jewelled and plumed saffron turban, brocade cummerbund, gold-hilted ceremonial sword, medals, and decorations, including the Star of India. His ancient sandalwood throne, brought from the original Rashtrakuta kingdom in what is now modern Karnataka, was flanked on his left by low, silver-gilt chairs on which sat his three immediate heirs, Robin, Pat, and Raj Kumar Kishen Singh.

On his left were ranged identical velvet-cushioned silver chairs for the nine hereditary chiefs of Chattargadh, whose attendance at Dussehra Durbars was mandatory to renew their oaths of allegiance. Two of these seats, however, were conspicuously empty. The Durbar Hall, with its carved sandstone pillars, marble floors, pietra dura and mirror-inlaid walls and ceiling, was full of gaily clad men with respectfully covered heads, young boys eagerly jostling forward to get nearer the throne, and the usual contingent of sumptuously costumed and jewelled dancing girls with veiled faces. Incense sticks and perforated *attar* bowls scented the air as the occasional overwhelmed *charan bhaat*, or old Brahmin high priest, burst forth into loud praise of their beloved Maharajah, invoking blessings on him and his clan.

Impressively sturdy, moustached bodyguards with spears stood at every entrance arch, for, in keeping with tradition, the Durbar Hall was open to the public and had no doors. The British Resident, Military Secretary and other State officials, including judges, doctors and college principals, sat in strict order of precedence across the hall from the chiefs. Behind them were ranged the wealthy *Seth-Sahukars* who also formed an important part of every native State's hierarchy. Chattargadh's economy and welfare services benefitted greatly from their contributions. They had also served their rulers well as ministers, advisers, and bankers over the centuries.

Two *chawari* bearers flicking gold-handled yak-tail whisks, two soldiers with drawn swords, two *mor chari* bearers holding peacock feathers in four-feet-high gold cylinders, a nobleman with the Maharajah's shield, and another carrying the saffron-and-crimson Chattargadh standard, stood behind Jai Singh. The dignified old Durbariji with his impeccably groomed white, fan-shaped beard, tight pink *pugri*, and old-fashioned, pleated *mulmul fargal*, stepped forward. Tapping his great golden mace on the floor, he began calling out the names and titles of the chiefs in order of seniority. Each got up in turn, delving into pockets before advancing with stately dignity to the Maharajah, to present the traditionally stipulated token tribute of 21, 11, or 5 silver rupees which were laid out on brand new brocade or silk kerchiefs.

'Jobner Raja Saab Lakhan Singhji! *Chattargadh Riyasat ka Sirayti Rathor Sardar! Dolaadi tajeem ka haqdar! Sava saat lakh koh patto! Takhat ka Mujra wastey haajir howo saa!*' cried the Durbari.

In keeping with customs forged by their fiercely independent and outspoken nature, and the immutable *primus inter parus* spirit of all the Rajput clans which had emerged after the fall of the Gupta and Vardhan empires, Maharajah Jai Singh rose to receive the youthful chief's tribute. They exchanged a few smiling words. The Maharajah remained standing till the young chief backed away with folded hands and resumed his seat.

The Durbariji tapped again with his gold mace. 'Bhainswara Raja Saab Natwar Singhji! *Takhat ka Mujra wastey haajir howo saa!*'

At this, the mood changed instantly. A ripple of laughter ran through the Durbar: the aristocrats exchanged amused glances and quips; old timers smiled and muttered invectives; and several people, including Robin, openly relished the all too familiar joke.

Glancing at his wristwatch, and then at the main entrance arch, the Chattargadh Dewan, R.K. Kishen, rose almost on cue. '*Gareeb Niwaz*! Bhainswar Raja Saab is absent again from our Dussehra Durbar without Your Highness' permission.'

For a moment the Maharajah sat considering this information. Then he decreed: 'Let the absent *jagirdar* be fined 2,000 rupees as usual for failing in his duty, and setting a bad example to our Bhaipa, and Chattargadh's other *Sirayti* Sardars.'

His curiosity thoroughly aroused—for he knew that the Rajputs prided themselves on their close-knit blood brotherhoods or Bhaipa, and loyalty to the head of their clan—the Resident asked the Military Secretary sotto voce: 'Who's this misguided chap?'

Grinning widely, Colonel CP whispered, 'Nutty Pisshengunj!'

Comprehension dawned on Gerald Redverse. 'Ahhum. This explains a lot. I must read my 'Tod' more carefully to get a clearer perspective.'

Seven handcuffed prisoners, clad in spotlessly clean handloom clothes, were ushered into the Durbar by smart policemen. Although Jai Singh had tried his best to eradicate crime from his State, he still had to reckon with human nature. But the statistics were noteworthy, and his justice system exemplary. From the time of his accession, he had tried to remember the advice given to Rama, the Hindu epitome of the perfect king, by the dying Ravana, himself one of the greatest scholars, rulers, and mystics of his era: 'The primary duty of a king is to give justice, temper justice with mercy, protect his subjects, provide for their material and spiritual needs; and pause before doing anything contrary to the advice of his kinsmen and ministers.'

At a signal from the Maharajah, Kishen Singh rose to announce: 'Today, at this Dussehra Durbar held in honour of Bhagwan Ramchandraji's victory over evil in the *Treta yug*, our gracious Maharajah Jai Singhji Bahadur sets these prisoners free. They have been reformed, and having sworn on the Ganga *jal* and the Koran Sharif to amend their ways, they will be rehabilitated at state expense. That is, all except Maan Singh *Daku*.'

After the others were set free to loud cries of '*Khamma, Baapji!*' and '*Raj amar ho Maharajah Jai Singh koh!*', a solitary bearded youth with an impressive physique and pugnacious stance, was left standing in the hall, flanked by two guards.

'Maan Singh, don't you want a better life for yourself and your family?' Jai Singh asked with genuine concern.

The bandit responded with perfect equanimity. 'Baapji knows that I have never done anything dishonourable even though my *sanskar* turned me into a dacoit at the age of 14.'

Nodding agreement, for he knew the all too familiar story of treachery, injustice and vendetta flowing from affronts to ancestral *aan-baan*, Jai Singh continued. '*Sanskars* can be changed through right action, Maan Singhji. You too can go free on one condition. Give me your word of honour as a Rajput that you will stop looting the Princely States.'

Maan Singh looked the Maharajah in the eye with an impudent smile. '*Raghu kul reeti sada chali ayi, pran jayi par vachan na jayi!*'

At a signal from the Maharajah, the dacoit's handcuffs were removed. 'You're free to go anywhere you like. But having your welfare very much at heart, I'd like to know how you're going to live now.'

His dark eyes gleaming and teeth flashing, Maan Singh answered with perfect aplomb. 'Really, Your Highness! By looting British India, of course!'

Loud guffaws of laughter greeted this sally, and by the time the Maharajah and the Raj representative recovered, the dacoit had vanished.

With a finger on his lips indicating silence to the two elderly maids gossiping with the governess busy knitting in a quiet sunny corner, Maharajah Jai Singh stood watching his agile and scruffy daughter Kitten and his grandson turning handsprings and cartwheels across the lawn. They were laughing and calling instructions to each other. Their discarded sweaters lay draped over a lady's bicycle, and their warm woollen trousers and plaid shirts were badly stained. Some sixth sense made Mrs Rawlins look over her shoulder. Seeing the Maharajah, she sprang up, apologising profusely. Jai Singh silenced her with a rueful smile, commiserating with her for having to take charge of an incorrigibly tomboyish sixteen-year-old *enfant terrible*, who seemed to be enjoying herself just as much as four-year-old Pat.

One look at her husband striding across the walled *zenana* bagh without having bothered to shower and change out of his polo kit, told Maharani Padmini that something was up. She immediately stopped the brisk walk she enjoyed almost every winter evening, when roses, poinsettias, oleanders, hibiscus, and bougainvillea were in full bloom.

Kitten and Pat sprang up from the grass before the Maharajah could reprimand them for their rowdy behaviour. But since he seemed preoccupied, they both went off indoors to wash and tidy up.

'Hello, darling. How did your game go today?' asked the Maharani, rearranging her bright blue silk sari to cover her head, and buttoning up her Jaeger cashmere cardigan.

'Your beloved son tried to ride me off again. One of these days he's either going to hurt himself, or ruin a perfectly good horse,' was the tart rejoinder.

'Nothing could be worse than that,' agreed Padmini, amused, as usual, by his warped priorities.

'I think it's time to send Robin off to Sandhurst, where he'll learn discipline and self-control.'

Waiting till they were seated on garden chairs placed to catch the welcome warmth from the setting sun, Padmini said, 'He seems keener to join the RAF.'

The Maharajah waved his hand dismissively. 'Tiger's reprehensible influence, no doubt. He made Cambridge fashionable among the younger lot; then Paris and the Riviera in preference to London. And now it's flying over the more usual cavalry or artillery units.'

'And everyone knows who moulded Maharajah Tiger Fateypur's likes and dislikes!' teased his wife.

Aware that she was referring to his very determined and modern sister, Princess Diamond—who had assumed charge of her seven-year-old nephew Tiger's upbringing after the tragic deaths of both his parents when their ship to Europe sank in one of those terrible typhoons just off the Malabar coast—Jai Singh quickly changed the subject. 'But that's not what I wanted to discuss with you. Would you like to visit Pisshengunj next week with me?'

Surprised, she asked, 'What on earth for? There is very little for ladies to do in Pisshengunj. The three Maharanis are always in purdah! It's all right for you, though, because of the duck shoots, and so on. Besides, I thought we were going to spend some time in Delhi before going to Calcutta for the Christmas polo season?'

Jai Singh hastened to explain. 'We have to treat it as a State emergency, sweetheart. Because Nutty's third wife is Koodsu Rao Saab's sister, and because I exiled him just before Dussehra, Nutty has retaliated by throwing all our engineers and construction workers out of Pisshengunj.'

'That's carrying family feuds too far,' observed Padmini. 'You should ask the Viceroy to stop His Nutty Highness from taking undue advantage of our disadvantage at a time like this.'

'Nutty has turned the Viceroy against me by complaining that I publicly humiliate him every year at the Dussehra Durbar! The British simply refuse to understand that Nutty's great-grandfather was just a younger brother, with a small *jagir* in Chattargadh before grabbing Pisshengunj. He merely took advantage of the fact that the Mughals, Marathas, and Sikhs were busy plundering each other early in the last century.'

'Which still makes him your brother prince, and ruler of our nearest riparian state,' retorted his wife with her usual candour. 'Isn't it time to stop this childish game of tit for tat? Just savour the fact that our branch of the family will end up inheriting Pisshengunj if Nut-Bolt Singhji continues to remain childless.'

'Uh-humm. But I often feel that Nutty wouldn't resent us so much if we had a younger son whom he could adopt, and bring up as his own,' mused the Maharajah.

Clasping her hands together, the Maharani rejoined: 'Then for that reason alone I'm glad there's only Robin. Unless you are thinking of handing your grandson over to His Nutty Highness for the sake of your famous canal!'

'You *know* I wouldn't do that. But tell me, why is Pat always stuck in the *zenana*?'

'Because neither he nor Kitten can be left alone for a minute. And Sister Rawlins can't be in two places at the same time. I think you saw that gymnastics display just now!'

Jai Singh couldn't help chuckling at the memory of all the childish pranks the two managed to pull off, in and out of supervision. He also knew that they took advantage of the lack of Ratna's restraining influence whenever she went home every year during the winter, summer, and Dussehra break to spend time with her own parents in their little state of Buggery near Mount Abu. But there was no need to spoil Pat, or encourage him to emulate his aunt just because his mother was still in hospital after a difficult Caesarean section.

'What a pity Pat won't be ready for Mayo College for three more years. What he needs is the challenge of studying and playing with boys his own age in an atmosphere where he's just another schoolboy, and not the Maharajah's grandson,' said Jai Singh briskly.

Nodding agreement, Padmini smiled as she observed the governess escorting a beaming nun (wearing the long white habit, starched wimple, veil, rope cord, crucifix, and the long brown woollen mantle of her Franciscan order) through the garden.

Rising, she said, 'Then you'll be happy to see Mother Angelus, who's here to discuss Pat's admission—and our donation—to Saint Mary's.'

After exchanging hearty greetings, handshakes, and kisses, the Maharajah and Maharani sat exchanging news with Mother Angelus. Kitten joined them for the lavish high tea on two trolleys wheeled in by two elderly women who had come more than 25 years ago as wet nurses to Robin, remained to care for his younger siblings, and then his son. The assortment of hot cauliflower *pakoras*, crisp little *samosas*, perfect fruit cake, lemon tarts, and salmon sandwiches disappeared as the Maharajah, the nun, and the princess helped themselves. The Maharani poured aromatic Earl Grey tea into virtually transparent Royal Doulton cups from a crested silver service.

Wiping her mouth on the dainty organdie serviette Mother Angelus continued, 'So I said to the Bishop, we must keep trying till we find a way of touching the Maharajah's heart. We've got branches in every Rajput State here except Pisshengunj . . . .'

'My dear Mother Angelus, Nutty has no heart!' swore Jai Singh, 'And he's very anti-missionary.'

'All the more reason to pursue our plan,' responded Sister Angelus with a decided twinkle in her intelligent Irish eyes. 'Going where we are most unwanted is the first duty of all missionaries!'

Everyone laughed. Psychologically and socially in tune with any aristocracy, Mother Angelus had been born Lady Anne FitzGerald. She was rated as the most popular nun in north India. She had come out as a young woman of 21 to visit her uncle, the Bishop of Ajmer, and stayed on to found a Franciscan teaching and nursing order which was immediately confirmed by the Pope, who believed that the lively former debutante had found her real vocation. Having a gift for languages, Mother Angelus had endeared herself very quickly by speaking the local dialect with the parents, students, native princes, and the poorer persons who flocked to the free dispensaries attached to every convent she opened. Since her avowed aim was education, not conversion to Christianity, she soon forged a special friendship with the progressive Maharajah and Maharani of Chattargadh, who were dedicated to the cause of modernisation and female education.

'But Pisshengunj is frightfully backward, Mother,' warned Padmini.

'Really, Your Highness. Then we shall start by emancipating the Maharajah's children,' Sister Angelus stated with a firm little nod.

A huge grin split Kitten's face. 'He hasn't got any, Mother—thank God!'

Setting down her teacup on the hand-embroidered tablecloth, the nun considered this information. 'But surely he has nephews and nieces? And, there must be several good, well-to-do families besides all the State officials who want their children to learn English, the international lingua franca!'

The Maharajah gave her a rueful smile. 'Believe me,

Mother Angelus, I really want to help you. But Nutty
Pisshengunj can't be coaxed or bullied . . . .'

'Our Mother Superior could try taming him, like
Androcles and the Lion,' interposed Kitten.

Jai Singh gave his impish daughter a pat on the arm.
'Yes, but first we'll have to put a thorn in his paw!'

Feeling that the garden had become rather chilly after
sunset, Padmini suggested that they move inside so that
they could chat a little longer, and persuade Mother
Angelus to play the piano for them.

A cosy coal fire had been lit in the Maharani's drawing
room, and an electric heater was switched on to warm the
adjoining chamber where the grand concert piano stood.
The Maharajah pushed open the connecting glass double
doors while Kitten dug up some leather-bound music books
from a corner cupboard. The Mother Superior, who gave
them piano and singing lessons besides teaching them
English and elocution, always stressed the importance of
following an original score as closely as the composer
intended. She disapproved of thumped out variations which
most of her pupils seemed to prefer. After entertaining
them with two charming Chopin mazurkas, she coaxed the
Maharani to play her favourite Mozart piece. The
entertainment ended with a stirring Spanish bolero played
in quick tempo by Mother Angelus as Kitten turned the
pages.

Enjoying her polished performance, which reminded him
of concerts he had attended in various European capitals
and American cities, Jai Singh was suddenly struck by an
idea. As Mrs Rawlins came in to say that the car was ready
to take the Mother Superior back to the convent,
Maharajah Jai Singh exclaimed, 'By Jove, I've got it! You're
coming with us to Pisshengunj, Mother Angelus. And we'll
leave the rest to God—plus the psychology of the
individual!'

The Resident almost lost his much vaunted sang-froid when he first set eyes on that abysmally original and undeniably colourful display of porcelain pisspots brimming with hardy English annuals, ferns, and cacti lining the Pisshengunj Maharajah's terraced riverside garden.

'This chap's incredible,' he said to CP. 'Why don't people call him Potty, instead of Nutty?'

Shrugging expressively, the Colonel responded: 'Can't say. But Nutty's an aberration of Natwar, and His Nutty Highness is notorious for his practical jokes. So watch out, Reverse Gear.'

Nutty stood talking to Baron Tikemoffsky on the marble terrace overlooking the river even as he studied his dogs taking their afternoon exercise on leashes around the ample lawns. His eyes were alert to the least sign of neglect on the part of their handlers. It gave him great joy to see that the perfectly matched pair of St. Bernards he had plotted and schemed to acquire, had begun to tolerate each other, and that he could hope to mate them as soon as they came into season. These pleasant reflections were broken when Nutty spied Bhoorji escorting his detestably cocky cousin towards him.

The Englishmen strolled across to join the two Maharajahs just in time to overhear Nutty's cryptic utterance. 'A little conning, Tikky.'

'What's Your Highness' definition of conning?' Gerald asked Nutty.

Taking instant offence to the Resident's tone, Nutty swore, 'Mr Redverse, English may be YOUR mother tongue, but I speak it like a native!'

'Are you ready to take us boating, Nutty?' Jai Singh asked his host.

Folding his hands in mock servility, Nutty responded, 'Hukum, Hajoor! We've been patiently waiting for you to finish your afternoon nap.'

With admirable forbearance, Jai Singh resisted comment. Nutty knew that he hadn't been napping. He had, instead, been enduring a rather tediously tearful meeting with Nutty's third wife Neeru Baa, who was undoubtedly entitled to a hearing from the ruler of her own State. However, she was incapable of comprehending the virtue or sanctity of Chattargadh's anti-polygamy law, and was concerned only with getting him to reinstate her brother, Rao Saheb Koodsu.

The entire party proceeded towards the palace ghat, where the Pisshengunj Maharajah's ceremonial motor launch and other boats were moored. They were just in time to see the elaborately curtained and painted pleasure craft reserved for his wives setting off upstream. Kitten, Mother Angelus, and their escort Raj Kumar Kishen, were leaning over the double railings, and waving at them. The four Maharanis were seated decorously beneath the purdah awning, able to enjoy the view but remaining unseen by vulgar eyes. Nutty's own launch steamed in the opposite direction, its powerful engine roaring as it created deep dark furrows in the water, and sent up gold-crested waves and swirls of white water spray. The two Englishmen found this changing scenario particularly refreshing after having borne the dry, dusty monotony of Chattargadh for so long.

Pointing to the river bank lined with temple spires, Nutty said, 'Sir Aurel Stein tells me that these ancient Jain shrines are even more beautiful than those at Jaisalmer, Ranakpur, or Delwara. And our Hindu temples can only be compared to those at Konarak and Tanjore.'

His guests merely nodded, exchanging 'humour him' signals. Maharajah Jai Singh, Colonel Claude-Poole, and the Resident were all equally keen to end the impasse created by Koodsu Rao Saheb's second marriage and his subsequent exile from Chattargadh.

The 150-year-old palace complex created by Nutty's father and grandfather had simply been added on to the original 12th century citadel once ruled by the Parmar kings whose line was now defunct. Local legends credited them with amassing a huge horde of treasure collected by looting all the looters returning home to Afghanistan, Persia, and Central Asia over nearly seven centuries. This had fallen into the hands of Nutty's ancestors, and become the source of Pisshengunj's mysterious wealth.

The motor launch passed beneath a spacious concrete bridge spanning the river. It led to the opposite bank on which the ancient city stood. Narrow alleys zigzagged uphill through rows of colourful shops and white-washed houses. People wrapped in shawls and dhotis used the numerous ghats for bathing, praying, meditating, or simply lounging. Barefooted children played on the steps and platforms, while several women clad in colourful veils and flared *ghaghras* were beating soiled garments against the stones. Others were scrubbing brass and copper utensils and then rinsing them in the river. Groups of men and women carried gleaming water pitchers for religious rites and rituals, often pausing to pour out libations to various deities under the *peepul* and banyan trees thriving along the waterfront. Ferry boats carrying villagers with baskets of vegetables, fish, and fruit sailed across the river, with their passengers and rowers raising folded palms with loud salutations to their Maharajah. Camels, cattle, hobbled ponies, donkeys, foraging sheep and goats scrambled up and down the wooded banks. Peasant children could be seen bathing their buffaloes in the shallow sandy stretches.

'See that, Mr Redverse? I have even made the river safe for my people,' boasted Nutty. 'There is absolutely no danger here in Pisshengunj to anybody from dangerous things like crocodiles-shockodiles!'

'Really, Your Highness. And how, may I ask, has that been achieved?' asked the Resident.

The Maharajah of Pisshengunj pointed to several large sign boards. 'See those bright red signs in the latest American day-and-night glo paint clearly saying "Crocodiles Keep Out!"'

Choking back a laugh as he and CP exchanged a quick conspiratorial look, and recalling the fate of Sir Henry Higgins' crocs, the Resident couldn't resist asking: 'And what if some misguided reptiles do come swimming dangerously close to Your Highness' city limits?'

'Then, bang!' swore Nutty, raising an imaginary gun to his shoulder. 'My best shikaris soon turn such disobedient beasts into suitable gifts for a few lucky handpicked guests. Which reminds me, I must send some suitcases to your rooms, because matching alligator-skin luggage is very fashionable these days. But it's a pity that my dear brother, HH Chattargadh, can't have what's in vogue because he's terribly allergic to crocodiles in any shape or form!'

Shrugging, Jai Singh conceded that everyone had at least one weakness.

Nutty had instructed his boatmen to take them up to the canal headworks. He knew exactly how to soften his cousin. It was all too easy to withhold all those millions of cusecs of water for which his parched state was desperate.

'Tell me, has anyone succeeded in tracing this river to its source?' inquired Jai Singh.

'Really, Your Highness! Do you think that mortal eyes can find the source of the Guptaganga?' scoffed Nutty. 'Sanskrit scriptures say that this holy water falls down on Pisshengunj straight from heaven. Therefore, it cannot be polluted.'

Smiling, Jai Singh teased: 'Even though you bathe in it every day, Nutty?'

'Yes, Sir! Winter and summer.'

'Really, Your Highness. Isn't it rather chilly for river bathing these days?' asked the Resident, glad that he'd worn a tweed jacket rather than a lightweight blazer, as had CP.

'Not for people like me, Mr Redverse, who are steeped in the great Hindu tradition of yoga. It bestows unbelievable endurance and mental prowess.'

'Really, Your Highness, such an admirable orientation is too rigorous for lesser mortals from our gross European world!' Colonel CP declared, adjusting his checked peak cap to keep the sun out of his eyes.

A clangorous chorus of temple bells, conch shells, Sanskrit mantras, and orders shouted in the local Marwari dialect broke through all the sound barriers which cocooned Gerald Redverse in deep sleep. Torn between the desire to ignore or investigate this ruckus, the Resident switched on his bedside lamp, looked at his travelling clock, and found that it was already a quarter past six in the morning. Walking across the sumptuously appointed guest room warmed by an electric heater, he drew back the heavy velvet curtains of the alcove windows which overlooked the Pisshengunj palace ghat. And found himself looking down upon an incredible scene.

Three huge copper cauldrons simmered over brick fireplaces burning great logs of firewood. They were slowly dispelling the early dawn mist rising from the Guptaganga. A claw-footed white porcelain bathtub, clearly made in England, stood on a nearby temple platform. A relay of water carriers kept pouring steaming hot water into the tub, while the Maharajah of Pisshengunj stood wrapped in a warm woollen dressing gown, chanting mantras as he tested the water with something that looked like a large thermometer.

So this was His Nutty Highness' definition of ritual river bathing, winter and summer!

Rapping on the connecting guest room door, Redverse called, 'CP, you've got to see this!'

CP joined Gerald at the window just in time to see Nutty allowing an attendant to remove his dressing gown, and step into the steaming hot bathtub. He was clad only in a skimpy red silk dhoti. A thick gold chain with Rudraksha beads and jewelled charms hung around his neck, and glittered in the fire light. Another attendant poured something out of a large flat bottle into the tub. Priests holding coconuts, flowers, and puja *thaals* containing silver lamps and incense sticks, intoned with foggy breaths the right mantras for this cleansing rite.

Ever alert to photo opportunities which helped supplement his income, Colonel CP lost no time in fetching his camera. He clicked away merrily while his pyjama-clad companion kept passing amusing comments on the scene below. 'There! Now I've recorded His Nutty Highness' posterior for posterity!' he laughed, just as the butler brought in their bed tea.

It was barely seven o'clock.

While his guests enjoyed a lavish English breakfast, and after his *Peel khana* supervisor had made sure a *mahavat* had groomed his particular shikar elephant to perfection, Nutty strode into the sunny palace forecourt to where all the elephants were lined up. He was accompanied by his Dewan.

'Remember, Tikky. Let him choose his own elephant. And the psychology of the individual will take care of the rest.'

His Slavic soul delighting in conspiracy, Baron Tikemoffsky chuckled. 'A master stroke, Your Highness! Then neither HH Chattargadh nor the Resident, nor that Colonel, can blame us for anything that happens.'

The subjects of their conversation emerged from the

palace. They were laughing loudly as the Englishmen described the early morning bath scene in great detail.

'So that's why he smells so suspiciously bandagey every time we are forced to embrace formally! And this is despite his dousing himself with strong scents like *Chypre Coty* and *Je Reviens*!' Maharajah Jai Singh surmised, considerably amused.

'But how do you know it's Dettol?' demanded Kishen.

Tapping his nose, Colonel Claude-Poole explained. 'The trained military nose, Raj Kumar Saheb! After all those night patrol and recce exercises, one learns to navigate by scent while moving over enemy territory, sight unseen.'

'Perhaps someone should tell His Nutty Highness that Savlon works just as well for disinfecting holy Ganga *jal*!' the Resident remarked.

Jai Singh shook his head. 'One could, but he'd never make the switch. Because its not anglicised enough! Unless you can convince him that it's more in vogue now in your best stately homes!'

'Of course, Your Highness. But we don't want him to know that his version of the spartan holy Indian river bath is no longer a secret,' demurred the Resident.

'Oh yes, we do,' countered Jai Singh, clinching the argument with a single word. 'Leverage, my dear chap. Leverage. Specially with my Military Secretary selling me half a dozen copies of his candid shots for our intelligence files!'

With perfect timing, the *mahavats* made the elephants 'salaam' their Maharajah's guests. Soon they sank to their knees, allowing everyone to mount. The shikar party, consisting of three native princes and three white foreigners, were all clad in warm woollen round-necked coats with leather shoulder and elbow patches, ammunition slots and pockets, baggy buff or brown twill trousers, thick socks, comfortable laced-up walking boots, sola topees, and sun glasses. They carried handcrafted and specially made-to-measure Holland & Holland 375 magnum and other heavy bore guns, anticipating big game on their first day's shoot in the Pisshengunj Maharajah's reserve.

Two turbaned retainers stood ready with the short mounting ladder as Nutty bowed to Jai Singh with folded palms. 'Shall we sit together, my dear Bhai?'

'If you insist,' the Chattargadh Maharajah responded. 'But the slightest distraction can make one miss the easiest shot.'

'Of course, Bhai. I understand. You're our honoured guest, and we want to give you an unforgettable experience that will rival your African safaris.'

Patting one of the smaller elephants suggestively, Tikky intervened. 'Really, Your Highness, on behalf of our Maharajah, may I suggest that you ride our best shikar elephant, Bhagwati? Steady as the Rock of Gibraltar, as His Britannic Majesty's representatives would say.'

Casting a disparaging eye on that particularly unimpressive little Nepali elephant, Maharajah Jai Singh of Chattargadh strode over to the largest tusker among the six lined up. 'One elephant is as good as another, Baron Tikemoffsky.'

Exchanging triumphant glances, Nutty and his Dewan blessed the psychology of the individual as they too mounted.

The city was soon left behind as the sure-footed shikar elephants moved deeper into the thick jungle, where some cattle-lifting tigers had been reported. They proceeded in single file, with the two Maharajahs leading the way. The Resident, Colonel CP, and the two Dewans followed. They could hear the beaters doing Haka, to make the tigers break cover and head towards the shikar party. They beat their drums and cymbals loudly, whistled and made weird hooting sounds as they beat the bushes and the rocks with stout bamboo sticks. Villagers clad in round red or white turbans, homespun dhotis and kurtas, and carrying *dahs,* swords, and spears, accompanied their Maharajah's shikaris armed with loaded guns and cartridge-stuffed bandoliers. Everyone was ready to take action at the least sign of danger. Disturbed by the infernal din, all the birds in the vicinity flew off, with eagles and kites soaring over them. Peacocks screeched and scattered before the beaters. It was all very exciting. Several sambar, neelgai, chinkaras, and blackbuck bounded across the pathless jungle. Ignoring the large wild boar rushing wildly within easy shot, Jai Singh and the Resident concentrated on sighting a tiger through the tall patches of thatch and ochre elephant grass.

Suddenly, Jai Singh saw a full-grown tiger break cover, streak across their path, and head towards the river. He immediately tapped his *mahavat* on the shoulder, signalling him to follow the tiger.

When the *mahavat* seemed reluctant to obey him, the Chattargadh Maharajah urged him on. '*Chalo sa, bega chalo*'!

With utmost deference, the *mahavat* whispered over his shoulder to the Maharajah. 'Baapji, it's too dangerous. This elephant . . . .'

Jai Singh reassured him with a mixture of encouragement and arrogance. 'Don't be afraid, son. I've never missed a single shot in my life.'

But instead of obeying, the *mahavat* kept trying to take the elephant back into the forest. The tiger turned at bay, diving down the river bank. Suddenly, Jai Singh's elephant trumpeted and charged headlong into the river, spraying water with its trunk in great arching jets. It gambolled playfully, flapping its ears in sheer joy. The *mahavat* lost control, and the entire shikar party watched as the elephant began to roll in the shallow water, unceremoniously tossing its *mahavat* and Maharajah Jai Singh off its back.

Even though they saw that he was still clutching his gun, the Chattargadh party realised that Jai Singh was in real danger. The tiger was very close. But Nutty and Tikky sat guffawing and pointing at their hapless guest with smirks and snide remarks. They knew the dark secret the *mahavat* had tried to hide. This particular tusker, born by the great Brahmaputra river, always found water irresistible, and had the nasty habit of rolling in water, be it river, lake, or pond. Nutty Pisshengunj congratulated himself at finding that his theory about the psychology of the individual had been proved right. He had succeeded in setting Jai Singh up for a ducking, and having a tiger swimming so close by had only added to his enjoyment of his cousin's discomfiture.

Alarmed and apprehensive for his relative's safety, Kishen Singh swore an oath, and told Nutty to do something. The Colonel suggested that they must divert the tiger's attention by riding into the river with weapons ready, and thus putting their own elephants between HH Chattargadh and the tiger. But even as they spoke, the tiger whipped around in a flash of yellow and black. Roaring fiercely and with its tail thrashing, it seemed ready to attack the Maharajah floundering in the slithering mud of the freezing cold river flowing down from the Shivalik range of the Himalayas.

Determined to prevent Nutty Pisshengunj's abominably thoughtless prank from turning into a tragedy, Gerald Redverse lifted his loaded gun, exhaled, and took careful aim. A single shot to the neck killed the tiger, slowly turning the water around him bloody red. Colonel CP was off his elephant in a jiffy and gave Jai Singh a hand as he clambered up the river bank, sopping wet.

Forced to spend their first evening at Pisshengunj upstairs in the *zenana* with the three Maharanis while a formal banquet—complete with bands and *natch-gaana*, (dance and song) honouring her father and the Resident was in full swing downstairs—Kitten was frankly relieved to find His Nutty Highness compelled to entertain them properly afterwards. He had been informed that his elder sister-in-law, HH the Maharaniji Sahebah of Chattargadh, would be dining downstairs en famille and would like her dear brother-in-law, Pisshengunj Durbar, to join them. With all the foreigners, of course, for the sake of Mother Angelus. They could look forward to something slightly more stimulating than listening to stories about recent pilgrimage trips taken by her three aunts. Looking at numerous albums full of carefully mounted snapshots of their childhood homes and weddings, or playing games of Scrabble to impress the nun with their proficiency in spelling English words was much too boring.

The dining table at which they were seated—'quite informally, of course,' as their host kept repeating—was dominated by a silver toy train chugging around on specially laid metal tracks, controlled by a foot button hidden from view. Each coverless wagon contained some delicacy from the royal Pisshengunj kitchens, supplemented by culinary treats from the kitchens of the Maharaja's three wives, who hailed from such distinctly different places as Nepal in the high Himalayas, Bundelkhand in Central India, and, of course, Chattargadh right next door.

Maharani Padmini was elegantly dressed in a narrow brocade-bordered powder blue sari set off by an exquisite Jamewar shawl, pear-shaped diamond eardrops, a diamond-studded pearl choker, and bracelets. She was sitting between Nutty and the Resident, and presented a striking contrast to the nun seated between the two Maharajahs. Mother Angelus admired the large Lalique bowl with red poinsettias and white snowball chrysanthemums. It was flanked by perfumed candles in branching candelabras. The service was superb silver and Rosenthal bone china, and perfectly trained butlers and bearers stood behind each chair, ready to replenish the Waterford wine and water goblets before they became empty.

Though urging his guests to try a little of everything, Nutty kept his 'gravy train' moving round so rapidly that it was difficult for any one to be selective. Even though formally attired in black ties and dinner jackets, the Resident and Colonel CP had reverted to boarding school behaviour and were helping themselves liberally to whatever they could, be it mutton, fish, pork, or fowl. Kitten managed to spear some seekh kebabs on to her plate; and Baron Tikemoffsky removed a wagon load of chicken à la Kiev on to his while continuing to regale Mother Angelus with an anecdote about Nadia Boulanger's backstage instructions to the great Pavlova at the Paris Opera about how to put more life into her Dying Swan.

Knowing his cousin Kishen's partiality to grilled grouse, Nutty would cunningly press the foot button every time he was on the verge of helping himself, with the result that the Chattargadh prince constantly found his favourite dish flying out of reach. Fuming silently, he notched up another score to settle with His Nutty Highness, quite oblivious of the fact that the Pisshengunj Maharajah might also be indulging in some score-settling of his own.

Even though her parents had decided not to allow Nutty the satisfaction of referring publicly to that morning's near fatal episode and so spoil the rest of their short visit, Kitten couldn't let it pass. At the first lull in the conversation between her mother and the Resident, she said with her warmest smile, 'Mr Redverse, we can't thank you enough for saving Father's life today.'

'My dear child, someone would have got the tiger before it harmed His Highness,' he answered with a deprecating shrug.

'Of course, Resident Saab,' Nutty added instantly. 'With so many crack shots accompanying him, I can swear by all the *taintees crore Devi-Devatas* present that not a hair of my dear Brother Maharajah Jai Singhji would have been harmed. It was such a small little tiger—hardly more than a cub, as anyone could see. Chattargadh Durbar could have strangled it with his bare hands! Fortunately, it was not one of our huge man-eaters. Though, of course, we couldn't prevent the little ducking. For this the *mahavat* has already been dismissed, you'll be happy to know, Bhabisa Hukum.'

Padmini hastened to protest that she saw no reason to deprive a poor man of his job just because HH Pisshengunj's elephants went berserk. She made him promise to reinstate the *mahavat*. Asked if there was anything else he could do to win his sister-in-law's approval, the Chattargadh Maharani remarked that she would have been delighted if, instead of staying cooped up in the *zenana*, his wives had also been included in this select dinner party because now times were changing.

'*Vajeb farmavno*, Bhabisa Hukum,' agreed Nutty blandly. 'But tonight they are all busy entertaining Chota Maharanisa's brother. You understand, of course, that I'm forced to keep Koodsu Rao Saab out of sight because I would never do anything to provoke any guest, let alone my esteemed elder brother. *Ateethi Devo Bhava!*'

Jai Singh let this pass, and continued chatting cheerfully with Mother Angelus. Their dialogue was frequently punctuated with the nun's 'God bless you!' every time R.K. Kishen sneezed. The latter was having a difficult time keeping his turban at the right angle on his head after every sneezing bout. And, there was no question of taking it off out of deference to his sister-in-law.

'Really, Kishen. I fall into the river, and you catch a cold!' joked Jai Singh.

'He should go to bed immediately after dinner, with a hot water bottle and some brandy, plus some of the eucalyptus oil I never travel without,' the Mother Superior recommended.

As the cheese, fruit, and nuts followed dessert, Nutty suddenly announced, 'Let's have a shooting match after dinner to make up for this morning's disappointment. Everyone will stand in line on the terrace with lighted cigarettes in their mouths! And we'll take turns putting out the glowing tips with our pistols!'

'Certainly not, Nutty. None of us are in the mood for any more childish games. Let's just spend a civilised evening listening to some music.'

Kitten sprang up from her seat the instant an ADC, (summoned no doubts by some overzealous retainer) entered the dining room with the Maharajah's pistol. Snatching it out of his hand with a determined sparkle in her eye, she turned towards Nutty.

'Come on, Uncle Nutty. I'll make you happy by playing William Tell.'

'Really, Princess!' the Resident chided her. 'Let's not take our jokes too far.'

'Joke?' she flashed scornfully, quickly taking an apple from one of the large silver fruit bowls on a sideboard, and holding it over Nutty's turbaned head. 'Unless HH Pisshengunj tells us that he's afraid. And he'd never do that, would he, being a Ranbanka Rathor?'

Incredulous, Nutty blanched. He was completely unable to frame a response. The ADC's jaw dropped, and Tikky froze at her impudent smile and aggressive tone. Knowing from experience that Princess Kitten could neither be curbed nor cajoled once she got going, Mother Angelus and Colonel Claude-Poole refrained from comment.

Her mother protested. 'Legends are one thing, but you can't put your uncle through this ordeal!'

Thinking of the ordeal Nutty had subjected him to only that. morning, Jai Singh sat silent. He could, of course, have easily defused the situation merely by smiling and shaking his turbaned head negatively at his daughter. But he did no such thing.

Cornered, Nutty asked: 'Is Kitten a good shot?'

'Unfortunately, very!' replied R.K. Kishen.

Impervious to the consternation and tension in the room, Kitten took off the pistol's safety catch. Supporting its weight by putting her left hand under her right wrist, she took careful aim, and shot the apple right off the Pisshengunj Maharajah's head. He sat stock still for several minutes, recovering slowly from the trick so publicly inflicted on him by his horrid niece. Obviously, Maharajah Jai Singh's thoroughly spoilt daughter didn't know how to behave like a well-bred girl, let alone a princess. Silently, he thanked all the gods for his narrow escape. He remembered how often he had regretted the fact that she was not a boy, so that he could have adopted her. But she had turned out to be a hell-born brat who had humiliated him in front of everyone, including foreigners who happened to be no less than the representatives of the Raj. In retrospect, he was glad that the Almighty in his wisdom had kept his State safe from such a girl.

Vowing silent revenge, Nutty decided that, one of these days, he would teach Kitten a lesson.

A very strong sense of *déja vù* hit the Resident as soon as he stepped into the Pisshengunj Maharajah's private drawing room. It was full of crystal furniture upholstered in scarlet and gold brocade, gold-fringed swagged and valanced yellow velvet curtains; gaudy custom-made Aubusson carpets; cabinets decorated with pietra dura panels of flowers and birds and gilt-wood bases carved with fantastic creatures; and colourful Bohemian glass bowls stuffed with tight bunches of flowers. Chandeliers sparkled. Ormolu-encrusted pagoda clocks stood before the tall gilt-framed Venetian mirrors above both fireplaces, flanked by several bronze dogs. Three life-size marble cherubim mingled with a pair of enormous silver-mounted elephant tusks carved with celestial nymphs, Tibetan and Nepali tantric statues, Messien figurines, lapis lazuli and malachite ashtrays, crested and filigreed gold cigarette boxes, and the inevitable spittoon next to Nutty's seat.

While he was still trying to figure out where he had seen just such an unharmonious mélange of Italianate *trompe l'œil* ceilings, Rococo and Second Empire furnishings, and Byzantine bad taste, Redverse chanced to meet Kitten's wickedly twinkling eyes.

'He has been to the Turkish Sultan's Dol-ma-bahch, Dol-ma-bahch, Dol-ma-bahch, and brought it all home!' she trilled.

'Of course,' laughed the Englishman. 'They say you have a formidable memory, Princess.'

'That's because I collect facts the way other girls collect bangles and baubles. And I haven't learnt the art of making small talk,' confessed Kitten, with beguiling honesty. 'Tell me, was your father actually Ambassador to Turkey when Kemal Ataturk seized power? And at Vienna just before the War?'

Butlers brought in demitasse cups of coffee and a tray full of choice liqueurs in beautiful crystal stemware while the Resident and the Princess discussed the not-so sublime Porte, the demise of the Ottoman and Hapsburg empires, the resulting chaos in Mittele Europe, and Communism's onward march.

Nutty sat talking to the Maharajah and Maharani of Chattargadh. They spoke of the Calcutta polo season, discussing the various Indian and foreign teams which participated on a more or less regular basis. Nutty remarked that his nephew Tiger Fateypur was already there, commandeering, as usual, the best stabling from the Turf Club. Jai Singh mentioned his forthcoming interview with the Viceroy regarding several matters, including their water-sharing agreement. R.K. Kishen had been sent off to bed to nurse his cold by his solicitous sister-in-law. And, Mother Angelus was having a grand gossip session with Baron Tikemoffsky and Colonel CP about all the people she hadn't seen in nearly two decades, but whom they kept meeting frequently in the Indian and European social circuit.

Peeved by the prolonged conversation the Resident was evidently enjoying with his abominable niece, the Pisshengunj Maharajah asked: 'What's that strange costume you're wearing, Kitten? Good for a fancy-dress party, but a little out of place for a family get-together, don't you think?'

Kitten swung around with a scoffing look, touching the paisley-patterned chiffon dupatta draped scarf fashion over the perfectly tailored jade green velvet *ghararah*-kurta outfit that she had chosen to wear instead of the usual unmarried Rajput girl's informal tunic and pants, or a formal sari. She informed Nutty that if he wasn't so backward, he would have recognised the latest fashion from Bombay, Lucknow, Lahore, and Hyderabad.

While Jai Singh had no compunction about his daughter taking Nutty down a peg or two, he forced himself to intervene. Uppermost in his mind was the dual mission that had brought them to Pisshengunj. Catching his daughter's eye, he signalled to her.

Detaching herself from the group around their host, Kitten walked over to the gleaming grand concert piano at the other end of the chamber, opened the lid, and tried the keys. Satisfied that it was kept in tune, she played a few chords, trying out the popular theme song from a film that she had so enjoyed seeing recently.

Listening to her critically while sipping his almond-scented Amaretto, Nutty couldn't resist walking across to inform his niece that he also knew some good tunes. Highly amused to see him swallow the bait she had laid, Kitten immediately got off the long piano stool, courteously offering to find HH some pieces he might like to try. His full mouth pursing in concentration, and his rotund fair face gleaming with the warmth of two fires, good wine, and spicy food, the Maharajah of Pisshengunj started picking out a tune with one finger.

'Come on, Nutty Kaka! Who wants to hear Baa Baa Black Sheep!' said Kitten, laughing as she leafed through a stack of music books arranged on a nearby bookshelf. 'Here, try La Paloma, which everybody loves.'

Anxious to hide the fact that he couldn't sight-read musical scores, the Maharajah waved it aside. 'With my God-given gift of musical ears, I don't need scores-fashcores. Just hum it, my dear Kitten, and I'll play any tune in the world for you.'

The Chattargadh Princess immediately started humming La Paloma, keeping time with her tapping foot, and swinging her right hand up and down like a music teacher. Mother Angelus sat shuddering through the Maharajah's dismal performance till she couldn't bear to hear another false note.

To the amusement and great delight of Maharajah Jai Singh, Maharani Padmini, and the two Englishmen, Mother Angelus materialised at HH Pisshengunj's elbow, gave him the right chords, and then simply asked him to move over. Settling her robes, the Irish nun touched the keyboard with magic, imbuing every listener with a special feeling for this most recognisable of gypsy melodies.

Everyone clapped. Baron Tikemoffsky cried 'Bravo!' and Colonel CP said 'Hear hear!' Redverse walked over to stand by the piano, smiling down at the Mother Superior.

Turning to Kitten, Mother Angelus said, 'Shall we play a duet, my dear? I see that HH Pisshengunj has the Sugar Plum Fairy score.'

As Kitten took her place beside her music teacher, Jai Singh remarked: 'Ah, the Nutcracker Suite. How appropriate.' Tikky responded that Tchaikovsky was always appropriate for light entertainment, but he himself preferred more substantial masters like Beethoven, Liszt, and Mahler.

When everyone had stopped clapping and complimenting the performers, Nutty insisted they have another round of cognac. 'I'd give anything to play the piano like that, Mother Angelus. Can you teach me tomorrow?'

'Really, Your Highness,' demurred the nun. 'Music can't be taught overnight, you know.'

'But in two-three months? If this monkey Kitten can do it, so can I,' Nutty persisted.

Jai Singh exchanged a happy, knowing smile with his wife. Things seemed to be going exactly as he had predicted when he had spoken about the psychology of the individual at Chattargadh.

Determined to outshine Kitten at the piano, Nutty continued. 'I'll do anything you say, dear Mother.'

'Then, first of all, Your Highness, you must get a good music teacher.'

'But you are already here, Reverend Mother.'

'Really, Your Highness, I can't neglect my work. It involves supervising ten convents, three hospitals, eight orphanages, and several dispensaries all over Rajputana.'

The Chattargadh Maharajah hastened to assure his cousin that he could easily find some European lady who'd be willing to teach him anything.

'Yes, but they don't stay,' confided Nutty, turning petulant. 'They get bored and elope with the first foreigner who comes along, start preaching Christianity, or steal my puppies and open kennel clubs!'

This confession drew smiles and laughter from the Pisshengunj Maharajah's guests. Colonel Claude-Poole suggested that Baroness Tikemoffsky might like to take up the challenge of turning her husband's employer into a concert pianist.

'Russians are so musical, as we well know,' added Her Highness Chattargadh.

Bowing to the Maharani, the Baron demurred. 'Too gracious as ever, Your Highness. Unfortunately, besides becoming arthritic due to river damp, my wife happens to be away on an extended visit to her sisters in Shanghai.'

He did not add that the trip had become necessary after his generous patron and his beloved wife had almost come to being daggers-drawn over her refusal to let His Nutty Highness interpret the Tarot cards his way, instead of the ancient way she had been taught by her master, Alistair Crawley.

'May I suggest that Your Highness gets a man this time,' said the Resident.

'I don't want a man-shan. Or another woman-shuman. Only Reverend Mother Angelus, even if I have to petition the Pope!' declared the Maharajah of Pisshengunj.

Maharani Padmini tried to reason with their host. 'Perhaps Pisshengunj Durbar doesn't understand that nuns have very strict rules about mixing with outsiders. They have to live in convents, not palaces . . . .'

'Yes, Bhabisa Hukum. Then I'll build her a convent! I'll force all the good families of Pisshengunj to send their children to your school, Mother Angelus. But you'll have to stay here and teach me how to play duets all by myself!'

Mother Angelus drained her tiny glass of Benedictine with a triumphant smile which also signalled Thank You to Jai Singh. 'Really, Your Highness,' she said to Nutty. 'I'll have to ask the Bishop's permission, you know.'

On the Pisshengunj Maharajah's orders, the migratory water birds for which his state was renowned, were kept off the river and adjoining *jheels* so that they were forced to swoop down for their early morning drink at Sur Sagar, a lake situated a few miles outside Pisshengunj. Hundreds of duck, geese, and sandgrouse came from every direction, skimming low over the lake to dive down for water. Their wings created a splendid susurration of sound that was music to the ears of the various guests positioned in the butts concealed in the broad fringe of vegetation around the lake. Nutty's duck shoots were notorious for being difficult because this vast sheet of water was dotted with islets and clumps of tall reeds in which waterfowl found ample cover. Since shooting birds on the wing was mandatory (hitting sitting ducks was considered unsportsmanlike and therefore anathema), only outstandingly keen marksmen could hope to collect respectable bags. A dug-out canoe was assigned to each gun for retrieving the fallen birds, and printed cards were provided on which the number and species of his bag were recorded by each shooter.

Kitten's keen eyes followed the flight path of several mallards, snipe, and geese. She could easily distinguish these in the pure early morning light from the pochards, shufflers, and large mandarin ducks. Suddenly, the silence was shattered by volley upon volley of double-barrelled shotguns going off. She looked around. Fortunately, the sun was behind her. Taking up a comfortable stance with her right cheek resting on the butt of her perfectly balanced 12-bore, and carefully allowing for flight and wind factors, Kitten brought down two bar-headed geese and some ducks within the first half hour. She then concentrated on snipe-shooting—just to train her eye and improve her aim, for these flying targets were truly challenging.

In the butts around her, Jai Singh, Redverse, Colonel CP and Baron Tikemoffsky were all busy firing, ejecting, and rapidly loading their custom-made Purdy guns with LG cartridges guaranteed to bring down anything within range without needing to be very selective. As the sun climbed higher, Nutty began to fret at his small score, critically examining his ornate ivory-inlaid 'Made-in-England' shotgun.

Turning to the ADC standing just behind him and acting as his loader, Nutty demanded, 'Kalu Singhji, did you get this gun properly zeroed before we came here to play shikar?'

'Hukum, Anta!' he responded.

'Then there's something wrong with these cartridges.'

'*Sharatiya* (you bet), Hukum! I can see the pellets hitting the birds, but they refuse to drop dead. And it will soon be 12 o'clock,' intoned the sycophantic ADC.

The Maharajah studied his watch, thought for a moment, and made a quick decision. 'Never mind. We'll stick to the rules, and have the bugle blown at noon like civilised shikaris. But we'll still manage a larger bag than anyone else's.'

At a signal from Nutty, the bugle sounded precisely at midday, and all the guns fell silent. The shooters emerged from their butts to watch the Maharajah's retainers and retrievers going into action, collecting the last of the day's bags in their row boats. The well-trained dogs dashed into the bushes or waded into the water to retrieve every single bird shot down that morning. These were loaded into an open pick-up van. Guns and cartridge boxes were collected and carefully stored in the waiting Bentley and Rolls Royce while Jai Singh, Redverse and Colonel CP compared counts with Nutty, Tikky, and Kitten.

By the time his guests had driven back, washed, and tidied up for lunch, the Pisshengunj Maharajah's shikaris had laid the day's bags out in neat rows on the marble terrace overlooking the river and palace garden. The shooter's name, butt number, and kill were clearly written on small blackboards. Two butlers wearing pure white uniforms with red bow ties and gloves served beer, gin slings, and fresh fruit juice from heavy silver salvers.

Raising his beer mug, Nutty smiled at Jai Singh. 'Congratulations, Bhai. You've got a very respectable bag today, though it's not the highest I've known.'

'Duck-shooting is always a chancy sport, Nutty. But I must confess that I was using a loader and two guns.'

'The average count is pretty good, considering there were only six guns out today, with Raj Kumar Saheb forced to stay in bed nursing his cold,' said the Resident.

Setting down his movie and still-life cameras on a table shaded by a garden umbrella, Colonel Claude-Poole remarked that, unlike most of the famous wildfowl preserves in north India which were shot over only four or five times in the entire season, Pisshengunj provided great shooting throughout the winter.

Hearing this, Kitten had something to say. She pointed out that the credit for this abundance had to be attributed to the fact that Pisshengunj lay in the path of migrating duck and geese, and not to His Nutty Highness' marvellous *bandobast* (arrangement). Before anyone could say anything to this, she had strolled off to count coup against all the scorecards she had collected as souvenirs from the others. Her father, a superb shot (and the person who had taught her the trick of hitting moving game, flipped coins, and stationary targets), had brought down 90 birds.

But Nutty Uncle seemed to have beaten him by shooting no less than 94!

Scrutinising the huge heap of duck, grouse, geese, and snipe clearly marked as HH Pisshengunj's bag, Kitten couldn't help feeling that something was dashed fishy. Monitoring his precocious niece's movements, Nutty was not at all happy to see her bending down to examine critically an extremely fat pintail and a rather stiff mallard. Hurrying over, the Maharajah of Pisshengunj playfully tugged the sleeve of Kitten's padded shooting jacket.

'Come along, Princess. Colonel CP wants our photographs for posterity.'

But his niece shook herself free and grabbed a duck. She began shaking it till pieces of charcoal spilled out of its stomach, all the while laughing in demonic glee. 'Colonel Claude-Poole! Get here fast before you miss a million-pound photo opportunity!'

Almost incoherent with laughter, Kitten pointed to several dead birds whose stomachs had been already cleaned out and stuffed with charcoal for preservation. As Colonel CP happily clicked away, recording His Nutty Highness' unsportsmanlike perfidy, Gerald Redverse found it difficult to sustain the required diplomatic tact. Tikky and Kalu Singh knew from experience that their chagrined master, so ruthlessly exposed by the Chattargadh Princess, would inevitably blame them for this debacle witnessed by no less than the two Raj representatives, *and* recorded for posterity by the Colonel and his camera.

'I say, CP, these days ducks seem to be falling ready gutted out of the Pisshengunj sky,' observed the Resident, perfectly straight-faced.

'AND stuffed with charcoal from His Nutty Highness' pantry!' chortled Kitten, enjoying herself hugely.

Jai Singh added in a congratulatory tone, 'You're truly becoming capable of performing miracles, Nutty.'

The Pisshengunj Maharajah stood glaring at his laughing guests, convinced that Kitten was his bête noire. She had brought him nothing but bad luck. Twice in 24 hours she had made him appear foolish when everyone knew he was nothing of the sort. Soon, very soon, he would find a way of wreaking vengeance on her. She—and her father—would

rue the day they tangled with Maharajah Natwar Singh
Bahadur of Pisshengunj.

As the special train between Pisshengunj and Delhi (to
which the Chattargadh Maharajah's saloon had been
attached) prepared to move out of the well-lit private
palace siding, soldiers in Pisshengunj State Force uniforms
blew a trumpet fanfare. The sound of a 17-gun salute being
fired could clearly be heard over the puffing, whistling
train as the saloon door painted with the Chattargadh crest
(and colours) shut behind Jai Singh. Maharajah Natwar
Singh of Pisshengunj stood with his Dewan, Koodsu Rao
Saheb, Bhoorji, and Kalu Singh, and waved goodbye to the
Resident and the Chattargadh party.

As the train drew away, Nutty grinned broadly. He gave
his brother-in-law a familiar nudge while they put their
turbaned heads together, and shared a joke in Marwari.
'*Humey karo beti ra baap Latsaab sou Panchayati* (Now go
and have a conference with the Viceroy, you son of a gun!)'

As they walked towards the waiting cars, the Maharajah
asked his Dewan, 'Tikky, did you issue proper instructions
to the railway staff?'

'Of course, Your Highness. It's exceedingly generous of
you to lay on a special for HH Chattargadh instead of
having his saloon cars attached to one of our regular
passenger trains.'

'Well, what else could I do as a responsible host? My
brother, Maharajah Jai Singhji of Chattargadh has a very
important meeting tomorrow, exactly at 8 a.m. with the
Viceroy! And you know how particular the Brits are about
punctuality.'

Gravely nodding his head up and down, Koodsu Rao
Saheb added, 'After all, it is a Rajput's solemn duty to provide
for all his guest's needs. *Ateethi Devo Bhava!*'

Laughing uproariously, Nutty and his brother-in-law drove back to the palace.

Up as usual before dawn, Maharajah Jai Singh had already shaved, showered, and dressed in his formal white uniform with orders, medals, and sky blue silk turban (to match his Star of India sash) for his forthcoming visit to Viceregal Lodge when his personal attendant brought in the silver tray bearing his light poached egg and fruit breakfast from the train's pantry.

Inclining his head in thanks and stirring the tea poured out for him, Jai Singh inquired: 'Meghji, isn't Raj Kumar Saab ready yet?'

Meghji shrugged. 'He's still resting, Baapji. Pisshengunj's strange climate made him rather unwell. He ordered us to wake him up only at Rewari station.'

The Maharajah glanced at his watch. 'We should have passed Rewari long ago if the train left Pisshengunj at 10 o'clock last night. Please tell the pantrywallahs to send Raj Kumar Saab his tea, or we'll be in Delhi before he wakes up!'

Later, as the train moved through the foggy countryside, R.K. Kishen, Gerald Redverse, and Colonel CP joined the Maharajah in the luxuriously appointed saloon drawing room. While the others sat discussing the forthcoming meeting, Jai Singh glanced through the document Nutty had been coerced into signing the day before. He had allowed work on the CP canal to commence without any of his own demands regarding Koodsu Rao Saheb's reinstatement being conceded. Kitten's marvellous discovery of the ready gutted birds so obviously procured from his own pantry, had done the trick. Nutty couldn't possibly afford to have his reputation destroyed by impeccable eyewitnesses possessing evidence of his unsporting conduct. The Rajputs and the British took such things rather seriously. Knowing Nutty, Jai Singh had made sure that Colonel CP's cameras remained in

the Resident's safe custody, for no Maharajah would dare
tamper with a Crown Agent's luggage.

Finding the train slowing down, Jai Singh again glanced
at his wristwatch. 'Kishen, could you please look out of the
window on your side and tell me the name of this station?'

Sniffing and dabbing his nose with a soft white
handkerchief smelling strongly of eucalyptus oil, Kishen Singh
rose, drew the velvet curtain apart, pushed up the glass window,
then the wooden shutter, and thrusting his head out, frowned
at a looming oxidised water tank just near the platform.

Laboriously he read the white lettering barely visible
through the winter mist and railroad steam. 'Kapa-shitty.'

'Some of our villages have such peculiar names,' said the
Maharajah to the Resident.

'I'm sure Your Highness would also find some of our
English village names quite funny,' responded the Resident.

'There's Dumboulton, and Gurglewood, or Humperdingle,'
added Colonel CP.

Finding the train halting too frequently, and chugging
along at a disastrously slow pace even after it was long past
their arrival time at Delhi, Jai Singh became increasingly
uneasy. 'Kishen, can you step outside and discover where
we are? Ask the guard, or the engine driver. A journey
between Pisshengunj and Delhi takes exactly eight and a
half hours by train, and slightly less by road.'

'Hukum Hajoor,' responded Kishen, once more walking
to the window and peering out. 'Bhai, you can come and
read it for yourself since you don't trust me. Even for people
who didn't go to Oxford, there it is . . . in big white letters
even a blind man can't miss! KAPA-SHITTY!'

In order to forestall one of those all-too-frequent
altercations between the two cousins, Colonel Claude-Poole
stepped over to the window, looked out, and swore an
oath. 'Really, Your Highness! You won't believe this! Do
you know, we are still where we were yesterday.'

Jai Singh's dreadful suspicion was confirmed by one swift look. Pisshengunj's palace, river, and other landmarks were clearly outlined by the rising sun. Ruefully realising that Nutty had really given them tit for tat, Jai Singh immediately put an arm around his cousin's shoulder.

'Sorry, Kishen. We've been going round Pisshengunj in circles.'

'And earning demerits by missing an important conference fixed weeks in advance with the Viceroy,' Gerald Redverse surmised, torn between irritation and amusement.

Elephants Ahoy!   3

Standing in the middle of a storeroom packed from floor to ceiling with numerous almirahs, steel trunks, wooden chests and crates, discarded furniture, damaged paintings, long tables loaded with old-fashioned silverware, lanterns, brass lamps, and other bric-a-brac, Maharajah Jai Singh regretted not having followed Colonel Claude-Poole's advice about turning the new wing's entire basement area into a series of connected storerooms for his growing collection of personal possessions and household effects. Confident of his own unmaterialistic and non-acquisitive nature, Jai Singh had ignored his architect's suggestion. But conspicuous consumption and being à la mode went with the territory of self-respecting Maharajahs who were obliged to refurbish their palaces periodically, regardless of their own reluctance. There was also the folly of indulging in needless expenditure such as buying Rolls Royce cars, not so much to impress their own subjects, but to show Raj representatives, foreign guests, and visiting royalty that they also knew how to surround themselves with the latest and the best from every corner of the world.

Torn between his devotion to the Maharajah and simple common sense, Thakur Ganpat Singh was vociferous in lamenting his total inability to cram any more stuff into this particular store, no matter what Durbar said or thought. 'Baapji, you've made me your *Shikar khana* and *Toshakhana*-in-charge even though you call me *Gadbad* (faulty) Singh! I may have many faults, but sycophancy is not one of them. Where do you want me to keep all that stuff you keep on buying? On top of my head?'

Obliged to pacify his literally loyal-unto-death kinsman, Jai Singh said, 'It's only that stuff which we got on our last trip to Europe, for heaven's sake.'

'We have no place here even for brand new *samaan* from *bilayat*, Baapji.'

Roopji and the other *farrashes* standing behind him awaiting instructions, kept their eyes downcast as they absorbed every word of the altercation between their Maharajah and his outspoken ADC. They could hear the sound of trucks reversing, heavy crates being unloaded, and someone calling them loudly in Marwari to hurry along.

Having an inborn knack for cajoling people into instant obedience, Jai Singh smiled. 'Gadbad Singhji, there is always place if you are willing to fit in a few more things here and there. You know that I depend on my *Toshakhana*-in-charge.' Walking over to a row of locked cupboards, he asked: 'What's in there?'

'Unwanted Savile Row suits, silk shirts, scarves, ties, T-shirts, riding breeches, some *achkans* and other *poshak* items brought down from Baapji's dressing room.'

Jai Singh nodded his head decisively. 'All right, clear out everything. And what's in those boxes piled up over there?'

'Games, toys, paper hats, balloons, Christmas crackers, and other gifts for guests . . . .'

'Store the valuables in those almirahs, and send all these old things up to my study. But make sure everything is in tip-top condition. We'll distribute them to our staff, and some of the *kabilawalas* (relations). Then, have the new pictures and ornaments, bronzes, clocks, vases, lamps, marble statues, silk screens, silverware, dinner services, tea sets, easily breakable cut glass decanters and wine goblets carefully unpacked, and ready for inspection by tomorrow.'

Folding his hands, the ADC responded: 'Jo Hukum, Baapji.'

If there was one thing Redverse had learnt to respect and enjoy after his chaotic first year as a district officer in cyclone- and other calamities-prone Bengal, it was the peaceful Sunday ritual of doing nothing after Church except catching up with reading, letter writing or the odd game of bridge, billiards and tennis. Since his wife was still away, he and CP had fallen into the habit of lunching with each other on Sundays. Since a cold winter drizzle (considered so beneficial by the locals for lawns and crops alike, and for settling the dust) had driven them indoors from the partially restored Residency garden, they decided to play snooker.

The Resident looked on as his childhood chum kept increasing his lead with one lucky break after another. 'Another fluke, CP!'

'Call it what you like, Reverse Gear,' said the moustached redhead, moving buoyantly to the scoreboard. 'But actually it's my scientific approach. Trajectory, old chap. Trajectory.'

Conceding that for a soldier, CP was a tolerable engineer, Gerald chalked his cue, wondering if he should try potting the blue ball into the right centre pocket, or go for the higher value red with a cannon off the cushion. Straightening up with a genial smile after a successful shot, he wondered: 'How on earth did my predecessor wangle a billiard table out of His Majesty's Government for this Residency?'

'His Majesty's Government?' Colonel CP scoffed. 'This table was provided by the Chattargadh Maharajah to keep Residents from popping in and out of the Palace uninvited.'

'Well, who can blame HH for wanting to keep a chap who kept crocodiles in his bathtub at arm's length, specially when Sir Henry must have known they're the one thing he's allergic to!'

Colonel Claude-Poole bent over the table, steepling his fingers on the green felt and taking careful aim. Sudden loud knocking diverted his attention, making him muff an easy shot. On the verge of winning the day's second frame of snooker, the Colonel quipped: 'I say, old chap, you've certainly trained your staff to create a well-timed disturbance to spike the competition!'

Going to the heavy flush door, Redverse peered out of the glass spy panel, and admitted his beaming bearer.

'Saar, Palace telephoning, with Maharajah Saab Bahadur's voice!'

With a brief apology to his guest, Gerald replaced his cue in the stand, and went off to take the call.

Comfortably clad in baggy corduroy trousers, open-collar shirts, Argyle sweaters, socks and brown brogues, the two Englishmen debated whether to take the Maharajah's 'come as you are' seriously. Changing into more formal attire would keep Highness waiting and make for another kind of *faux pas*.

'Does he ring you up often, Reverse Gear?'

CP was aware of the special relationship which had sprung up between HH Chattargadh and Reverse Gear after the latter had saved his life in Pisshengunj a month earlier. There was also the fact that he was the Crown Agent, and not the Maharajah's employee like himself. This put him on a footing of greater equality than a mere Military Secretary, even though he had put in more selfless service to this State.

'Not really. But how many people can the Maharajah talk to in this one-horse town?' replied Gerald as they both got into their well-worn tweed jackets.

Speculation rife in his mind, for Maharajah Jai Singh never did anything without a specific purpose, CP pursed his mouth.

'But what does he want to see his Resident and his Military Secretary about on the Sabbath, for Christ's sake?'

Redverse responded with an airy wave of his hand. 'Oh, he just wants to show us some of the stuff he bought in London and Paris, and get some helpful suggestions on interior decor. I do wish Dorothy was coming back a bit earlier, for fiddling about with rooms and furnishings is just the sort of thing she enjoys. But I say, isn't it a great relief to be around a rational ruler like Jai Singh after all that we endured last month in Pisshengunj, not to mention Calcutta with its wild horsy bunch of perpetually partying princes like Tiger?'

'Show me one ruler who's really rational in this country, or in the entire history of our world, since they started crowning the biggest bully AND endowing him with divine rights!' scoffed CP. The youngest son of a high church Anglican bishop blessed with an ancient Norman-Plantagenet pedigree and numerous progeny, Cedric Claude-Poole delighted in voicing opinions calculated to trigger disputes and acrimonious debate in his immediate social circles. But having practically known him forever, Redverse, naturally, didn't let himself fall into that particular trap.

Even before the Residency Humber Snipe provided by the Maharajah drove into the carved sandstone portico, Redverse and CP could hear all the commotion going on in the nearby ADC Room.

Acknowledging his salute, Colonel CP asked the bodyguard *sipahi* on sentry duty: '*Kai ho riyo hai* (What's happening), Ram Singhji?'

The *sipahi* could not repress his broad grin. '*Aap khud dekh lo sa*, (See for yourself), Kernull Saab.'

Driven by curiosity, the Military Secretary and the Resident walked up to the ADC Room, and watched in growing astonishment as several Rajput chiefs, retired State force officers, and the ADCs unpacked the boxes and packets they held with happy anticipation. Their jovial banter turned into scoffing remarks and scathing criticism as disappointment with the Maharajah's gifts grew. One dhoti-clad chieftain held a box of bow ties. A little boy had received a dozen dress shirts. A white-bearded Sardar wondered what to do with so many tennis shorts. A touchy Rajvi held a bunch of suspenders, while another royal relation had got nothing but several packs of playing cards! The recipients of too many silk ties, monogrammed handkerchiefs, cummerbunds, vests and paper hats complained loudly against those who'd had the good fortune to corner all the better things like coats, trousers, and breeches.

Zorji spotted the Englishmen he should have received in the portico standing among the curious *farrashes* and retainers crowding the doors and windows of the ADC Room.

'*Lo sa, Rejdunt Saab bhi aa gaya tamasho dekhan ney* (The Resident Saheb has also come to watch the fun)!' he cried.

Depending on their individual natures and the nature of the item each had received, the gathered 'beneficiaries' immediately started making humorous comments or complaining.

'Is this a joke or generosity?' demanded a down-at-heel World War veteran holding up four felt hats.

Ganpat Singh tried to pacify everyone and save face before the outsiders. '*Bhagwan ri sogun* (By God), I swear this is a mistake about which Baapji knows nothing. I should have checked every box and packet before Durbar started presenting them to you.'

'Well, how else would you live up to your name, Gadbad Singh?' the bearded old Sardar scoffed.

'Is it my fault if the *bilayatis* have strange ways of packing? *Set ra set toh mata rakhey koni* (They don't keep things in sets)!' he protested.

This drew a spontaneous peal of laughter from the two Englishmen, who had manfully suppressed their mirth so far for fear of giving offence to the notoriously touchy and vindictive Rajputs.

'Savile Row suits, my foot!' swore a burly brigadier.

'What shall we do with all this *kuchura* (rubbish)?' demanded a man with too many pairs of socks.

'Throw it back in Rajaji's face!' said an angry, impoverished prince. 'We didn't come here to be insulted.'

Surmising that things were about to get out of control, the Resident said in his most conciliatory manner: 'I'm sure His Highness will be most upset and apologetic when he hears of this unintentional mix-up. So may I be permitted to make a suggestion? If all the Princes and Sardars pooled their resources with their military brothers, each one of you would have a complete European wardrobe.'

'Plus a pack of cards!' Colonel Claude-Poole added, with a solemn nod.

Having turned a potential noblemen's revolt into a boisterous scramble resembling an English parish jumble sale-cum-school lucky dip drive, the Resident and the Military Secretary stood watching as people started togging themselves out in the most outlandish combinations.

On their way to the drawing room, they met Kitten and Ratna about to set off for their evening *hawa-khori* (airing) in the waiting Rolls Royce, chaperoned by Mrs Rawlins and a senior ADC.

The Resident courteously doffed his hat. 'Good afternoon, ladies. Where are you off to?'

'We are going to see the Gogaji fair today,' replied Kitten.

Colonel CP greeted them individually, adding, 'Its good to have you back with us, Ratna.'

'Yes, indeed!' exclaimed Kitten. 'Its so much nicer when there's someone to share things with.'

'Like homework. And running errands!' teased Ratna, dimpling as she raised velvety brown eyes to the Colonel, and gave Kitten a little nudge.

'Oh yes, one of Father's numerous chits,' remembered Kitten, pulling a note out of her tunic pocket.

The Resident received it from her with a murmured 'Thank you.' He learnt that the Maharajah would join them as soon as he could get away safely from the visiting female relations he was being obliged to honour alongside Her Highness.

Observing that the princesses were eager to be off, Redverse said that he wouldn't detain them, and would be quite happy to meet the local scribes having tea with Raj Kumar Kishen on the lawn until the Maharajah appeared.

'It's not that we wouldn't enjoy staying and talking to both of you, but we don't want to miss all the funny things that keep happening at our fairs,' said Kitten.

'If that's all you want, just step into the ADC Room, children!' laughed the Colonel.

Their governess immediately protested. 'Colonel Claude-Poole, you're perfectly aware that the princesses are not allowed to go there for obvious reasons—such as ensuring other people's privacy.'

'And dignity!' added CP.

Turning around to find a group of gesturing and arguing chiefs and officers clad in the oddest mix of Indian and European clothes, Kitten, Ratna, and Mrs Rawlins burst into laughter. The Resident wondered which combination looked the most ludicrous: dinner jackets over riding breeches, the ruffled dress shirts tucked into tennis shorts, or the plus fours girdled with red cummerbunds?

Kitten guessed that her father's generosity had been motivated more by pragmatism than true philanthropy. It had turned these simpletons into fashion freaks of a kind guaranteed to provoke rude laughter and a loss of face for everyone concerned. She immediately knew that she would have to undo the damage. And set things right.

Chivalrous to the core, she marched down the colonnaded verandah, exchanging greetings and jolly banter with her kinsmen. Courteous suggestions and instructions followed.

The ADCs protested that the suit lengths she seemed so keen on giving away were still 'on approval' from Mr Jackson, the Ajmer-based Anglo-Indian shopkeeper who did profitable business with all the Rajasthani princes every winter when they collected there for the Mayo College prize-giving.

'Consider them approved,' responded the smiling Princess. 'Didn't Baapji promise to turn our *bhai-bandh* (kinsmen) into suited-booted gentlemen, just like English Lat Sahebs?'

Once the suit lengths were fetched, she mollified the chiefs by implying that her absent-minded elder brother, Robin, must have forgotten to convey Baapji's wishes to Thakur Ganpat Singhji. The hastily summoned Palace *durzis* (tailors) arrived, and started measuring them for brand new *bilayati* suits. To be made free of charge, of course!

The Resident was quite impressed by Kitten's knack for handling a rather sticky situation and turning it into a marvellous public relations ploy for herself and the Maharajah. But what truly intrigued him was the fact that her impetuous and, at times, high-handed behaviour was not only affectionately tolerated by her own family, but also actually admired by everyone around her.

Declining the Household Comptroller Zorji's belated escort, the Resident and the Maharajah's Military Secretary proceeded past the lily pond towards the Croquet Bagh. When they were perfectly safe from eavesdroppers, Redverse observed: 'Isn't it amazing how successfully Kitten shatters all the stereotypes about Rajput princesses that one reads and hears about?'

'My dear fellow, Kitten *is* the aristocratic female Rajput prototype personified!' retorted CP.

His friend conceded that she had all the qualities they seemed to value. She was a fearless rider and crack shot with nerves of steel. She was also generous, good-looking, and bright enough to take full advantage of the educational opportunities her progressive parents provided.

'When you've been here a bit longer, Reverse Gear, you'll begin to realise that it is tradition that moulds girls like the Chattargadh princess, not modernisation—or Europeanisation. D'you have any idea why even His Nutty Highness is forced to endure Kitten's attacks and naughty put-downs? Because it's their custom to treat sisters, daughters and nieces with indulgence, and a deference which went out of fashion elsewhere in the prehistoric era, you know.'

Realising that CP was in one of his disputatious, information-dispensing moods, the Resident refrained from comment.

They reached the group gathered round the tea table on the lawn just in time to hear R.K. Kishen exclaim: 'I don't understand you people. It's almost as though we don't speak the same language.'

Resisting the temptation to add that he often thought so too, the impeccably dressed Parsi proprietor of Chattargadh's English paper simply sighed: 'But today is Sunday, Raj Kumar Saheb.'

'We all know that. Otherwise I wouldn't be free to have tea with you and Gopal Dasji here, because His Highness has made it a rule that everyone and everything except the dutywallahs must rest on Sundays! Which is a great pity; for the ground is good today, the dust having settled thanks to our welcome winter shower. But orders are orders!'

'Precisely,' continued Mr Modi, who also owned Chattargadh's only cinema house. 'Because it's Sunday, there is no one to do composition at any press.'

'But this is not an essay competition, my friends,' the prince pointed out. 'Just print the news without worrying your heads about unnecessary things like composition-womposition.'

Openly chuckling as they exchanged amused glances with the editors of the local English and Hindi weekly tabloids, Colonel CP and Redverse sat down and accepted cups of tea from an attentive butler.

'That's just the problem, Raj Kumar Saheb,' said the Resident, without allowing a mocking note to enter his voice.

Kishen frowned at him, adjusting his dark glasses. 'What problem? It's simple, straightforward news. And it should be on their front page tomorrow. Not next week.'

Concluding that this incredibly naive prince was utterly ignorant of printing techniques, Colonel Caude-Poole pointed out that before anything could actually be printed on paper, the typeface would have to be composed.

'But surely you chaps can make some *bandobast* to print the scoop I'm giving you,' the prince persisted.

'Indeed, Raj Kumar Saab? Don't you see, according to our Maharajah, progress equals time off even for bonded labourers in his State, and a six-day working week,' countered Gopal Das, the committed nationalist permitted to publish a radical political weekly combining news, views, and entertaining local stories. 'Besides which, what you've just told us is hardly hard copy.'

'Journalistic jargon aside, everybody already knows that the Prince of Wales is coming to India next month for an extended tour, just like his father, grandfather, and great-grandfather. The Indian and British press have been full of it for weeks,' added Mr Modi.

'Of course. But the paperwallahs in Bombay, Delhi, London, and Calcutta don't know the real story. The Prince of Wales is going to spend four out of those 40 days cementing the British Empire in Chattargadh!' announced R.K. Kishen triumphantly. 'A personal cable from Buckingham Palace confirms this.'

Half an hour later, the Englishmen joined the Maharajah without revealing by word or gesture that this was the first intimation they had received about British royalty honouring this insignificant desert state with a personal visit.

When he had finished apologising for disturbing them on a sacred Sunday afternoon and then failing to receive them due to circumstances beyond his control, Maharajah Jai Singh got to the subject uppermost in his mind. Pointing to the newly unpacked paintings, bronzes, cut glass, porcelain, ivory, jade, silver ornaments, ormolu clocks, and embroidered silk screens, Jai Singh said that he would appreciate helpful advice about arranging all these things without overcrowding either of the drawing rooms, the dining halls, the writing room, the guest rooms, or the library.

'Your Highness has such excellent taste that one would hesitate making suggestions,' protested the Resident.

'Thank you, Mr Redverse. But you see, my staff have no idea about colour combinations, or what's appropriate where.'

Redverse nodded his head in agreement. 'CP and I have just seen a delightful display of their exotic tastes. But since every home is a reflection of its master, it would be easier to make suggestions if we understood Your Highness' preferences.'

'Well, I believe in combining comfort with dignity. I do my best to avoid our rooms resembling Nutty's version of the Turkish Sultan's Dolmabahace . . . or the stodgy stuffiness of the Indianised Italian-Gothic palaces so popular in Hyderabad, Gwalior and Baroda . . . or the psychedelic splendour of the Mysore palace!'

A couple of years ago, Maharajah Jai Singh and Colonel CP had embarked on a remarkable collaboration which had transformed a minor retreat into a palace of great comfort and charm. The choice of furniture and the conception of the interiors showed considerable Continental influence and clever Indian touches. They had effectively reconciled original Rajasthani architecture with European additions.

The muted mauves and greens of the main drawing room were perfect in this land of harsh sunlight and frequent sandstorms. Elegant silk-upholstered Rococo and Regency-style sofas and armchairs, gilded consoles, Venetian style mirrors; glass-fronted giltwood cabinets displaying rose quartz, amethyst, amber and jade pieces; superb Indian ivory boxes and figurines; embossed silver lamps, gold-crested cigarette cases, onyx ashtrays embellished with enamelled bronze birds and beasts; and locally woven Oshag-style carpets on the marble floor proclaimed the Maharajah's good taste. And attention to detail.

CP's enthusiasm for historic houses, furniture and works of art matched the Maharajah's. Therefore, apart from admiring particularly impressive items like a two-foot tall French pagoda clock, and a tall pair of jasper and lapis lazuli inlaid alabaster lampstands, Gerald maintained a discreet silence while they strode from room to room, conferring about where to put all the new stuff in the already overcrowded apartments.

'Wait till you see my crowning glories,' beamed Jai Singh, ushering them into a large unfurnished chamber seemingly enlarged by panels of nine-foot-high mirrors between the French windows.

At a signal from the Maharajah, turbaned *farrashes* simultaneously lifted the white dust sheets off three huge Bohemian cut glass chandeliers. The sparkling prisms and lustres made a tinkling sound as the cloth shrouding them was carefully removed. The Resident indicated his admiration with a complimentary nod, smile, and quirk of his eyebrows.

Colonel CP was equally impressed. 'Absolutely smashing, Your Highness!'

In one quick movement Jai Singh stepped sideways, rapping his knuckles on the door. 'Touch wood!'

'Quite extraordinary. One doesn't usually come across three identical Bohemian cut glass chandeliers of this size,' declared Redverse. 'These were custom made, no doubt?'

Immensely pleased by their reaction, Jai Singh confided: 'I found them at a Paris auction, in the Chevalier Gallery on the Boulevard St. Germaine. The owner assured me that they used to hang in the Tuileries ballroom till the end of the Second Empire.'

'Really, Your Highness?' said the Resident rather sceptically.

The Maharajah laughed, and indicated that he was perfectly aware of the ploys used by antique dealers and auctioneers to enhance the value of their exorbitantly overpriced wares. He'd lost count of the supposed personal possessions of British and French kings, Russian queens and tsars, Austrian archdukes, Chinese and Mughal emperors, Italian popes and princes, and all the Caesars, Christ and Cleopatra that he'd seen on sale—and often been urged to acquire.

Turning to his Military Secretary, the Maharajah asked, 'Now tell me, how soon can you instal them?'

CP strolled around the enormous chandeliers, taking in their design and dimensions. 'As soon as Your Highness tells me where you want them hung. I suppose one goes up here in our Durbar Hall, one in the Hajoor Niwas Banquet Hall—and the third in the main Drawing room.'

The Maharajah immediately dispelled these notions. 'I think not, Colonel CP. As you can see, these chandeliers are a unique set of—shall we say—identical triplets! Therefore, they cannot be hung in three different rooms, and lose their impact. I'd like them all right here in this Durbar Hall, where I propose to hold a grand reception for the Prince of Wales.'

'Really, Your Highness!' countered CP, after considering the Maharajah's words for a while. 'As the great modern master Mies Van Der Rohe says, "Less is always more for creating a real impact!"'

Jai Singh directed one of his piercing glances at the Englishman, polite and persuasive as ever. 'Colonel CP, shall we say that I'm rather keen to have them hung as they always were.'

Disconcerted, but still determined to make the Maharajah
see reason, Colonel CP sighed ruefully, raising his hands in
a helpless gesture. 'Really, Your Highness, I can't possibly
hang *all* these chandeliers in one room.'

'Why not?'

'Rather risky, shall we say. There would be too much
stress, and the roof would collapse.'

The Resident tactfully strolled away across the chamber
to examine an interesting wall fresco depicting a medieval
Rajput court and hunting scenes, aware that battle was
truly joined when the Maharajah countered CP's Euclidean
logic by wondering if he had really cast a flimsy roof. The
Colonel refuted this unwarranted assumption, but stuck to
his guns.

Jai Singh pointed out that Colonel Claude-Poole had
not really designed or built the entire Jai Mahal complex.
He had only extended and renovated it. And that too, only
slightly. CP immediately said that that was precisely why he
knew exactly what he was talking about without being
impudent, or contradictory to His Highness in any way.

'No one has a better notion of your Palace's structural
strengths and weaknesses. Therefore, Your Highness, I
repeat. It may seem like a simple exercise, but I regret to
say it can't be done.'

Things did not always run smoothly between the
Maharajah and Colonel CP. But if he'd merely wanted a
Yes man, he could just as well have appointed one of his
royal relations as Military Secretary—just like he'd made
Kishen his Dewan, thought Jai Singh. The British officer
could really be very aggravating at times!

But then, Maharajah Jai Singh recalled how the
confident young military engineer (sent along by the
Viceroy's Political Department) had speeded up the process
of modernising the State's old-fashioned army by
eliminating dead wood, and expanding the Chattargadh

Camel Corps. His ability to get things done on a war footing had also helped complete the CP canal—which Nutty insisted on calling the Pisshengunj-Chattargadh canal—in record time. And well within the budget. His practical and artistic skills also came in handy whenever Jai Singh came up with new projects, like the High Court, the Assembly buildings, or the new Stadium. The Maharajah knew that CP could never resist a professional challenge.

'You know, Colonel Claude-Poole, I didn't expect such a defeatist attitude from a distinguished and achievement-oriented soldier like you.'

At his most congenial the Maharajah was always hard to resist. But CP knew he had no other option. 'Right now, Sir, I'm in my architect avatar!'

Jai Singh appealed to the Resident. 'Mr Redverse, perhaps you could persuade your friend in this little matter? After all, these chandeliers have hung together from the same roof for centuries without causing any problems even when revolutionary mobs overran the Tuileries!'

'Really, Your Highness, architecture's hardly my cup of tea,' he replied.

The Maharajah was thoroughly put out by this lack of support. 'Colonel Claude-Poole, you should be cooperating instead of raising objections and obstructions to my wanting to beautify my home for British royalty!'

CP knew that the British royal family had achieved cult status among the Indian Maharajahs. But he wasn't going to risk his own reputation—and other people's necks—in order to pander to any prince.

'Indeed, Your Highness? Perhaps I too have a reputation to protect. I intend making sure that your palace keeps standing, instead of coming down like the walls of Jericho! As the chap who put it up in the first place, I happen to know without a shred of doubt that the Durbar Hall roof simply cannot take the weight of three elephants.'

Immediately seizing this face-saving ploy, Jai Singh cried: 'That's it! You wouldn't have any objections to installing my crowning glories if the Durbar Hall roof withstands the weight of three elephants?'

Colonel Claude-Poole shut his eyes and took a deep breath. 'Really, Your Highness. Elephants are hardly the issue here.'

With a condescending smile to his Military Secretary, the Maharajah commanded: 'Roopji, tell Thakur Ganpat Singhji that I wish to see him here as quickly as possible. Mr Redverse, you're a witness to this gentlemen's agreement.'

'What agreement?' wondered the Resident, absolutely puzzled.

'The one we just made,' said the smiling Maharajah.

Grasping his intention, the Resident drew an audible breath. 'Really, Your Highness, you can't be serious!'

Two days later, Maharajah Jai Singh summoned the Resident to witness the triumphant march of his elephants to the Durbar Hall rooftop. This, if nothing else, would oblige his Military Secretary to get off his architectural high horse, and instal his crowning glories exactly where he wanted them.

Colonel Claude-Poole, Robin, Raj Kumar Kishen, Ganpat Singh, Zorji, several gardeners, guards, and other Palace servants stood watching as the Chattargadh Raj Purohit smashed a coconut over the ramp constructed in record time from the Maharajah's private garden to the Durbar Hall's roof. Three beautifully painted and ornamented baby elephants were led up to this ramp by their *mahavats* to the chanting of auspicious mantras. Two high priests distributed rice and flower petals to the Maharajah, his son, grandson and cousin. They were to be sprinkled on the elephants before they took the first step on their significant journey. The bells round their necks began tolling as the elephants began to climb.

When he had first seen the waiting animals, Colonel CP had protested. But the Maharajah had simply countered his argument by saying that there had been nothing about size in their agreement. Jai Singh had had the good fortune of acquiring three unweaned, one-year-old elephant calves (along with their mothers) as an added bonus from his Mysore cousin. They had come along when he had been compelled to expand his *Peel khana* in anticipation of the grand processions customary during the Prince of Wales' visit, when the other attending Maharajahs would also have to be suitably mounted.

'I told my chaps, let's have a ramp like the ones constructed by the Pharaohs of Egypt!' Jai Singh confided to the Resident.

Since CP refused to have anything to do with this preposterous affair, he had been compelled to let Robin wield the camera instead of recording this absurd scene for posterity himself. Robin found it difficult to simultaneously compose, click, wind the film, and continue commenting on this silly situation.

'Let's cross our fingers and pray that this *tamasha* is over soon. I don't know what has come over your father,' Kishen Singh told Robin.

'A touch of Rajput madness, Hukum!' the heir apparent retorted, with a conspiratorial wink.

His wife Wendy, his mother, sisters, and their governess watched this *tamasha* with mixed feelings. They stood behind an arched and domed upstairs window that certainly screened them from view, but also amplified everything they said. Kitten and Ratna made frequent gleeful comments about Colonel CP's encounter with the Maharajah over something so trivial. Opinion was sharply divided over who should give in to whom. For nearly everyone in the Palace (excepting the Maharani), this was just another wonderfully entertaining interlude enlivening their daily routine.

'Mama, have you ever seen anything so crazy in this house?' demanded Kitten.

'All Rathors are crazy. Since I've been forced to put up with so much nonsense, I've forgotten half the shocking things they've done. But I never thought I'd see the day when your father would be acting like your Uncle Nutty! These stubborn Rathors! You can't expect them to back down, because they think it's below their dignity to admit defeat! I can't understand why Colonel Claude-Poole doesn't see reason, and give in gracefully without turning the entire place upside down over some silly chandeliers!'

Considerably taken aback by the Maharani's critical tone, the governess suggested: 'Your Highness, perhaps his professional pride won't let him compromise either.'

Encouraged and prodded along by their *mahavats*, the baby elephants marched in single file. They were almost halfway up the ramp when suddenly they stopped, refusing to budge. Maharajah Jai Singh ordered them forward. The priests chanted louder. The patient *mahavats* coaxed them *sotto voce* with secret invocations handed down to them from father to son in the jungles where elephants were trapped and trained. The Resident wished they'd get a move on, so that he could call it a day.

However, just then CP heard the first ominous sound.

He marched up to the Maharajah. 'Your Highness, may I suggest that the elephants go up one by one.'

'Why? Do you think this is Noah's Ark?' countered Jai Singh, raising his brows.

Kitten watched in horrified fascination as the timber planks of that hastily constructed ramp began cracking under the collective weight of the baby elephants. They were rather tiny ones, quite unlike the large tuskers used for weddings and state processions. But the wooden supports swayed. There was an unmistakable crackling sound as the heavily burdened bridge developed a gaping jagged hole in the middle where the planks had obviously been weak, and where the elevation had not been adequately supported.

Their ears alert and trunks upraised, the elephants had sniffed out potential danger. Nothing could force them forward. Trumpeting a protest, they turned around resolutely, and speedily scampered to safety on the grass below. Peacocks perched on a nearby kiosk flew off, screeching. The Maharajah's grandson, Pat, added to the hullabaloo caused by this unforeseen disaster by running up to examine the damage with some of his boisterous companions.

As the ramp disintegrated before their eyes, Kitten exclaimed between spurts of loud laughter: 'I knew this was not the way to get those elephants on the roof!'

'Ha! D'you have a better suggestion?' scoffed Ratna.

'I'll think of something,' promised Kitten.

Maharani Padmini agreed that the whole thing had been mismanaged from the start. She wasn't one bit surprised that it had all turned into a shambles laughed at by everyone.

Treating the whole thing as a huge joke, Robin continued clicking photographs. This exasperated Jai Singh. 'Give me that camera,' he ordered.

But the young man swiftly dodged out of his father's reach.

'I *knew* this would happen,' lamented the Military Secretary. 'But nobody listens to me. And the same thing will happen to the roof if some misguided fool succeeds in forcing those elephants where they don't belong!'

Jai Singh reluctantly admitted to himself that things hadn't gone according to plan. He would have to evolve a new strategy for achieving his objective. Glancing at his wristwatch, he quickly invited the Englishmen in for a drink. The garden was filling up with more than half the Palace staff, including the male and female labourers employed to build the ramp. They were all hugely diverted and more than ready to cut jokes about this set-back. By evening they would undoubtedly be singing new songs poking fun at him.

But this too was part of their fond feudal relationship, as the Maharajah well knew.

R.K. Kishen was the only one to decline the sherry served by the butler. 'Bhai, how could you forget that today is Tuesday? I can't annoy my *Ishta Devta*, Hanumanji, by drinking on this day.'

Saying that he was sorry but there were more important things on his mind, the Maharajah asked his cousin to order coffee or tea instead. They disposed themselves on the sofas and chairs in the large entrance hall, and Jai Singh sat down facing the wide marble staircase sweeping up to the first floor.

'Come on, Kishen. Think of something.'

'Sorry, Bada Bhai,' began the Dewan in his usual blunt manner. 'But I can't think of anything except one stubborn man getting off his high horse!'

The Maharajah nodded emphatically. 'Indeed, that would solve this problem immediately.'

Colonel Claude-Poole promptly added: 'I entirely agree with Your Highness.'

His good humour restored by this seeming capitulation, the Maharajah declared, 'So you've decided to see reason after all?'

'I think we all know what Raj Kumar Saheb means,' retorted CP.

The outraged Maharajah set down his sherry glass on a carved rosewood table. 'Did you hear that, Mr Redverse? Now my own Military Secretary starts casting aspersions on me, when Heaven knows I'm the most reasonable man alive . . . .'

'Really, Your Highness! I'm just an impartial observer.'

Both were being equally uncompromising. CP claimed that with him, it was a question of integrity. The Maharajah accused him of vanity. As they argued back and forth, Redverse found that the perfect princely paragon for whom he'd developed a great liking, was degenerating before his eyes into a childishly obstinate autocrat determined to have his own way. He longed to end this deplorable stalemate. But a Resident's role demanded hefty amounts of detachment, and diplomacy, even at the best of times.

'I shall take immediate steps to get those elephants up, and make Colonel Claude-Poole eat professional humble pie!' swore Jai Singh.

Rising to take leave, the Resident cautioned, 'I hope they won't be very drastic steps, Your Highness, because this story is all over Chattargadh already. And we don't want the newspaper *wallahs* making mountains out of molehills!'

'I thought what happened out there was the other way around!' teased Robin.

Standing up to bid his guest goodbye, the Maharajah happened to glance towards the staircase, and a brainwave hit him. 'Now why didn't I think of that before?'

Word of the Maharajah's latest orders spread through the Palace, bringing Kitten and Ratna rushing downstairs to join their family members arguing vociferously in the hall. Unable to depart, the Resident stood silent, watching the *mahavats* actually bring the three baby elephants indoors, unable to say anything that might dissuade HH.

This was too much for the Colonel, who swore an exasperated oath, and glared at the Maharajah.

Robin pleaded one more time with his father, telling him that their ancestors might have ridden horses upstairs and downstairs and jumped them off the ramparts of nearly every historic fort in India. But elephants were another story!

'Robin, you obviously know very little about the inherited traits of these animals. Elephants can move through dense jungles without disturbing a single leaf or snapping any twigs. Have you ever seen them put a foot wrong, either on shikar or at any circus?'

'But this is not a circus, Data Hukum, and those poor little elephants are absolutely untrained! Think of the damage they might cause.'

'Don't worry,' said Jai Singh scornfully. 'Trained or untrained, you'll inherit this place intact when I die.'

Abashed by this totally crushing and undeserved put-down, Robin retreated to a safe distance.

Kitten told the Raj Purohit to use his most powerful mantras so that those chandeliers brought across the seven seas could be lit up for The Prince of Wales. The priest assured the princess that he had already asked Ganeshji, Jagadamba Mata, and Pashupati Nath Mahadev Shiv Shankar to get there with Bajarang Bali Hanumanji Maharaj to clear up all the obstacles, and fulfil Baapji's little desire.

It soon became clear that the elephants, who had happily toddled upstairs behind their handlers without mishap, had encountered a set-back as soon as they reached the corridor leading to the roof. When the Maharajah ordered the *mahavats* to hurry up, for they were now close to their goal, his grandson suddenly leaned over the bannister, shouting: 'They're stuck! They're stuck!'

'The elephants might be having a few navigational problems, but I'm confident they'll finally sail through,' Jai Singh said to everyone.

'Camels might pass through a needle's eye. But I doubt if elephants can squeeze through marble and sandstone walls!' said his irrepressible daughter, making everyone laugh.

Kitten's rude comments about the preposterousness of her father's idea included the observation that he seemed to have ignored the flexibility factor. Instead of ignoring her, the Maharajah asked his favourite child to clarify this sweeping statement. She cheekily informed him that in their natural habitat, elephants could breeze through the densest forests because even the tallest trees and the thickest undergrowth bent or parted, allowing them to pass!

Having said this, Kitten crossed the hall, whispered in her brother's ear, and approached her father, brandishing a silver coin. 'Data Hukum, a toss of this coin can settle this affair without loss of face for anyone,' she said.

But the Maharajah and his Military Secretary both refused.

After a hasty consultation with Colonel CP, the princess suggested that a compromise could be arranged if HH agreed to having two chandeliers in the Durbar Hall, and one in any other room of his choice. But Jai Singh drew himself up to his full height, looked down his nose at Colonel CP, and informed his daughter that although he appreciated her effort to resolve this business, it still had to be all three.

Thus, efforts to get the elephants through the corridor and on to the Durbar Hall roof continued.

Considerably embarrassed and irritated by the noisy hullabaloo caused by her husband's stubborn attitude, Maharani Padmini decided to remonstrate with him after lunch. A message had been brought to Her Highness while it was being served that Baapji had commanded the elephants to remain upstairs—'With Maharani Saab's permission, of course!'—till he could figure out a way for having them transported to where they would defeat Kernull Saab.

But, he had not allowed for the fact that the little ones had to be fed at regular four-hourly intervals, and given at least two gallons of water to keep them happy.

Kitten and Ratna were only too ready to jump up from the table with all the fruit they could carry, asking the laughing upper-caste Brahmin women serving them to organise buckets and basins full of water. They ordered Her Highness' *Badaranji* to the *zenani dyodhi* to summon Butler Saab, who was told to immediately send up jumbo-sized helpings of bread and milk, plus all the fruit in the pantry for the poor hungry little animals till their own afternoon feed arrived from the *Peel khana*.

As soon as they were alone, Padmini pointed out to her husband that for a ruler whose kingdom was populated largely by animal-loving Jains and Bishnois, his attitude was strange. Jai Singh immediately countered by saying that he had fulfilled his duty towards his land and his people by providing them with sufficient water, conserving and planting forests, protecting wild life during the closed season, and absolutely prohibiting any killing or trapping of helpless deer and peacocks—the two species his Rathor ancestors had sworn to protect when the Bishnoi chief Gogaji had put the Raj *tilak* on Chattarsal's forehead in 1483.

The noise and commotion grated increasingly on Padmini's nerves. Everyone in the *zenana* was rushing around to gape, fondle, and play with the cute little elephants once it was established that they were perfectly harmless and didn't mind having their trunks stroked. Her naughty grandson had unleashed all the four dogs belonging to his father and grandfather. Their incessant barking, scampering, and jumping up and down round the elephants added to the ruckus. Since the Maharani prided herself on running a household that was a marvel of organised efficiency, she took exception to her entire staff behaving as childishly as all the three generations of her assembled family. In unmistakable terms, she requested her husband to have the calves immediately restored to their mothers in the Fort.

However, he continued to cudgel his brains for the next two days, trying to get his own way, instead of compromising like a sensible man.

Subsequently, Kitten and Ratna were kept busy carrying chits back and forth between Maharajah Jai Singh (who had immediately retreated to his own apartment downstairs) and his wife, who had sworn that she would go on an indefinite fast and observe complete silence in the fashion of Mahatma Gandhi's *maun vrat* (silent fast) if he did not see reason.

When Kitten suggested that HH use someone else to put up those chandeliers since there didn't seem to be any way of getting the elephants to the roof of the Durbar Hall, her father retorted that just by virtue of being an Englishman, Colonel Claude-Poole had subverted all the master masons, electricians, and carpenters, who had eaten Chattargadh salt. He had filled them with so many superstitious doubts that now no one was touching this task even at the risk of offending or disobeying their Maharajah. They simply refused to take responsibility for damaging Baapji's home—a greater mortal sin in their eyes than humbly begging to gainsay him just this once.

Returning from a thoroughly enjoyable evening ride with her brother and cousin, Kitten went to fetch a book from the music room, also used as a private library by the Chattargadh royal ladies. Still clad in her cream-coloured riding breeches, checked hacking jacket, and dusty, dark brown boots, Kitten browsed through the built-in, glass-fronted marble shelves full of books in Sanskrit, Hindi, and English. Several Tamil tales treasured by her grandmother, and Dingal sagas belonging to her mother and great-grandmothers were also there, alongside translations of European, Arabic, Persian, and Chinese classics. A voracious reader, Kitten spent more time reading fiction after the Senior Cambridge exam, which had ended her schooldays at St. Mary's. She finally picked *Around The World In Eighty Days* by Jules Verne, whom she always enjoyed re-reading because he was such an original, futuristic writer.

Refreshed by a lovely long soak in the steaming hot water scented by generous handfuls of her favourite Penhaligon's bathsalts, Kitten dressed informally for dinner with the help of her doting personal maid, Jamna Jiji. Her entire suite, including the bath and dressing room, was done in shades of blue, with contrasting peony-patterned upholstery covering the armchairs, stools, and chaise longue in the large bedroom, which also contained her writing table. Beautiful bird paintings hung on the walls, and silver-framed family photographs stood among the porcelain statuettes, lamps, and flower bowls. The heater had been switched on. Kitten adjusted the silk-shaded pedestal lamp, settling down to read on the inviting chaise longue piled with feather-soft cushions as soon as her maid left the room.

Suddenly, her firm rosebud mouth flew open and her huge black eyes brightened as she stared at the illustrated title page.

'I've got it!' cried Kitten, smiling at the hero, Phileas Fogg, and his valet, Passepartout, off on their great adventure round the world in an air balloon.

In one swift motion she tossed aside the hand-knitted Afghan rug covering her legs, thrust her feet into fur-lined embroidered Kashmiri slippers, and, without bothering to tidy her tousled hair, rushed out of her room with the book.

Downstairs, the exuberantly fiesty princess surprised her father and uncle by bursting into the Maharajah's study, hiding something behind her back and claiming that she'd just found the perfect solution to the impasse between her father and his Military Secretary. They both rose automatically when she entered, Jai Singh with an inquiring look and raised eyebrows and R.K. Kishen with a softened expression on his rugged brown face.

'If it's another note from your mother, you may tell her that she should use the telephone so that we may speak to one another directly.'

Apart from reminding him that her mother, a true-to-her-word Sisodia by birth, had refused to speak to him till he complied with her wishes, Kitten exercised great forbearance, foregoing a golden opportunity to enlighten her father about the grim realities of eavesdropping in the palace, which fed city tittle-tattle. Everybody in Chattargadh relished inside gossip about every little thing that their rulers said and did.

Instead, she showed him the leather-bound book she had brought.

Waving Kitten down into a leather armchair, the Maharajah sat up and took a sip of brandy. 'Kitten, I'm really not in the mood for any of your silly pranks. And you're much too big for fairy stories.'

Kitten's slender sensitive nose flared as she tilted her pointed chin at her father, proudly showing him an illustration in the book in her hand. 'Look at this, Data Hukum! That's the perfect solution to your little problem.'

Perfunctorily glancing at the sketch and reading the title, Jai Singh returned the book to his daughter. 'So? What does this have to do with anything?'

Kishen Singh set down his brandy balloon and leaned forward, studying the picture. 'Bhai, it's so obvious! I'm supposed to be the dim-witted one in this family, but even I can see what she means. Kitten, you should have been a boy. Here, take a sip of my brandy.'

Grinning and accepting the honour given her, Kitten declared, 'A second son? No thanks, I'd rather be an only daughter.'

Jai Singh's gloom vanished as he realised that his beloved daughter had once more resolved a formidable problem. With one of those quirky flashes of brilliance that illuminated her mind and the lives of people around her, Kitten had found the perfect solution to the ongoing impasse between himself and Colonel Claude-Poole.

Fortunately, reflected the Maharajah, the warfare, vendetta, and *johar*-prone Rajputs had always known that without equally cultivated and fiercely assertive women capable of taking over their kingdoms and fiefdoms, their dynasties were doomed. So they had trained them accordingly. A Rajput girl child was either given oblivion through opium at birth, or brought up alongside sons to become a reasonable scholar, a knowledgeable art patron, a benevolent ruler, and a formidable warrior capable of leading armies in battle. They were also taught how to organise embassies and control regency councils. *Rawlas* (queen's courts or houses) were sacrosanct power centres and fountains of charity, and everyone in Rajputana knew this. Purdah had been observed only at the Mughal court and not in their own homes. Their incarceration behind *zenani dyodhis* came with the British Raj, when Residents and Crown Agents preferred undermining astute Rajput dowager queens in order to assume direct control of their ancient, wealthy kingdoms.

Mulling over her suggestion, R.K. Kishen observed that it would take several days before Baapji could lay his hands on hot air balloons and persons capable of flying them in from Delhi, where the English had a Meteorological station.

Obliged to concede this, Jai Singh smiled and added: 'But there was no Statute of Limitations on our agreement! It should be done before the fourteenth of February—which gives us enough time before the Prince of Wales arrives.'

After their usual game of tennis that evening, Gerald accompanied CP into the spacious bungalow adjoining the Chattargadh Camel Corps officers' mess and parade ground. The Colonel's efficient batman immediately wheeled the tea trolley out to the screened verandah where the Englishmen lounged on large round *modas*.

'This is getting ridiculous, CP,' began Gerald as soon as they were alone. 'I'm told that astrologers and pundits were summoned to the palace, and a favourable *muhurat* (auspicious time) was sought for Operation Jumbo!'

CP passed his friend the fruitcake. 'Standard procedure, old chap, whenever the Maharajah starts a new venture or sets out on a journey. But this time, they've also cast my horoscope in order to find out which planets must be propitiated, because my negative vibes seem to be hindering HH's business!'

Redverse rolled his eyes, barely able to contain his feelings about this whole silly charade. 'Although I appreciate your stand, CP, why don't you give in like a good chap? We both know that *he* won't because its against his Rajput dharma!'

Swallowing the sausage roll specially prepared for his visitor, CP gave him a scathing look. 'Reverse Gear, there may have been times during our long association when I've thought you were making an utter ass of yourself. But have I ever told you how to do your job?'

'No, I must say you haven't'.

'Then just stay out of this. I'm a builder, not a demolition squad!' snapped CP, adding a few uncomplimentary comments about princes in general, and this Maharajah in particular.

'Eccentric? Would you go so far as to actually label him eccentric?' protested Gerald.

'My dear fellow, then how, pray, would you justify his present behaviour? It's time someone read him the riot act, y'know.'

Younger than Maharajah Jai Singh by nearly nine years, the Resident disliked the idea of confronting him on something so silly. He simply shook his head and turned the conversation to a much more intimate and pleasant subject.

'Ah, so she's coming back at last. That's great news, Reverse Gear. I was afraid Dorothy had deserted you forever to stay home with those twins.'

Redverse explained that his wife had been detained in England first by her sister's wedding to that American tycoon, and then by her mother's fracturing an arm while riding an imperfectly trained hunter on their Scottish estate. She had been away too long, and he would be only too glad to have her back. CP said that in that case, why hadn't he hurried off to Bombay to meet her boat?

'Because the date had coincided with an important conference of Agents to the Governor General, Residents, and Crown Agents at Delhi regarding the final details and protocol for the Prince's Indian tour,' explained Gerald. 'Dorothy can always be relied upon to handle everything satisfactorily.'

Clever, capable Lady Dorothy Frazer, with her cliquish family connections in high places, had become the perfect Civil Service wife. The statuesque Scottish debutante had refused four proposals before marrying Gerald Redverse, merely a second son serving in India. Their passionate love had turned into real devotion with the sharing imposed by eight years of prolonged sojourns in remote, isolated places.

When she stepped off the Rajputana Express at Chattargadh, her husband was the first person she spotted on the busy platform. Since the Residency, like the Palace, lay a good distance from the railway station—beyond the temple-dotted old walled city, and away from the modern section with its well laid-out public park, superb sandstone buildings housing schools, colleges, hospitals, the *Kuchehri* (Court), the Assembly, the museum, the cinema and Town Hall—Redverse had decided to drive Dorothy home in his own one-horse buggy, leaving the chauffeur to attend to her considerable luggage.

As soon as they finished talking about their sons Samuel and David, various friends and family members, her voyage, and his recent trip to the capital, Lady Dorothy turned her attention to the local sights, taking in the cavalcade of camels and turbaned men, the women's splendid swinging *lehngas* and colourful veils, the hawkers and cyclists and bullock carts driving past the occasional motor car, and donkeys loaded with bricks or bundles. Temple bells pealed from a vermilion-daubed shrine near the post office. The easy-gaited chestnut trotted past large, single-storeyed bungalows surrounded by huge trees, bougainvillea, and henna hedges. There were peacocks, pigeons, parrots, kites, mynas, silver grey doves, little sparrows, bulbuls, and those ever-present crows everywhere—plus several other birds she couldn't name.

She absorbed the smells and sounds of the new place around her. She had frankly been dreading it despite all she had heard and read about romantic Rajputana. But now, the

Scotswoman smiled at her husband. 'Not bad at all after your dreadful descriptions of Chattargadh as a desolate desert!'

'You've come at a good time, my love. And though the place gets abominably uncomfortable in summer, there's never a dull moment.'

'Sounds as though you really like it here, Gerry.'

Checking his horse to let a group of pigtailed girls lugging schoolbags cross the narrow metalled road, Gerald responded: 'It grows on you. I hated coming, and I'll hate going.'

'What's the Maharajah like?' asked Dorothy, adjusting her wide-brimmed hat.

Redverse gave her a rueful, revealing look. 'Perfectly charming as long as he gets his own way.'

Lady Dorothy's shrewd hazel eyes gleamed. 'In other words, a typical Indian prince.'

'Certainly not, old thing,' her husband protested. 'He's a cut above the rest, a sort of Rajput Kemal Ataturk who's frightfully keen on modernisation . . . .'

He stopped mid-sentence, for his well-bred wife was clutching his arm in public and pointing skywards over his shoulder as she gasped. 'Gerry, I'm either going mad, or hallucinating, for I can't possibly be drunk!'

Redverse followed the direction of her pointing finger, and saw three elephants floating above the Palace, suspended from bright orange air balloons. His cool blue eyes crinkled as he began laughing. He assured her that she needn't fear for her sanity because this joke was on CP. Still shocked and slightly puzzled by his strange response, Dorothy cried: 'Can't you see what's in plain sight? One is prepared for anything in India, but flying elephants are a bit too much even for me!'

Patting her arm as they watched the elephants landing right on target on the designated roof, the Resident puzzled his wife even further. 'Really speaking, my love, you're looking at the Maharajah's chandeliers!'

The Prince of Wales
in Princely India 4

Harmony speedily restored after the ridiculous elephant and chandelier incident, the Maharajah and Maharani of Chattargadh reverted to thcir custom of lunching together as often as possible outdoors in the *zenana* bagh on fine winter afternoons. Aware that protocol prohibited royal wives from seeking or summoning their husbands (though everybody else in the kingdom had the right to do so), Jai Singh had always been meticulous about enhancing Padmini's status (and dignity) by simply popping in and out of her domain in the *rawla* as often as possible.

Maharani Padmini still had not acquired the knack of being able to do three things at the same time like her husband. Every time he read aloud some interesting bit of news for her benefit while going through his *dak* (mail), she lost track of the precise line in the pattern she was knitting (out of a Patons and Beehive pamphlet) for Kitten's compulsory handicraft project. Her optimistic daughter always chose the most complicated patterns and designs when everybody knew that nothing bored her more quickly than knitting and sewing. She inevitably ended up cajoling other people to complete the sweater (or piece of embroidery) every senior was expected to submit before the school's annual exhibition and prize-giving ceremony. These were fast approaching. So her mother, her governess, her cousin, and sister-in-law were together trying to finish the four parts of an impressive sports sweater, which Kitten had no compunction about passing off as her own work!

Jai Singh threw up his head with an oath, laughing loudly as he set the *Court Gazette* he had been reading on the table between them.

'What's so funny about this year's Birthday Honours list? Have they ennobled the Mahatma?' asked the Maharani.

Amusement glinting from his eyes, Jai Singh gave her the *Gazette*. 'Even the Brits wouldn't be so obvious. But you've now become a knight's daughter!'

Puzzled, Padmini said: 'Impossible.'

'Not if it pleases the King of England. He has knighted Dudu Durbar, Maharawal Sir Bakhat Singh!'

Understanding dawned on his wife, who also chuckled, showing perfect white teeth. 'That so-called honour won't impress HIM. He's quite capable of informing the King that he doesn't need foreign titles to enhance a self-esteem which comes from performing every Indian Raja's dharma.'

'Bravo, Padmini! You should join the Indian National Congress,' teased her husband.

'No thanks. Agitational politics would be more appropriate as another hobby for you,' rejoined the Maharani.

'We must send your father a congratulatory telegram just for fun.'

His wife smiled. 'You've forgotten that he refuses to allow telegraph or railway lines to mutilate his state.'

'Backward chap,' sighed Jai Singh. 'But we must still invite him here to meet the Prince of Wales.'

'He can't accept Chattargadh hospitality without incurring some sort of sin and loss of prestige because I'm your wife,' protested Padmini. 'You know how he sticks to our old customs and traditions.'

'Don't worry, we'll coax him by pretending that he's only Raj Kumar Kishen Singh Saab's guest, for I'm sure that the Prince would enjoy meeting a real history-book Rajput.'

Abandoning the knitting till she could give it her undivided attention, Padmini asked, 'Whom else do you propose inviting?'

'Just family members,' replied the Maharajah. 'My sister Diamond, her husband Sir Pratab, their son Arjun, and, of course, their nephew, Tiger Fateypur.'

Aware that Maharajah Tiger Fateypur and the Prince of Wales were close cronies belonging to the same high-spirited, horsy international set, the Maharani wondered aloud how they could be kept entertained for three whole days with Chattargadh's meagre resources. When her husband outlined the programme he had in mind, she couldn't resist asking, 'And what about the Maharajah of our upper riparian state?'

'What about him? Haven't I just explained that I haven't invited other Maharajahs because I don't want protocol problems and silly squabbles over precedence to spoil the Prince's visit? Do you think I'm going to have that Nutty chap running loose around the heir to the British throne with two dozen dogs?' demanded Jai Singh.

'Darling, knowing him . . .' began Padmini.

'Sweetheart, knowing Nutty, I refuse to invite him to Chattargadh at a time like this,' interrupted the Maharaja. 'And even he wouldn't dare gatecrash an event controlled by the British Foreign Office.'

Every one who was gathered around the conference table in Maharajah Jai Singh's study, quickly endorsed his plans for making the Prince of Wales' visit a memorable affair. Except, that is, his son.

'Data Hukum, couldn't we be a bit more original?' begged Robin.

'Originality can often misfire, Robin,' countered the Maharajah. 'Personally, I think that every State should stick to its own speciality. What do you say, Mr Redverse?'

'Quite so, Your Highness,' said the Resident.

But young Robin continued protesting. 'It's so predictably stale and boring to make the Prince play polo, shoot grouse, lay foundation stones, and go pig-sticking just like every other royal visitor to Chattargadh before him. Let's do something different this time.'

'There really is no need—and no time either—to go off on wild tangents just to introduce novelty into a very tightly structured royal visit in which nothing can be left to chance,' replied the Maharajah.

'Our only problem will be how to entertain HRH successfully when he's not actually out there, doing something entertaining for our people,' added R.K. Kishen.

Assuring the Dewan that the hectic programme chalked out by the Maharajah would keep even this hyperactive Prince of Wales completely occupied every minute he was awake, Colonel CP began reading from a printed card in his hand. 'Twenty-third February. Arrival by train, 9 a.m. Procession to Fort, 10 a.m. Durbar in HRH's honour, followed by a luncheon organised by the Chiefs of Chattargadh. An hour's rest, followed by the polo match at 3 p.m. The Canal opening ceremony at the auspicious time, 5.15 p.m. followed by the State banquet and torchlight tattoo by the Chattargadh Camel Corps.

Second day: Twenty-fourth February. Grouse shoot at 7 a.m. followed by review of State Forces, 10.30 a.m. Distribution of gifts and medals to Boxer Rebellion and Great War veterans before lunch with State Force officers in the Risala Mess. Rest, then Her Highness' family reception, 4 p.m. followed by a ritual fire dance and dinner, 8 p.m.

The third and last day of the royal visit: Twenty-fifth February, 1939. Pig-sticking and lunch at the shooting lodge. Laying the foundation stone of the Maharani Padmini Women's College 3 p.m. followed by a football match between the Chattargadh and Fateypur teams. Tea at the British Residency, 5.30 p.m. Then a traditional Rajput feast with singers and dancers, 8 p.m. Departure of royal party by train, 10 p.m.'

'Splendid now that's what I call a beautifully planned schedule,' exclaimed the Maharajah. 'But make sure the Prince has enough elbow room for sowing the usual wild oats.'

R.K. Kishen assured Jai Singh that everything would be done in a manner befitting Chattargadh's renowned traditions of hospitality. 'But Bhai, we still have to sort out the accommodation for everyone, and appoint extra ADCs to look after the royal party and our visiting relations.'

'Pity the chap who'll be looking after HH Pisshengunj,' the Resident remarked with a slight shudder.

The Maharajah hastened to reassure him. 'He's not on our guest list, Mr Redverse.'

The Resident gave the Maharajah a perturbed glance, pursing his lips while he speculated on the repercussions this might have. 'Is that really wise, Your Highness?'

'Indeed, Mr Redverse, I can't afford to have that Nutty chap ruining my reputation with his strange eccentricities and odd behaviour. Now, let's iron out all the minor details. Kishen, where are the files and photo albums of Their Majesties' previous visits to Chattargadh?'

The Dewan waved his hands airily. 'Being ironed out, Hukum.'

'Kishen, stop repeating everything I say.'

'Sorry, Bhai. I keep forgetting that you like hearing the real truth only from the horse's mouth.'

Deftly intervening before they got sidetracked by another one of those pointless arguments so common between these blood brothers, Colonel CP said, 'Your Highness, what Raj Kumar Saheb really means is that your grandson Pat somehow got hold of those lists, and . . . .'

The irritated Maharajah interrupted. 'I bet he found them lying on your office floor, Kishen, where you throw everything you're too lazy to read. You go around pretending to be illiterate like Akbar just to give me a bad name. Didn't we share the same tutors as boys? Didn't we both go to Mayo College for seven years?'

'But only YOU were sent to Oxford!'

'Because you jumped ship in Bombay,' retorted Jai Singh.

The next instant he winced as something hit him on the neck. Turning around, he found his grandson Pat performing a balancing feat on the window sill behind his desk. He was tossing paper darts and planes clearly made of the missing files and photographs into the room. Horrified at this mutilation of valuable historical records, the Maharajah rose menacingly from his seat to pounce on him. But the boy swiftly jumped to safety, laughing over his shoulder at his grandfather as the latter leaned out of the window, uttering dire threats.

Nutty continued to remain silent as his Dewan talked about various subjects. One of these was his relief on hearing that his wife was still on a shopping spree in Hong Kong, and unlikely to reach Japanese-occupied Shanghai or the rather more vulnerable Singapore; another was the rapid progress (since the labour had been tripled) of the convent under construction for the Maharajah's designated music teacher, Mother Angelus. Nutty leaned back on the drawing room's bright brocade sofa, stretching out one foot after another for his *poshaki* (valet) to unlace and remove his tennis shoes and white socks. Respectfully placing the Maharajah's feet on a fluffy folded towel and sprinkling them liberally with Johnson's Baby Powder in order to prevent athlete's foot, the retainer placed a pair of soft, pearl-encrusted slippers on his feet. The butler respectfully handed the Maharajah his custom-made, gold-crested Limoges cup and monogrammed Irish linen napkin.

Since the game, set, and match had gone exactly as his exacting master liked, and no minor mishaps had marred the day, Baron Tikemoffsky couldn't quite figure out why HH sat brooding and pondering instead of tucking into the excellent energy-restoring spread provided by the palace pantry.

Declining the delectable ham-stuffed sandwiches, Nutty demanded, 'Tikky, are you absolutely sure the Resident did actually speak to HH Chattargadh?'

'Yes, Your Highness. I booked a personal trunk call to Reverse Gear . . . what a silly name, ha ha . . . but then silly nicknames have always been an English speciality. They call their kings Bertie, and their dogs Rex!' Consuming another coconut cake, Tikky continued, 'And I have it from the horse's mouth that the Viceroy is very much looking forward to seeing you at the Delhi celebrations honouring the Prince of Wales.'

Nutty clicked his tongue and gave his Russian confidante a dismissive flick of the fingers. 'Tikky, I'm not at all worried about the Viceroy's banquet, where all the 19-gun salutes will automatically appear. But what about Chattargadh? Because going there is my birthright!'

Setting down his quarter-plate and adjusting the sleeves of his white V-necked sweater, Tikky conceded that HH was absolutely right. But there was the little matter of protocol between brother princes, whose ancient lineage and dignity made formal personal invitations de rigueur before they could even think of showing up in each other's States. This was so no matter how closely they were related. Clearing his throat, Tikky concluded: 'I'm afraid HH Chattargadh's response on this occasion remains negative, Your Highness.'

As this piece of information sank in, the Pisshengunj Maharajah let loose a tirade against his cousin, recalling past disagreements and every damaging recent encounter. 'Do you want to know his real problem? He's scared that I'll outshine him, everywhere, every time. Therefore, he doesn't dare take the risk of having me around during the Prince of Wales' visit, because the whole of Europe knows who's closer to Their Majesties, he or I. And if he's going to be so obstinate and unreasonable, and refuse to recognise my right to visit my ancestral home whenever I like, Prince or no Prince, I'll teach him a lesson he won't forget even in his next birth!'

Nutty thumped the sofa for emphasis, startling the two miniature Spitz snuggling under the down-stuffed cushions. He demanded to know whether he was less worthy of a personal invitation than young Tiger Fateypur. 'He's not even remotely related to HH Chattargadh because he's Princess Diamond's nephew only by marriage. They've conveniently forgotten that, in actual fact, he's MY real sister's son! And, how could Jai Singh so thoughtlessly set about ruining the Rajput dharma of his father-in-law, Maharawal Bakhat Singhji, by forcing him to eat Chattargadh salt when everyone knows that this heinous sin guarantees his being reborn as a dog in his next birth?'

The Baron chuckled and conceded that most persons would give anything to rub shoulders with British Royalty.

'That's right, Tikky. But I don't believe in compromising my principles, only in triumphing over people who take disadvantage of this simple soul called Maharajah Natwar Singh of Pisshengunj.'

Wholeheartedly agreeing with the Maharajah, Tikky suggested they put on their thinking caps.

'Huh,' scoffed Nutty. 'I don't need any caps-shaps to activate my brain.'

'Just a figure of speech, Your Highness.'

'Did you manage to get hold of a copy of their programme for the Prince's visit?' demanded Nutty.

'But, of course, Your Highness.'

Ordered to fetch it immediately from his safely locked office, Tikky left the room. By the time he returned, the drawing room fires had been lit, the shimmering scarlet and gold damask curtains drawn, and several well-groomed dogs brought in to enjoy their fond master's cossetting and company.

Avidly scanning the list and announcing that he would soon find Jai Singh's Achilles' heel—for surely everyone had one—Nutty began plotting his revenge on the Chattargadh Maharajah for being so petty-minded as not to invite him to share the privilege of entertaining their future King Emperor.

Anticipation electrified everyone waiting to welcome the Prince of Wales as they heard the royal special clattering towards the railway station with its whistle hooting. Maharajah Jai Singh, Robin, Kishen, Maharawal Bakhat Singh of Dudu, Sir Pratab, and Tiger Fateypur stood waiting, resplendent in multi-hued brocade *achkans*, jewelled turbans and swords. The British Resident and Colonel Claude-Poole were also dressed in full ceremonial regalia, including orders, ribbons, and feathered high hats. Behind them stood the seven hereditary Chattargadh chiefs, its ministers, the various ADCs, and all the European and Indian State officials, looking forward to meeting this world-famous royal visitor. Chattargadh's brass and bagpipe bands were ready to strike up the minute the Prince of Wales stepped off the train.

They could clearly hear the wheels grating to stop as the puffing train reached the platform. But to Jai Singh's utter consternation, the royal saloon stopped short of the profusely patterned Persian carpet, specially designed for hiding historic footprints.

'Damn it!' swore CP. 'After all the instructions and rehearsals, it stops one compartment too early.'

'And one Prince too late,' murmured the Resident.

Tiger's long-lashed almond eyes twinkled. 'They can always Reverse Gear, y'know!'

Jai Singh cast his Dewan a significant look. R.K. Kishen pantomimed an SOS to the badly rattled Station Master, who frantically began waving both his flags, and blowing his whistle in an effort to avert disaster from his own head. Baapji could really get annoyed. But it was no fault of his! It was the engine driver who was responsible for halting the train in the right place.

Mopping his profusely perspiring brow, the engine driver began adjusting the brake lever with careful concentration, cursing his fate and mumbling: *'Satyanaash ho gyo Maataji Maharaj! Ram bharose chall bhai gaadi* (Disaster, my Mother Goddess! God guide my train)!'

Since the drill drummed into the royal retinue never varied, the door of the saloon painted with the Prince of Wales' feathers was flung open as soon as the 31-gun salute began booming. Clad as a British admiral (in order, no doubt, to stand out among the usually over-jewelled Indian Maharajahs), the Prince put his best foot forward. But the royal boot remained suspended in mid-air because the train began shunting unsteadily back and forth even as the band began playing 'God Save the King'. Completely alarmed, the rapid response team of British officers accompanying the Prince immediately hung on to his sleeves and coat-tails.

Those standing beneath the cloth-of-gold canopy to welcome the imperial heir, struggled to suppress their smiles—and even laughter—at such a rollicking arrival. But Jai Singh, who prided himself on the smooth efficiency with which everything—specially royal visits—in his State ran, smarted under this dreadful loss of face. He watched helplessly as the

Prince of Wales was forced to play tick-tack-toe all because of Chattargadh's overenthusiastic Band Master.

At last, the train screeched to a halt. The Prince stepped down to shake hands with his host. Graciously turning the near-fiasco into a joke, he remarked laughingly that no one could henceforth accuse him of failing to uphold King and country! Maharajah Jai Singh complimented him on his excellent balance even as the Guard of Honour presented arms. The Prince shrugged, murmuring, 'Really, Your Highness, one picks up these little survival skills while being shunted around the blessed Empire!'

A great shout from the assembled multitude greeted the Maharajah and his guests as they emerged from the railway station. Waving and smiling to the people crying, '*Khamma, Baapji!*' and '*Bilayat Ro Rajkumar, Jindabad!*', the royal party moved over the carpeted steps to the specially erected elephant platform which allowed them to mount the kneeling animals without ladders. Sunlight made their brocade trappings and embossed silver-gilt ornaments glitter and sparkle. The Prince of Wales sat beside Maharajah Jai Singh in a golden *howdah* with swan-shaped armrests, atop a magnificent 10-foot tusker painted with auspicious designs. A scarlet-turbaned *chawari* bearer, perched ceremoniously behind them, whisked gold-handled yak tails over their heads. The others followed in equally splendid style, their *mahavats* guiding and prodding the huge animals through the roads crowded with spectators. Marigold garlands, tinselled streamers, colourful paper flags, and buntings decorated the entire route to the Fort. Horsemen and camel riders in their uniforms mounted guard all along the route to ensure the British heir's safety.

Cheering men in bright turbans and caps (accompanied by excited boys of every age) pushed against the bamboo barriers for a better look, pointing, gesticulating, smiling, and raising folded palms as the elephants marched past. Thousands of villagers had also flocked to Chattargadh to participate in this *tamasha*. Their exuberant outpouring of love and adulation for their ruler (who served them so well) exceeded anything the Resident had witnessed (so far) in Princely India. Women in festive costumes and ornaments filled every window, balcony, and housetop along the route, giggling, pointing, adjusting their veils, and tossing flowers on the Maharajah and the Prince, often spontaneously calling out blessings and greetings.

The Prince of Wales positively beamed as he glanced around appreciatively from the *howdah*. 'Your city's colourful atmosphere is absolutely matchless, Your Highness. And the public response is so touching, especially after my recent experiences in Bombay.'

'Well, actually, my dear Prince, Indians adore the British Royal Family. It's only British rule that we resent,' explained Jai Singh, smiling pleasantly.

The Nishan elephant, carrying Chattargadh's ancient saffron-and-crimson standard, led the procession. It was followed by eight riderless camels (wearing wonderful cowrie shell and tasselled silk necklaces), pulling gleaming brass salute cannons. Three other elephants followed, carrying the Mahi Martab, the Golden Hand, and Orb insignia presented by the Mughals. Five sturdy ponies bore the musical instruments which had been used to sound the charge for battle in the not-so-distant days when Chattargadh's Rathor rulers went to war. Next came the silver-gilt Khasa palanquin borne by eight retainers in yellow costumes, and two velvet-canopied *raths* (chariots) drawn by unblemished white long-horned bullocks. Platoons of the State's light infantry and lancers on horseback escorted the procession.

The chiefs and nobles who had arrived from their *thikanas* formed a splendid train behind the elephants carrying Royalty and the Resident. They were mounted (according to preference) on fierce chargers or lavishly adorned camels, each escorted by mounted retainers carrying their respective Chief's standard and flags, swords, shields, and spears. Every chieftain was preceded by camel-mounted drummers to which he was traditionally entitled when entering his overlord's walled city and fort.

The slow, stately movement of the elephants, the deep tones of their bells, the tinkle of silver anklets, the shuffling of camel feet, the clopping of horse hooves and clicking harness, the skirling of bagpipes played by men in leopard-skin capes, the brass band marching in tune with its drummers, and the punctuating sounds of the desert minstrels' reverberating *duffs* (tambourines) and cymbals created a splendid cacophony of sound. It made conversation impossible. Still, Gerald Redverse couldn't help wishing that protocol hadn't paired him off with Raj Kumar Kishen with whom he couldn't share any of that day's capital jokes—like the one about the triumphal arch looming ahead which said 'God Shave Our Prince'. He guessed that this amusing little *faux pas* could only have occurred because the Maharajah had been far too busy to personally check out every banner. He must have entrusted that task to his dyslexic Dewan for whom spelling correctly was absolutely impossible. Reading and writing were certainly not R.K. Kishen's forte.

Colonel Claude-Poole also noticed this from the open carriage he shared with the Prince's chief equerry. 'Obviously, only the best barber in the world will do for His Royal Highness!'

They laughed again when they spotted another banner calling for 'A GAL A DAY for our future King!'

'Did you ever see anything like that, Tommy-Rot?'

'You won't get the rotten inside story from anyone on the staff, CP! But that banner headline indicates a leak somewhere, you know,' grinned Major Thomas.

The incredibly handsome and modern young Maharajah of Fateypur and the old-fashioned, white-bearded Maharawal of Dudu made an incongruous pair on the elephant they shared (as ruling princes) just behind the Royal mount. Just then, Chattargadh's prize tusker suddenly stopped and began merrily snacking off the banana leaf arch between the newly completed Public Park and the Fort. Tiger wanted to laugh aloud; but he controlled himself. He dared not share his amusement with his formidable companion, even though Maharajah Jai Singh's first class *bandobast* had acquired yet another black mark.

But the Maharawal noticed this and immediately scoffed derisively in his own dialect. 'It seems that my son-in-law's elephants are not only badly trained, but also kept hungry before a procession. It makes all Indians, specially Raja-Maharajahs, look like incompetent fools before these foreigners!'

Kettledrums, war horns, and trumpet fanfares began sounding the moment Maharajah Jai Singh's elephant marched through the moated Fort's spiked outer gate. The ramparts, terraces, and galleries overlooking the Chattar Mahal courtyard were crowded with privileged citizens and dignitaries, all agog to watch a part of this historic event, particularly because they were not entitled to a seat in the actual durbar on this occasion.

Since this was not an open public Durbar, the ceremony honouring the Prince of Wales was being held in the beautiful old throne room, with its double row of scalloped sandstone arches and slender fluted pillars, surrounded by exquisite lacquered ceilings and walls in soothing blues, greens, and gold. This design was duplicated in the superb Persian-style carpets which covered the entire floor. Shafts of sunlight shimmered in through the wraparound marble fretwork gallery above the throne room. Here Maharani Padmini sat with several female family members and guests, including the aristocratic ladies from all the *thikanas*; the Resident's wife Lady Dorothy, and the four British beauties accompanying the Prince's party.

The Prince of Wales and Maharajah Jai Singh sat on golden thrones on the single-stepped marble dais. The other Indian rulers and princes also had similar ornate seats to the right. Chattargadh's heredity chiefs sat on their usual velvet-cushioned silver chairs, strictly according to precedence. The British Resident, the Military Secretary, the State's various Indian and European ministers and officials, sat facing them. Impressive orange-turbaned attendants stood behind the thrones, bearing the ancient Rathor heirlooms and insignia of kingship, including Rao Chattarsal's massive double-edged sword and embossed shield; the State's crimson-and-saffron standard; peacock feathers in four-feet-tall gold cylinders; and golden handled yak-tail whisks, which they kept swinging from side to side.

After Maharajah Jai Singh performed the ceremony of welcome, Tiger—as Maharajah of the very ancient and important 21-gun-salute State of Fateypur—was invited to present the first *nazar* (symbolic offering) to the Paramount Power represented by the Prince of Wales. Holding his turbaned head at a jaunty angle, Tiger presented his gift with a graceful flourish.

The Prince retained his studiously cultivated public expression as he swore softly at this long-standing member of his inner circle. 'Just one lousy diamond from your famous horde, Tiger?'

'Take it or leave it,' countered Tiger, equally sotto voce. 'Protocol only entitles you to a couple of gold coins!'

'Ah, so it's actually true. The Rothschilds HAVE coloured Your Highness's views!' retorted the Prince.

This clearly refered to a joke going around Continental playboy circles that the exuberantly extravagant young Maharajah of Fateypur had been forced to study international financing and banking systems by his uncle-cum-regent, Sir Pratab. The latter wanted Tiger to shoulder full responsibility for their fabulously wealthy coastal kingdom, and exercise the full ruling powers confirmed by the Crown more than five years earlier when he had turned 21. But Tiger was perfectly content to let his uncle remain Regent while he enjoyed cutting a swathe through international society and effortlessly acquire a Master's degree from Cambridge in Astrophysics. The other loves of his life—besides fast horses and dashing memsahebs—were aeroplanes, astronomy, and sports cars.

Raj Kumar Kishen then requested Maharawal Bakhat Singhji of Dudu to come forward and also perform the ceremony of *nazar*. The imposing old Maharawal rose, and accepted a heavy brocade bag from his ADC, Abhay. He informed everybody that no one in the 1200-year-long history of Dudu had ever offered *nazar* to any overlord. But he was ready to do the decent thing by showering coins over the Prince. Of course, in this way his servants could also go home with some Indian gold in their pockets!

Everyone waited, watching the old Maharawal do as he had pledged. However, instead of proceeding towards the guest of honour, he stood there, trying obviously to figure out something with a perplexed expression on his bearded face.

'Abhay Singhji, I feel we are forgetting something important.'

'Oh Baapji,' protested the ADC.

Kitten watched her grandfather's straight-backed, upright figure striding majestically towards the dais. She was as surprised as everyone else in that throne room when he suddenly stopped, fixed his sharp eyes on the Prince's feet, and thrust his empty hand inside his *achkan* pocket. 'Oh yes, I remember now!' he said loudly.

A mixture of curiosity, amazement, and amusement rippled through the hall as the Maharawal—completely ignoring the occasion and everyone present—pulled out a pair of bright pink silk socks out of his pocket. He sat down on the marble step slowly, and with perfect aplomb, began putting them on, completely oblivious of the fact that he was committing a frightful breach of Royal protocol.

Suppressed giggles and smothered chuckles were heard from the *zenana* gallery upstairs even as those downstairs tried manfully to control their own laughter. The Resident avoided the Military Secretary's eyes as he held his white gloves before his face.

After showering the Prince of Wales with 101 gold coins, Maharawal Bakhat Singh beamed. 'Wait. Say sorry, son.'

Jai Singh hastened to intervene. 'Sir, he means . . .'

The Prince of Wales chuckled. 'I know he means well, Your Highness!'

As they drove back to the palace after the opening ceremony of the canal—with Tiger driving HH Chattargadh's Rolls Royce through the traffic-free desert roads as though he was under starter's orders at the Monaco Grand Prix—CP regaled HRH with stories about the convoluted schemes and stratagems which had made it possible for HH to complete the world's longest cement-lined canal in an unbelievably short time. Maharajah Jai Singh added that it was Colonel Claude-Poole who deserved most of the credit for this engineering feat. The Resident's role had also been invaluable. It had even included tiger-slaying to save his life!

The Prince of Wales was reminded of his mother's partiality towards Maharajah Jai Singh when the latter began enumerating all the other admirable schemes for converting his desert State into an enviably productive and progressive role-model for the surrounding region.

'Our up-to-date power house supplies electricity to all wells and main roads; public buildings and institutions; hospitals, schools, colleges; the jail and railway station; railway workshops; our flour mills, and factories; the officers' bungalows and thousands of private houses; besides our Fort and Palace. I've been extending the scheme to our district towns. It involves the laying of high-tension transmission lines. I have sworn to provide running water and affordable electricity to every household in Chattargadh. But we know that that's impossible without an adequate powergrid, don't we?'

Maharajah Jai Singh and Colonel CP were as perplexed as was the Prince of Wales seated in front, at the curious sight they encountered as they drove into the Palace. The usual sound of kettledrums, war horns, trumpets and eulogistic·bards, as well as sentries presenting arms met them as they approached the portico. However, the driveway was crowded with a double file of huge, humped camels (loaded with goatskin water bags) marching merrily up and down the forecourt. They were led by turbaned men urging them along with tugs on rope halters and taps of short sticks, all the while exchanging jests with each other in the fast falling twilight.

Jai Singh was completely taken aback. What WAS happening here?

The only explanation that occurred to him was that, perhaps, the Chattargadh Camel Corps contingent had arrived rather early to take up positions for the torchlight tattoo scheduled for 8 o'clock. But he couldn't figure out why nobody was in uniform, or why the animals hadn't been properly accoutred in their ceremonial *Lavajma* (ornaments).

Colonel CP quickly glanced at his wristwatch as they stepped into the confusion. 'Really, Your Highness, there's plenty of time for everyone to have a refreshing bath. And in any event, the entertainment will only begin when His Royal Highness emerges.'

But one look at the grimacing face of HH Chattargadh's ADC Ganpat Singh clearly suggested that there was another, bigger, problem. It was enough to give Maharajah Tiger Fateypur's thoughts a deliciously irreverent turn. He needed to do this especially after the modernisation monologue he had been forced to endure during the long drive back to the Palace from the canal headworks after the Prince had smashed a coconut to open the floodgates.

From the overheard protestations in rapid fire Marwari, Tiger drew the all too obvious conclusion—the Palace water supply had suddenly failed. Something had gone wrong with BOTH the tubewells, which no one, except Colonel CP, could fathom. And fix. But, Princess Kitten had saved their Baapji's face by immediately contacting and commanding the Chattargadh State Force duty officers to deploy the whole Camel Corps as well as use every available *degchi, bhagona* and *patila* (pots and pans) to ferry cauldrons of boiling hot bath water to the Palace from their Messes and *Langars* (community kitchens). Every conceivable means, including trucks, tongas, and bullock carts, had already been used.

Tiger immediately also understood that no one would have known that the camels had been running a relay race between the city's water tanks and the Palace bathtubs at her insistence, if Baapji hadn't been inconsiderate enough to allow a guest—meaning himself—to bring them back to the Palace way ahead of time!

A cheerful coal fire warmed the drawing room of the Royal suite where the Prince of Wales, Maharajah Tiger Fateypur, Gerald Redverse, and Colonel Claude-Poole sat sipping nightcaps, and mulling over the day's fantastic events. Silver salvers laden with crystal decanters, brandy balloons, liqueur glasses, jugs and shakers (in which Tiger enjoyed concocting his lethal cocktails), stood on elegant ivory-inlaid tables amidst cigarette and cigar boxes, heavy Bohemian cut glass ashtrays, nut bowls, and flower vases filled with fragrant roses.

'Honestly, Tiger,' continued the Prince. 'I've seldom been ENTERTAINED so much! At last I'm beginning to understand why Chattargadh figures so prominently in family goodwill tours!'

The twinkle in Tiger's eyes belied the asperity of his tone. 'Of course, Prince. We do realise that only Royal goodwill keeps the Union Jack flying from Gibraltar to Hong Kong, over India and Australia!'

The Prince savoured the vintage Armagnac known to be his preferred after-dinner drink. 'Dash it, Reverse Gear, from the little I've seen of India, everybody seems addicted to processions, banquets, balls, durbars, polo, shikar, or tennis parties. Don't you chaps ever work?'

'Indeed, Sir,' countered the Resident, adjusting his black tie. 'Those are the very occasions when our main work—representing His Majesty's Government—gets done.'

Everybody chuckled. However, the Prince was still curious about several aspects of life for Crown Agents and British officers among the Rajput Maharajahs, whom he was visiting for the first time.

'Is it always so hectic, CP?' he asked.

The Colonel responded with a wry smile. 'Well, Sir, there are slow days and busy days like everywhere else. But you'll find that everything seems like a crazy *tamasha* to first-time visitors, till they get used to our pukka style of doing things.'

'Dorothy told me a very interesting story about crocodiles in your bathtub on the first day of your arrival, Reverse Gear.'

Redverse smiled, recalling the commotion caused by CP's obedient soldiers dumping those crocodiles in the Palace lily pool. 'Did she tell you the one about CP's flying elephants on HER first day here?'

'Oh yes,' said the Prince. 'She still seems a bit shell-shocked, you know, because you insisted on calling them the Maharajah's chandeliers. But I told her that Her Majesty says one must be prepared for anything in India.'

'Like that quaint old Maharawal putting on his socks right in the middle of a formal Durbar, completely oblivious of the fact that he was committing lese-majesty!' chuckled CP.

'Not to mention being hit by 101 gold coins,' said the Prince of Wales.

Tiger immediately retorted that no one was to blame if foreigners refused to follow the sensible native custom of keeping their heads covered indoors AND outdoors, particularly when attending functions where ANYTHING could fall on their heads!

The Resident added that HRH might have found things even more entertaining if the guest list had included the real joker in the Princely pack. The Prince immediately demanded his name, and Tiger confided that this was none other than his dear maternal uncle, His Nutty Highness Pisshengunj.

'Oh, you mean the Dog-gone Maharajah!' exclaimed the Prince. 'You must ask Tommy-Rot what happened when he came to stay at Windsor during Ascot week.'

Tiger was ready to bet that, knowing Their Majesties, this would be permitted for the first and last time.

In the Resident's opinion, it was rather late for someone to be knocking on the door. He was just about to suggest that HRH retire, since they had another hectic day ahead of them. Bidding whoever it was enter, the Prince of Wales turned an amiably enquiring gaze towards the ivory-inlaid doors, flung open with a flourish. His eyebrows soared when in marched the strangest of all processions. It was led by the Chattargadh Maharajah's cousin-cum-Dewan. The High Priest followed him, loudly chanting some Sanskrit mantra, clad like a true yogi in just a saffron silk dhoti, with a white Hare-Rama-Hare-Krishna patterned scarf draped round his shoulders, the *janeuw* (sacred thread) slung across his torso, and an impressive array of *rudraksha* beads, tiger claws, sacred medallions, and gem-studded talismans round his neck on thick gold chains. Behind them came turbaned retainers carrying a silver tray holding an earthen dish full of garden soil, and an antique silver-gilt bowl full of grain.

The Prince queried his friend Tiger with a look. The Resident and Colonel CP also looked askance at this strange midnight intrusion. No one had anything to say. Finally, the

Prince of Wales seized the initiative by affably enquiring, 'What's all this, Raj Kumar Saheb?'

Kishen Singh bowed politely with folded hands. 'Wild oats for Your Royal Highness, with our Maharajah Saab Bahadur's compliments.'

Tiger gave a spurt of appreciative laughter as Colonel CP tried his best to intervene. He realised that, as usual, R.K. Saheb had taken the Maharajah's words—spoken in jest at their meeting to finalise the Prince's programme— too literally. But Chattargadh's High Priest kept chanting his mantras even as he continued to hold out handfuls of the oats to the Prince. Grinning widely, the bemused British Prince sportingly received them from the Brahmin.

The Resident turned to Tiger, demanding, 'And what, may I ask, is His Royal Highness to DO with these wild oats?'

Still continuing to laugh, Tiger said, 'Sow them, old boy!'

'With benefit of clergy!' added the Prince with that ready wit which his detractors often described as deplorable levity.

As the priest and the retainers retreated, Kishen Singh courteously enquired, 'And now, if Your Royal Highness will kindly indicate which room you would like us to prepare for your Elbow?'

His enjoyment increasing with every passing moment, the Prince stuck out his elbows, peering at them in turn. 'Which elbow?' he wondered with a deadpan face, as the Resident, CP, and Tiger guffawed heartily.

It was evident to Mrs Rawlins that Kitten was in one of her naughty, contradictory moods. She showed no inclination to learn how to make a proper Court curtsy, and had no intention of allowing Ratna to do so either. She was deliberately striking ludicrous poses, which drew giggles from her cousin, and several watching maids.

'Now, girls,' said Mrs Rawlins, beginning her demonstration once again. 'It's really very simple. Back straight, heads held at precisely the correct angle, skirts delicately held just by your finger and thumb, and cross your . . .'

'EYES as the Prince approaches!' interrupted Kitten, suiting action to words.

'Enough of that nonsense, Kitten. Your ankles, child. Cross your ankles! Bend both knees . . . and sink gracefully. But not as low as if you were greeting the King or Queen.'

'Imitating one's conquerors IS pretty low,' scoffed Kitten.

'Nonsense. It's nothing to be ashamed of, or make a song and dance over. EVERYONE curtsies to Royalty. Now Ratna dear, don't pay any attention to Kitten. But keep a . . .'

'Stiff upper lip!' quipped the irrepressible Kitten. 'Curtsying in these clothes! It's enough to drive anyone crazy!'

Both the princesses were dressed in splendid brocade costumes with *zari* work veils. Ratna's was in royal blue, and Kitten's the palest lemon. Elaborate Rajasthani jewellery, consisting of diamond-studded *rakhris*, anklets, pearl chokers, bangles, and lovely long earrings (set with sapphires and emeralds), enhanced their appearance. But the pearl-embroidered slippers on their dainty feet, and their flaring Oriental skirts looked distinctly incongruous as each dipped low in a stately English curtsy.

'Can't we just shake hands with the Prince?' demanded Kitten.

Ratna, as usual, exhorted her to stop making such a fuss for nothing.

Just then, the senior-most maid brought a message requesting the governess to attend Her Highness in the *zenana* garden where the tables had not been laid satisfactorily for the Royal reception. As she left, the two princesses returned to their toilet.

It struck Ratna—as she watched her cousin carefully stick on a crescent-shaped black and gold *bindi* on her forehead and lavishly splash Worth's latest cologne on herself—that she had rarely seen Kitten so keen on beautifying herself. Guessing the reason for the glow of excitement in her friend's eyes, Ratna tried to caution Kitten. Her lifelong infatuation with Tiger Baapji really had no future since he was already married to a very well-connected, good looking, and wealthy Nepali princess.

'But she's not here!' countered Kitten when this was pointed out.

Ratna reminded her that Her Highness Fateypur had not accompanied her husband only because she had to attend her sister's wedding to the King of Nepal. 'Escorted by your fiance!' teased Kitten. Ratna blushed as she carefully wiped the extra kohl off her lower eyelashes, protesting that Kitten shouldn't say such things even as a joke.

'I know for a fact that Mama and Diamond Aunty had matched your horoscopes,' continued Kitten. 'And what's more, you've been approved by Arjun Baapji AND his brother, HH Fateypur!'

A few minutes after the Palace clock tower struck five, Maharajah Jai Singh escorted the Prince of Wales into the *zenana* garden where Maharani Padmini and her sister-in-law Princess Diamond stood ready to receive him. Followed by Tiger, Sir Pratab, and Maharawal Bakhat Singh, the Prince walked through a double row of beautifully costumed and jewelled girls, some carrying silver pots stuffed with coconuts and mango leaves on their heads, and others baskets of flower petals. Still others held rose water flagons with which they sprinkled the British heir and the Rajput princes accompanying him. They were all in riding boots, breeches, and blazers, having come straight from the exhibition polo match. HH Chattargadh had insisted that there was no time to be lost in changing, for it got dark by six o'clock on winter evenings; and he knew that the ladies would not like to have their garden party curtailed. They would, in any case, all have to bathe and dress in time for the evening entertainment before dinner.

Robin had begun taking photographs the moment he saw the Prince coming. Ratna garlanded the Prince with artistically entwined red and white roses, smiling shyly when he murmured, 'Thank you, Ratna,' and complimented her on her costume. Then the Chattargadh Princess performed the *arti* ritual, waving the lamp and incense-laden silver tray five times around their guest. Resplendent in a shimmering apricot silk costume and traditional jewellery (including diamond amulets), the Maharani came forward to put a saffron paste *tikka* on his forehead. Equally well-ornamented, her sister-in-law Princess Diamond, R.K. Kishen's daughter Princess Sita, and Robin's deeply veiled wife Wendy, threw rice on the British Prince.

The Prince looked appreciatively at the winter annuals in full bloom, and the fountains playing around the marble pavilion which formed the focal point of this private garden for Chattargadh's queens and princesses. The moment a young girl took the prayer tray from Kitten, he shook her warmly by the hand.

'My dear Kitten, it's too late to get you on this year's birthday honours list, but I shall do my best to have you dubbed Knight Grand Commander of the Order of the Bath!' swore the Prince of Wales, praising her resourcefulness for organising yesterday's sorely needed bath-water relay via the Camel Corps.

A roguish grin split Kitten's face. 'Your Royal Highness might find that much harder to do than mustering a camel cavalcade, for they seem to have sworn to keep the Order a male bastion, you know!'

The Prince promised to have such antiquated rules changed especially for her, only to have Princess Kitten warn him that she would tattle to *The Tatler* if he didn't keep his word!

Before the Prince could think of a fitting rejoinder, the Maharani came up with the Resident's wife. 'Your Royal Highness, may I present Lady Dorothy Redverse.'

The Prince smiled graciously at his hostess, and held out a hand to the curtsying lady. 'No need, Your Highness. We're kissing cousins who've known each other all our lives.'

The Prince of Wales leaned forward and gave his kinswoman an affectionate peck on the cheek. They stood chatting and exchanging gossip about mutual friends and relations back home, till Princess Diamond claimed the Prince's attention.

'Even HH didn't mention that you're so closely connected with British royalty,' remarked Padmini.

The willowy auburn-haired lady gave a deprecating shrug of her shoulder. 'Really, Your Highness! Everybody is cross-connected back home, just like everybody one meets in India.'

Several round tables, swathed in beautiful convent-embroidered white organdie, were scattered around the central damask-draped tea table laden with succulent snacks, silverware, and blue Wedgewood china identical to the one ordered by Catherine the Great for her Petersburg palace. The Maharani served the Prince of Wales with the items he indicated, aware that his bland British palate couldn't cope with the spicier Indian delicacies. Nearby, Princess Diamond urged her brother's father-in-law to at least taste a sweetmeat or two, since the customary taboo only applied to the consumption of salt in his daughter's home. When the Maharawal protested that he never ate between meals, the Chattargadh Princess immediately offered him some tea. However, this beverage was also cordially declined. '*Baisa Hukum, cha-copy toh aanpa kadeej nee peedi. Haan, jadi daru kee manwar karwawoh, toh chaal jailee* (Princess, I never drink tea or coffee. But I'll gladly accept some wine)!'

Laughingly confiding that, under *bilayati kanoon* (foreign rule), they had to wait for sunset before bringing out the whisky and brandy decanters, Diamond strolled off to chat with Mother Angelus, who stood undecided between an

Asprey cake stand stacked with strawberry tarts, and another piled with chocolate éclairs. Kitten, Ratna, the Yuvrani, and Mrs Rawlins were kept busy pouring tea for all the other guests, while Maharajah Jai Singh and his wife made sure that everyone was presented to the Prince.

In another corner, a crease marred Lady Dorothy's brow as she struggled to comprehend Maharawal Bakhat Singh's cryptic utterances. His atrocious English, and her non-existent Marwari was making communication impossible. But she was too well bred to walk off while he was in mid-sentence. 'Hujbaand got name?'

'But of course, Your Highness. Gerald Redverse,' she said.

'No Saar?' queried the Maharawal.

Quite unaccustomed to such vulgar queries, the Scottish aristocrat merely begged his pardon.

Not understanding a word, the stately old Maharawal inclined his head with a rapidfire 'Khamaghani!'

To Lady Dorothy, this all-purpose Rajput greeting sounded very much like 'Come on, honey.' Gasping at his effrontery, the Resident's wife became red in the face and tried to think of a crushing rebuff.

Bakhat Singh studied her blazing face with a concerned eye. 'Bloody bad, Lady Saab. Un Phitt to bharr shunj . . . .'

Unwilling to hear any more nonsense, Dorothy strode off with a swish of her elegant taffeta frock, bumping into Princess Diamond whom she did not see because her best flower and feather-trimmed hat had slipped down over her eyes in all this annoyance and agitation.

But she immediately composed herself with a murmured apology.

Inferring that something was very wrong with this remarkably poised person, Princess Diamond urged the Resident's wife to reveal what was upsetting her.

'I really don't know how that awful old man had the gumption to say "Come on honey" to me!'

Somewhat taken aback, the Chattargadh Princess protested. 'My dear Dorothy, he couldn't possibly have said that. He can hardly speak any English, and certainly no Yankee slang!'

'But you've got to believe me, Princess. He also had the super-colossal cheek to tell me—the mother of TWO boys— that I was, quote: "Bloody bad, and unfit to bear sons!"'

Secure in her knowledge of the Maharawal's linguistic shortcomings as well as a generally benevolent paternalistic nature, Princess Diamond still demurred. 'I'm terribly sorry that you've been distressed, but please don't be offended because you probably misunderstood what he said.'

But Lady Dorothy continued to fume, promising to tell Gerry exactly what that awful old Maharawal had said.

Before Diamond could say another word, the Scotswoman's attention was peremptorily claimed by Kitten. 'Lady Dorothy, Grandfather seems to have taken a great fancy to you. He wants me to get you into the shady pavilion, because he feels that you're much too fair and delicate to bear even our setting winter sun!'

Princess Diamond wrinkled her jewel-studded nose at their disconcerted guest, and laughed. 'Dorothy, you goose! Wait till this story gets around.'

Kitten demanded that she share the joke.

'Ask the Resident Saheb's Memsaheb, Kitten. But *Khamaghani*, Baapji, because you've just averted a major diplomatic incident between the Crown Representative and Dudu State!'

A little distance away, the Prince of Wales and Tiger Fateypur were swapping stories about the weird encounters each had had just a few months ago at Palm Beach and Santa Barbara, where too many American heiresses and Hollywood queens vied for the collective attention of all the high-handicap polo players absorbed in more important things, like winning major tournaments. Robin was busy filming the garden party, having acquired a new movie camera of his own which made them all no longer dependent on Colonel CP's equipment.

As he came nearer for a close-up shot, the Prince of Wales said, 'Robin, I'm going to try my Hindustani on your grandfather, Batak Singh.'

Robin put down the heavy movie camera on the nearest table, exchanging a quizzical glance with his friend, Tiger. The Maharajah of Fateypur gave a broad grin. 'Pardon me, Prince. BAKHAT, not BATAK! Bataks are things which go quack-quack in our language. Not to be confused with buttocks, which go wiggle-waggle.'

'That's called getting a duck in any language, Tiger. Guess I'd better stick to titles after all,' said the Prince.

As soon as she saw the Prince of Wales in conversation with her grandfather, Kitten rushed to Tiger's side with a plate full of desi (local Indian) delicacies. This made her brother comment sarcastically on her penchant for muscling in even where she was least wanted.

'Who wants to even look at you?' retorted Kitten. 'I'm simply looking after our guests, unlike you.'

Tiger took the plate out of her hand, and began sharing it with Robin. 'Bad strategy, Kitten,' he said, speaking as they ate. 'Get your brother eating out of your hand, because he'll be here when all your guests have gone!'

Robin protested with a show of fake revulsion. 'Good God, Tiger, I have enough problems keeping Miss Sticking Plaster out of my hair without you giving her any of your idiotic Machiavellian advice!'

Rising to the bait as usual, Kitten forgot both occasion and decorum, and jabbed her brother in the back with the tiny silver snack fork in her hand. But Tiger prevented injury by clutching her bangled and braceleted wrist in a ruthless grip. Familiar with Kitten's antics since she could toddle, Tiger had no compunction about treating her exactly like a spoiled brat.

'Don't you think she looks just like a lemon drop in that awful yellow *poshak*, Robin? Or, a sour puss waiting to claw our eyes out?'

Kitten let out a squeal as her brother and the Maharajah of Fateypur lifted her right off her brocade-slippered feet by grasping both forearms in a typical schoolboy trick, and began swinging her between them, reciting: 'Ding dong bell, Sour puss in the well!'

Before this horseplay could get out of hand, Maharajah Jai Singh signalled to his son to join the group seated informally on garden swings and cane chairs around the guest of honour. Several birds twittered as they tried to find perches before the sun finally set in a blaze of glorious colours, outlining the romantic domes, pavilions, and crenellated palace walls on which peacocks and pigeons were coming home to roost.

Maharajah Jai Singh asked the Prince of Wales if he would like to try his hand at pig-sticking the next day. 'Certainly, Your Highness. If you can mount me suitably.'

'You needn't have any worries on that score, Prince,' quipped Tiger. 'It won't be like Canada, where the Mounties' best town-patrol horse let you down like a ton of bricks!'

The Prince gave a deprecating shrug. 'He couldn't take the tumultuous welcome, old chap.'

'No such problems here, Sir. HH Chattargadh has the horses—as well as the crowds—perfectly trained.'

'In fact, one might safely say that horsing around is Chattargadh's speciality,' added Sir Pratab, making everyone chuckle.

'And what is your family speciality, Prince?' inquired Kitten.

'Carrying the burden of Empire, I suppose,' HRH said, and turned to his host. 'Any field tips, Your Highness?'

'About the burden, or the empire?' asked the Maharajah.

An appreciative twinkle in his eye, the Prince said lightly, 'Shall we stick to pigs for the moment?'

Jai Singh leaned back in his chair. 'Remember, Prince, wild boar invariably charge in a straight line, just like rhinos. And nothing can turn a charging boar . . . . So keep your horse just a few degrees out of his path.'

'And spear him like that!' said Tiger, jabbing the teaspoon held like a javelin in his hand. 'Get him quickly on the flank or shoulder. He'll tear you apart, if given half an opportunity.'

'At the gallop,' advised Sir Pratab.

'Never dismount in wild boar country for any reason. And most important, never ride away from a charging wild boar, because he's genetically programmed to give chase,' continued Jai Singh. 'A good Rajput heads straight FOR the pig.'

'So that's why they're called pig-headed!' laughed Lady Dorothy, her sense of humour long restored.

The early morning haze slowly dissolved as Maharajah Jai Singh led his guests and relations at an easy canter (away from the ancient fortress he'd turned into a hunting lodge) into the surrounding scrub forest and ravines considered perfect wild boar country by all keen horsemen. All the riders, including the ladies, wore khaki drill jodhpurs and side-slit shikar jackets. The Indians were distinguished by their turbans, and the British by their pith helmets. Everyone carried shoulder belts with loaded revolvers, in addition to their pig-sticking spears. Their hoofbeats disturbed and alarmed the sambar, neelgai, cheetal, chinkara, blackbuck herds, rabbits, partridges, and bustards in their desert habitat. But the shikaris ignored them, searching keenly for a rideable pig.

Tiger's hopes of first spear were dashed when he found that the wild boar streaking past a *keekar* tree had several piglets in tow. By that time, Maharajah Jai Singh, riding effortlessly alongside the Prince of Wales, had taken his perfectly trained horse down a familiar track into a deep dry gulch where he knew (from experience) wild boar often rooted.

'We're miles ahead of the others, and should be spotting a rideable pig very soon,' promised the Maharajah.

'Really, Your Highness, I'm enjoying this. Rather like steeplechasing, y'know.'

Although she had initially kept up with the men even over the unfamiliar thorny and dusty terrain, Lady Dorothy soon began having problems with her highly excited, fast mount, whom she could not calm, encumbered as she was with a heavy spear, her riding crop, and recalcitrant goggles which kept slipping down her nose. Figuring that she needed both hands free to check and soothe the horse, Dorothy wished that her husband or Colonel CP were close by to lend a helping hand.

At that very moment, the most experienced and alert rider present happened to notice the young woman having difficulties with her horse. Swiftly urging his mount alongside hers, Maharwal Bakhat Singh said, 'Lady Saab, Lady Saab, you ride me. I ride you!'

Some instinct made the Resident glance back over his shoulder just in time to see the heavily tipped spear slip out of his wife's hand even as she tried to keep her seat and control her rearing horse. 'I knew it!' he swore to his companion. 'But try telling a woman that she can't do something, and that's the one thing she'll attempt even if it means landing up in hospital.'

Redverse had spent a futile evening trying to warn Dorothy that pig-sticking in Rajputana was utterly different from hunting in England or Ireland, or even riding to hounds in Virginia. But she had remained adamant about joining the hunt.

As he turned his horse around to rescue his wife, CP reassured him. 'Don't worry, old chap. She's in excellent hands!'

In one smooth, fluidly effortless movement, Maharawal Bakhat Singh hurled his spear to the ground, dismounted, and scooped Lady Dorothy off her horse. Then, as the two

Englishmen watched, he deposited her on his own perfectly motionless roan mare. Recovering her poise, Lady Dorothy wiped sand off her face with a white lace-edged handkerchief even as her husband and CP trotted up.

'Really, Your Highness, I don't know how to thank you,' began the Resident.

The Maharawal retrieved his spear, and waived him off with a kind smile. 'Go off for quicky-quicky. Shock everybody!'

Convulsed with laughter at the Maharawal's words, Colonel CP added: 'Guess you better do what His Highness says, Reverse Gear!'

'We both know exactly what he means, CP,' retorted his friend. Admiration, amusement, and understanding burgeoned in Lady Dorothy's mind as she saw how effortlessly the old-fashioned bearded and turbaned warrior had controlled her wickedly wilful former mount.

'*Khamaghani*, Your Highness!' she cried as he galloped off, giving her a brief salute with his javelin.

Hot and dusty after a whole morning in the saddle, the Prince of Wales rode into a patch of open scrubland where nothing stirred. Finding himself alone for a few moments, he looked around for signs of the shikar promised by his host. The place was quiet, and seemed perfectly safe to him. Looking around once more, the Prince dismounted. He dropped his spear and reins, wiped the sweat off his forehead, whistled merrily, and began strolling behind some jungle bushes. In a minute he had disappeared. Just then, Maharawal Bakhat Singh rode up. He saw the riderless horse, heard the whistling, *and* a sudden sharp squealing. Didn't all this herald disaster?

Before he knew it, the British heir found himself subjected to a loud and angry tirade even as he emerged into the open, buttoning his jodhpurs. '*I* know you Prince of Wales! *Horse* know you Prince of Wales. But bloody-fool

PIG not know, not care you Prince of Wales-Shales!' he said, in his typically broken English.

The Prince of Wales looked up sheepishly. He barely had one foot in the stirrup and his spear held awkwardly when he heard hooves pounding closer. Maharajah Jai Singh thundered up in a flurry of sand at the head of a cavalcade of keen shikaris including Kitten, Tiger, Colonel CP and R.K. Kishen. They were galloping neck to neck with spears poised for the kill.

The Chattargadh Maharajah urged his royal guest to remount. 'Quick, Prince! Here it comes!'

Kitten was the first among them to rein in her supremely sure-footed, favourite cross-bred Kathiawari mount. She raised her javelin to signal the others waiting behind her, all attention. An enormous pink thing was shuffling out of the thorn bushes a few yards ahead. As it came closer, she saw that it was only a pathetically puzzled-looking Yorkshire pig. It also had an enormous crimson and orange ribbon tied round its neck.

Aghast and amused in equal parts, she immediately guessed what had happened, and began laughing.

However, the more his daughter laughed, the more Maharajah Jai Singh felt that his worst nightmares as a host were coming true during this royal visit.

The Prince of Wales, however, remained unfazed. Urbane and humorous as usual, he said, his face deadpan: 'Really, Your Highness, our Empress of Blandings seems to have usurped your wild boar territory.'

'And our State colours too!' added Colonel CP.

R.K. Kishen demanded furiously who it was who had dared to use THEIR State colours to humiliate them thus before guests.

'Come on, Uncle Kishen,' teased Tiger. 'Even HH Pisshengunj wouldn't be Nutty enough to use his OWN State colours!'

Horsing Around 5

It was weeks before Maharajah Jai Singh could venture anywhere in polite princely circles without being greeted with cries of 'Hot Dog!' and 'Yorkshire Ham or Pork Pie, Your Highness?' Egged on by Nutty, his Mysore relations baited him so mercilessly throughout the Bangalore polo season that he quickly cut his visit short. He proceeded to Ooty with a few family members many days before Race Week held usually towards the end of April when true horse lovers came up to the Nilgiris. Since Jai Singh and his sister Princess Diamond had both inherited considerable estates there from their long-deceased mother, they preferred this southern hill station over popular Himalayan summer resorts like Simla, Mussoorie, Darjeeling, and Nainital. They also avoided Mount Abu because they found it much too provincial, being part of Rajputana. It was also too intrigue-ridden, being the AGG's headquarters. And, as for visits to Srinagar, they involved too much protocol with HH Kashmir.

'We should come to Ooty more often, Bhai,' observed R.K. Kishen. They were sitting in a white balustraded balcony overlooking a splendid vista of cypress, pines, blue gum, mauve jacaranda, pink acacia, and red rhododendron trees in full flower. But they were much too busy examining, selecting, disentangling, and discarding the jumble of fishing rods and tackle stored since their last visit, to admire what was rightly considered one of the finest views of Ooty's downs and *kundas*.

'What's the use of having this beautiful house in the hills if it's kept locked up most of the time?'

The Maharajah admitted that although he also found Ooty's cool green hills, lakes and eucalyptus-scented air most refreshing compared to the one in their own home in the desert, he simply couldn't afford to neglect their State. 'But you can come up whenever you like, Kishen, and stay as long as you please even without me.'

'But everyone takes holidays, Hukum! We know that the British Royal Family goes to Sandringham and Balmoral. President Roosevelt takes weekends away . . .'

'From Mrs Roosevelt at Mercer-side!' interrupted the Maharajah.

Both chuckled, and his cousin continued, 'Nicholas the Second and Empress Alexandra religiously went to Tsarkoeselo . . .'

'Once too often!'

'And even Hitler, I hear, likes skating . . .'

'On thin ice!' added Jai Singh. 'Which reminds me. Have you seen that urgent telegram which came from Bombay?'

'No. Nor do I have to. It was part of our agreement when I became your Dewan, that I wouldn't be forced to read anything except warrants of precedence.'

'And death. But this concerns your nephew, Kishen. Do you know what that fool has done?' demanded Jai Singh.

Just to aggravate his cousin, Kishen protested. 'I don't have any fools in MY family, Hukum.'

'No?' cried the Maharajah. 'Then tell me, what d'you call Robin?'

'Your only son and heir.'

'Who deserves to be disinherited for fracturing his hip bone just before the polo match that blasted Nutty Pisshengunj has challenged us with after losing the prestigious Hyderabad Gold Cup. He has the audacity to call our win the umpire's partiality!'

'Tch-tchh, tchh-tch!' responded Kishen, suitably concerned, for he was rather fond of Robin, having no sons of his own. 'How did he manage that, Bhai? A riding accident, I suppose?'

Jai Singh tossed down the feathered silver-gilt bait he had finally located at the bottom of the compartmentalised velvet-lined box. Such things were supposed to be neatly kept, instead of being jumbled up together so that one was bound to suffer cut fingers and bleeding thumbs. But it was too much to expect illiterate retainers to understand that one needed one kind of bait and tackle for successful carp-fishing in the Paikara river, and another for hooking rainbow trout at Gadalu.

'Do you think I'd feel so badly let down if he'd had the decency to fall off a galloping horse? But to fall on his own behind on some stupid wooden floor in a public skating rink proves that he's a disgrace to the Rajput race!'

This was too much for R.K. Kishen, who disliked all family disputes and controversies except with His Nutty Highness. 'Really, Your Highness, isn't that condemning the poor boy without proper *jaanch-partaal* (enquiry)?'

'*Jaanch-partaal*? Several delighted eyewitnesses who had watched the entire *tamasha*, lost no time in booking urgent trunk calls to inform me that the blundering idiot had "broken his ass" as the Americans say, while trying to teach the Resident's niece skating!'

'He must have fallen really hard for her, Bada Bhai. Now, everybody can't be a Rama avatar like you!' teased his cousin, referring to the Chattargadh Maharajah's extraordinarily exemplary monogamous marriage.

Jai Singh ignored this attempted levity and, setting the box he had finished sorting out on a nearby table, said that a young man's harmless flirtations could always be tolerated. But Robin's irresponsible behaviour in hurting himself had destroyed the team on which he was depending to thrash Nutty. 'He's spoilt everything. *Aanpni toh team chopat ho gyi saa* (Our team has been destroyed)! Where are we to find a good substitute almost overnight? Colonel Claude-Poole is on leave . . . .'

'What about our brother-in-law, Sir Pratab Singhji?'

'He can't join our team after refusing to play for Nutty along with Tiger! Besides, the Ooty Equestrian Federation has asked him to umpire the match because he doesn't take any nonsense from anyone on the field.'

By now R.K. Kishen was convinced that Nutty had put a *tantric* (occult) jinx on the game. But Maharajah Jai Singh wouldn't even discuss such things, let alone allow him to catch hold of somebody who could be paid to use *jadoo-toona* counter-measures for clearing away all the obstacles Nutty took such diabolical pleasure in creating. His ultra-modern cousin refused to accept or appreciate the true significance of all this bad luck. As it is, one disgraceful event had piled up on top of the other despite everybody's best efforts to uphold Chattargadh's reputation for perfect hospitality, sportsmanship, and efficiency during the Prince of Wales' disastrous visit. And now, Nutty had injured Robin, knowing fully well that he was master of the balancing act both on and off horseback.

'*Bajarang Bali Ki Jai*,' resolved Kishen Singh, determined to nullify Nutty's tricks through his own tried and tested *upachar* (remedies).

The Maharajah, however, was also mulling over the sticky situation. He was wondering if it would be appropriate to fall back on their Resident, who was, fortunately, still in Bombay which wasn't as far from the

Nilgiris as Chattargadh. There was no time left to summon any of the other excellent players he himself had trained. The inducement of a free holiday for the Resident's entire family as the Chattargadh Maharajah's honoured house guests—and that too in a place he knew they'd never visited before—could do the trick.

'Let's hope so,' said Kishen. 'But there's an even better rider sitting right here in Ooty, if you care to consider him. He'll come running and jumping for joy if you simply summon him, Hukum. We lost a very good player when you exiled Koodsu Rao Saab. And our loss became Nutty's gain!'

Jai Singh heaved an exasperated sigh. 'When will you chaps realise that principles are more important than polo handicaps? I want to cure this country—or at least as much of it that's under my direct control—of its medieval mentality. Polygamy is inexcusable when a 58-year-old grandfather, who happens to be one of my *sirayati* Sardars, goes and marries a 16-year-old orphan! And you seem to have forgotten what a rotten time Koodsu Rao Saab gave your own daughter and son-in-law over the issue of *jagirs* and male heirs!'

Several shoppers scurried out of the way as the Pisshengunj Maharajah rode right into Jackson's Store through shelves piled with merchandise varying from woollen shawls and sweaters, pots and pans, medicines, baked goods, chocolates, fruit, soaps and cosmetics, flower vases, porcelain ornaments, dinner services, tea sets and south Indian bronzes. Young Jackson smothered an outraged gasp when he saw his father bowing and calling for chilled lemonade to refresh His Highness.

'Really, Your Highness, we always look forward to having you back in Ooty. And this shop feels doubly honoured by your personal visit in this real royal style, on horseback no less!' beamed old Mr Jackson.

The Maharajah of Pisshengunj was soon joined by his Dewan, Baron Tikemoffsky, leading the two famous St. Bernards on leashes and his brother-in-law, the Rao Saheb of Koodsu, who had (quite correctly) insisted on leaving his own horse hitched outside. Ooty boasted a strong doggy set, and the annual dog show was a great local event, with the doggone Maharajah of Pisshengunj virtually in control of the organising committee, the judges, and the prize-giving, to which he contributed lavish purses and silver trophies. Everyone treated the harmless St. Bernards as mascots, for there wasn't another pair in the Nilgiris.

Nutty glanced around the shop as they all sipped lemonade from fluted crystal tumblers. Literally rubbing his hands and swaying from side to side as he smiled ingratiatingly up at the wonderfully spendthrift Maharajah, the angular Anglo-Indian shopkeeper said that he merely awaited His Highness's commands.

Nutty ordered his restless mount to stand still. He pursed his florid mouth as his large protuberant eyes lit up on seeing some attractive new radiograms, indoor games, and puzzles. They would keep all his wives happy when they couldn't go boating or picnicking on rainy days, and prevent their clamouring to go to the cinema, or to visit other royal families who were best kept at arm's length (like the one from Chattargadh).

'Ahh, now let's see . . . . This, that, and ALL those. Yes, of course, I mean those *bajas* (players) with every latest record you can supply; but separately gift-wrapped. And by the way, I hope you've got that English plum cake my darling Sunny and Bunny adore?'

Immediately assuring him that Jackson's took great pride in procuring anything and everything that all the great Maharajahs demanded, old Mr Jackson took out a two-pound fruit cake from his confectionery counter.

Unable to turn his horse around in the restricted space, Nutty commanded over his shoulder: 'Tikky, please give Sunny and Bunny half-half right away because my hands are not free.'

'Sit, Babies, sit!' crooned Tikky. 'Papa give you cakey!'

Kitten and her father Maharajah Jai Singh strolled into Jackson's Store just as the salivating dogs had begun to bark. They were leaping up to catch the pieces of cake lobbed at them by the Pisshengunj Maharajah's White Russian Dewan, who had momentarily dropped their leashes in order to carry out his master's orders. Speedily devouring the cake, the greedy dogs went completely beserk hunting for some more tasty treats. They barked joyfully upon sniffing the sausages and sliced ham just delivered from the Richmond piggery. The enormous St. Bernards jumped right over an intervening counter, scattering several baskets of fresh strawberries. Their bushy, yard-long tails sent an assortment of china ornaments and displayed toys crashing to the ground.

Their playful behaviour created complete pandemonium in the store. Besides alarming the shopkeepers and shoppers, it set their master's horse shying and plunging so badly that it dashed into the shelves and slipped on the waxed wooden floor. Nutty slid off the saddle and landed with a thud on the polished floorboards littered with crushed fruit, broken glass, and other debris.

A first-rate horseman, Koodsu Rao Saheb immediately grabbed the reins of the shying horse, soothed it down, and led it out of harm's way. However, as he led it outside, he found R.K. Kishen among the curious persons standing there, watching the whole *tamasha*.

Jai Singh immediately went forward to help his cousin up, while Kitten tried to suppress her gleeful grin as Baron Tikemoffsky chased the two naughty, disobedient dogs from aisle to aisle. Old Jackson kept shouting at the wretched animals wreaking havoc in his shop while his infuriated son advanced towards them with a measuring rod.

This was too much for Nutty. 'How dare you?' swore the Pisshengunj Maharajah. 'Are you trying to kill the goose that lays your golden eggs? First you made my horse throw me off! Now you want to beat my dogs! Even my shadow won't cross the threshold of your horrid shop unless—unless you . . . .'

His words demolished Kitten's self-control. She immediately began chuckling and chanting. 'Love me, love my dog. And my dog Tik too!'

The elder Jackson started beseeching Maharajah Jai Singh for justice. 'Really, Your Highness, it wasn't our fault! The Maharajah of Pisshengunj is very much free to hurl his accusations, and deprive us of our humble livelihood, but Your Highness can see how much damage his dogs have caused even though we go out of our way to pamper them! They are squarely responsible for causing the downfall of such a great rider like Maharajah Natwar Singhji of Pisshengunj! And I haven't even said a word about the entire strawberry crop they've destroyed or all my broken glass. Not to mention all that contaminated bacon, ham, salami, and sausages meant for my most esteemed regular customers, like His Excellency the Governor, and the Mysore Maharajah, who trust Jackson to spare them the rabies!'

'You'll be shot if you go around spreading propaganda about my dogs having rabies!' swore Nutty, advancing menacingly towards the agitated shopkeeper.

Kitten stepped neatly between them, humming, 'Humpty Dumpty sat on a horse! Nutty Uncle took a little toss!'

A huge grin splitting her face, she advised him to take some anti-rabies AND anti-tetanus shots, just to be on the safe side. She completed his discomfiture by extracting immediate obedience from the thoroughly spoilt, outsized dogs (each larger than a Shetland pony), who, by now, were happily grovelling at her feet. Then, with a mocking flourish, she presented her royal relation the riding hat and stick he had dropped.

Thanking her curtly, Nutty snapped, 'Still at the nursery rhyme stage, my dear niece? And Bhai, as a brother Prince and the head of our house, you of all people shouldn't be siding with these ill-mannered Anglo-Indians against me even in this *ghor kalyug* (evil time)! My beautifully trained horse would not have slipped if this man Jackson had spread a carpet instead of butter on his bloody floor.'

Jai Singh smiled down at his silly cousin. 'Nutty, don't blame poor Mr Jackson for your own sins of omission and commission. Everybody knows that getting buttered up is your favourite hobby!'

Clenching his fists, Nutty retorted through sneering lips: 'Even the hereditary pillars of Chattargadh State know where to find buttered bread when they are uprooted lock, stock . . .'

'And wives!' added Kitten.

When Nutty narrated his own true version of that afternoon's shocking mishaps, all the three Maharanis of Pisshengunj were convinced that someone must have cast an evil eye on Annadata, who couldn't be unseated even on the polo ground by the world's toughest riders. They decided to keep a 24 hour fast with *jagran* and *akhand jyot* (non-stop hymn singing and glowing prayer lamps) in order to protect their beloved husband from future occult attacks.

Only Koodsu Rao Saheb ate dinner with His Nutty Highness that night, while his sister, the third Maharani, talked to them and supervised the service. Occasionally, she flicked a gold-handled whisk to shoo off the odd insect and firefly which had managed to sneak in despite all the efforts of the staff and servants, and all the closed wire mesh doors and windows of Pisshengunj House. Ever eager to out do (or at least keep up with) his Chattargadh cousin, Nutty had bought this large English-styled gabled mansion with well-tended gardens from Miss Molly Elphenstone's descendents, who had moved on to Australia.

Observing her husband wince as he reached for the cruet set, his third wife passed it to him, and asked: '*Hajoor*, I hope you didn't hurt anything?'

'Can anything be worse than hurt pride?' he replied.

The Rao Saheb of Koodsu waved his fork full of fried fish smothered in tomato sauce backwards and forwards like a red flag. '*Jawaisa* Hukum, in order to apply the healing touch we are all here to take revenge on all those who dared to laugh at you! What is a Rajput without pride, even though I personally still feel that Your Highness should have parked your horse outside the shop, Hukum!'

Nutty instantly took exception to his brother-in-law's last remark. Koodsu Rao Saheb furrowed his forehead and patted his greying moustache, trying to think of some rational response to this notoriously unpredictable Maharajah whose patronage he simply couldn't afford to lose until his own Maharajah reinstated him.

His sister thought it wisest to refocus her husband's attention and annoyance on his original targets. Rearranging her super-soft shahtoosh shawl over her slippery silk sari, she said, 'Bhai, please tell me, who all were there in that shop when all this happened?'

Pausing a little while buttering his seventh dinner roll, her brother responded, 'Chattargadh Durbar, Raj Kumar Kishen Singhsa and our spoilt Princess.'

'Do you remember what Kitten Baisa was wearing?'

'Stop asking typical *zenana* questions, Chota Maharanisa!' objected Nutty. 'You seem to be more interested in those awful Chattargadh people than in your own husband!'

The junior-most Maharani gasped. '*Hajoor* shouldn't say such things even as a joke. Here I am, sitting hungry and thirsty, because I'm praying heart and soul for your welfare! AND, of course, for revenge on Chattargadh Durbar, who stood by and did NOTHING to prevent your downfall, when he's the head of your clan and your nearest blood relation after Tiger Baapji! AND for the burning grudge I hold against those who've branded my elder brother an exiled criminal, thanks to some silly foreign law about polygamy.'

'Ladies can't understand these political pulls and pressures,' her husband interposed. 'Your beloved Maharajah is an expert at cooking favour-curry with the British Raj by copycatting Kemal Atatürk! And just because Turkey has thrown off fez caps, and shamelessly started showing women's legs with frocks just like Kitten Baisa, Jai Singh thinks he too can turn our society topsy-turvy.'

Neeru Baa placed another perfect mutton chop garnished with fresh mint leaves on his plate, and demanded, '*Hajoor*, did you explain all this to the Viceroy when you took my brother to see him? According to Hindu custom, every man has the right to remarry . . . but only three times, of course . . . if he happens to fall short of heirs due to bad luck.'

Nutty informed his third wife that that was exactly what he'd told His Excellency, besides pointing out the fact that their own holy book, the OFFICIAL King James' English Bible, preached that all marriages were made in Heaven. Therefore, it was not her brother who had done something unlawful, but Maharajah Jai Singh, who had committed a grave excess by confiscating her brother's *jagir*.

The Pisshengunj Maharajah also believed that HH Chattargadh would swiftly change his tune—and his law—if one of his own idiotic children were to be caught in a similar situation.

Maharajah Tiger Fateypur roared towards Ooty in his custom-built black Alfa Romeo at a speed he considered confoundedly slow, but which made his cousin-cum-heir, Arjun, grimace and keep grabbing the seat, door, or dashboard at every elbow bend on the steep uphill road cut along dangerously deep ravines. Tiger preferred this shorter route from the Mysore side into the Nilgiris to the tedious rail or road journey from the Coimbatore side which most other regular summer visitors used. However, given a choice, he would always much rather fly.

'I still think we could have done it,' swore Tiger.

Arjun cast him a derisive look. 'What? A crash-landing at Ooty, Tiger Baapji?'

'Nothing of the sort!' the Maharajah retorted. 'You've flown with me often enough to know that I would get you safely across the Atlantic or Pacific in record time, provided I had the right aircraft. And refuelling facilities. If the Met report hadn't let me down at the last minute, I'd have taken you to Ooty in style.'

Arjun said that falling out of the sky in bits and pieces was not his idea of arriving in style anywhere. 'And if you continue handling this crazy low-slung sports car like an aeroplane, I don't have to be an astrologer to predict a regretfully short life for both of us!'

'Mind that black tongue!' swore Tiger as he narrowly averted collision with a Bedford truck loaded with timber which came on to the main road from a *kuccha* side-track, just as two tribal women carrying baskets full of tobacco leaves suddenly strode smack into their path from the thick jungle.

Arjun scoffed at his notoriously superstitious cousin, and pointed towards the accelerator. 'Really, Your Highness, why don't you mind that foot? You know, at times, you sound just like your Nutty uncle.'

This remark effectively spiked the usual bonhomie prevailing between these two look-alike princes who were closer than most identical twins because of the circumstances surrounding their upbringing. It was Arjun's parents who had provided protective nurturing to Tiger, when he became an orphaned Maharajah at a very tender age.

They drove in silence through the foothills, with the hood down, and the wind ruffling their perfectly barbered hair. They often spotted elephant and bison herds; the occasional tiger, panther, or leopard swiftly retreating into the thick forest cover; a few wild boar; several spotted deer; monkeys; colourful macaw parrots; and other birds moving through the Mysore Maharajah's strictly protected private preserve. Soon they reached the Wynaad swampland. Beehive-shaped Toda and Kunda huts were clustered along river banks, perfumed by wild orange trees in flower. The bamboo groves, paddy fields and bogs dotted with wild bananas, areca palms, and spiky native cedars merged into the great towering cliffs surrounded by dense evergreen forests. The higher they drove into the Blue Mountains, the more beautiful became the vistas on all sides, with terraced tea gardens and coffee plantations merging into the horizon.

After fording the Sandy Nullah, Tiger broke the silence. 'Arjun, I'm beginning to wonder why I chose the pleasure of your stimulating company on this long drive.'

'For the simple reason that none of your usual fair companions were available today, and none of the other memsahebs this side of forty would risk her neck—and her reputation—with you!'

'You'll be punished for slandering me,' swore the playboy Maharajah, tapping his cousin's forearm with a playful punch.

'Before you do that, could we stop at Colonel Murphy's tea estate for beer and a bite, *Hajoor*?'

'If you insist, Raj Kumar Saab. But I'll even tie your bib for you if you condescend to share the packed lunch provided by your doting grand aunts!'

'You're welcome to their superb south Indian hospitality. But I'm a bit tired of eating everything smothered in tons of *curry patta* (curry leaves)-flavoured coconut chutney, or tamarind paste,' objected Arjun, wrinkling his replica of Tiger's nose. 'Colonel Murphy's beer has some special—body—you know what I mean, Bhai.'

'I certainly do,' grinned the Maharajah, showing perfect white teeth. 'His first wife's, they say.'

'Really, Your Highness,' Arjun admonished with well-bred distaste. 'Jewels in the Crown can't go around repeating such dreadful gossip.'

'It's gospel truth, Younger Brother. Heard it from those missionaries who run that school near our place in Ooty.'

It was late afternoon by the time Tiger reached Church Hill Road, where the Collectorate, Higginbotham's Book Shop, Spencer's, and Jackson's Store stood close by the St. Stephen's Church. The latter marked the beginning of Ooty's main bazaar named, for some odd reason, Charing Cross by the first British settlers back in 1827.

Suddenly, Tiger was forced to apply the brakes and swerve sharply to the right. A roll of grass-green carpet had come hurtling out of Jackson's shop.

This strange spectacle was also watched with varying degrees of curiosity, chagrin, and amusement by several other people, apart from the two Fateypur princes. R.K. Kishen was escorting the Resident, his wife, and his niece Elinor, towards the famous Botanical Gardens when their leisurely stroll was interrupted by the sight of old Mr Jackson bustling out of his shop, and exhorting his swarthy assistants to do a pukka job.

'Pull! Pull! Another foot over the pavement. Yes, yes, over the entrance! But NOT till the middle of the road, you bloody idiots!'

Redverse raised his brows, glancing quizzically at the Chattargadh Dewan. 'I say, Raj Kumar Saheb, is this part of

Ooty's seasonal face-lift, or some special town beautification project?'

'Talk of Indian extravagance!' added Lady Dorothy. 'Carpeted sidewalks in one of the rainiest places in the country!'

Elinor blinked her dazzling, cornflower blue eyes. 'But Uncle Gerry, what's it actually for? Are they expecting Royalty? Or the Viceroy? Nobody referred to anyone special arriving in Ooty, because the Madras Governor practically lives here around the year, I hear.'

Kishen Singh chuckled, gesturing with his turbaned head at the two horses trotting towards them. 'There's your reference to context, Miss Elinor!'

Enjoying himself hugely, Arjun almost stood up in the front seat of the Fateypur Maharajah's car for a better view of this unexpected high-street drama unfolding before the eyes of several visitors, planters, and permanent residents out shopping or taking their evening walk. The road was lined with Victorian pillar boxes and wrought iron lamp-posts which were surrounded by beds of geraniums, begonias, impatiens, and petunias.

'I should have guessed it. The Ooty Municipality is spreading carpets not to honour Maharajah Tiger Fateypur, but to humour ANOTHER Nutty Maharajah!'

Tiger also grinned back. 'Okay, but the question is why does everybody kowtow to my crazy uncle, thus actually encouraging him to make a perfect cake of himself?'

'Really, Your Highness, because just like you, he's got the stuff in sackfuls.'

Nutty beamed as he surveyed the carpet spread out to cushion his horse's hooves and rule out any further mishaps. 'See this, Rao Saab? It pays to throw your weight around, and refuse to take any nonsense from anyone, especially shopkeepers. Now there's no danger of my prize polo ponies or thoroughbreds slipping in my frequent shopping zone.'

His brother-in-law merely nodded. But Nutty's horse started nibbling at the carpet, snorting and hoofing it playfully, and pulling out tufts of green wool. No matter how hard he tugged at the reins or however much he cajoled it, HH Pisshengunj couldn't get its head up. This made Jackson's son click his tongue in sheer exasperation, and rush forward to save their brand new carpet.

'Stop, you fool!' ordered his father, restraining him by forcefully clutching his coat.

'But that bloody horse is ruining our brand new carpet!' protested the young man.

'It's only a carpet, not the Governor's lawn before a garden party,' old Jackson snapped.

Just then, Kitten and her aunt Princess Diamond emerged from Higginbotham's where they had been browsing through the bookshelves. The commotion created outside by HH Pisshengunj, mounted on another uncontrollable horse, had drawn their attention. Sir Pratab followed them, stopping only to sign for the books and magazines they had selected. But as soon as they came out of the typical colonial tile-roofed and shuttered brick building, Kitten saw the mud-splashed Alfa Romeo convertible parked across the road.

Only one man could have the dash and gumption to drive all the way into the Nilgiris in such an unsuitable car. And that was Tiger Baapji.

Kitten was effectively prevented from streaking across the road in her joyful enthusiasm by a gentle restraining touch of her uncle's hand. Well aware that all the Rajput princesses and maharanis who holidayed in the Nilgiris revelled in south India's total freedom from purdah, he still couldn't allow any female relation in his charge to go dashing off to accost young men—not even blood relations—in public bazaars.

At that very moment, Tiger, who had been looking around

appraisingly, caught sight of Elinor. 'Arjun, who's that absolutely stunning girl over there with our Resident?'

'The girl who broke my cousin Robin's hip. And heart!'

Oblivious to the fact that his stentorian, high-pitched voice could easily be heard beyond the Club's private bar— named after the first Master of Ooty's famous Hunt, Colonel Jago—Nutty continued exhorting his team-mates Tiger, Koodsu Rao Saheb, and Baron Tikemoffsky. He ordered them to use every subtle device they could think of to make sure that his dear elder brother's players got in such bad shape that they wouldn't even be able to win a ping-pong match, let alone a polo tournament.

Unknown to him, the players he was referring to were standing just outside the door, able to hear everything. But the Pisshengunj Maharajah continued to unfold his dastardly plot. He planned to wine and dine the Chattargadh players until they all got indigestion; then he would forcibly keep them awake by hiring two Goan brass bands and several bagpipers to take turns in serenading them all night.

'I'll make sure that they don't get any sleep before Sunday's all-important match.'

'You needn't go to all that trouble, Nutty,' Maharajah Jai Singh said from the doorway. 'I intend calling on the Collector, along with the Resident to arrange fishing and hunting licences for my guests. And I shall see to it that he imposes Section 144 around the entire area, with police pickets and a night patrol to check noise pollution!'

The Maharajah of Pisshengunj spun around, spluttering protests as he faced Jai Singh and the laughing Redverse, Arjun, and Kishen. His rotund fair face became flushed with annoyance at their unforgivably sneaky and wicked eavesdropping on his private conversation in a private bar which he had hired for his personal use for the entire week.

He would have to tell the Club Secretary that even such high-and-mighty gatecrashers had to be forbidden from violating the rights of other members.

The Chattargadh Maharajah and his party returned to the large lounge with its glassed-in verandah, inviting sofas and armchairs, and a grand piano on which Lady Dorothy and Elinor were playing chopsticks in double-quick rhythm. The polished wooden floor was carpeted with first class Kashmiri *kaleens* (carpets). Impressive hunting trophies of tigers, brown bear, elk, horned bison and jackals were mounted on the walls between portraits of British Kings and Queens, former Viceroys, boards listing Club presidents and Hunt Masters, and some water colours of local scenic spots. Butlers with starched white turbans and red cummerbunds, served tea to some elderly ladies wearing floral frocks. They looked quite at home as they sat chatting about their gardens and grandchildren in one of the deep bay windows. Three retired Englishmen wondered aloud if someone could be found to make up a bridge foursome; and some British army officers up from Wellington stood discussing their chances of recouping that day's losses at the Race Course the following day.

Gerald Redverse knew that although the Snooty-Ooty Club was patronised by all the Civil Service *wallahs* from Madras and Bombay, and all the cavalry officers posted at Wellington and Bangalore, plus the European coffee and tea planters who worked in the Nilgiris, membership was severely restricted only to selected persons of the white community, which included Americans and Australians. The only Indians allowed reciprocal membership were the Maharajahs and Nawabs who cared to apply through the Governor of Madras.

Looking out of one of the bay windows which provided a good view of the churches and cottages around Club Hill, the Resident thought that the neo-classical facade gave a much-needed imperial touch to the otherwise modest single-storey clubhouse. The driveway was lined with weeping willows, cedars, rhododendrons, and pine trees, with a profusion of white Arum lillies, blue Agarpanthus, drifts of daffodils, narcissus, and crocus growing under them. All this reminded him of the Devonshire manor house now belonging to his eldest brother, and Elinor's father, Viscount Redverse. Rare tulip trees, camellias, roses, lilac and hydrangea bushes dotted the sloping lawns lined with fuchsia hedges. Containers spilling over with the season's first freesias, begonias, primulas, geraniums and every conceivable type of fern were grouped on all the steps and verandahs, giving a very Anglicised atmosphere to the whole place.

'Your Highness, has anyone agreed to umpire tomorrow's tournament?'

'Yes, Mr Redverse. Sir Pratab, and Brigadier Roberts of the Madras Sappers have finally been roped in. So we can expect fair play, even though the Brigadier is frightfully sticky about offside balls, opponents hooking each other's sticks from under their ponies' necks, and rough riding. And your father won't allow anyone—specially not you or your brother Tiger—to get away with crossing the line of play or committing the slightest foul. So watch out, Arjun,' cautioned the Chattargadh Maharajah.

'Oh come on, Bhai,' protested R.K. Kishen. 'We are lucky to have a low handicap player on our team, because you know it gives us an advantage over the other team. Arjun, just give us those long hits of yours! They will come as a bolt out of the blue for our dear doggone relative. He can't even control a standing horse these days!'

Redverse had heard varying versions of the incident leading to the carpeting of Jackson's Store. But he didn't think that this proved anything because Nutty was a fairly good player. Nevertheless, he still wanted to know what the other team's form was like.

Jai Singh assured him that he needn't take any of them—except Tiger—seriously. 'Their entire game plan revolves around pleasing Nutty!'

Tiger had seen the look of dismay on Lady Dorothy's face as he strolled across the lounge towards Elinor, the irresistible deb of the year 'doing' India like any other fashionable young European. Reckoning that someone must have imparted a lot of bogus information to make the Resident's wife wary of his effect on their niece, the lethally suave Maharajah decided that he would first have to work to disarm the entire family.

He greeted everyone who crossed his path with just the right degree of warmth or courtesy till he came to the Chattargadh group. Shaking hands with Elinor as they were introduced, Tiger asked: 'Is this your first visit to our country, Miss Redverse?'

'Yes, Your Highness.'

'Please call me Tiger. Everyone does. And before you say what a funny name it is, let me tell you that my English nanny, Miss Mackenzie . . . .'

'Scottish,' corrected Lady Dorothy.

Tiger thanked her cordially for setting him right, and continued. 'Well, my pukka British nanny, Miss Mackenzie, couldn't pronounce my actual name . . . .'

'Christian name,' interjected the Resident's wife.

'You really mustn't mislead people, Lady D,' said Tiger with deceptive deference. 'I've never been baptised, you know!'

This made the ladies laugh. But Elinor demanded the full story of how he had been given his name.

'Being scrupulously efficient and economical in every way, she translated Nahar Singh literally, and I became Tiger in English.'

'And in earnest, Elinor. So beware,' cautioned Arjun.

Elinor changed the subject by asking if anyone knew

whether snooker had been conceived and popularised by Colonel Sir Neville Chamberlain at the Ooty Club, as was claimed by all the guidebooks, or by Lord Kitchener at Woolwich's Royal Military Academy, as the Field Marshal insisted. They then digressed into a discussion of how the British had acquired Ooty for the princely sum of two rupees from the Toda chiefs after the defeat of Tippu Sultan during the Mysore Wars. Gerald Redverse said that, after seeing the Nilgiris, he no longer found it strange that Macaulay chose to spend several months here (compiling the Indian Penal Code) instead of returning to hot and muggy Madras to his gubernatorial duties.

'Have you noticed how many of our eminent men got their start in India, Elinor,' asked Dorothy. 'The Duke of Wellington, Churchill, Lawrence . . . .'

'Indeed, Your Ladyship?' teased Tiger. 'I hardly thought someone like you would publicly admit to having read and admired his naughty books!'

'I was referring to Lawrence of Arabia. Not D.H!' said Dorothy.

'Quite,' continued the Cambridge-educated Maharajah in his perfectly enunciated English. '*Lady Chatterly's Lover* seldom appeals to stuffed shirts. I saw you both coming out of the Nilgiri Public Library empty-handed this morning. Why don't you try ours at Fateypur House, which is so much better supplied with the latest fiction. Please feel free to drop in any time. And if your aunt is busy, I can always pick you up, Elinor.'

Elinor fingered the knotted pearl string dangling over the baby blue cashmere cardigan she had slipped over her box-pleated silk dress. 'That's terribly kind of you, Tiger, but HH Chattargadh has put a sweet little Baby Austin at my disposal. So I'm quite mobile, you know, and shall certainly come visiting whenever Princess Diamond is ready to receive me.'

At 21, Elinor had emerged unscathed from two London seasons before succumbing to wanderlust. She had perfected the art of handling such transparent ploys from the loftiest potentates, maharajahs, and Arab sheikhs without loss of face for anyone, specially herself. With a dependable scattering of blood relations around the world—which ranged from London loafers to Palm Beach playboys, taipans, diplomats, and top brass up to (and including) India's current Viceroy—her path had been enviably smooth so far. And this despite the dreadful handicap of being both beautiful and rich.

As she turned towards Maharajah Jai Singh, her cool composure secretly amused the worldly-wise man. But it exasperated the handsome young Fateypur Maharajah, considered irresistible by females on no less than four continents. 'Your Highness, I can't recall the name of the person who built this clubhouse,' she asked.

'Sir William Rumbolt,' replied Jai Singh.

Tiger lost no time in reclaiming Elinor's attention by adding that Sir Willam was grandfather to the present Madras Governor, and had acquired his fortune by marrying Lord Rancliffe's frightfully eccentric daughter, who'd gone not only 'native', but 'tribal Toda native,' with all the proper ceremonies. He had also become senior partner in William Palmer & Co., financiers to the Nizam of Hyderabad.

By this time Tiger's uncle, Nutty, had joined the Resident's family and began talking. He pointed out that nobody had any business building anything on Toda sacred ground because it definitely brought on divine retribution, or nemesis of the truly Greek kind. Completely misunderstanding Tiger's attempts at levity, the Pisshengunj Maharajah continued expounding on the enduring effects of nemesis. 'You can bet that THAT is why Rumbolt's business collapsed; why his wife died in childbirth; and why he himself did not survive beyond 46—which has to be the prime of life, for it is my own age, you know.'

He also added that he was compiling a book on those Magic Mantras which would ward off evil influences and help attain one's innermost desires. 'People have to learn to chant them correctly, at the right time, and at the right place. And of course, wear the right clothes.'

'Of course,' agreed the Resident's wife, pursuing her own chain of thought. 'There is nothing more maddening than turning up on holiday with the wrong clothes.' She regretted having changed into a scoop-necked, sleeveless, lavender cocktail dress for an evening at the club. The draughty old place (which even the two log fires lit as early as at 6 o'clock didn't do much to warm) needed something more suitable.

Elinor nodded. 'One doesn't realise that India can also be cold enough for coats in the middle of May.'

'Depends on where you are,' said Jai Singh. 'This hill stands more than 8,000 feet above sea level!'

Elinor mentioned her desire to visit Pondicherry on the Coromandel coast, which, she had heard, was quite close by. Somerset Maugham's wife had told her quite a bit about Sri Aurobindo, the famous freedom fighter-turned-Guru who had cleverly evaded imprisonment by living in the French enclave. The talk turned to Anglo-French rivalry since the days of Dupleix and Clive, the annexation of Arcot, and Hyder Ali. Tiger couldn't resist baiting all the British present by informing Elinor that, like the church beams of St. Stephen's, the roof of the Savoy Hotel had also been stripped from Tippu Sultan's palace at Sri Rangapatnam by that other empire builder, Wellington, when his brother was the East India Company's Calcutta representative.

'Lady Dorothy, what do you think of this place?' inquired Jai Singh.

'I'd think better of it, Your Highness, if someone added a porch! Now we all get soaked when it starts pouring. And the Nilgiri rain is as unpredictable as our desert sandstorms.'

Jai Singh gave her a sympathetic smile. 'I'll get the Club committee to do something about it.'

'About sandstorms?' teased Tiger, making everyone laugh.

The pace of play became faster and more furious after the second *chukker*. Chasing the ball at great speed, Tiger tried to hold the line and right of way towards their goalpost. But the Resident was marking him so closely that he had no choice except to feed the ball to his Nutty uncle. Polo sticks flashed as some of the other players galloped up, pushing, shoving, swearing, and trying to ride each other off. Four of them tried to get away with the ball without committing a foul. But Arjun made the mistake of hooking Baron Tikemoffsky's stick under his pony's neck, endangering and obstructing the Russian in a manner that immediately resulted in a whistle blown by his hawk-eyed father, Sir Pratab, who came cantering up with the other umpire. A free penalty hit was awarded to Nutty's team amidst oaths and protests from some of their opponents. Baron Tikemoffsky had a try at three successive 60-yard penalties. But he did not score even once.

Despite the one-and-a-half goal advantage conceded to the Pisshengunj team in handicap, the latter was unable to block off the daring raids initiated by the Chattargadh players. But, before the end of the second *chukker*, a deft backhander from Tiger scored the first goal for his side.

The spectators who had turned up to watch the friendly exhibition match between the Pisshengunj and Chattargadh Maharajahs, were completely caught up in the enormous amount of aggression, sheer physical courage, and stamina displayed by horses and riders in the furious pursuit of a small bamboo ball. The teams were quite evenly matched, even though the 10-handicap Maharajah of Chattargadh was considered to be one of the most brilliant tacticians in the international polo set. Though having lower handicaps, Tiger and Arjun displayed impressive acrobatic skills in the saddle. They were too youthful and fearless to worry about nasty falls or bruises.

All the eight players kept changing one superb mount after another after every *chukker*, but Jai Singh could be clearly distinguished even in the thickest mêlée, because he was always mounted on yet another of his famous Chattargadh greys. At half time, a phalanx of uniformed syces marched around the ground, treading in the divots kicked up by the ponies.

There was a fair sprinkling of Indian royalty among the European sahebs, memsahebs, and *babalog* surrounding the Governor's party. They were well aware of the undercurrents of animosity between the two Maharajahs, and it added extra spice to that afternoon's play. While the three younger ladies, Kitten, Ratna, and Elinor seated in the central front row, were caught up in the sheer exuberance and excitement of a faster-than-usual polo game, their older chaperones, Maharani Padmini, Princess Diamond, and Lady Dorothy, felt anxiety mingle with justifiable pride as they watched their menfolk caught up in the brutal contest. The tuc-thwack of mallets, the crescent-shaped turf clods thrown up by pounding hooves, the Resident appearing so controlled, Tiger leaning dangerously halfway over his pony's neck to the left to get in his shot, and Maharajah Jai Singh perfectly balanced in the saddle as he got away with the ball repeatedly— were all part of that exciting afternoon. Each team had scored exactly six goals. Everyone knew that, for the team captains at least, it was going to be a ruthless, no quarter fight for that one winning goal. And each hoped and prayed that no one would end up in hospital with broken bones.

A little behind them to their left, the effeminate little Nawab of Jabberali was being quite catty about the huge hats and umbrellas obstructing his vision. While one or two of the Englishmen in front of him had adjusted their sola topees and felt hats, some ladies carrying bright silk parasols (to filter out the afternoon sun and prevent sudden rain from spoiling their wide-brimmed, ribbon and flower-trimmed Panama boaters) had simply ignored him. The afternoon sky was full of scudding clouds, and a growing cold wind rippled through the strands of blue gum, cypress, cedar, and rhododendron trees that surrounded the polo ground on three sides.

Kitten was glad that she hadn't followed Ratna's example by turning up outdoors only in a fluttery thin sari minus cape or cardigan. She had insisted on wearing her lightweight, houndstooth jacket and classic Capri pants with the Italian silk scarf she'd pinched from HH Fateypur. For Kitten, the unparalleled enjoyment of watching good polo players in action was enhanced on that particular afternoon by the presence of Tiger even though he was playing on the enemy's side. His effortless ability to intercept and propel the ball into terrific arcs whenever he got a clear hit had true polo enthusiasts cheering and clapping loudly.

But Kitten did not allow herself to clap too much for fear of causing scandal or inviting reprimands.

'Oh, isn't the Maharajah absolutely smashing,' cried Elinor, unable to restrain herself at a particularly tense point as the players rode right opposite the stands, valiantly trying to keep the ball from going out of play.

Maharani Padmini gave her an amused half smile. 'Which Maharajah do you mean, my dear Elinor?'

Princess Diamond merely quirked her fashionably plucked eyebrows at her sister-in-law as Lady Dorothy informed her niece that there were at least three of them present out there.

'Of course, she means Tiger Baapji!' exclaimed Kitten with a glowing look as she flipped back her windblown hair.

'Whatever gave you that impression?' quizzed Elinor, adding that SHE for one wasn't addicted to hero worship.

After an amazing about-face at a furious gallop, the gutsy veteran player Koodsu Rao Saheb managed to get the ball away from his bête noire, R.K. Kishen. The umpires and referee closed in to monitor the play, and once more Maharajah Jai Singh showed his mettle. He scored a diagonal hit under the neck of his horse, a move which called for a high degree of equestrian skill, and control over stick and ball. Soon they were into the hottest part of the game. With the fourth *chukker*, Chattargadh was leading. All semblance of gentlemanly restraint had long since vanished. The spectators followed the thundering horses hurtling up and down the 300-yard field, egged on by players waving 4-feet long polo sticks, and yelling incomprehensible instructions to each other. The seasoned ponies responded heroically to their demanding riders as the two Maharajahs battled it out for victory.

Confident of making the score even, Nutty concentrated on the ball for a clear hit without allowing himself to be distracted by the rider crowding him from the left. Arjun managed to manoeuvre his heavier horse alongside HH Pisshengunj. He began ramming him with his leather-capped right knee, while simultaneously digging his elbow into the Maharajah's ribs just as their ponies' rumps collided full force. By the time Nutty's team-mates rode to his rescue, it was too late. Unwilling to let go of the ball and right himself in the saddle, the Maharajah of Pisshengunj took a header under the fascinated eyes of the watching crowd.

The moment Nutty hit the ground, his team-mates

Koodsu Rao Saheb and Baron Tikemoffsky spontaneously catapulted themselves off their polo ponies, thus bringing the tournament to a sudden halt. Kitten doubled up with laughter as the stunned, confused, and angry referee, umpires, and opponents began berating Arjun. Tiger deftly manoeuvred his horse out of this unprecedented mêlée, hoping that the bugler would end this farce. Nearly all the spectators also began laughing, jeering, and hooting derisively at his Nutty uncle, who seemed to be on the verge of having an apoplectic fit.

'But why did the entire Pisshengunj team fall off?' demanded Dorothy.

'For protocol reasons!' gurgled Kitten, echoing precisely the very explanation that the two well-bred aristocratic exiles, Baron Tikemoffsky and the Rao Saheb of Koodsu, were offering to their livid team captain and their aggravated opponents.

The unprecedented and bizarre behaviour of HH Pisshengunj's team-mates provided much mirth the following evening to the guests gathered at Chattargadh House for the party Jai Singh usually held before leaving Ooty. A lesser person than Nutty would have been deeply mortified, but the Pisshengunj Maharajah merely excused his team's appalling breach of International Polo Federation rules by praising their staunch sense of loyalty. He lauded their praiseworthy devotion to the finer points of propriety, and a protocol which were in grave danger of disappearing from the world just because everyone was clamouring for equality.

'Even real Brahmins, like that Kashmiri chap from Allahabad—what's his name? is debunking the caste system!'

'Nutty Uncle, can't you tell the difference between protocol and the shocking sycophancy that led to yesterday's foul-up?' countered Kitten with her usual candour.

'At least get the terminology right, my dear niece,' he said, pinching her nose. 'Pile-up. Not foul-up!'

Overhearing this, Maharajah Jai Singh cast his daughter an admonishing glance. But before he could remonstrate with Kitten any further, drums rolled, and a bugle fanfare from the military band positioned outside alerted him to the Governor's arrival. The Maharajah went forward to receive him. Renowned for his superb hospitality, gracious manners, and awesome intelligence, Jai Singh had already managed to make each of the forty carefully selected people invited to dine and dance that evening, feel extra special. He addressed everyone by their right names and titles, and had an appropriate word and smile on his lips for each guest.

Just as the Governor of Madras and his wife stepped into the room full of faultlessly attired, punctual and protocol-conscious guests, their escort, Raj Kumar Kishen Singh, proclaimed loudly: 'Sir Charles and Lady Hugging-his-Bottom are here at last!'

Nutty was not the only one who guffawed loudly at this shocking *faux pax*. However, Kitten saved the situation by grabbing the hands of her cousin Arjun, and the Resident, who happened to be standing near her and breaking out into a spirited rendition of 'He's a Jolly Good Fellow' in her clear contralto voice. Others, including the orchestra, followed the Princess's lead, completely drowning all the choked-back titters, coughing, and comments. Jai Singh, as usual, maintained his composure, smoothly offering his guests of honour the drinks of their choice without referring to the linguistic boulder dropped by his well-meaning but malapropism-inclined cousin.

Apart from this slight contretemps, the formal sit-down dinner went off without a hitch. Course followed succulent course, served with nothing but the correct Grande Reserve wines imported from Alsace, Bordeaux, and Burgundy. And the conversation, which perforce had to be confined to the persons seated on either side at this rather formal princely party, was animated and jovial enough to please both guests and hosts.

The well-sprung parquet-floored hall, with its over-hanging wrought iron balcony designed like a minstrels' gallery for musicians, also served as a ballroom. It was decorated with masses of scented orchids banked against lush potted palms. Colourful flower arrangements consisting of locally grown gladioli, carnations, roses, and lillies stood on the marble-topped tables flanking several sofas on which people, exhausted by their exertions on the dance floor, could rest. The bright, tinkling chandeliers and gilt wall sconces highlighted the ladies' ornaments, thus adding an extra dimension of glitter to the gathering of Indian royalty, British officialdom, European planters, Hyderabadi nawabs, aristocratic horse breeders, and Parsi industrialists present in Ooty at that time.

Through the open French windows and the long verandahs draped with jasmine garlands ordered all the way from Coimbatore, the guests could enjoy the sight of the lovely little Chinese paper lanterns strung from tree to tree in the well-kept gardens surrounding Chattargadh House. All the lamps and lights were reflected in the large lake in the middle of the gardens. Fires had been lit in all the three drawing rooms. The one with hand-carved teak panels furnished with marvellous mother-of-pearl and ivory inlaid Coromandel settees, bureaux and screens had been set aside for the old-fashioned Maharanis and Begums who did not care to mingle with the others.

Princess Diamond added considerable zest to the party when she wasn't taking turns to be with her sister-in-law, her niece, and her daughter-in-law-to-be. She was doing her best to ensure the comfort and entertainment of the other royal ladies, including Nutty's three wives, and the

Travencore Regent, Setu Rajye Laxmi. Responding to a solicitous query from her gossipy old aunt, the Maharani of Mysore, Princess Diamond admitted that Tiger's miscarriage-prone bride was better off under her own mother's care in Switzerland. After nearly five years of disappointment, they were all hoping for an heir to Fateypur.

Maharani Padmini looked as elegant as usual in her carefully colour-coordinated coral and cream sari draped over an elaborately jewelled top knot. But she couldn't help eyeing her sister-in-law with a twinge of wistful envy. Princess Diamond radiated a sophisticated glamour. She was tall and sleek, and was wearing one of her one-of-a-kind saris bought from the best chiffon, Benaras, Kanjeeveram, Tanchoi, Dhakkai, Kotah, and Chanderi specialists in the country. Her jewellery, apart from all that heirloom stuff, was custom-made by Van Cleef and Arpels or the Crown jeweller, Garrard. Her perfumes were specially bottled in Grasse. Her silk scarves, handbags, and shoes came from France and Italy; her riding togs from London. Other princesses were quick to copy her clothes and her famous bobbed, face-framing hairstyle. And inevitably ended up looking like Princess Diamond clones.

'The coconut can definitely be sent,' she informed Padmini as they stood watching Arjun and Ratna chatting together with the palpable ease of young people who had known and liked each other all their lives.

Maharani Padmini bowed her head in grateful assent. 'We couldn't have found a better match for Ratna. But you were quite right about avoiding awkwardness between them—and postponing the final decision and the formal engagement ceremony—until Arjun agreed with the family's opinion that they would make an ideal couple.'

While this dialogue was in progress, Ratna had turned to answer a query from another young lady who wished to know how often the Ooty Club screened English films. Unable to share their enthusiasm for Clark Gable, Errol Flynn, Stewart Granger, Gregory Peck, or Gary Cooper, Arjun strolled off to join his cousin. Both accepted chilled pink champagne from the turbaned retainer standing deferentially before them with a loaded silver tray.

It was soon evident to Arjun that Tiger had eyes only for Elinor, looking stunningly beautiful in a creamy silk, halter-necked cocktail dress. Sapphire and diamond drop earrings and strappy silver sandals completed the fashionable picture. Tiger wondered what Elinor was saying to make Brigadier Roberts laugh so loudly.

'She's always so serious and standoffish when I'm around. Can you imagine, she asked me what Mahatma Gandhi is really like because she thinks we're neighbours.'

'And what did you tell her?' asked Arjun.

'Told her I knew even less about him than she did! And that a few hundred miles separated Fateypur from both Porbandar and the Sabarmati Ashram.'

A lull in the noise level permitted Arjun to overhear the English girl. 'My dear brother, you aren't likely to get anywhere with her. Just listen to that . . . .'

Like Tiger, Lady Dorothy too could scarcely believe her ears. Only yesterday their niece had been sneering at Kitten about adolescent hero worship, and today she was doing the same thing!

'Now look at her,' she told her husband in an anxious undertone. 'She's got it so badly, Gerry, that I shall have to watch her all the time she's in our charge. One never knows with Maharajahs.'

But Redverse disagreed with her. 'Relax, and enjoy the party, old thing. She's chasing the wrong Maharajah. Now, if it was young Tiger Fateypur, even harem guards couldn't have prevented the inevitable. But our chap's the soul of discretion.'

'You really think so?' mused Dorothy. 'But I can't blame the poor child. If I wasn't married to you, Gerry, I'd fancy him myself, because he's absolutely mesmerising!'

The Resident was prevented from making a befitting rejoinder to this sally by the arrival of Kitten, who joined them just then. She said something complimentary about Dorothy's beaded crêpe de Chine claret evening gown which was offset with a shimmering Benaras brocade stole.

Referring to Kitten's beautifully hand-painted chiffon sari, the Resident's wife wondered how she had been permitted to wear white.

Kitten informed her that the taboo involved only unrelieved black or white. Elinor's smashing dress, for instance, would be considered appropriate only for Eastern widows. 'And Western brides,' she added with a disarming grin.

Once the musicians picked up their instruments, Kitten lost no time in carving her way towards Tiger through the throng of animated guests who were in the process of abandoning their glasses, cigarettes, and cigars. One look at the tiresome young girl's eager, animated face was enough to prevent the Fateypur Maharajah from going off in search of a much preferred partner. Princess Diamond and Sir Pratab had certainly reared the prince well. He knew how to be kind to animals, children, dependents, and ageing relations. The dancing began as usual, with husbands and wives partnering each other. Only the most dashing (or depraved) Indian socialite would dare to be seen enjoying herself in the arms of anyone but the most closely connected escort.

Since the first dance was a sedate foxtrot, Kitten conducted herself with perfect decorum, delighted with the fact that she had actually managed to make HH Fateypur ignore all the other females who were dying to dance with him. But as soon as the band struck up the Blue Danube, she couldn't resist the temptation of forcing Tiger to follow her lead, performing the most flamboyant variations with great style and in perfect tempo.

Exasperated beyond belief, Tiger let her know who was in charge, firmly propelling her backwards and controlling her with a finger touch so tight that her spine tingled. 'My dear Kitten, if you try to guide me again, I'll simply pick you up and dump you on the nearest sofa!'

Effectively snubbed, Kitten allowed HH Fateypur to manoeuvre her through the clapping couples. They soon reached Arjun and Elinor, who seemed to be on the friendliest terms. 'Thanks a lot, Kitten. Shall we change partners, brother?'

'No, thanks,' retorted Arjun. 'You can keep Miss Sticking Plaster!'

Kitten's smouldering black eyes flashed as she tried to think of an equally rude rejoinder.

Maharajah Jai Singh joined the group. He complimented Elinor again on her ability to turn heads, hoped the Fateypur princes were enjoying themselves, and told Kitten to come along and chat with the Governor's wife who had sat down to catch her breath after the demanding Viennese waltz. Tiger lost no time in claiming Elinor's hand for the next dance. He was keenly aware of all the British officers in their scarlet regimentals, and other aspiring chaps in black dinner jackets and *bandhgalas*, keen to prevent him from dancing with this sensational newcomer.

But, without any excuse or explanation, Elinor suddenly hurried off after Jai Singh.

Looking at his chagrined cousin with a good deal of amusement, Arjun began reciting: 'Would you like to sin with Elinor Glynn on a tiger skin? Or would you rather err with her on some other fur?'

'If you say one more word, Arjun, I'll knock you out!'

'Really, Your Highness. That would be a breach of feudal privilege. And protocol. Maharajahs can't afford to go around hitting their younger brothers and dependents, especially with all those Raj representatives watching.'

Tiger tapped Arjun's chin playfully with a clenched fist, swearing softly that he didn't give a damn about princely protocol or public relations.

Elinor's attempts to monopolise her husband's attention all evening had not been lost on Maharani Padmini, who stood chatting with Nutty while he quaffed yet another glass of champagne to revive himself after his exertions on the dance floor with the Governor's unusually tall and hefty daughter. Exchanging a provocatively amused glance with his wife, Maharajah Jai Singh led the Resident's niece up to them. 'Few people know more about Indian mythology, music, and dances than HH Pishengunj. I'm sure he'll be only too happy to answer all your queries regarding the lack of keyboard instruments in our country while he dances with you.'

The minute Kitten overheard this, she made a beeline for the bandmaster. Ripples of laughter and frissons of sheer fun ran through the ballroom as Nutty tried to get the hang of what his partner was doing to the strains of a jazzy Xavier Cugat rumba. 'There was a rich Maharaja of Maggadore,' sang a loud baritone voice. 'Who had ten thousand camels, and maybe more! He had rubies and pearls, and the loveliest girls, But he didn't know how to doo-OO the rumba!'

Nearly everyone joined in singing the chorus. Most of the couples stopped dancing to form a circle around Nutty and Elinor, whose sporting spirit prevented her from walking off the floor and exposing her partner to more jibes and jolly banter from the younger guests. These were led by that madcap Kitten who always enjoyed creating mayhem wherever she went. The perfectly proper English aristocrat had already discovered this during her stay at Chattargadh House.

Tiger was also watching Kitten's gleeful face as she disrupted the sedate function, and turned it into an adolescent romp. She seemed bent upon ensuring HH Pisshengunj's discomfiture with her fiendish ability to lure people into making ludicrous spectacles of themselves under the guise of playing party games.

Princess Diamond was rather daunted by her nephew's sudden query. 'Does your favourite niece always act so crazy, Aunty?'

'My ONLY niece,' she countered instantly. 'And since when have you become the arbiter of proper female behaviour, Tiger? Kitten is just a normal child having some fun, even if it is at your Nutty uncle's expense!'

The Viceroy's Visit 6

Although Koodsu Rao Saheb's fondest hopes had been
realised when he became the proud father of a second
son at nearly sixty from his seventeen year-old second wife,
what the people gathered in the Chattargadh Palace ADC
Room couldn't comprehend was Maharajah Jai Singh's
complete volte-face over this affair. For some inscrutable
reason, the high-principled and progressive Rathor ruler had
not only reinstated the Shyani chief, but restored all his
hereditary rights. He had even granted him the privilege of
personal audience with the Maharani on special occasions
like family weddings and births.

Several male and female retainers in festive costumes—
carrying brocade-covered *thaals* and fruit baskets—sat in the
verandah outside, waiting for the summons from the *zenani
dyodhi* (Queen's portico).

Colonel CP hailed him from the door, adding to the
room's increasingly rowdy atmosphere. 'Congratulations,
Rao Saheb! You really pulled a fast one . . . .'

In high spirits because the unnecessary tiff between
himself and his feudal overlord was over at last, Koodsu
interrupted: 'Begetting sons involves more than THAT,
Kernel Saab.'

'I didn't mean to disparage that achievement of yours! But I was referring to your secret clout with HH.'

'Yes, Rao Saab,' added Zorji, lounging on the sofa, the enamelled gold buttons of his smart white *bandhgala* jacket left deliberately undone. Despite the *khus*-scented air being blown into the room by the large desert cooler fitted to the north-facing window, it was a frightfully hot May day. 'Baapji has returned your *jagir* and reinstalled you fully as a pillar of Chattargadh State *only* because of your polo handicap. He seems to have forgotten that you're prone to falling off horses for protocol reasons!'

Everyone laughed, and continued to tease Koodsu as iced *nimboo pani*, biscuits, and the crested silver cigarette case were passed around. Still trying to fathom the real reason for Maharajah Jai Singh's unusual behaviour, Colonel CP commented on the land speculation deal in which Koodsu Rao Saheb and his brother-in-law, HH Pisshengunj, had bought up most of the barren tracts through which the famous canal was being built.

'Yes, Kernel Saab. I'm no longer fair game for our Maharajah, specially after producing a posthumous son!'

Howling with laughter, Colonel Claude-Poole protested: 'PREmature, Rao Saheb! Not posthumous, Heaven forbid!' The British officer bade him invest in a dictionary, and a copy of Roget's *Thesaurus*. As the Rajput chief tried to comprehend the difference between the two rather similar-sounding English words, the phone rang.

Ganpat Singh tilted his chair towards the writing table, and picked up the telephone. 'Hello, ADC Room speaking . . . .'

The other three persons relaxing on the sofa were at first puzzled, then amused by the sudden yet complete transformation in the bearing and attitude of Ganpat Singh. He sprang up from his chair, quickly stubbed out his cigarette in an ashtray, covered his bare head with the nearest sola topee from the hat stand, and switched from arrogant, heavily accented English to the most deferential Marwari. 'Hukam *Hajoor, hajeer hai*!' he said loudly.

Colonel CP raised his brows questioningly at Zorji, who was busy buttoning up his jacket with a reverential look on his face. But Koodsu Rao Saheb chuckled softly, put a forefinger againsts his forehead, and made the universal 'screw-loose' gesture.

Worried that their rude laughter and jesting words might get relayed over the telephone, Ganpat Singh glared at them over his shoulder. 'Jo hukum, *Hajoor* . . . Yes, he's very happy after meeting Durbar . . . . Yes, I'll escort Koodsu Rao Saheb and his sons up to the *zenani dyodhi. Khamaghani*, Hukum.'

As he put the phone down, the ADC, popularly known as Gadbad or Faulty Singh, shook his fist belligerently at his mocking companions. 'You think that's a joke, *daakiras* (devils)? Couldn't you chaps see, that was our Maharani Saab Bahadur speaking DIRECTLY to ADC Room!'

Colonel CP continued chortling. 'Yes, Thakur Saheb. But Her Highness couldn't see you!'

'That is not the point,' he retorted. 'Among us, custom is custom. And protocol is protocol.'

'Never thought I'd see Koodsu Rao Saheb getting the full-fattened calf treatment,' mused the uniformed Englishman as he watched the turbaned aristocrat proceeding upstairs for an audience with Her Highness. He understood the paternalistic principles and the purpose behind this interaction, for among the Rajputs, the Maharajah and Maharani actually became guardians of minor *jagirdars*, acting *in loco parentis* as long as a court of ward was deemed necessary. In Koodsu Rao Saheb's case, a formal recognition of his newborn second son's rights was even more necessary because Maharajah Jai Singh had taken such a strong stand against polygamy. He had even enacted a law against this ancient practice. And HH Chattargadh was the last Rajput on earth who would deviate from a stand, no matter how uncalled for or absurdly pig-headed it was. The abysmal 'chandeliers for elephants' affair before the Prince of Wales' visit was a case in point. But no matter how persistently he pursued the subject, his usually knowledgeable cronies Reverse Gear, R.K. Kishen, and Robin were either pretending ignorance, or were as baffled as himself. And the Maharajah, of course, was being extremely tight-lipped about the whole affair, behaving as though nothing out of the ordinary had ever happened between himself and Koodsu Rao Saheb, even when everyone who was anyone in Princely India, including the Viceroy, had been dragged into that extraordinary muddle by His Nutty Highness.

All this made CP realise that it was time he toddled off for that inspection of the Royal suite and guest wing which HH had redecorated before the Viceroy's forthcoming visit. Though, why the Viceroy had chosen the worst time in summer to descend upon Chattargadh was anybody's guess!

Princess Kitten stood tiptoe on a stool planted on top of a massive carved sideboard. She was busy scraping a stuffed and mounted rhinoceros's horn with a small Swiss pocket knife. Her concentration was so intense that she didn't hear the dining room curtains parting even though they made the distinct metallic sound of brass rings sliding against gleaming brass rods.

'A rhino's horn, two tiger claws, the beloved's hair, and a peacock's eye . . .' she chanted, oblivious to the four pairs of astounded eyes watching her with varying shades of disapproval.

The full glare of two large chandeliers that had suddenly begun blazing down on her almost made Kitten lose her balance. She turned to reprimand the intruders who had so rudely disturbed her at this vital moment. But, as she gazed down at her father, brother, uncle, and the Military Secretary, the words died unspoken on her lips.

'Kitten, what on earth are you up to now?' demanded Robin, horrified to see his sister perched on the sideboard.

'Just a little scientific experiment,' said Kitten, with perfect aplomb.

Maharajah Jai Singh advised her sternly to climb down before she fell off. Colonel CP gallantly gave her a hand without batting an eyelid or permitting a hint of the laughter lurking in his eyes from touching his twitching lips.

Robin picked up the open book lying face down on the sideboard, glanced at the title, and read it out with a puzzled frown. *Magic Mantras?*

Kitten made a quick dive to rescue the book from her brother's hand, and in the scuffle, a pair of tiger claws fell to the carpeted floor. Aware of his younger sister's hopeless infatuation with Tiger Fateypur, Robin immediately put two and two together, and burst out laughing.

But Maharajah Jai Singh was not amused. Nor was R.K. Kishen. 'So YOU stole the tiger claws for which those poor *farrashes* were blamed.'

'What rubbish, Uncle Kishen. Taking what belongs to you isn't called stealing!' she retorted.

Colonel Claude-Poole had seldom seen the Chattargadh Maharajah looking so displeased. 'Kitten, is there no end to your thoughtlessness? Wasn't it bad enough you pinpointing a lacuna in our State legislation, but actually giving Nutty's Dewan—a foreigner, and a Russian at that—my personal copy of Roget's *Thesaurus!*'

'Really, Your Highness, there was no other way of convincing them that English is a very precise language,' stressed Kitten with airy nonchalance. 'You yourself admitted that there IS a difference between polygamy and bigamy.'

The Englishman was immediately all attention. This remark had suddenly solved the great mystery of HH Chattargadh retracting his stand on the Koodsu affair. But it left him wondering about what Kitten's real motive was in providing a solution to a problem so closely connected with Nutty Pisshengunj, whom she so heartily disliked.

As they stood in the trophy-hung room used for formal banquets, Maharajah Jai Singh continued to look aggrieved. But his unabashed daughter continued to behave as though she had done nothing unusual. 'This is too much. My own children behaving like vandals! As if the Viceroy's coming— like a wolf descending on the fold—isn't bad enough!'

Grabbing this opportunity to change the subject, Kitten asked her brother what this cryptic reference meant. Robin impatiently explained that it was clear to everybody, including their father, that she was as bad (if not worse) than the new Viceroy who was as notorious as Byron's Assyrian. 'He comes, he sees, he admires, and acquires . . . .'

'Art treasures for himself, and heirloom jewellery for his wife,' added Jai Singh.

Kitten said that she was not in the least bit surprised to hear this. 'After all, he's a soldier—nothing personal, Colonel CP! On top of which, both his wife and his mother happen to be American robber-barons' daughters! Very *Veni Vidi Vici*. But we can still save our real treasures from this chap.'

'How?' demanded her father.

'By pocketing your pride, hiding all the collector's items, and trotting out only the State's accumulated junk,' said his daughter in a manner normally reserved for explaining things to halfwits.

Robin very generously conceded that, as usual, his

brainless sister had hit the nail on the head, and should be forgiven for damaging a hunting trophy even though it had great sentimental value.

The Maharajah fixed Kitten with a stern eye and tapped the confiscated book. 'I can see that we'll be beholden to the Princess yet again; but I'm still going to get to the bottom of this *Magic Mantras* rhino rubbish inspired by His Nutty Highness!'

Mrs Rawlins shot the Maharajah an aggrieved look as she sat facing him on an armchair in the Maharani's drawing room. Didn't the man understand that nobody controlled Kitten? As usual, parents were the last to know the truth about their children. But heaven knows, thought the governess, they ought by now to have learnt their lesson as far as the Princess was concerned.

Waving the heavily gold embossed and privately printed leather-bound volume, Jai Singh demanded, 'Where did Kitten get this awful book from, Mrs Rawlins?'

'From the author, I believe, Your Highness.'

The Maharajah opened *Magic Mantras* and read the florid inscription inside the first page. It was exactly as he had feared. That blasted Nutty had even tried to brainwash his daughter for some unfathomable nefarious purpose of his own.

'But it's your *duty* to prevent the Princess from accepting unsuitable gifts,' said Padmini.

'Really, Your Highness, I don't see how I can prevent the Princess from doing anything during my annual holiday, or whenever I leave her temporarily in your far more capable and safe hands! As Your Highness can see, the book was autographed and given to Kitten only very recently, at Ooty. Of course, I do admit to having taught her that there's nothing objectionable about accepting books, flowers, and candy from one's friends and relations. This is permitted even in Royal British circles!'

'My dear Mrs Rawlins, all I'm trying to say is that we don't want all your efforts to turn Kitten into a rational, well-behaved and modern young lady to be undermined by negative influences like this silly, superstitious book, written by HH Pisshengunj of all people,' protested Padmini.

The Maharajah added that they depended on her to keep Kitten out of mischief now that she was out of school, and at a loose end after finishing her Senior Cambridge. He was doing everything he could to arrange a suitable marriage (at least as good as Ratna's) for her, which they would all be attending in a couple of weeks.

The governess sighed and shrugged her shoulders. She wondered whether it was dereliction of duty or sheer self-preservation that prevented her from informing her optimistic, ultra-modern employer about his frightfully determined little daughter's horrifyingly anachronistic intentions regarding that particular subject. How could she tell him about all the stolen scarves and photographs and the rabid hero worship she knew everything about?

No premonition of looming disaster cast a cloud over the cheerful countenances of the princes waiting under the fluttering windsock to receive HH Fateypur at Chattargadh's brand new airstrip. It was 4 o'clock in the afternoon, when only mad dogs and Englishmen were normally seen outdoors. They heard the aircraft before they saw it streaking out of the desert sky. The loud drone and whirr of its propeller-driven engines became ear-splitting as Tiger brought it down in a perfect landing, which nevertheless created a small sandstorm, flattening the parched grass tufts and the few scraggy trees around.

But Robin was rather surprised to find that his hyperactive friend had refrained from jumping out of the cockpit as he usually did, and was, for once, actually condescending to wait for the steps to be rolled up to his plane. R.K. Kishen also remarked that he was happy to see Tiger behaving like a sensible chap, because they all had more than enough on their plates already with the visit of the Viceregal party. Where was the time to babysit any relatives with broken or sprained hands and legs in this heat?

'Surprise! surprise!' cried an all-too-familiar figure stepping out of the Fateypur Maharajah's personally piloted aeroplane.

The welcoming smiles were instantly wiped off the healthy bronzed faces of the Chattargadh Maharajah's heir and cousin.

'Robin, who invited *that* chap?' demanded Kishen.

'Does His Nutty Highness *wait* for invitations, Hukum?'

Since Tiger also emerged with a rather meaningful twinkle in his beaming almond eyes, they had no option except to welcome the unwanted Maharajah, notorious for creating international intrigues and protocol snags.

Slapping Robin on the back as he only half-heartedly made the customary feet-touching gesture, the Pisshengunj Maharajah said, 'Your aunts said I musn't go gatecrashing, specially when Viceroys are around. But I assured them that you would all be very happy to see me pay a flying visit to my ancestral home!'

'*Ateethi Devo Bhava* (Guests are Gods)!' intoned Robin, rolling his eyes and bowing low with folded hands.

Tiger stood back enjoying the farce as R.K. Kishen and his Nutty Uncle's White Russian Dewan stood arguing near the Rolls Royce which had come to fetch him. Nearby, their ADCs supervised the loading of their luggage in the Bedford lorry.

'Baron Tikemoffsky, you're the last man on earth to teach me protocol-shrotocol in my own country!'

'Really, Raj Kumar Saheb, would it be expecting too much to ask you to abide by international protocol procedures approved by the League of Nations, involving Heads of State? And the Imperial British Blue Book? And please don't tell me you haven't read it . . . .'

'Get to the point, old chap,' interposed the dyslexic Chattargadh Dewan.

'You are duty bound, for protocol reasons, to strike down that junior Maharajah's flag from your Rolls Royce, and fly the Pisshengunj flag instead. Otherwise, we'll not only report this breach of privilege to HE the Viceroy—who is a military man, as you know, and rather rigid about such things—but also impose economic sanctions against your State,' said Tikky.

'But we didn't expect Pisshengunj Durbar to land up here out of the sky, just like that,' protested Kishen, clicking his tongue in exasperation at this blatant blackmail. 'Therefore, nobody is carrying his flag-shlag.'

'I am, Raj Kumar Saheb,' said Tikky, pulling out from his coat pocket a small car pennant in the Pisshengunj State colours and crest.

It took Kishen some time to convince Ganpat Singh that he was neither joking nor making a frivolous request.

'But *how* can a car with only one metal flagstick fly *two* State flags at the same time, Raj Kumar Saab?'

Kishen heaved a deep sigh, and told the ADC to improvise something, since their State's *izzat* (respect) and well-being were at stake.

Ganpat Singh swore in sheer disgust. 'I should have become a magician before becoming ADC to Chattargadh Durbar! Whom do I obey? Yuvraj Saab says that Fateypur Durbar's flag stays exactly where it is, on this royal Rolls.'

By now there were three distinct groups on the uncomfortably warm airstrip waiting to get to the palace: Tiger, Robin, and Nutty; their ADCs; and the two arguing prime ministers of the two adjoining sister states. All these were being watched with considerable curiosity and relish by the various drivers, retainers, and ground maintenance staff.

'Absolute nonsense!' swore Nutty even before Tikky stopped speaking. 'How dare they suggest anything so humiliating? Maharajahs *don't* sit in follow cars! Thakur Ganpat Singhji may not have two flagpoles, but God gave him *two* hands. If I can't get precedence over my own sister's son, then I insist on being treated at par.'

Thakur Ganpat Singh stared at the Pisshengunj Maharajah, absolutely appalled by the latter's outrageous suggestion. R.K. Kishen began fiddling with his Ray Bans while Robin tried to pacify the ADC, requesting him to think of something that would help them out of the ridiculous impasse created by the abominably inconsiderate, uninvited guest who had landed on their heads. Tiger strolled off to examine some striped squirrels chattering at an aggressive magpie before irrepressible mirth choked him.

Chatting affably with Tiger, Robin drove his father's Rolls Royce through Chattargadh's busiest street with perfect élan. It wasn't the quickest or the only route from the airstrip to the palace. But Nutty's odious behaviour had triggered off the devilry lurking under the surface of every Rathor carrying Rao Jodhaji's genes. Nearly all the activity in the busy bazaar around Kote Gate came to a virtual halt as the cavalcade approached. Turbaned men in flapping dhotis frowned, then gestured. Word spread from camel riders to tonga drivers and bullock-cart *wallahs*. Boys began to laugh loudly, pointing fingers, and clapping as though some circus had come to their town. Shoppers jostled shopkeepers to see what the commotion on the road was about. Veiled women turned to peep, point, and giggle, calling to each other in the local dialect to 'look quickly', because they would never see anything like this again!

On the bonnet of their Maharajah's famous car sat his equally well-known ADC Thakur Gadbad Singhji, the Rolls

Royce's silver-lady logo between his legs like a saddle pommel, and his booted heels braced against the fender in a perfect horseman's stance. From his hands fluttered two shimmering pennants emblazoned with the royal crests of the Pisshengunj and Fateypur Maharajahs, who could clearly be seen seated inside.

The people playing croquet on the palace lawn were alerted to their impending arrival when the trumpet fanfare, drum rolls, and royal gun salute began.

Unable to contain her joyful excitement, Kitten cried, 'Ah, here comes Tiger Baapji at last!'

Maharajah Jai Singh strode towards the portico, accompanied by his grandson, Pat. Lady Dorothy drove the ball through the hoop, and continued to follow through on her advantage because she knew that there was enough time before Tiger got around to greeting her. Elinor made a moue, interrupting her other aunt, the Vicereine, in mid-sentence. Colonel CP gave a puzzled frown as the guns kept booming even after he'd definitely counted off the proper number. The Viceroy, Field Marshal Lord Axeminster, swivelled his lanky, loose-limbed frame westward to peer at the motorcade drawing up to the palace porch. For a full minute, he stared in perplexed bewilderment at what appeared to be one of the Maharajah's ADCs perched on the Maharajah's Rolls, holding up a couple of flag-like things rather gingerly by his fingertips—as though they were contaminated.

'I say, Reverse Gear, isn't that rather odd, what?'

Having perceived the Pisshengunj Maharajah claim precedence over the other one, who was, in fact, the only ruler invited to meet the Viceroy, the Resident gave a diplomatic rejoinder. 'What we might consider rather strange back home seems to be quite normal among these Maharajahs, Poozle.'

Kitten knit her thick black brows when she saw Tiger immediately latch on to Elinor, who seemed to have taken up permanent residence at the Chattargadh Residency, in spite of having a much more influential uncle to entertain her in Viceregal style elsewhere in India. But Tiger, used to being the irresistible playboy prince, had felt more challenged than piqued by Elinor's indifference at Ooty. He had immediately seized the heaven-sent opportunity to pursue her by accepting HH Chattargadh's invitation to come along and help entertain the Viceroy even if it was the wrong time of the year to be in the desert.

That the possibility of war in Europe could lead to his instant recall by His Majesty's Government had compelled the Viceroy (whom everyone called Battle Axe behind his back) to undertake a Viceregal tour of Chattargadh even in the hot month of May. Normally, May was the month meant for enjoying a well-earned rest in Simla among the Himalayan snow peaks and pines. But he was not going to allow anything to frustrate his determination to take home an Indian lion to match the stuffed African one gracing the Great Hall at Axe.

Jai Singh understood completely his guest's convoluted motives for coming to Chattargadh at this most inconvenient time. His arrival had turned things topsy turvy. It had come in the way of other more important things— like his favourite niece's marriage to his only nephew; the Prince of Wales' wedding to that Dutch Princess who was bringing him more colonies (and Burmah Shell oil) as part of her dowry; and the prestigious polo tournament for which he had to be in London before June 6 of this year of 1939.

Moreover, he hadn't expended his energy and juggled his resources to stand in his own drawing room, listening to that utterly uncalled-for argument with Tiger, who was like his own son. The Viceroy should have known better than to provoke that notoriously irreverent young man!

Rattling the ice cubes around in his whisky glass, the Viceroy continued: 'Really, Your Highness, His Majesty's Government doesn't approve of Maharajahs running wild all over Europe.'

'But gathering first-hand knowledge of the outside world can't be called running wild, y'know,' countered the Maharajah of Fateypur.

'Quite unnecessary, I should think,' continued the Viceroy in his loud parade-ground voice, which made the other people in the reasonably cool, softly lit, khus-scented drawing room draw nearer to enjoy the increasingly heated exchange.

'How else can we catch up with a rapidly changing world, Your Excellency?'

'By reading, listening to the radio, particularly the BBC, and watching newsreels, not films, Your Highness. What I object to is the financial aspect of all this flying around.'

The irrepressible Tiger waved an airy arm around the luxurious lavender, green, and off-white apartment full of foreign paintings, furniture, and bric-a-brac. 'But we don't mind giving Europe's economy a shot in the arm, old chap.'

Jai Singh and Nutty laughed outright, and even the Resident smiled as he sipped his drink.

But the Viceroy was not amused. 'Come, come, Tiger. D'you know what I'm getting at, Reverse Gear?'

'Not quite, Poozle,' said Gerald Redverse, more than the Viceroy's social equal as a British peer's son (he hadn't sprung from shady Irish stock) and a closer-than-liked connection through the marriage of their respective siblings, now Elinor's parents.

Wagging his finger in lieu of an officer's stick, Lord Axe said, 'Don't you see that the people can't go on paying for the gratification of their Maharajah's whims in this day and age!'

'Well, in my case, it's not the people, but the place that pays!' came the cheerful response.

The Viceroy looked to the Resident for clarification.

'HH Fateypur is merely referring to his coastal kingdom's three thousand-year-old gem, jewellery, and textile trade, which pays for everything,' explained Redverse.

'And which has turned Fateypur into a super-nannyfied welfare State,' scoffed the Pisshengunj Maharajah.

Jai Singh gave his uninvited upper riparian relative—with whom he had yet another score to settle for poisoning his daughter's mind with his rubbishy book—a wry smile. 'Which is a great deal better than merely letting it go to the dogs, Nutty!'

This sally made everyone, except Nutty, laugh. The Resident thought it a great pity that Dorothy and CP were both missing this drawing-room drama. It would have given them something new to talk about till the next rumpus inevitably took place in this crazy place. But he knew that the Maharajah's Military Secretary, R.K. Kishen, and Robin were all busy organising the next day's review of the State Forces. And the ladies would only be joining them for the formal banquet with the Viceregal party, and all the Chattargadh chiefs and officers much later in the evening.

'Coming back to the point, Tiger,' said the over-zealous Viceroy, 'diamonds aren't forever, y'know.'

'Obviously you haven't seen De Beers latest ad!' said Tiger in immediate response.

Nutty eyed his nephew with pronounced asperity. 'Do you think a Viceroy (who's also a Field Marshal) has the *time* to go around reading advertisements in women's magazines? We are talking about image projection . . . .'

'Precisely!' said the Viceroy as Maharajah Jai Singh exchanged a very significant 'Look who's talking!' glance with his Resident.

'And tradition,' added Nutty.

'Traditions aren't enough, Your Highnesses. You've got to modernise your States, and update your forms of government.'

Tiger blew smoke rings as he stood facing the Viceroy. 'What *form* of government does Your Excellency recommend? The fascist regime of Nazi Germany? The totalitarian dictatorship of Marxist Russia? The ineffective oligarchy of Republican France? The Mafia lobby feudalism of liberated North America? Or the defunct democracy of Great Britain?'

Maharajah Jai Singh gave Tiger a thumbs-up sign as Lord Axeminster sputtered. He had been completely unprepared for such a scathing denouncement.

Tiger's confidence had a great deal to do with his early training by his own sister Diamond, and her husband. Under the debonair playboy exterior, Tiger had an extraordinarily sharp and enquiring mind, a limitless energy, and a complete contempt for sham and sycophancy. The ability to combine cheerful levity with incongruously incisive political insights was one of Tiger's many endearingly paradoxical qualities.

'Really, Your Highness, what I had in mind was something more suited to your own native genius—local self-government, y'know.'

'Oh, you mean *Panchayat Raj*?' said the amiable young Maharajah of Fateypur. 'But we've always had that, except under the British Empire, which makes Collectors out of Kings, and Kings out of Collectors!'

The stadium was packed to capacity the next morning. Eager spectators, including young and old veiled women (most of them holding babies and small children), were keenly enjoying the rare treat of witnessing a Viceroy reviewing their State Forces with full military paraphernalia. The public also felt proud of their Baapji, Maharajah Jai

Singh, poised like an elegant equestrian statue, holding his drawn sword without a tremor in his hand, arm or back. The Maharajahs of Pisshengunj and Fateypur also sat their horses with practised ease, like true Rajputs. The Resident was distinguished by his feathered high hat and full diplomatic dress, which stood out among the row of mounted Military Secretaries and ADCs in uniform.

Redverse felt that the State Forces undoubtedly presented a picture of great martial beauty and efficiency. Colonel Claude-Poole silently congratulated himself, plus all the officers and men, for practising so hard to make everything go perfectly. If the truth were told, he had devoted himself just as much as the Maharajah to improving this army. Together, they had transformed it into a highly efficient fighting force, well equipped, and well seasoned by intensive training.

If the rumours about mobilisation repeated by the Viceroy's staff had any kernel of truth, what did the future hold for the Chattargadh troops and officers like himself.

Maharajah Jai Singh's heart swelled with pride as he watched the main units of his army marching past in review order. First came the Chattargadh Lancers—led by his heir-apparent, Robin—in their sky blue and gold tunics and turbans, their silvery lances and stirrups all glinting in the first sunbeams. The sound of hoofbeats, jingling harness, bits, and creaking saddle leather merged with the stirring martial music as the beautifully groomed horses, held in check by riders born to the saddle, filed past. But they were immediately overshadowed by the splendid Chattargadh Camel Corps, with Raj Kumar Kishen Singh at its head on the finest camel in the *risala*. Flaming orange turbans, gold-braided white tunics, polished muskets and long boots, white cowrie shell and scarlet silk-tasselled leather accoutrements, and monogrammed saddle cloths filled the parade ground. More than four hundred healthy, humped camels marched past with proud disdain, indifferent to the spectators and the dust raised by their padding feet.

Then, the Chattargadh Light Infantry, in khakhi uniforms and red turbans, entered the stadium with colours flying. It was followed by the brass and bagpipe bands playing tunefully. The musical ride by the camel-mounted Bijey Battery provided the grand finale to the military review. Each cannon was drawn by two pairs of camels performing the most intricate manoeuvres to music, including racing at a fast trot without falling out of step. They frequently cut into each other's path with only a foot or two to spare. The public cheered and cried out in admiration at every turn. The Viceregal party was also thoroughly impressed by this splendid show. Very few outsiders knew that these thoroughbred Marwari camels responded to music. In a fashion similar to the famed Austrian Lipizzaner horses, they also kept in step with the utmost precision as long as the band played a particular, familiar tune at a particular tempo.

On their ride to the Officers' Mess for breakfast, the Viceroy complimented the Maharajah. 'Really, Your Highness, you've got some of the most colourful State Forces in India, I say.'

'Thank you, Your Excellency. We also have one of the proudest war records, as I hope you'll bear in mind whenever the Allies need our soldiers to fight the fascist tide in Europe.'

The Viceroy inclined his head noncommittally, smiled, and turned to address a remark to the other Maharajahs riding alongside.

But to the great chagrin of this British soldier (who had seen much active service in the Household Cavalry permanently stationed at London), Lord Axeminster was appalled to find Tiger Fateypur flaunting shoulder pips identical to those of the Colonel of the famous Life Guards. 'Really, Your Highness, as an Oxbridge man rather cosy with our Royal family, I presume you do know that only *one* person in the world is entitled to wear the Guards' Colonel's pips.'

'Oh yes, Your Excellency. The King of England,' admitted Tiger.

'Then how do you explain this lese majesty?' the Viceroy demanded, pointing to Tiger's polished rank badges with his Field Marshal's baton.

'By my original oriental touches, Sir,' said Tiger, tongue-in-cheek.

Nutty glared at his nephew, but Jai Singh knew that young Tiger had worn that particular uniform just to needle the Viceroy.

On closer inspection, anyone could see that the heraldic device on the shoulder pips bore little resemblance to any British regimental crest.

The Maharajah of Pisshengunj sat cross-legged on the huge, black velvet-draped, Victorian brass bed, placed directly under the ceiling fan going full blast. He was vainly trying to dry off the perspiration pouring off his recently, ritually bathed torso. Except for the sacred *janeuw* (thread) slung across his chest, and the thick gold chain loaded with all the nine lucky gemstones, tantric talisman and charms he always wore to ward off evil and attain his dearest desires, his chest was bare. A *rudraksha mala* (beads) held between thumb and middle finger in the prescribed manner, lay in Nutty's lap on the folds of his saffron dhoti, which matched exactly the quilted saffron *puja* cap he wore over his curly locks, also in the prescribed manner.

Tiger moved restlessly around the bedroom while his uncle, instead of concentrating on his evening prayers, continued to lecture him.

'Stop prowling around, Tiger! You've ruined my concentration,' fumed Nutty. Mumbling a Sanskrit mantra, he demanded: 'Where was I?'

'Heavenward bound, I think!'

'On the Viceroy—*Om aiyeng Chow Cheem Choo hreem kleem phat Swaha*! . . . . It is pointless pretending to pray when you are standing there without paying attention to a word I'm saying. Why are you being so offensive to the Viceroy?'

'Because he puts me on the defensive every time he lectures us, *Hajoor*. And didn't their greatest General, Wellington, say that attack is the best form of defence?'

'You silly ass, don't you realise that Maharajahs can't afford to alienate Viceroys? Didn't your guardians teach you anything?' demanded HH Pisshengunj. He well knew where to lay the blame for all the gaps in Tiger's training.

In fact, Nutty had jockeyed very hard to get himself appointed guardian-cum-regent to his deceased sister's one and only son. But Sir Pratab's own kith and kin, particularly Jai Singh, had lobbied just as hard, convincing the Viceroy and the King Emperor to opt for the age-old Indian custom of granting guardianship of minors to the nearest male relation on the father's side.

'Speak for yourself, Uncle Nutty. I have no skeletons in *my* stately cupboard!' replied the Maharajah of Fateypur, continuing to stand and eat the bunch of grapes he had picked from the crystal fruit bowl provided in every guest room.

'I'm warning you, Tiger,' said Nutty. 'You never know when you'll need his signature on some piece of paper to further your own schemes, as every Maharajah discovers to his cost when its time to go, cap in hand, seeking favours from London.'

'But I don't have a scheming mind like yours, dear Uncle. And, I'll still be a Maharajah when he's no longer the Viceroy.' He leaned over to examine a rather splendid enamel and gold box lying on the counterpane near his uncle's knees. 'What's this? One of your latest *Jantar Mantar* (magic) stuff?'

The Pisshengunj Maharajah began telling his beads. 'Oh, it's just a little gift I'd promised Princess Kitten. Will you give it to her personally as soon as you see her? I want to make sure that it doesn't fall into any unlucky hands. You can see that mine are busy just now.'

The Princess, however, had gone off for her daily drive, accompanied by her governess and nephew. Instructing his ADC Phool Singh to inform him as soon as she returned, Tiger went to his own guest suite overlooking the main porch and lily pool, for a leisurely tub bath in lieu of the swim he usually enjoyed on summer evenings after schooling his horses, or playing tennis.

Informed of Kitten's return, Tiger decided to get the errand over with so that he and Robin could go off to pay a surprise call at the Residency. They knew that Elinor was going to be home alone that evening. And they didn't want Miss Sticking Plaster pestering them to take her along. Holding the enamelled gold gift box, Tiger greeted the Governess pleasantly, inquired after her family which lived in Bombay, and asked if she'd enjoyed her annual holiday away from the infantile Chattargadh brats. Kitten took immediate umbrage at being lumped with her nephew Pat, especially when she had been doing everything possible to seem grown up including draping herself in different saris several times a day all through HH Fateypur's visit.

'Ah, Kitten. I've been waiting for you,' began Tiger.

'You could have come with us to the Residency for tennis, and done the driving too, Hukum, instead of waiting here, doing nothing.'

'I really couldn't. One has to keep up appearances, you know, with an uncle here, and an uncle there, to say nothing of hostile Viceroys!' countered Tiger. 'But here's something to make you happy.'

Kitten eagerly accepted the box held out to her. She was watched by several curious eyes from nearby windows and corridors. 'What's in it?' demanded the Princess.

The Fateypur Maharajah shrugged with a quizzical expression on his handsome face. 'Some good luck charm, I was told.'

Kitten couldn't believe her good luck as she stood holding up the impressive double tiger-claw pendant suspended from a gold chain against her neck in front of the triple mirrors of her dressing table. It couldn't have been easy for Tiger Baapji to reveal his hand, she thought, when there were so many blood relations present, not to mention her father's well-known aversion to second marriages. But at long last, things were beginning to go her way. The absence of their extremely perceptive relatives, Aunt Diamond and Sir Pratab, had really helped. They were, thankfully, much too busy finalising the finer details of their own son's wedding to be held in Fateypur a few days later. They always kept an eye on everyone, and had, so far, scuttled all her attempts to fulfil her lifelong dream.

The Maharajah of Pisshengunj insisted on accompanying the Viceroy and Vicereine when Maharajah Jai Singh took them to visit the museum in one of the disused wings of the old Fort. The Resident, his wife, and R.K. Kishen also accompanied them for another *dekkho* of Chattargadh's famous treasures. They walked through a vaulted sandstone chamber into a spacious mosaic-floored courtyard around which ran deep shady verandahs, lined with hand-carved wooden chests, swings, and chairs. Several silver-embossed double doors led to the exhibition rooms crammed with sculpture and statues from abandoned ancient Harappan, Buddhist, Jain, and medieval Hindu towns and temples situated in the Chattargadh region. Jai Singh drew the Viceroy's attention to the swords and armour of his ancestors. Comparisons were made with Saracen steel and Spanish chain mail, said to be the finest in the medieval era. The Vicereine and Lady Dorothy discoursed knowledgeably about the silverware, lacquer work, brocade costumes and splendid jewellery, which they naturally found far more attractive and interesting than 'all those frightful weapons and things'.

'Really, Your Highness, I've seldom seen such exquisite enamelled gold and stone inlay work during our tours of other princely States,' the American born Vicereine said, gazing covetously at a particular necklace and identical emerald-and-pearl bracelets.

Maharajah Jai Singh bit his lower lip as he exchanged a significant glance with his cousin, Kishen. 'Your Excellency, allow me to present you these simple samples of local craftsmanship, which you've praised like a true connoisseur.'

His other cousin immediately seized the opportunity to cause friction between the Crown representative and HH Chattargadh, with whom he had so many scores to settle. 'I wouldn't be seen dead wearing such second-rate stuff, Lady Axeminster. Wait till you see the real treasures, which my brother has hidden out of sight.'

'Nutty, have you forgotten how often all of us have been looted in the last century?' countered Jai Singh.

But Nutty continued with a supercilious smile. 'Don't be so modest, my dear Bhai. Chattargadh's heirlooms are the envy of every other Rajput ruler, because our Fort has never been conquered or looted. Even the marauding Pathans, Afghans, Marathas, and other thugs didn't risk raiding this desert kingdom. So show us the real stuff, instead of wasting everybody's time on this show-cased rubbish.'

Pausing to replace the replica Mughal miniature in the alcove full of similar ivory paintings, the Viceroy began: 'Well, Your Highness? I'm sure you know that African antiques are a little hobby of mine, to which I've added Indian stuff since His Majesty's Government saw fit to send me here, instead of Canada. I do prefer the snow to the sand, you know.'

'Indeed, Your Excellency,' HH Chattargadh responded. 'And we're doing our bit just like Lord Curzon, and the Royal Asiatic Society, to make Indian art—not just yoga— more fashionable abroad.'

'You and your wife will be happy to know, Poozle, that HH Chattargadh has loaned some of the exhibits HH Pisshengunj so doggedly recalls, to the White House on Mrs Roosevelt's explicit request,' the quick-witted Resident intervened.

'Oh yes,' corroborated Lady Dorothy. 'Gerry and I spent hours convincing the Maharajah's museum management committee that anything lent to our Yankee allies would fetch us handsome dividends in the shape of technology transfers through Hollywood blockbusters!'

Maharajah Jai Singh was too good a host to leave anything to chance, especially when he had to take Viceroys hunting. He personally checked the four machans, and all the 375 magnum guns that were normally used for big game. He double checked to ensure that the *Shikar khana* in-charge had provided them with brand new imported cartridges, and gave the khakhi clad shikaris a word of praise before returning to the shooting lodge in time for lunch with his guests.

'*Shabash*, Ganpat Singhji. But please remember, everything must be perfectly timed, or I'll be disgraced in front of all our guests,' said the Maharajah, getting into his Shooting Chevy and preparing to drive off.

The ADC shut the convertible's door. 'Why do you worry, Baapji, when I'm your guaranteed sure shot?'

'Thakur Saab, Baapji means that you must synthesise

your actions with the Viceroy's when the lion comes on the kill,' Kishen cautioned him as he also got into the car. 'We can't afford any *gadbad* with our dear blood brother Maharajah Nut-Bolt Singhji around!'

'Raj Kumar Saab, you should know that my foolproof *bandobast* is famous all over the world!'

The machans, cunningly hidden among the branches of six huge banyan trees, were allotted in advance. Despite having to share his company with the Vicereine, Kitten revelled in her proximity to Tiger. The latter couldn't help envying his friend Robin, who had undoubtedly manipulated the shikar party's seating plans to ensure his own proximity to Elinor. But Lady Dorothy too was perched up there with them, and would surely prevent Robin from playing the oversolicitous host. In any case, everyone had to sit absolutely quiet, moving as little as possible so that the lion was not warned off the kill.

By one of those strange ecological quirks, Chattargadh was the only other region besides Junagadh with a forest full of lions. These had almost completely disappeared from other parts of India in the last century. Thanks to stringent protection from Chattargadh's Maharajahs, the open scrubland and evergreen *keekar* and *bargad* forests adjoining Gujarat boasted more than 70 lions. In the daytime heat, prides lay mostly in cover around the few waterholes and rain-fed nullahs. They emerged only at dusk, choosing to stalk stray goats, cattle or camels, which they preferred to chasing the much more fleet-footed sambar, cheetal, neelgai or wild boar.

Elinor dabbed her face with a cologne-scented handkerchief. She was rather uncomfortable on the wooden platform, which was hard, despite its velvety mattress. Worst still was the fact that there was scarcely place to change posture. Neither was there anything to lean on, except the Maharajah's son. So far, she had succeeded in maintaining a proper distance between herself and Robin, though he wasn't being half as presumptuous or persevering as Tiger Fateypur.

The cuffs of her turned-up trousers dug into Elinor's calf muscles, and she longed for a lounge chair. Her sleeveless linen blouse left her arms exposed to attack from flying gnats and other insects, although thankfully, there were no mosquitoes in the desert at this time of year. Her skin itched and burned dreadfully. The Maharajah had told her that this was the only time he permitted very special guests to shoot one or two lions, because they mated in October-November and had their cubs in January-February.

On Elinor's other side, Lady Dorothy sat gently fanning herself with the squashable cotton sunhat that no European lady in the tropics could do without.

Kitten, however, had perfected the art of sitting comfortably on machans. One never knew how long one would have to stay perched quietly before anyone shot anything. A printed full-sleeved voile shirt tucked into baggy, elastic-waisted fawn pants protected her from insects, ants and spiders. Her hair was neatly tucked away by a hairnet to keep it from blowing into anybody's face in the confined space everyone had to share. Kitten's special affinity with this forest preserve was enhanced that evening by Tiger Baapji's within-touching-distance presence. She was also glad that her father had forbidden the usual shikar haaka here, so that the lions had a sporting chance. They could keep to cover if they scented man, or could make a feeding foray right under their guns. She sat stock still, listening to the wind song blowing through the trees, and the last hooting calls of the local herdsmen driving their goats and cattle home to safety behind the high thornbush stockades. Roosting partridges, parrots, peacocks, pigeons, mynas, crows, and other birds also gave their typical territorial cries before settling down for the night. As the blazing, golden-orange and indigo-streaked desert sky darkened, several crickets and cicadas broke the silence. Now she could distinctly spy the cooking fires of nearby Rebari and Raathi villages twinkling beyond the trees.

Suddenly, Kitten's attention was diverted to the Vicereine who had begun cringing, moaning, and fluttering her chiffon scarf ineffectually while clutching Tiger's arm. The Fateypur Maharajah knew from long experience what that indicated. Running his eyes over her exposed arms, neck and fair freckled bosom, he quickly brushed away the harmless moth giving her the heebie-jeebies. Nothing could convince these *firang* memsahebs that in India, you needed to cover up as much as possible to avoid discomfort.

Maharajah Jai Singh grew alert as soon as the male buffalo calf, tethered to a stunted tree just opposite their machan, started snorting, lowing, leaping with fright, and desperately trying to break its rope and flee from death. The Viceroy clutched his gun, and hoped that the fast fading twilight would allow him an accurate shot. He knew there would be no chance of a second shot if he muffed the first one. At the other edge of their machan, Nutty Pisshengunj craned his neck from side to side in his keenness to be the first to spot the lion, since it had already been clearly understood that no one except the Viceroy was permitted to bag it.

Jai Singh could virtually smell the lion before it broke cover, making all the monkeys, birds, and deer in the vicinity nervous and noisy. The Maharajah alerted the Viceroy as the silently padding lion took one graceful leap to bring down its helpless prey. His entire body tensing with expectation, Field Marshal Lord Axeminster brought the heavy gun up to his shoulder, took careful aim and pressed the trigger.

To his utter consternation, it simply refused to fire.

Yet, everyone also heard the instantaneous loud *disshum-*

bang-slam which made the lion fall dead, and the buffalo stay miraculously alive. The astounded Viceroy cast a puzzled eye over his gun—which hadn't fired because somehow unlocking the safety catch had completely slipped his mind—and then at HH Chattargadh, who certainly knew how to make excellent provision for all contingencies! And before he know it, the great hunt was over.

Simultaneous cries of 'Good shot, Sir!' 'Well done, Poozle!' and 'Darling, I'm so glad we've got our pair at last!' greeted him. But, while everyone else in the shikar party gathered around to congratulate the Viceroy as soon as they had scrambled down from the machans, the Pisshengunj Maharajah gave a hoot of derisive laughter. Grabbing Ganpat Singh by the arm while several shikaris were arranging the lion to Colonel CP's satisfaction for the obligatory photographs, Nutty announced: 'My dear Bhai, the secret of your sure-shot, foolproof *bandobast* is right here! And I'm going to enjoy letting *this* cat out of the bag . . . .'

However, before he could finish his sentence, Kitten intervened.

'Nutty Uncle,' she whispered with sweet menace. 'One word more, and the secret of *your* ready-gutted, charcoal-stuffed ducks out of the pantry will be all over the world. And, with picture proofs!'

Soon after, flash bulbs popped as the Maharajah's Military Secretary took several shots of the Viceroy posing proudly with his wife and host beside a lion he knew he hadn't shot.

Just as Lady Dorothy and Elinor joined the Resident and his friend CP for a leisurely breakfast the following morning, the Residency chowkidar appeared in the dining room carrying a large brocade-wrapped packet on a massive silver salver.

'Yes, Bhoot Nath?' said Redverse, breaking off a discussion with Colonel CP about the complicated and crazy arrangements Maharajahs invariably made to entertain Viceroys. His wife had been equally determined to lay on something memorable, in addition to the dinner party they were holding that evening for the Viceregal party and all the Maharajahs. And, his niece had insisted that she couldn't possibly leave Chattargadh with her more eminent uncle and aunt without seeing its famous fire dance.

The elderly, crimson-turbaned chowkidar bowed with a beaming smile. 'Urgent messenger from the Palace with something, Hajoor.'

'Put it on my writing table, will you,' said the Resident, eating a slice of papaya.

But Bhoot Nath shook his head from side to side with the confident impertinence of irreplaceable retainers. 'Uunhun. This is only for the eyes of the two memsaab-*log*. That ADC told Bhoot Nath before going back to the Palace, which is so busy dancing round the Lat Saab!'

'Aren't we all!' quipped Dorothy. Aware that Elinor at least shared her ferocious curiosity, she began unwrapping the brocade bundle as soon as the door closed behind the chowkidar. Inside it were two identical, flat velvet boxes with gilt clasps. Their gasps of pleasure forced the two men to also focus their attention on the exquisite Rajput-style diamond and pearl necklaces in their hands.

The Resident's eyes narrowed as he looked down his long patrician nose at the shimmering jewels in their intricate antique setting. 'My dear Dorothy, you can't possibly keep those, y'know.'

'I say, Uncle Gerry, don't be such a spoilsport,' protested Elinor. Not that she needed more stuff to add to her king's ransom in jewellery. But she wasn't going to part with any memento from this wonderful Maharajah, no matter what her stodgily upright uncle said.

'Dash it, Reverse Gear, you can't go around humiliating Maharajahs by sending their gifts back, y'know!' added the Maharajah's Military Secretary, abandoning his omelette to admire the jewellery thrust under his nose.

Redverse sat irresolutely behind the toast rack as he mulled over this unnecessary dilemma. 'I really can't see why such·a proper Prince has gone and done something so improper.'

'Improper my foot!' swore the other Englishman. 'This is merely our Maharajah's little way of thanking you and Dorothy for supporting him so staunchly while His Nutty Highness constantly tries to undermine him with the Viceroy.'

That evening, the willowy auburn-haired Lady Dorothy and her beautiful blue-eyed niece, decided to wear their new necklaces. Their fashionable spaghetti-strapped lace dresses in ivory and peach were perfect for both the occasion and the hot weather. Although Dorothy had agreed in principle with the Maharani to keep the party as informal as possible (because 'it would be such a change for everyone'), she knew from years of experience in India that such simplicity was incompatible with visiting Viceroys. Added to this were the three Maharajahs, (one utterly Nutty one!) and their entourage. Where was the scope for 'just a moonlight picnic on the lawn'?

True to expectations, the Maharani and her daughter arrived, looking regal in their shimmering Rajput *poshaks*, and jewelled from head to toe. The Maharajahs and their staff all sported turbans pinned with gem-encrusted aigrettes and spotless white *bandhgala* jackets with diamond and enamelled gold buttons. The British contingent barely passed muster in black ties and dinner jackets, and mess kits.

Acclimatised to Chattargadh over the past four months,

Lady Dorothy kept her fingers crossed throughout dinner, fervently hoping and praying that no sudden sandstorm would ruin the alfresco party.

Bright moonlight and several fat, foot-high candles, and the firepit glowing on the especially laid sand floor, made it easy for everyone to move around without bumping into each other. But Kitten still managed to do so. She was so often in Tiger's vicinity that the Maharajah of Pisshengunj assured his brother-in-law, Koodsu Rao Saheb, that everything was moving along splendidly towards their ultimate revenge on father and daughter, provided, of course, the Resident's niece continued to stay out of the picture. As the two girls stood exchanging opinions and giggling frequently, Nutty could not help remarking upon the strange similarity between the two. They matched each other in height and build, and in that indefinable self-confident stance that came naturally to both. The only difference was that Kitten was a black-haired Indian Princess, and Elinor, a typical golden-haired British aristocrat.

The Resident and his wife concentrated on the two Dewans after settling their chief guests down to watch the promised entertainment. Colonel CP made sure that all the ADCs and ladies-in-waiting had double helpings of the excellent hand-churned mango ice cream. They determinedly ignored all the turbaned heads, veiled faces, and eager-eyed children peering through the densely planted canna, oleander and henna hedges separating the Residency's front garden from its kitchen yard. They were aware that the Lat Saheb's presence, along with their own Maharajah and Maharani, was a not-to-be-missed, once-in-a-lifetime occasion for them also.

Maharajah Jai Singh chatted effortlessly with the Vicereine (displaying a shimmering cleavage) while they sipped iced after-dinner liqueurs in their hostess's prized Waterford stemware. The Viceroy was busy telling Maharani

Padmini that all Germans were confirmed kleptomaniacs because they hadn't a clue about respecting another chap's personal property.

'. . . including borders, which are absolutely concrete and can't be moved around y'know, no matter what that Hitler chap says about lend-lease and *Lebensraum*,' he concluded in disgust.

Well informed and well travelled, thanks to her peripatetic polo-playing husband, Padmini politely said she'd heard that the former was an American invention, like chewing gum.

Her attention divided between the amazing fire dance—which had just begun after the Siddh Nath clan chief finished invoking his Deity—and the Maharajah, whom she found more fascinating with each passing day, Elinor kept fingering her necklace.

Kitten · had always wanted to join the dancers striding with such superb self-confidence over the blazing coals. But their chief had invariably protested that the secret mantras and methods invoked could only be imparted to blood brothers. Moreover, her entire family had vetoed all her brainwaves about blood pacts on the spot. But she was always thrilled by the spine-tingling energy of the finely synchronised acrobatic leaps that formed the fire dance's core whenever she watched it. The tambourine, cymbal, and flute players urged them on with double-quick rhythms into more complex steps and twirls until everyone began clapping and congratulating their stunning performance.

As soon as Robin was unobtrusively summoned to take his father's place beside Lady Axeminster, Tiger moved close enough to inhale Elinor's expensive perfume. 'You're looking absolutely magnificent tonight.'

'Anyone wearing a king's ransom would be!' smiled Elinor, with an unintentionally provocative glance as she touched her lovely necklace.

Immensely pleased by her reaction, Tiger threw her a flying kiss. 'Come on, Elinor. It's you! Not those lifeless gems, which aren't good enough for you.'

But the British girl swore he would never know what they meant to her. She was trying her best to move towards HH Chattargadh while trying to cope coolly with such blatant flirting.

'That's nothing,' continued Tiger. 'I'll have Cartier design something special just for you.'

But Elinor had already moved away. And, the Maharajah of Fateypur was quite put out to find that she had been replaced by Kitten who was joyfully crying 'Promise!' as she clutched his arm.

Later, while thanking the Chattargadh Maharajah and Maharani for breaking tradition and for once accepting, instead of dispensing, hospitality, the Resident's wife added, 'Really, Your Highness, I don't know how to thank you for such princely generosity.'

Floating up alongside her aunt, Elinor too beamed a beatific smile at the graciously demurring Maharajah.

'Quite uncalled for, if I might say so, Your Highness,' said the Resident, adding his little bit.

Jai Singh was thoroughly puzzled by all this uncalled-for effusiveness. However, Dorothy continued to insist that although nobody wanted to embarrass him, they had to thank him properly for the beautiful necklaces which they would always treasure.

A quizzical glance and outright laughter from his wife drew the Maharajah's attention to Tiger, who was once more hovering around Elinor. It was then that HH Chattargadh got the true picture. 'You're thanking the wrong chap,' he said immediately.

'Really, Your Highness. The messenger *did* come from your palace, didn't he?' asked Lady Dorothy.

Thoroughly enjoying the joke, Jai Singh tilted his

magnificently turbaned head closer to the Englishwomen.
'But did neither of you bother to find out which Maharajah
had sent him?'

Elinor immediately protested that there could only be
ONE . . .

'Oh, no, my dear girl,' countered Jai Singh. 'You can
count three right here, and we're all in the same palace,
although it belongs to me. But; taking false credit is really
not my style.'

This obvious dig at the Viceroy, who had only the day
before coolly claimed a trophy lion shot by the Maharajah's
henchman, had them all laughing.

London Escapades

Maharajah Jai Singh paid no attention whatsoever to his Resident's advice about avoiding areas bound to be congested by a heavier-than-usual influx of visitors swamping London that week, thanks to the Royal wedding. He insisted on sticking to his usually preferred, much longer route back to the Ritz. But just as the chauffeured Bentley hired for his visit turned down the Mall towards Buckingham Palace, he found the road blocked by scarlet-coated guardsmen with their distinctive bearskin headgear, marching to the strains of martial music. Behind them rode the massed mounted bands of the Household Cavalry and the Guards Division, rehearsing, no doubt, for the forthcoming occasion.

Brightly polished helmets, staffs, and instruments gleamed. The sound of drums, fifes, trumpets, and bagpipes merged with the metallic clatter of horseshoes on the black tarmac, virtually muffling other city noises, including the excited babble of comments and chatter in several languages from the groups of men, women, and children crowding Victoria Memorial and the Palace's enormous iron gates. Today they could watch this additional free show besides the regular 11.30 a.m. Changing of the Guard. All of them were dead keen to catch a lucky glimpse of the British King or Queen, or any of the foreign crowns present in London for what all the newspapers and magazines had so vulgarly termed as the Merger Match of the century.

Redverse glanced at his watch, knowing from past experience that they would be stuck here till the guards rode back to the barracks. They were on rather a tight schedule, with a hundred things to take care of. But it was never any use expostulating with this Maharajah, as the International Polo Federation bigwigs had found when they had tried to tell him that 'having *two* Englishmen on the Indian team is hardly cricket, Your Highness.' Promptly reading out the names of all the Argentine, American, and German professionals who made up the British and French teams, HH Chattargadh advised the committee to forget about nationality, or nobody would be fielding any teams worth watching. Didn't they want to turn polo into a popular spectator sport, like football?

The Maharajah and the Resident were both relieved when the road finally opened to normal traffic. But, before their car could inch forward through the crowded circle, Gerald Redverse spotted an amazing procession which, once again, had encouraged everyone to stop and stare. A caparisoned elephant carrying a resplendent regal figure, preceded by camels ridden by saffron-turbaned retainers beating huge kettledrums, and Rajput horsemen flaunting historic standards, gold-handled peacock feathers, and other insignia of royalty dating back to Vedic times, wheeled smartly into the Palace.

'Really, Your Highness! Why on earth is the Maharawal Saheb of Dudu riding into the Palace through the Sovereign's gate with beating drums and flying banners?' exclaimed the thoroughly astounded and disapproving Englishman.

Jai Singh leaned forward to glance out of the window of the Bentley just in time to catch sight of his venerable

father-in-law acknowledging the sentry's salute with a
gracious inclination of his leonine head. 'Mr Redverse, he's
only exercising his treaty rights vis-à-vis the Paramount
Power. I confess though, that he didn't say a word to any
of us about a Royal invitation to England when we
collected at Buggery recently for his granddaughter's
wedding to my nephew.'

Redverse turned his suntanned face to give the
Maharajah a wry smile. 'Indeed, Your Highness, the Dudu
Maharawal is full of surprises. But that's part of his charm,
wouldn't you say?'

Major Thomas nearly had a giddy fit when he found
himself confronting the fiercely moustached, bearded and
turbaned Indian prince with his jewelled sword and dagger.
No one had dared disarm Maharawal Bakhat Singh of
Dudu, even though it was absolutely *verboten* to enter the
Sovereign's residence bearing arms. Evidently, this was not
one of those foreign rajahs one took lightly, or fobbed off
with tea with the Queen Mother. He correctly surmised
that one look at this formidable personality who had arrived
in such style—with ADCs flashing a handwritten invitation
from His Majesty—had been enough for all those idlers in
the Equerries Room to let Tommy-Rot deal with this
unprecedented situation.

'Welcome to England, Your Highness. Their Majesties
and my Royal master will be delighted at this unexpected
pleasure.'

Instead of shaking hands, Lord Rama's direct descendent
graciously folded his palms. 'Ram Ram, Major Saab.
Everything all right here?'

'First rate, Your Highness.'

The chief equerry to the Prince of Wales conducted the
Maharawal to an ornate red damask sofa in the antechamber
where debutantes usually fussed around with their feathers
and trains before being presented at Court.

While the Maharawal commented on the weather which he hadn't expected to find so bright and sunny in this country renowned for its sudden showers, several Dudu retainers staggered into the chamber, lugging enormous silver jars similar to those Major Thomas remembered seeing in the Arabian Nights pantomimes he'd enjoyed as a schoolboy.

The Englishman cleared his throat. 'Ahem. Huh—are those things meant to be gifts for His Royal Highness?'

'No no, Major Saab,' the Indian ruler reassured him. 'That's only my supply of drinking water. The Prince's wedding gifts will be unpacked later.'

Vastly relieved, Major Thomas offered him some tea. A Palace butler immediately appeared with a monogrammed silver tea service, and a plate of those special biscuits usually reserved for the Queen's favoured horses and hounds. Deftly pouring and passing the old Maharawal a cup of tea with plenty of milk and sugar, the Prince's equerry enquired: 'Your Highness, may I ask where you'll be staying?'

With perfect sang-froid Bakhat Singh replied, 'Here only.'

Completely taken aback, he still tried to maintain the tactful attitude drilled into him by all the Foreign Office *wallahs* popping in and out to sort out the seating lists and stabling for everyone according to the *Almanach de Gotha*. 'Really, Your Highness, I don't think that His Majesty actually expects any of the visiting Maharajahs to stay at Buckingham Palace, y'know...' began Tommy-Rot.

But the splendid old Maharawal, continuing to enjoy his biscuit dunked in tea, said with irrefutable logic, 'But natural, Major Saab. Where else will they make me stay? Do you think, if I invited your King or Queen to my State for my son's wedding, I'd allow them to stay in some hotel-shotel?'

The Vicereine was in raptures over their reception at the Drawing Room that evening as she chaperoned her friend's daughter—entrusted to her for entrée into haute European circles via the London season—back to their hotel to discard the ostrich plumes, fans, trains, and tiaras before going on to that new nightclub, where such things only got in the way. Both the American ladies wore enough diamonds to stock a shop window, though Honey Moneykurl's pampered patina needed no extra adornment. Lady Axeminster recalled her own presentation nearly thirty years ago as Honey chattered animatedly about what the King, and several other Royal personages, had said to her.

As they walked up the curving carpeted staircase to their adjoining first floor suites, her ladyship regretted the fact that the coming-out ball one *always* held for every debutante couldn't take place at Axeminster House, which had been leased out for five years. She hadn't had the foggiest idea that after firing off their own two daughters so successfully, Poozle would *want* to leave India. They would simply have to make do with the Cosmic hotel ballroom because those with more cachet were booked solid till July.

Suddenly, Honey gave a most unladylike loud screech and hiked her white silk gown right up to her knees. She also hurriedly began hauling in her trailing train. At the same instant, Lady Axeminster felt something hot and soapy soaking her stockings right through her high-heeled satin pumps. She looked around.

It was exactly as she suspected. There was enough bathwater gushing down the stairs to ruin their brand new gowns. And shoes. But before she could open her mouth to demand explanations from those fatheads in the lobby below, two dripping wet St. Bernards nearly knocked her over as they dashed downstairs, with their master brandishing a bath towel in hot pursuit.

Of course, she recognised him.

Her hazel eyes bulging as she leaned against the bannister, Honey demanded: 'Has the management gone bonkers?'

'It must have, dear child, or they wouldn't have had that doggone Indian Maharajah staying here right alongside people like US!'

Summoned to dine with his uncle that evening, Tiger Fateypur arrived at the Cosmic accompanied by Colonel Claude-Poole, whom HH Pisshengunj had been cajoling with bribes and threats to swap places with him. Since R.K. Kishen was too ill in India to play any games, Nutty wanted to be the third Maharajah on the Indian polo team, and CP to become a mere reserve in the Coronation Cup finals. The two were just in time to witness the mayhem caused in the hotel lobby by several persons engaged in a war of words over his Nutty uncle's dogs. The latter's faithful henchmen, Baron Tikemoffsky and Koodsu Rao Saheb, were still trying to collar and leash those unruly animals while they blamed each other for the bath-time fiasco, completely oblivious to the objections raised by the black-tie and ball-gown brigade who were used to an altogether quieter Cosmic as their London pied à terre. But Sonny and Bunny kept tearing around the grand piano in the foyer, playfully butting the Russian baron and the Rajput chief who were trying to catch them. Grumbling waiters and grinning bellhops were busy clearing up the debris of broken crockery, splattered food, and overturned pot plants littering the place.

The harassed hotel manager looked distastefully at the mess at his feet, mentally cursing himself for forgetting to invoke the hotelier's invaluable 'Terribly sorry, but we're *absolutely* full!' clause, especially applicable to foreigners (travelling with large entourages and utterly untrained pets) who wanted entire floors sealed off for their exclusive use. 'Really, Your Highness, the ruined carpets don't matter too much. But we can't let your mad dogs annoy our other guests.'

Quickly taking advantage of the reinforcements provided by his nephew and the well-known British officer from back

home, the Maharajah of Pisshengunj cried, 'Did you all
hear that? This man has labelled me!'

'Libelled, Your Highness,' Colonel CP corrected.

'Say what you like, Colonel Clod-Pole. But this man will
be really sorry he got tangled up with me and cast
aspersions on my dogs, who are saner than most of us
standing here!' swore Nutty.

The indignant Vicereine insisted that the Pisshengunj
Maharajah's dogs be removed immediately to the nearest
kennels before they shattered her nerves, and did grievous
bodily harm to the other guests and hotel staff. When
Nutty dared anyone to try laying a hand on his pets, Lady
Axeminster asked HH to kindly produce their quarantine
certificates right away, unless he wished to have this matter
taken up by the Viceroy, who was just around the corner,
waiting to be picked up as usual with the Secretary of State
for India. The Maharajah of Pisshengunj informed her
ladyship that since he too enjoyed diplomatic immunity
throughout the British Empire, there was no question of
putting anyone travelling with him through any
inconvenience like quarantine-shorentine.

'Ask them!' continued Nutty, pointing his finger at Tiger
and CP. 'Haven't *they* brought shiploads of polo ponies to
England from all sorts of places, without anyone ever trying
to stop them?'

But even Tiger's charmingly rendered apology refused to
budge the disgruntled Vicereine, who was used to having
her tiniest whims fulfilled wherever she went. Lady Axeminster
remained adamant about having the dogs removed from the
hotel premises. The Maharajah of Pisshengunj was in a
quandary, because it was against his Rajput dharma to act in
such an unchivalrous, disobliging manner when any female,
let alone the Crown Representative's wife, made such an
impassioned demand. But in this case, animal rights
triumphed over womens' rights. He simply couldn't send his

darling dumb babies off to suffer untold hardship and neglect in some foreign kennel. And he couldn't move out as a goodwill gesture either, because all the hotels where he preferred staying, like the Savoy, Ritz, Claridges, and even the Carlton were fully booked due to all the people crowding the city for the Royal wedding, various Imperial conferences, and other fashionable events.

Heartily bored by her chaperone's refusal to terminate this silly wrangle, Honey demanded an introduction to the frightfully dishy young man everyone else seemed to know so well.

'Darling, he's just another of those married Indian Maharajahs, so we're not wasting our time on him!' hissed Her Excellency.

CP too made a manful effort to defuse the situation. 'Really, Your Highness, I'm sure this little misunderstanding can be resolved by—by . . .'

'Buy! That's right, Colonel CP!' cried Nutty, snapping his fingers. 'I will buy up this hotel just now. And then let me see who's going to throw whom out!'

The Manager groaned. The Vicereine shut her eyes, took a deep breath, and exhaled with great exasperation. Honey chuckled mirthfully at this extravagant announcement. But knowing this Maharajah rather well, Colonel Claude-Poole protested that this was hardly the time to invest in European property.

'Come on, Uncle Nutty. The owner may not want to sell,' added Tiger.

HH Pisshengunj gave a derisive snort. 'Tiger, when will you learn that everybody sells if the price is right? And specially if the buyer happens to be a determined Rajput!'

The next day, several publications, including *The Financial Times* duly recorded the acquisition of this London landmark for an astronomical sum by an Indian Maharajah for the sole purpose of housing his dogs. The *Mirror's* front page story also carried a picture of the hotel, which seemed to have been renamed the COMIC.

When Tiger regaled their aunt Diamond and her parents with the true story about HH Pisshengunj's latest venture, Kitten's ready laughter pealed out. She insisted on going to see the sign immediately, before someone brought the missing S to their Nutty uncle's notice. 'Then he'll have it put back.' But her cousin Arjun assured her that there was no need to skip the more-sumptuous-than-usual Savoy Grill lunch they'd just begun, because they'd already taken care of those trade union *wallahs* who did neon signs and stuff. His bride Ratna looked a little flushed, and even prettier than usual, as Arjun continued playing footsie with her throughout the meal.

Maharajah Jai Singh tried to figure out why anyone would sell off such a prize Park Lane property, while Tiger recounted other amusing incidents involving other visiting Maharajahs. He told them why Dudu Durbar had been singled out for such special treatment. For the Sailor King had confessed to his staff that while the Jodhpur Regent might have led the cavalry charge at Haifa, 'THIS was the chap who'd fished us out of that crocodile-infested river when our dinghy overturned during that state visit back in . . . .? Never mind.' And since Lord Rama's descendents never attended other people's coronations or durbars, His Majesty had thought it more appropriate to invite him to the Prince's wedding, without actually expecting him to attend.

But Dudu Durbar did not know this. So what if he expected to stay? Surely there was room for one more guest at the Palace!

Giving Maharani Padmini one of those disarming grins after hoping that he hadn't triggered Maharajah Jai Singh's C-R-O-C-K allergy, Tiger continued: 'And when Her Majesty kindly buttered his muffins yesterday at tea time, guess what Maharawal Saab said? "You have buttered me up, dear Queen, now let me milk you!"

The others were considerably amused, but Her Highness Chattargadh protested that he'd made all this up just to tease her. Tiger teased her even more by a meaningful shrug and sidelong glance, swearing that he wasn't the only witness around. HH Chattargadh had also been invited to the Palace, though whether it was to entertain his father-in-law or the Queen, was anybody's guess.

'I would have given anything to see the King's face when Grandfather said that!' cried Kitten, recalling her grandfather's propensity for enraging the British with his unintended but inevitably maddening misuse of the English language.

'The Prince of Wales had the presence of mind to put the milk jug in his hands immediately,' concluded Tiger.

Kitten blessed her cousin Arjun's determination to show his bride Europe in style, for this enhanced her own enjoyment of their first foreign trip. Not only did Tiger Baapji frequently accompany them on their daily outings, but she was also spared the stricter chaperonage of her mother and aunt by Ratna's elevation to a position of responsibility through marriage. She was now considered fit to escort Kitten on jaunts around the city, without a governess or ADC tagging along. London became a continuous source of splendid shopping and sightseeing delights for the two princesses. Even entering and leaving shops and restaurants alone was a heady, new experience for both of them. They couldn't imagine being allowed to do so in India. Like so many other little things, it gave Kitten in particular her first taste of freedom.

Kitten was most impressed by the total absence of litter and all quadrupeds in the areas they visited to meet various London-based relatives and acquaintances. She wished that some social reformer backed by *force majeure* would put all the cattle, dogs, and donkeys roaming every Indian street, back where they belonged. Walking through the noisy, pulsating streets was a pleasant experience because of the organised manner in which buses, cars, trams, motor cycles, and even cyclists moved along without endangering pedestrians, under the watchful eye of a perfectly-willing-to-help Bobby's directions. There were plenty of striped awnings for people to duck under if it got too warm and sunny, or started pouring all of a sudden. There were window boxes everywhere, spilling over with summer flowers usually called winter annuals in India. Even strolling through Hyde Park or St. James's in the swirling fog (which followed London's frequent thunder showers) was quite an adventure for her and Ratna, for they absolutely refused to stay cooped indoors merely chatting or listening to the radio. Bursting with vitality and curiosity, the two seventeen-year-old girls were determined to see everything they had heard and read about. However, Kitten was frankly disappointed by the narrow river Thames, which simply didn't measure up to the historic hub of imperial shipping and hair-raising adventures described by so many of the British writers she had read.

She managed to see several Oscar Wilde, Shakespeare, and Shaw plays being staged in the West End theatres, every single ballet performance at the Royal Opera House, and some of the musicals, murder mysteries, and drawing-room farces everyone talked about. Once, she even dragged her honeymooning cousins to two shows on the same evening. She also broke her self-imposed resolve to wait and see the most popular Hollywood films only when they came to their own Indian city cinemas months later.

Since the Chattargadh and Fateypur families were rather popular in British sporting circles, they were invited to all sorts of interesting events. They were there at the dinner party at which the Marchioness of Dufferin gave Oswald

Mosley a black eye when he tried to make a pass at her, and at Lords where the Aussies played better cricket than the British. They also attended a party held by the Rumanian ex-queen Olga, cousin to the Windsors, Romanovs, Hapsburgs, and Bourbons. She always made it a point to include her son Crown Prince Rudolf's particular friends Tiger and Arjun Fateypur at all her rumbustious evenings where the fun began after midnight. Lady Dorothy and Elinor Redverse did their bit to point Kitten and Ratna in the right direction, sharing shopping secrets and information about the plays and shows they had enjoyed, and the places with the best jazz bands. For Maharajah Jai Singh had very generously flown the two British ladies back to England in his chartered plane, along with his team-mates, Redverse and CP. The gesture had delighted Dorothy with the prospect of seeing her sons again so soon after packing them off to boarding school; and Elinor with the opportunity of sharing the same confined space with the Maharajah for a few more precious hours while flying from Karachi to Cairo for refuelling, and then on to London without another stop.

When senior family members had other things to do, Kitten and Ratna often joined other wealthy women wearing cashmere twin sets, pearls, and scarves tied under their chins like the Queen, strolling through the wonderfully quaint little shops lining Oxford Street, Bond Street, Regent Street, and Kensington. They found famous stores like Harrods, Fortnum, Rigby and Peller, and the White House a treat in themselves. Discreet saleswomen conducted them over floors full of exquisite fripperies and a profusion of tempting things they simply had to buy. They wandered from one inviting window display to another, buying just the right gifts for relations and friends back home. Generous charge accounts, allowances and cash presents from all their relations and elders, including HH

Pisshengunj, allowed them to splurge on Penhaligon's fragrances in scrumptious silver flasks; enamelled gold hairbrushes, handmirrors and trinket boxes which replaced their childish, old-silver, monogrammed ones; quantities of lacy lingerie and nightgowns; perfumes and bath salts in cut-glass bottles; boxes of dusting powder with huge swansdown puffs; jewelled compacts and the latest shades of lipsticks and nail polish from Yardley, Elizabeth Arden, and Revlon; the trendiest shoes, sandals, and extra-soft riding boots; and lots and lots of silk scarves, handbags, monogrammed lace handkerchiefs, slacks and sweaters, perfectly tailored coats, French chiffon saris, porcelain figurines, brooches, and charm bracelets.

They accompanied Maharani Padmini, who loved painting, to the National Gallery and the Tate to see the Wallace Collection; and Princess Diamond to Christie's and Sotheby's. Colonel Claude-Poole got roped in to escort them around the Tower and Windsor Castle. He told Kitten it wasn't fair to compare them to those monstrous Rajput forts back home, 'because Britain isn't such a big country, y'know.' One day, Elinor took the two cousins to Foyle's book store at Charing Cross. Kitten was so engrossed in browsing through the millions of books, maps, and prints displayed that she lost track of time. She had to be literally dragged back to the Ritz for a reviving cup of tea, where they were just in time to see Maharajah Jai Singh driving off in style from the Picadilly entrance for some investiture ceremony; and for Maharajah Tiger Fateypur to insist that they all accompany him and Arjun to the new Noel Coward comedy opening that night at the Dolphin because he had booked a box.

There was no need for the Maharajahs of Fateypur or Chattargadh to own a box at Ascot. They invariably had special invitations (and the badges giving them entrée) to the Royal Enclosure for the entire week, through the kind courtesy of HM the Queen, and HRH the Prince of Wales. On Gold Cup Day, the craggy Maharawal was there too, undaunted by the sea of top hats, elaborate frocks, and bonnets surrounding his Royal hosts. Chatting affably with the Aga Khan and Sir Pratab, he confessed he'd never betted before, and asked their advice on which horses to back.

Still miffed by their refusal to swap places with him, Nutty ignored the Resident and Colonel CP, who were being congratulated (alongside Maharajah Jai Singh and Tiger) on their phenomenal 7-goal victory over the American team at Smith's Lawn in Windsor Great Park the evening before. Nearly all the aristocrats and royalty had turned up to watch the game from the Guards' Clubhouse. Forgiving unkind persons who had raised his hopes sky high was out of the question. That careless chap Kishen had been incapable of sitting astride a horse, let alone *playing* in one of the world's most prestigious polo tournaments, or representing his country. He would put on his thinking cap and soon find a way of getting even with all of them, including Tiger. At least *he* should have deferred to his maternal uncle's wishes in this matter!

The Chattargadh contingent was standing close enough to overhear the Queen, renowned for her contagious gaiety, asking the Maharaja of Pisshengunj, 'Really, Your Highness, won't you invite me also to one of your comic—oops—cosmic seances?'

'Not yet, Your Majesty,' Nutty beamed back in deadly earnest. 'But it won't be long before I can guarantee face-to-face encounters with all the spirits of your choice.'

It wouldn't do to give the British Queen any wrong ideas about his powers just in case she decided to check him out. He had only just begun giving free Tarot card and astrology readings to all those debs, designing mums, and dethroned monarchs in an effort to improve his own predictability ratings.

Maharajah Jai Singh stopped wondering how Nutty had managed to procure the badge giving him entrée to this usually exclusive Royal enclosure when he found that his cousin was on jolly good terms with the Vicereine. She had obviously dropped all her objections and inhibitions about sharing a hotel with HH Pisshengunj's dogs. He found out later that the doggone Maharajah had assured her that everything, including Her Excellency's racing bets, would be on the house if she took him under her social wings.

Even those who came to Ascot primarily to boast of having rubbed shoulders with Royalty, were caught up in the heady excitement engendered by the intoxicating aroma concocted out of the world's most expensive perfumes, sweating horseflesh, green turf, saddle leather, cigar smoke, and that indefinable whiff of wealth and power emanating from all those famous owners and breeders having a last word with trainers and jockeys before each race. Lesser racegoers and punters crowded around the paddocks, rails, and bookies; while those who had already backed the odds on favourites sat munching, smoking, and chattering in the public stalls. They stood up to cheer and swear as each race began, cursing or backslapping with great gusto. As everybody knew, many fortunes were lost and made at Ascot.

Kitten's love of horses and her beguiling natural breeziness made her an instant hit with the Aga Khan. He invited her along to the saddling stalls with her father, grandfather, Tiger, and his old friend Sir Pratab, to see his horse Sikander carrying the King's colours, and all prepared to scoop the Gold Cup from Africa. At lunch time, these Maharajahs, in their distinctive tunics and turbans, and the beautifully groomed, sari-draped princesses accompanying them, discreetly disappeared into the Aga Khan's box. He promised them a far better repast than anything to be found in the overcrowded marquees and bars of even the Stewards' Enclosure. Over the superb luncheon (served by perfectly trained butlers on properly laid tables and accompanied by champagne chilled in ice buckets), they talked of likely contenders for the Prix du Jockey Club at the upcoming French Derby, and the unlikelihood of anyone attending Iffezheim that year because those Nazis had absolutely ruined Baden-Baden.

And, when they went back to watching the races through huge binoculars slung round their necks, the Aga Khan encouraged Kitten to bet, explaining how the odds worked. Tiger however, snubbed her, saying: 'Brats don't bet.' But her ability to back a string of winners—including the outsider who stole the Gold Cup—after deliberately disregarding the world-famous racehorse owner's insider tips—impressed Tiger more than he cared to admit.

Having an intuitive understanding of human nature, Princess Diamond could see that her niece Kitten was besotted by her nephew Tiger. It was also evident that Kitten's mischievous charm, flashing wit, and ricocheting repartee held absolutely no allure for him. This was just as well, for her brother would never forgive her if Tiger, famous for his love affairs, made Kitten the target of his devastating gallantry. The problems created by his delicate young wife Yasho Rajya Laxmi's inability to provide an heir for Fateypur, were bad enough.

While Tiger might have brushed aside any such demand from Kitten, he found it impossible to ignore a softly articulated regret from Ratna—a refreshingly deferential and decorous addition to his close-knit but irreverent family— about leaving London without seeing Westminster Abbey. The princesses didn't dare venture unescorted into the frightful crowds surrounding the place before the wedding. Since Ratna never complained or cajoled people into doing the ten things they'd rather not (unlike her bosom pal Kitten), Arjun felt compelled to explain that even their combined chivalry couldn't get her anyway near the Abbey. It was off limits to the ordinary public due to all the last-minute work, and decorations going on there.

'Since when have *we* become the ordinary public?' scoffed Kitten, giving HH Fateypur her full nose-in-the-air with tilted-chin and imperious-glance treatment. 'I can get you *in*, if *you* can get us safely there and back!'

'How?' demanded Tiger, amused by her usual childish posturing and preposterously tall claims.

'Simple,' said Kitten, with one of her most provoking grins, because she knew he didn't believe her. 'All of us know Colonel Claude-Poole. But I also happen to know his father. And you can't say that the Bishop of London hasn't got enough influence to get us into Westminster Abbey, and also arrange a specially conducted tour, including tea in the Chapter House, for us.'

'No tea!' the two Bhati princes stipulated with one voice. Kitten might enjoy sauntering around cloisters, and impressing captive priests with her own interpretation of the Reformation and Christ's avatar but *they* had better things to do. They had to attend the Prince of Wales' bachelor party.

The well-bred young cleric deputed to escort the Maharajah of Fateypur's party around the Abbey was agreeably surprised to find them quite familiar with British history and church decorum. The polite princes kept their shoes on and remained bareheaded, unlike several Asian visitors who insisted on following their own customs. Both the pretty little princesses covered their heads with their shimmering silk saris, dipped their fingers in holy water, and genuflected towards the altar before beginning their tour. They began with the royal chapels. The four Indians talked knowledgeably with their guide about the saints and kings depicted on the soaring stained-glass windows, exclaimed over the gilded woodwork, and the ancient stonework dating back nearly a thousand years to the Norman conquest. When they came to Henry

VII's famous fan-vaulted and filigreed wood chapel, hung with banners belonging to the Knights of Bath, the others made fun of Kitten. Tiger said that no matter what the Prince of Wales had promised her, only *two* Indians had been made Knight Commanders of this famous Order—her father, and the other Rathor ruler she was very fond of referring to as 'Gunga Din!'

After seeing the Coronation Chair with the Stone of Scone under its seat, several tombs, including those of the renowned Tudor and Stuart queens who'd never met, they returned to the main sanctuary. Florists were busy arranging masses of beautiful flowers and ferns around the altar which was adorned with gold-fringed crimson velvet and massive silver gilt candlesticks, and where the actual ceremony would be taking place the following day before an extremely select audience of crowned heads and other celebrities. Indicating one of the pews, the Anglican priest said: 'This is where the Indian Princes will be seated, Your Highness.'

'It's so unfair that they forgot to invite the Maharajahs' families,' cribbed Kitten.

Arjun turned away from the plaque he was reading. 'My dear sister, it's your own fault. You should have become a Maharani in time to participate in all the fun.'

This made his wife and Tiger laugh. It also immediately planted an idea in Kitten's head. 'That's it!' She beamed, happily clasping her hands. 'I could pretend to be Her Highness Fateypur! Then no one would know I'd gatecrashed this fabulous Royal wedding.'

Her suggestion shocked everybody, specially the Maharajah of Fateypur. 'Out of the question, my dear child. You've become rather well known, and some busybody would be bound to tell my wife that the Chattargadh Princess was masquerading as my Maharani, and trying to take her place just because she's unable to move around yet.'

Tiger knew it wasn't her fault that his soft-spoken,

adoring little wife had proved too fragile to carry even one of her five pregnancies to full term. But it would be shockingly unchivalrous to cause Yasho needless pain, particularly after that dedicated team of Swiss specialists— who had saved her life—had made it absolutely impossible for her to provide him with an heir. It was only ten days ago, that he had been present at her bedside (along with his aunt Diamond and her parents) when Her Highness Fateypur had had that gruelling Caesarean section-cum-hysterectomy. He had flown down from London in his new plane to see her. And despite all his engagements, he telephoned her twice a day to cheer her up.

If things were different, he might have indulged young Kitten.

Kitten, however, was unwilling to relinquish her harmless treat. She gave the Maharajah of Fateypur a blatantly entreating look out of her long-lashed, black eyes. 'But it would only be temporary, Hukum.'

Arjun couldn't resist taking a dig at her. 'Who knows, Kitten, you might want to make it permanent!' Ratna giggled. Shaking his head and shuddering eloquently at the very thought of any such thing, Tiger began walking out after thanking their guide.

By the time Kitten had forced them to traipse round St. Margaret's Church, which she managed to locate even though it was virtually obscured by the Abbey and the Houses of Parliament, raindrops had begun to fall. The sunny June weather which had seduced Tiger into driving out in this particular car, had turned into a typically blustery, uncomfortably chilly, English afternoon.

It had been love at first sight when Tiger saw and test-drove the new Bugatti Royale, with its 12.7 litre, 8-cylinder engine, guaranteed to produce 250 bhp. Though the sales representative at their Michelin Building showroom swore that there were hardly four or five of these custom-made

Napoleon-type Bugatti coupés in the whole world, the Maharajah of Fateypur had insisted they take the entire top *off* if they wanted him to buy one. He had found it absolutely exhilarating to manoeuvre this superfast car through the city traffic, confident that it could have taken him round Le Mans in record time. But driving around London in the rain catering to Kitten's whims, was not proving to be an enjoyable experience for HH Fateypur.

Kitten was, as usual, optimistic about making it safely to some reasonably decent place close by where they could stay dry and tuck into a proper English high tea. After walking down miles of church aisles, she was hungry. First she suggested dashing into the House of Lords next door, where they were bound to run into someone they knew. Tiger vetoed the idea by informing her that everyone needed passes to enter the British Parliament—even if they had to meet their own MPs.

'Then let's pop into the nearest pub,' she said, as Big Ben struck five.

Tiger told the ignoramus seated by his side, huddling into her light lemon sari as if it were a sweater, that, unfortunately, there *were* no pubs between Victoria Street and Whitehall. Switching on his wipers while Arjun fussed over his bride in the back seat, Tiger decided that if he drove fast enough, they could make it to the Strand and have tea at the Savoy without getting too wet.

But halfway there, the billowing dark clouds broke with an ominous thunderclap.

Rain began falling in earnest, drenching everybody caught without umbrellas, hats, or raincoats. People dashed under arches and doorways, and disappeared into buildings. Passing cars and buses kept splashing the four young people trapped in the low slung car with filthy street water, and slush. They could hardly stroll into one of the official establishments lining Whitehall (without a prior appointment) merely because they didn't like getting wet. So, instead of turning towards Charing Cross, the Maharajah of Fateypur turned towards the Admiralty Arch, where they could at least take shelter from the rain without embarrassing anyone.

Tiger parked his car, took off his suit jacket, and gave it to Kitten with a slight smile. 'Please remember to return it eventually, Princess, even though I do have lots of other suits!'

Before she could think up a befitting rejoinder, she saw a hefty figure in a dripping mackintosh and the familiar oval helmet worn by British Bobbys, watching them.

The policeman shook his stick disapprovingly at the four frightful foreigners who had no business being here. 'Might I ask what you blokes is dhh-dhooing here?'

The Maharajah of Fateypur answered as pleasantly as he could. 'That's rather obvious, isn't it?'

'Move on,' ordered the minion of law and order, honking into his handkerchief. 'This hain't a barking place.'

Brushing water off his face, Arjun glanced around significantly. 'I don't see any No Parking signs here, Constable.'

Ratna hoped they could get off without further arguments or unpleasantness. She simply wanted to get back to their hotel and change into something dry. She wished she had never suggested this outing in the first place because rain water was making the red of her ivory wedding bangles bleed all over her bridegroom's coat.

'Hainnyone but a bunch opp ferrinerrs khnows this is a hissterical mhourn-you-mhent, snot a bubblick barffing blace! Acch-heu.' Sergeant Dobbins of the CID knew where his duty lay even when he was coming down with pneumonia as anyone except his superiors up at the Yard could see.

The Maharajah of Fateypur gave his cousin Arjun a restraining look, and fished his wallet out of the perfectly tailored coat now draped round Kitten. 'Thank you, Constable. We'll soon be on our way. Meanwhile, have a nice cup of tea.'

The outraged Sergeant looked at the hundred-pound note held out to him, and blew his whistle. 'You're bitched!'

The more Kitten tried explaining things to the supercilious young Inspector who confronted them after locking up HH Fateypur and R.K. Arjun for interrogation, the worse it got. 'I don't *want* to know how things are done in your country, young lady. In fact, I want *you* to know that attempting to bribe members of His Majesty's police force is a serious crime in *this* country!'

Kitten smothered her exasperation and continued in a more placatory manner. 'It wasn't a bribe, Officer. Just . . . *chay-pani inaam*, you know. A little money for a cup of tea, because the poor chap's obviously suffering from a very bad cold as anyone can see. In fact, he shouldn't have been forced to go out in his condition!'

The cheeky little foreigner really offended Sergeant Dobbins. 'Ell, I nab-her herd of an un-red-hound cuppa! NO SIR, no mhatter whott thiss lill 'eathen says.'

He had already informed his senior officer about his misgivings regarding the Indians. They were undoubtedly a bunch of ignorant anarchists who called themselves freedom fighters. He was sure they had identified the next day's route by the simple expedient of following all the gay banners, flags and bunting put up by HM's loyal subjects. He was also sure they were plotting a blow against his King and country just as the grand procession of coaches and carriages passed through Admiralty Arch.

All the details he had noted about them fitted in with his suspicions. First, their ring leader had tried to bribe him. Then, his equally oily crony had tried to con him into believing that, because of diplomatic immunity, they couldn't be arrested. Thirdly when he had looked at their licence plates to confirm this unlikely story, he had found that the car had none at all—not even the regular CD plates usually found on all embassy cars. To top all this, that mighty aloof, ultra-refined young lady with the tell-tale, blood-stained hands and clothes, and kohl-smeared face had piped up, saying that the licence plates were Applied For because the Maharajah of Fat-poor's car was out of the showroom only on trial. Not that *he* had believed a word she said: who had ever heard of a Maharajah driving around without his jewelled turban or at least ten ADCs?

Finally, when he had asked for their passports, of course they hadn't had any! No identification meant that they could be anyone from anywhere. But they had taken great offence when duty prompted him to ask whether they were Africans, Arabs, or Eyetees?

'We're Aryans!' is what they had proclaimed proudly.

THIS had clinched the matter. The Inspector was sure they were self-confessed Nazi agents driving around in a foreign getaway car. But the pugnacious, dark-eyed girl with the dripping wet, dishevelled hair had tried to floor him by saying: 'Dash it, even your King drives around in Daimlers, which are foreign cars! You can't go around arresting people just because they're driving *foreign* cars. I thought Britain was a law-abiding country!'

And to make matters worse, the cocky young lady had spun him such absolute drivel about their gang's real identities and relationships, that he'd had to exercise the utmost restraint about locking her up immediately for interrogation. The family resemblance between those two Indian males clearly established the fact that they were brothers.

'Of course, they are brothers', said Kitten.

And yes, Prince Arjun was undoubtedly her brother too. But HH Fateypur? Definitely NOT. Stepbrother? No they didn't have such things, or cousins either, in India. Only among Muslims and Christians did these exist. And indeed, her sister Ratna was the Maharajah of Fateypur's sister-in-law because she was legally married to her brother Arjun.

And, when he'd said that, except for the ancient Pharaohs, he didn't know of any civilised people who considered such unnatural alliances legitimate, Kitten said that she probably knew more Egyptian history than him, even though she could tell from his accent that he was a University man.

The Inspector tried to digest all that he had been told. But gave up. It was all too confusing. He merely read out the list of infringements for which the two gentlemen, with their amazing Oxonian accents and expensive Savile Row suits, were being charged and booked, in strict accordance with the law. No, they could not be released on the personal bond of two self-confessed minor girls who carried no identification whatsoever, and were no doubt trying to pull the wool over his eyes by giving the Ritz as their London address. He did not care what their Status was. Or their state of funds. They ought to thank him for keeping this matter confined to Scotland Yard, which followed due legal processes.

He could, of course, hand them over to His Majesty's Secret Service on account of the Sergeant's extremely serious allegations. These listed as: 'one, loitering with intent in a forbidden place; two, driving around without a licence in an unregistered car, allegedly stolen; three, assuming false identities, without a single passport or papers between the lot of them; four, being self-confessed Aryans!' They were all, in other words, Indo-Germanic Nazis, liable for deportation as soon-to-be ENEMY ALIENS. Finally, the worst was their claiming to be personal friends of HRH the Prince of Wales, and guests of HM's Government on Crown territory, whatever THAT meant!

Kitten, however, refused to be browbeaten by the overbearing policeman. 'That means that I'll have to make that phone call every arrested person is entitled to in all civilised countries. And since you refuse to believe a word I

say, kindly have the goodness to get me Buckingham Palace.
I'd prefer speaking to the Prince of Wales. But the King or
Queen will do if he's busy getting ready for tonight's party.'

When his equerry Major Thomas got the Prince of Wales
on his private line, he was in the bedroom selecting the
correct cuff links for his snow-white dress shirt. He had to
be very careful. It simply wouldn't do to send his Dutch
bride any negative signals, even though everybody knew
that their's was a political alliance which would, hopefully,
accomplish all that their mutual ancestors, William of
Orange and Queen Mary, couldn't.

'It could be a hoax, y'know,' HRH said, keeping one
arm extended for his valet to fix some splendid sapphires
unlinked to any of his much publicised girlfriends.

'No such luck, Sir. It's the Chattargadh Princess all right.'

'Well, what does she want?' asked the Prince, who had
been inundated with calls from disappointed persons trying
to cadge a last minute entrée to the Abbey for the
ceremony as if it were the Royal Enclosure at Ascot where
they could usually squeeze in just a few more people.

'A hot bath!' said the equerry.

The Prince chuckled, recalling young Kitten's resourceful
handling of that little problem during his visit to
Chattargadh in February. He had been rather rash in
jestingly promising her that Order, and knew she wouldn't
let him live it down if he broke his word. But dash it,
she'd caught him right in the midst of dressing for his last
night out as a bachelor, and it was already a quarter to
eight by the Fabergé clock his grandmother had pinched
from her cousin Nikki's Tsarkoeselo mantlepeice.

'Tommy-Rot, please tell Princess Kitten that I shall
definitely give her a tinkle as soon as possible if she leaves
her number.'

Major Thomas explained that she was insisting on

speaking to HRH right NOW. Something seemed to be up, because she had also been mentioning Paramountcy, and some rigamarole about treaties and Sanads compelling the Crown to go to the aid of distressed Native Princes.

The Prince of Wales laughed into the telephone, clearly detecting his mischievous friend Tiger's style in this jolly good try. 'Where exactly is she telephoning from?'

'Jail!' said the equerry.

The heir to the British throne wouldn't have believed a single word of all this, if he hadn't visited princely India. Now that he had done so he could believe anything involving Maharajahs.

After a word with the Chief Commissioner, the Prince of Wales got on the phone and was able to reassure Kitten between loud spurts of laughter.

'Scotland Yard's been able to rule out any IRA connection because they think that none of you looks Irish enough! And I've convinced them that although you're Aryans, you're neither Nazis nor Indian freedom fighters!'

Soon, Major Thomas reached the jail house with an armload of bath towels, sweaters and shawls sent by the Queen. The bonus was three last minute invitations to the Royal wedding. When Tiger gave her a grateful hug for getting them out of trouble without all their families (and the sensation hungry press) latching on, Kitten felt that she had really been rewarded for keeping her wits, and getting them out of a tight situation.

However, it was too good a story for the policemen to keep under their hats. The next morning, the tabloids were full of yet another escapade involving an Indian Maharajah and the Prince of Wales. And when a battery of extremely persistent camera-wielding American journalists pestered the Indian Princess outside Celestine's for comments, Kitten twinkled back, tongue in cheek: 'As they say in Chicago, amigos, I simply called in my Marker!'

Maharajahs in Europe   8

Nothing could have delighted Nutty more than the media spotlight on the rampant bonhomie between Maharajah Jai Singh's unmarried 17-year-old daughter, Kitten, and the extremely fast playboy set surrounding his nephew Tiger. The Maharajah of Pisshengunj concluded that he must strike while the iron was hot, and while Tiger was still feeling much too obliged to treat that preposterously precocious girl in his usual disdainful fashion. Sitting on the sofa opposite him in the Cosmic Hotel's most sumptuous penthouse suite overlooking Hyde Park, Nutty's devoted Dewan, Baron Tikemoffsky, and brother-in-law, Koodsu Rao Saheb, pointed out that although they agreed wholeheartedly with his current assessment, there were two tiny details HH seemed to have overlooked.

'Really, Your Highness, I doubt that anything—not even a gun held to his head—would compel HH Fateypur to even flirt with Princess Kitten, let alone marry her!' the Russian Baron observed.

Koodsu Rao Saheb swore that Maharajah Jai Singh would rather see his one and only daughter remain unmarried than compromise his stand on polygamy. 'Because—with all due apologies, Hukum—you Rathors are the most pig-headed of all our Rajput clans.'

'But that's just the point,' laughed Nutty, repeatedly tapping the newspaper pictures showing HH Fateypur and Kitten at the Epsom Derby, the Farnborough air show, Wimbledon, and dancing together at London's most exclusive for-members-only nightclub, Celestine's.

'Your stubborn Princess is absolutely determined to marry my nephew Tiger, even though he usually treats her like an annoying little puppy clamouring for attention! Why do you think Kitten Baisa explained to us the lacuna in HH Chattargadh's legislation regarding monogamy that day in Ooty with the help of HH Chattargadh's personal copy of Roget's *Thesaurus*? To establish a precedent, Rao Saab. Not to turn you back into a pillar of Chattargadh State! And don't tell me that any Rajput father will allow his daughters to remain unmarried. It's his dharma to marry them off as early as possible, before they become a liability and everybody starts laughing at them. Jai Singh may not know the *Veda-Puranas* and *Shastras* (Sanskrit classics of Aryan history, scripture, and literature) as well as I do, but even *he* knows the *Manu Smriti* (Hindu code of conduct).'

The Rajput chief nodded, but told his brother-in-law that Maharajah Jai Singhji would never agree to any matrimonial alliance which reduced his beloved daughter to the status of a second wife—even if there were no stepchildren or heirs, and however wealthy the State!

'Meaning Fateypur,' concluded Nutty. 'Trust me, Rao Saab. I'm banking on the psychology of all the individuals involved in this little *tamasha* (show). We both want revenge against HH Chattargadh for all the humiliations and injustice he's heaped on us over the years, don't we? And what could be better tit for tat than making him eat his own words about modernisation, progress and all that rubbish he loves lecturing us about?'

Completely knowledgeable about all the fallouts, feuds,

and public recriminations between the Pisshengunj and Chattargadh branches of the Chattar Singh Gotra Rathor dynasty, Tikky still felt that it wouldn't be easy to pull the wool over Maharajah Jai Singh's eyes. His Maharani Sahebah was also a formidably prescient person, and would never permit any situation involving her husband's prestige and her daughter's happiness to get so totally out of hand that HH Pisshengunj could enjoy the last laugh.

Nutty agreed that throwing mud in the eyes of his beloved blood relations was seldom easy. 'But the chief challenge in this particular case is my nephew Tiger's apathy towards a girl he's known since birth. She's not only ten years younger but also annoyingly indisciplined, tomboyish, and unsophisticated. We all know that he only admires perfectly poised and polished worldly-wise females—and the whiter the better!'

Tikky conceded that no one who had observed HH Fateypur cutting a swathe through haute international circles could fail to note this fact. Koodsu Rao Saheb added that he wouldn't be surprised if the Bhati Prince was unconsciously trying to emulate his amorous ancestor, Lord Krishna. Perhaps he was even trying to go a step further by marrying a few foreigners, and thus inflicting white Maharanis on his subjects. His uncles would have to do something quickly.

'Exactly!' swore Nutty, buffeting his brother-in-law's shoulder. 'Forget about Sir Pratab, because we know he's absolutely useless when it comes to controlling Tiger. But you can count on me to make sure that only another Rathor Princess takes the place of my dear departed sister as Maharani of Fateypur. And *that's* when the real fun will begin!'

Maharajah Jai Singh and his wife were entertaining the Resident's family and Colonel Claude-Poole informally over drinks in their luxuriously appointed Ritz drawing room before going on to see Uday Shankar's troupe perform classical Indian dances at the Royal Albert Hall, when the first cable from Chattargadh was brought in on a silver salver. Leaving it unopened, the Maharajah continued talking to his guests.

'So, what do you really think of those matched malachite urns and pedestals, Mr Redverse?'

'Top quality pre-Revolution stuff smuggled out of Russia, I imagine,' replied Redverse, surveying the gorgeous green-shaded, ormolu-rimmed objects. He signalled his wife to come over and take a look.

Dorothy set down her sherry glass, smoothed her close-fitting seagreen satin sheath over her hips, and strolled over to examine the Maharajah's latest acquisitions, which included some quite passable porcelain and bronzes. The price stickers made her turn around with an expressive shudder. 'Really, Your Highness, they've charged far too much for most of this stuff. I know a couple of places in the Old Brompton Road where one can get identical stuff at half the price!'

But HH Chattargadh merely smiled as he stood up to pour her another short drink. 'I'm sure you can, Lady Dorothy. But I'd still end up paying the price of being a Maharajah!'

Everyone was still laughing when his ADC Ganpat Singh entered the suite after knocking discreetly. He too held a cable, which he urged HH to read. Excusing himself, Maharajah Jai Singh tore open the first cable after reading the second. Maharani Padmini looked anxiously at her husband as his perfectly relaxed demeanour underwent a subtle change that only she could gauge. Elinor uncrossed her shapely legs under her ankle-length, apricot crêpe frock, while everybody waited for the Maharajah to finish reading his telegrams.

The first cable ran:

HH Maharajah Jai Singhji of Chattargadh
Ritz Hotel, London
England

Respectfully ask you ignore newspaper reports. Fighting famine, plague, and locusts with full State resources. But public wants Baapji back.

KISHEN

The second cable, from his son Robin, said:

Hajoor *may avoid change of plans by ignoring Uncle Kishen's SOS. Situation under control. Do not, repeat, do not, cut short much-needed vacation with Mama. Respects to both.*

ROBIN

Without a word, Maharajah Jai Singh handed both the cablegrams to his wife. Maharani Padmini was as unprepared for this unwelcome intelligence as her husband. But there was only one thing to be done when their people were facing such severe calamities. 'Robin can't be serious, darling. We must get back to Chattargadh as soon as possible, even if it means packing all night, and flying non-stop to India.'

Her words effectively banished the last lingering doubts in her husband's mind about whether to stay on in Europe or to return home. But upon cool reflection, the Resident suggested that an overseas call to India might not only set HH's mind at rest, but also clarify the situation.

Colonel Claude-Poole's grey eyes widened in astonishment as he also read the unwelcome news. 'Really, Your Highness, I can understand about acts of God like the plague and locusts. But how on earth can we have a famine when the buffer-stock State godowns are full, and there's sufficient canal water for humans, crops, and livestock to get through another drought, even if we were to be so unlucky?'

Lady Dorothy and Elinor offered their services to the Maharani for packing, writing notes of regret, cancelling invitations, and collecting undelivered valuables from the shops. Ratna and Kitten would also provide help once they got back from their motoring trip to Oxford.

When the Maharajah failed to get a satisfactory response from the hotel switchboard, Reverse Gear and CP took turns on the telephone, asking them to put through an immediate call to New Delhi—in India, where else?—in order to get first-hand information out of Chattargadh. They could see that it was pointless expecting even the efficient British telecommunication system to patch through an overseas call to that remote desert state. But all their reasonably worded requests proved futile. After repeatedly being told that the overseas cable lines to India were simply not functioning due to no fault of the Ritz staff, Redverse decided to call up one of his Foreign Office chums, and ask for a connection through abnormal channels.

Colonel CP said that instead of wasting valuable time wrangling with those grossly inefficient female operators, he would trot along and organise the aeroplane charter HH seemed to require. 'I'll take care of our transportation logistics while Thakur Ganpat Singh takes care of striking camp. Can't fool around London, listening to a bunch of gaga bishops going on and on about stuff which became obsolete way back in the Dark Ages when there's real work to be done.'

'That's mighty good of you, Colonel CP. There aren't too many British officers—or Indians for that matter— who'd cut short a holiday in England during the height of the season,' said the Maharajah. A couple of meetings with CP's father, London's latest Bishop, had made him understand why his Military Secretary had (as Whitehall often alleged) 'gone native'.

The Resident hesitated only for a moment before asking: 'Your Highness, would you like me to come back too?'

'Good heavens, Mr Redverse, I wouldn't dream of disrupting your holiday.' Residents were no earthly use during moments of crisis *within* the State, as the Maharajah well knew. Liaising with the Paramount Power, with unreasonable brother princes like Nutty, playing polo, tennis and bridge with the ruler, was their primary raison d'être.

Desolate at the thought of saying goodbye so soon to her Maharajah, Elinor pleaded with Padmini to leave Kitten behind, safe under the double chaperonage of her mother and aunt.

'That's really sweet of you, dear Elinor. I know your parents have been to a great deal of trouble in organising so many treats for the entire Chattargadh family, but burdening them with a house guest like Kitten wouldn't be at all fair! I shall telephone the Viscountess before leaving, and you must convey my warmest regards to them,' said the Maharani.

However, despite the fact that riot and rumpus inevitably followed the Chattargadh Princess, Lady Dorothy reiterated that they would be only too happy to have Kitten move into Redverse House. 'We'll do everything possible to keep her entertained, and bring her home safely to Chattargadh when Gerry's leave expires.'

The Maharani thanked her charmingly for this kind offer, and explained that her sister-in-law Princess Diamond had already promised to show Kitten Switzerland, Paris, and the Riviera. And they all knew how Kitten would react if anyone tried to rearrange her plans!

'Of course,' said Dorothy with a wry smile. 'Then we shall be meeting her again in Monte Carlo when we go down to visit my mother-in-law before sailing back to India from Marseilles.'

In Paris, Princess Diamond introduced her unsophisticated young niece and daughter-in-law to that rarefied world of progressive artists and writers, great jewellers and designers, haute cuisine, and enlightened European and Latin-American aristocrats among whom the Fateypur family felt totally at home. The French shops were so luxurious that they made the London ones look positively provincial in comparison. The Chattargadh princesses kept up so frenetic a schedule that it would have wilted women with lesser vitality.

Between their forays to the Ile de France, Versailles, Chantilly, and Longchamp, there was hardly any time for Kitten and Ratna to really pick and choose baubles for themselves at Cartier. This was also because Cartier was a jeweller Princess Diamond refused to patronise simply because nearly every Indian Maharajah already did so. However, once in Nice Kitten made sure she saw it. After strolling along the Promenade d'Anglaise (lined with numerous restaurants and brightly painted houses covered with vines, flower baskets, and flapping laundry), and comparing the views of the four famous Riviera ports and bays they had so far seen, Kitten cajoled her cousin Ratna into entering Cartier's Nice branch.

Only the language barrier prevented Cartier's deferential staff from transacting any business whatsoever with the two obviously well-born and wealthy Indian girls. Kitten's twilled silk slacks and matching scoop-necked jumper were as obviously haute couture as her simple stud earrings were flawless four-carat diamonds. Ratna, as usual, wore a perfectly draped crinkled chiffon sari in traditional bright colours out of deference to her in-laws. Since the Cartier show room was utterly unlike any of the jam-packed, overstocked jewellery shops of Bombay and Calcutta, it took them a little while to convey their preferences to the assistant manager, who spoke no English. They pointed out various items in the locked glass cabinets. After trying on every single tiara, dowagerish dog collar, and chunky necklace (which she evidently had no intention of buying), Kitten studied and discarded several salamander, snake, panther, and phoenix-motif bracelets and pendants. She then went through all the rings and earrings, rejecting every single piece until the Frenchman disappeared into the vault, and came out carrying several distinctive jewellers' boxes. It was then that the princesses were tempted to have some real fun. The boxes contained one-of-a-kind signature pieces composed of the finest gemstones in Cartier's exquisite invisible setting with *pavé* diamonds and platinum. Ratna was quite content with an elegant ruby and diamond bracelet she could see herself wearing quite often. But Kitten set her heart on a truly magnificent 18-carat, cushion-cut sapphire ring enhanced with two ribbons of diamond baguettes, and cunningly contrived diamond-and-pearl feather earrings. Both were much more glamorous than anything she possessed.

Aware of her aunt's stubborn stand about patronising Cartier's, Kitten knew that they would have to pay for their purchases instead of simply signing vouchers and having everything delivered to the Maharajah of Fateypur's 8-room, top-floor suite at the Cannes Carlton. Kitten took a handful of hundred pound notes (left over from her Ascot winnings) out of her purse, and offered them to the jeweller.

But the Frenchman shook his head from side to side, rattling off something in rapid-fire French, which the two Indian princesses couldn't even pretend to understand.

'*Je serais bien de choisir entre les deux. Pour l'du choix, elle no que l'de richesses. Deliberer de faire que-avec-precision-un objet grave de facture pour l'jeune fille!*'

From his eloquent gestures and frequent thrusting of

smaller rings and baubles towards her, Kitten understood that, for some reason, the jeweller was reluctant to let her have the ring she had chosen. Perhaps it had been especially made for someone else. But it fitted her so perfectly that she had no intention of leaving Cartier's without it. Since they had always been taught never to enter a shop unless they actually intended to buy something (to boost the shopkeeper's morale), and never to ask the price of anything they picked (because that was sheer bad manners), Kitten wondered if they had enough money between them to pay for their trinkets. She consulted Ratna in their mother tongue, Marwari; but found that her cousin was as ignorant about the exchange rate between pounds and francs as herself.

Just as the two disappointed princesses were deciding to return later with a French-speaking acquaintance, the Maharajah of Fateypur walked into Cartier's.

'Currency problems, children?' teased Tiger. He was greeted ecstatically by Kitten, and a little more decorously by Ratna. A palpably deferential and expectant atmosphere engulfed the jewellery shop as the entire staff recognised this seriously wealthy frequent patron. The Francophile Indian Maharajah and the jeweller conferred in French tinged with the mellifluous accent of *langu d'oc*. The items selected by the two cousins were examined, and although HH Fateypur quite agreed that the huge sapphire ring was totally unsuitable for an unmarried young girl, he was smart enough to know that Kitten would never concede this point.

It was also obvious that Kitten hadn't comprehended a word the jeweller had said to dissuade her. As HH Fateypur well knew, there were two things she couldn't do: she couldn't add and multiply (because she found arithmetic too boring); and, she had no ear for languages. This was just as well, perhaps, considering the price of the ring. It had sounded amazingly cheap in pounds. But after conversion into rupees (or francs), its price was outrageous.

Ratna bowed low with folded palms to thank her brother-in-law for the elaborate and valuable pair of ruby and diamond bracelets adorning her wrists. Kitten squealed with delight as Tiger gave in to her cajolery and slid the superb sapphire ring on her middle finger. 'Thank you so much, Tiger Baapji! I promise to pay you back as soon as possible.'

'Don't be silly, Kitten. Robin, Arjun, and I can always buy toys and trinkets for you children.'

Delighted with her gift, yet determined to prove that she had no intention of taking advantage of him and making him spend thousands and thousands of pounds on her just because he was obliged to provide for his family member Ratna, Kitten decided there and then that she would somehow find the funds to reimburse HH Fateypur. She still had some of the seventeen thousand pounds she had won backing winners at Ascot last month. She could easily double (even triple) the amount if Aunt Diamond, or better still, Tiger Baapji, took her to the famous Francois-Medici room at the Monte Carlo Casino where fortunes changed hands every night because the stakes were really high.

She would have to do something quickly about the fact that unsponsored or unescorted young girls like herself were simply not allowed in.

Tiger's remark that Kitten shouldn't be going around wearing pink pyjamas in broad daylight because it wasn't at all chic, effectively clinched one argument, and launched another. Informed that what she had on was a Schiaparelli original, Tiger countered: 'Yes, and quite *Shocking* too, just like your perfume! Hasn't anyone taught you that subtlety is the essence of feminine allure?'

'You don't know anything!' cried Kitten, lured as usual into a childish squabble defending the year's most popular perfume, Schiaparelli's *Shocking*. But before he could bait her further, Tiger spotted Elinor through Cartier's tall plate-glass window overlooking the Place Massena, and dashed off to have a word with her.

Even though she heard him call out to her, Elinor Redverse didn't stop for another encounter with Tiger. She felt that the Maharajah of Fateypur was behaving like a perfect chump, refusing to take any hint or snub. His reputation as India's most glamorous and irresistible Maharajah had obviously gone to his head, making him incapable of perceiving that she, for one, wasn't mesmerised by him. Clicking her tongue in exasperation, she compared him to the Hound of Heaven that followed ever after. She nipped into a side street, nearly colliding with a heavily made up woman walking out with a pair of poodles from the shadowy, tunnel-like street lined with shuttered houses.

The frustrated Fateypur Maharajah looked all around the palm-shaded public garden (and even behind the Fountain of Planets), wondering where Elinor could have disappeared. He couldn't spot anyone remotely resembling the unmistakable British beauty in the playground full of noisy families, elderly couples, and children accompanied by uniformed nannies. He would have to figure out just which fashionable shop or hotel lining the sea front had enticed her in.

Elinor reached the Negresco's arched entrance just as Tiger began stalking her up the Promenade d'Anglaise. She was at once engulfed by its *fin de siècle* opulence. Its Rumanian owner, Henry Negresco, had so embellished this hotel that it had become popular with Scott Fitzgerald, Picasso, the Churchills, Chanel, Charlie Chaplin, the Kings of Belgium, Spain, and Egypt; and renowned actresses and hostesses like Garbo, Dietrich, Elsa Maxwell, and Lady Astor.

Nutty observed the hurried entrance of the Resident's rather dishevelled, parcel-laden niece from the cool marble-flagged lobby where he stood conversing with his brother-in-law and the influential Jockey Club president Prince Alexandre, Duc de Nemours. He had been talking about creating a world-class polo field on the Riviera for people like themselves, who needed a little more physical challenge than what they normally got lolling around luxury hotels, casinos, yachts, and beaches.

The Maharajah of Pisshengunj quizzed Elinor as soon as the Bourbon prince departed. 'You came in here looking like someone escaping from a rampaging beast!'

'Your nephew Tiger, to be precise, Your Highness,' she retorted, unable to hide her growing exasperation even at the cost of sounding rude.

'Aah-ha! I'm delighted to discover a girl of character like you, Miss Elinor, who actually finds the irresistible Maharajah of Fateypur not just resistible, but positively annoying when compared to my beloved brother, HH Chattargadh. Rao Saab, we must help the young lady!'

Koodsu Rao Saheb immediately relieved Elinor of all her shopping bags and parcels. 'Certainly. But I thought you were quite safe in your grandmother's secluded Monte Carlo villa.'

The young Englishwoman explained that one could not go into purdah in Europe, no matter where one stayed.

'I too have bought a villa in Cap Ferrat, because these rude hotel *wallahs* refused to let my pets check in, just like those of any other paying guests!' said Nutty as he escorted her through the busy, antique-adorned lobby.

Elinor maintained a tolerably sympathetic expression as she listened to HH Pisshengunj's trials and tribulations in every European city he had visited. If only he comported himself with the dignity and restraint that Europeans expected, he'd get himself an unprecedented amount of politeness, amiability, and warmth, she reflected. Then, even his mania about everyone treating his dogs as if they were human would be seen as an admirably endearing trait.

The Pisshengunj Maharajah made his young companion comfortable in one of the cushioned and buttoned armchairs placed around several velvet-draped round tables in the crimson-and-cream royal salon where dangerous liaisons and hush-hush business deals could be conducted in style. The great oval hall, with its glass ceiling and marble columns, was famous throughout the Cote d'Azur. It was, perhaps, even more well known for its Baccarat chandelier which the last tsar had tried to buy from Negresco to hang alongside its twin in the Winter Palace.

Once the waiter who had brought their iced daiquiris had departed, Elinor made it abundantly clear to HH Pisshengunj that she found Tiger's enthusiastic pursuit quite galling. No one could accuse her of encouraging him. Except for that unfortunate mix-up over those necklaces in Chattargadh for which she couldn't be blamed—she had persumed they were tokens of esteem from their marvellous Maharajah—she had meticulously returned every single one of his extravagant gifts unopened the very same instant they had been thrust upon her.

Nutty assured the Resident's niece that such slip-ups were quite understandable. 'But they are regrettable too, because they have encouraged my infatuated nephew to think you're just like all the other memsahebs who find him smashing. The truth is that, after his parents departed so suddenly, hand in hand, for their heavenly abode when Tiger was only seven, his guardians Sir Pratab and Princess Diamond spoiled him so thoroughly that he has turned into a thoughtless playboy. With the best claim and intentions in the world, I had absolutely no say in the training and upbringing of my elder sister's only child. So you see how the damage was done?'

Elinor merely sighed as she continued to watch the doors for Tiger's unwelcome but inevitable arrival.

'I simply don't know how to make him see reason. Your

precious nephew refuses to pay attention to anything I say to discourage him from hounding me.'

'Simple,' said Nutty with an expansive gesture. 'I'll give you a magic mantra for taming Tiger. Hold out for marriage. Like Anne Boleyn, y'know!'

For a moment Elinor thought she couldn't have heard right. Was the Nutty Maharajah having one of his famous jokes at her expense? Holbein's portraits of Henry VIII and his executed, or discarded queens flashed through her mind. 'Really, Your Highness, even if I wanted to marry an Indian Maharajah, it certainly wouldn't be your nephew, HH Fateypur.'

Slightly bulging, canny brown eyes beamed back at the offended English girl. 'Just trust me to resolve your dilemma once and for all in my own way, dear child. You and I are going to have a bit of fun at Tiger's expense. Listen to Natwar Singh. He knows the psychology of this individual so well that he can guarantee sure-shot results.'

Honey Moneykurl's objective in assembling this strange assortment of people for a cruise aboard the elegant yacht she had inherited as part of her impressive fortune became obvious to some of her senior guests even before they sailed out of Monte Carlo's spectacular harbour. Sir Pratab, Princess Diamond, Nutty, their Resident, and Lady Dorothy didn't need any clairvoyant powers to see the obvious.

'It is really rather amusing, how many passion plays are being enacted right before our eyes,' confided Redverse to his wife as they left all the luxury liners, boats, and anchored yachts behind and headed for the open Mediterranean.

The heiress whom their common connection Lady Axeminster had successfully launched into haute European circles was targeting Tiger, who, in his turn, was vainly stalking their niece Elinor. The latter had sought cover behind the redoubtable Princess Kitten, who had long-term plans of her own regarding HH Fateypur. Dorothy's only comment was to advise Reverse Gear to steer clear of that imbroglio because everyone knew Maharajah Jai Singh's attitude to *that* outdated Rajput custom.

A distinctly euphoric sensation washed over Kitten as the yacht gathered speed, and a great rush of sea-spray laden air buffeted her body. Even the sharp, briny smell composed of salt water, freshly caught fish, seaweeds, polished decks and gleaming paint work, was unfamiliar. Each day on the Riviera was an altogether new and heady experience for her, a desert dweller. However, the Fateypur family, including her aunt, took all this in their stride because this coastal area undoubtedly evoked in them nostalgic memories of their far off seaside kingdom in India's Gujarat province. Kitten stood on the deck between Tiger and Elinor as the extremely tall and attractive Rumanian Crown Prince Rudolf told them disreputable stories about landmarks associated with such famous and infamous people as Hannibal, Julius Caesar, Nero, Caligula, Madame de Maitignon (Louis XIV's powerful mistress and second wife), Napoleon, and his gadabout grand-aunt, Empress Elizabeth of Austria.

Every shade of greeny-blue, silvery-gold, and deep amethyst shimmered, foamed, and merged together in great uneven swirls as the beautifully designed boat streaked through the historic Mare Nostrem waters in the opalescent morning light. Seagulls swooped and soared over all the curved bays, jagged red rocks, and lovely harbours sheltering boats of every shape and size. Holding on to the rails to keep from bumping into Rudolf, Kitten watched the craggy Esterel mountains, various hilltop villages, palm-fringed villas, grand hotels, crowded beaches, mimosa, olive and pine groves receding and advancing as they sailed south-west towards Cannes, the Riviera's best beach resort.

Kitten's talent for making new friends and finding fresh

amusements seldom surprised Arjun, who was keeping a watchful eye over her while his mother and wife had a jolly good time chatting with Queen Olga, the Aga Khan, and Baroness Beatrice de Rothschild in deck chairs placed in the shade. Connoisseurs of the wicked anecdote, these social luminaries knew at least one story about nearly everybody worth knowing in their cosmopolitan circle. His father was deep in some discussion with Baron Rothschild, the financial wizard who was advising them on global trends in banking and investment. Someone had to control Kitten's famous capers before they degenerated into infantile practical jokes, particularly when her bête noire, Uncle Nutty, and the two rivals for Tiger Baapji's attention were also on board and stood within striking distance.

'All that I require is the right opportunity to extract every ounce of revenge from my Chattargadh relations,' reflected Nutty. As he compared his niece and the foreigner his young nephew currently fancied, he grew more and more convinced that his cleverly contrived scheme simply couldn't go wrong. Kitten and Elinor appeared to be the same height and build when they stood side by side. Their upright posture, strong shapely shoulders, well-manicured hands, and small feet encased in crêpe-soled canvas shoes, were also similar. Of course, Kitten's darker volatile face, wind-blown black locks, and contagious gaiety were the exact opposite of Elinor's ladylike reserve, and permanently groomed appearance. A low, wide-brimmed raffia hat protected her spun-gold hair and extremely soft, pale pink skin from the ravages of sea breezes warmed by the strong southern sun.

The Maharajah of Pisshengunj noted the exasperated flaring of Kitten's nostrils as their hostess Honey clutched Tiger's arm instead of grabbing the guard rail to steady herself when the boat pitched up and down. Nutty studied the group around his nephew through gold-rimmed goggles as he took the crystal cocktail glass presented to him by one of the pursers dressed in a pure white uniform.

Kitten had been smart enough to resist the obviously nautical look sported by almost all the other ladies present. They had, predictably, come aboard wearing shades of blue with white. She had chosen to dress in comfortable cream slacks with a cool, cream-and-coral .cotton jumper (over a matching T-shirt) to protect her arms from sunburn. It never ceased to amaze her how all wealthy white folk sought opportunities to darken their skins in the sun, while every high-born Indian shunned sunlight, often seeking remedies to lighten their complexions as much as possible. Even people who ought to know better—like Lady Dorothy, Mr Redverse, and Baron Tikemoffsky playing shuffle board with the latest Begum Aga Khan near the pool which could be boarded over for dancing—did the same.

The day passed in a haze of deeply relaxing pleasures pursued in the civilised atmosphere of a perfectly organised boat boasting eight staterooms and six cabins apart from the crew's quarters. The cabins had been allocated to Honey's guests shortly on boarding so that those who wished to bathe, change, or take a nap after lunch, could do so in the privacy and comfort to which they were accustomed. As the party progressed from impromptu swimming sessions in the yacht's pool to the first-rate lunch served in the dining room designed to display several treasures from the Moneykurl collection, Kitten was struck by the fact that this small elite circle, existing well above national barriers and colour bars, enjoyed meeting each other as often and in as many different, fashionable places, as possible. They were the chosen few with the good karma, which allowed them to float through life buoyed up by an ocean of limitless funds.

That evening, Rudolf's mother, Queen Olga, was to

hold an informal party for friends to meet Lores Bonney, the first woman to fly 12,085 miles to London all the way from Australia, and the first person to fly non-stop from London to Cairo, and the Cape in South Africa. Between the lobster bisque and the ragout of ducks and grapes, the Crown Prince informed his fellow flying-freak Maharajah Tiger Fateypur that he would personally introduce him to entrepreneurs on the lookout for reliable test pilots.

For once in perfect accord, both his uncles immediately started raising several objections to this horrifying offer. Propriety forbade Tiger from contradicting them in public. But bestowing his most teasing smile on Sir Pratab and HH Pisshengunj, the Fateypur Maharajah announced: 'My uncles are absolutely right. We won't have time for dangerous hobbies like test-flying and driving once that chap Kitten calls Windmill Winnie, convinces his Allies to start fighting on the beaches, on the high seas, up in the air—and not with our bare hands, I hope—to fix those fascists.'

'And what about the Bolshies?' asked Honey, moving the conversation along like a good hostess once the laughter had died down.

'For the time being they're on our side, but knowing Winston, it won't be long before that *thing* he keeps talking about really drives us apart,' remarked Rothschild.

'Iron Curtain,' supplied Kitten, as the other guests speculated about the meaning of his baffling remark.

'What shall we do with this brat who always has the right answers?' demanded Tiger, flicking a chocolate mint at the Chattargadh Princess from the silver bonbon dish before him as he entertained his old mentor, Baron Rothschild, with the story of how she had literally used Agatha Christie's 'one phone call' leverage to get them out of prison in London just recently.

Raising his goblet in a toast as Kitten caught and ate the chocolate, the shrewd, heavy-set Aga Khan looked around the table asking everyone for suggestions about the theme for his masked ball next week. He listened courteously to their proposals, which ranged from Biblical figures, favourite literary heroes and heroines, characters out of the Arabian Nights, Wild West sagas, renowned kings and queens, and other historical personages from all countries, including China.

'Don't you think that historic persons have been done to death,' began Kitten in her most persuasive manner. 'How about some originality, Uncle Aga? Let's do a grand opera theme, with everyone dancing to overtures from stuff like *Der Rosenkavalier*, *The Marriage of Figaro*, or *Carmen*. There are endless possibilities for all your guests to come up with original costumes without too much trouble.'

The Aga Khan and his sensationally lovely young French wife immediately agreed, declaring that they would have the invitations engraved, requesting guests to come dressed as opera characters just as the Chattargadh Princess had so cleverly suggested.

'And no empire-building shorts or dress uniforms, Reverse Gear!' the snub-nosed Queen Olga added.

'Won't it be fun guessing who's who, before we all unmask at midnight!' said the Maharajah of Pisshengunj, delighted with the way Destiny was moving things along.

He grabbed the first opportunity for a private word with Tiger before they disembarked at Cannes. Both were freshly bathed and dressed in lightweight silk suits to attend Queen Olga's party. Shuffling his perfectly polished wing-tipped shoes around in his haste to escape from his tiresome relative, Tiger protested, 'Oh, come on, Uncle Nutty. We're enjoying a picnic.'

'Your entire life looks like a picnic to me!' swore his uncle. 'You have already wasted six years of your life fooling around the world aimlessly, instead of doing something useful like any other maharajah.'

'What else am I supposed to do? My uncle Sir Pratab virtually runs my State, and very efficiently too, as anyone can see.'

'Don't argue with me,' said HH Pisshengunj. 'Learn to assert yourself. How can Sir Pratab, who is merely your Dewan (never mind his being your father's younger brother) take you seriously and start thinking of his own *sanyas* (retirement Hindu style, preferably in the high Himalayas), when you can't even perform your basic duty by producing an heir for your 3000-year-old kingdom, in which, may I remind you, there has never been a SINGLE adoption, as history shows.'

Tiger took a deep breath to calm himself. He had no intention of rehashing this particular issue with anyone. If only his Nutty Uncle would remove his blinkers! He would be able to count two perfectly healthy, sane, and legitimate heirs to Fateypur in the direct line—his uncle Sir Pratab, and his son, Arjun, who would soon be having sons of his own.

But Nutty always refused to accept the status quo. 'Who's talking about another arranged marriage or dynastic alliance? Do you think I haven't got eyes to see which way the wind has been blowing since Ooty? You've tried your best to charm Elinor, but she's been leading you a merry dance just because of her silly father-fixation for another Maharajah, which any halfwit can see. But you are in a position to offer her an honourable marriage which my 'holier than thou' no-polygamy-allowed *Ram-avatar* brother—I'm naming no names—certainly can't. Or won't. Tell me, which girl in her right mind would throw away the chance of becoming your Maharani and gaining all the advantages flowing from your ancient title and fabulous wealth? Plus, pass up this enviable cosmopolitan lifestyle which very few Indian Maharajahs and British aristocrats can command?'

'That just proves how observant you really are,' scoffed

Tiger. 'Even if she said Yes, the British Government might refuse to recognise her as a Maharani, like that Frenchwoman HH Kapurthala married, or that Australian second wife of Palanpur Nawab Saheb. Sons of such marriages are automatically barred from inheriting the *gadi* (throne).'

The Maharajah of Pisshengunj urged his nephew to act like a *real* Rajput. 'Don't tell me that you lack the courage to fight the entire British India establishment! And the King's Privy Council too, because your treaty rights guarantee your freedom to forge matrimonial alliances without interference from the Paramount Power, even if the girl in question has influential uncles who go around calling themselves Viceroys and Residents! The only way to win Elinor Redverse is to lavish a great deal of attention on her and keep showering her with gifts which she can't resist. And when her rocky heart begins to melt a little with the warmth of your devotion, you should propose marriage to her in such an open, honourable manner, that you go down in history as the most lovable and romantic Maharajah, like your great ancestor, Shri Krishna Bhagwan.'

As soon as they began driving off from the quay towards the Rumanian Queen's stately mansion on the Boulevard Croisette, the Maharajah of Pisshengunj instructed his devoted Dewan Tikky: 'Get me a coconut as fast as you can.'

Rather puzzled, the Russian Baron inquired, 'What sort of coconut, Your Highness?'

'The kind that grows on coconut trees,' his master explained, with an airy wave of his hands.

'Really, Your Highness, I shall endeavour to carry out your command, if you would be so kind enough to explain exactly what SORT of coconut? Freshly diced, desiccated, chopped up, ground into chutney? Or scooped out for serving a Pina Colada, like we had this afternoon on Miss Moneykurl's yacht?'

'A proper, unblemished coconut,' cried the Maharajah so loudly that the English-speaking chauffeur engaged for their stay in the south of France, shot them a quick glance over his shoulder. 'If my brother-in-law hadn't gone underground pretending to be seasick, he would have understood exactly what I need. And why.'

'Really, Your Highness, I've yet to see the sort of brown-bearded, coir-matted, Indian ritual *puja*-offering coconut you seem to require, on the Riviera. Wouldn't an ordinary green one do just as well for whatever ceremony you have in mind?'

'Certainly not!' snapped Nutty. 'Which is the closest place selling such coconuts?'

'Africa, I imagine.'

The Maharajah of Pisshengunj ordered the chauffeur to stop the car.

'Then you will sail to Africa immediately, Baron Tikemoffsky. I don't care how you do it. Or what it costs. Charter a boat. Fly, if necessary. But get me a PROPER coconut before the Aga Khan's fancy dress ball!'

'You're going as WHAT?' Princess Diamond demanded.

'Mephistopheles,' repeated Kitten, treating everyone around the breakfast table—laid out on the balcony of their Carlton Hotel suite which boasted the best sea view in Cannes—to one of her devilishly innocent, wide-eyed looks.

Tiger Fateypur continued eating fresh strawberries sprinkled with a dash of cream and powdered sugar. 'Still under the influence of those people performing *Faust* yesterday at the Salle Garnier?'

Shaking her head from side to side as she patted croissant crumbs off her lips, the younger Chattargadh princess protested: 'Uhhn-huun. Not Goethe's Mephisto. Or Gounod's. But Boheetoh's . . . .'

'NOT before breakfast, please, Kitten,' implored her cousin Arjun, stopping her before she launched into a full-fledged discourse on their differing librettos, humming a few arias aloud for good measure. Dying to laugh, his wife Ratna maintained her demure, decorous attitude as she served tea to her mother-in-law.

A brisk breeze blew in the fresh fragrance of flowering orange and lemon trees and starry southern jasmine. It mingled pleasantly with their expensive perfumes and the strong coffee the three Fateypur princes preferred before facing the world after another inevitable, and unusually enjoyable, late night at the Monte Carlo Casino. Though the distance was nothing for men who thrived on speed, the hard drinking, gambling and socialising took their own toll when they were forced to drive back nearly 80 miles each way. But Princess Diamond, a seasoned traveller, believed that the secret of a happy, carefree holiday was to use one perfectly run, centrally located hotel as your pied à terre, and drive out to selected entertainments and events for which invitations poured in from all their famous villa-owning friends throughout the South of France. And since these three months in Europe gave her the only respite from running five palaces and a fort back home in India, she had vetoed all suggestions about buying their own place in Cannes. In any case, a large staff of retainers, which included personal maids, attendants, drivers, syces, cooks, and ADCs accompanied them on all their travels to pack and unpack, and cater faithfully to all their needs and whims.

Her aunt's irritation increased as Kitten paid no attention to her suggestion that she choose a more suitable costume for herself from other famous operas like *Aida*, *Joan of Arc*, or even *Porgy and Bess* if she wished to remain unrecognised. She wasn't going to have any of her blood relations capering around dressed as horned devils flashing tails and tridents at the Aga Khan's ball, making a laughing stock of themselves, *and* their guardians, in front of everybody who mattered on four continents. Diamond was forced to next urge her husband to speak to Kitten about preserving some decorum in public, and presenting at least a semblance of well-bred restraint.

Tall, upright and angular, Sir Pratab had an astonishingly large, high-domed forehead, a totally bald head (though only 44), and such a pointed chin that Kitten enjoyed comparing his face to a hard-boiled egg. This amused everybody except her aunt. But Sir Pratab was too well bred to lecture his wife's niece on what she should, or should not, wear to a fancy-dress party. These were *zenana* affairs in which he couldn't possibly get entangled. Naughty Kitten Baisa usually had excellent reasons for doing the most outrageously inexplicable things. She must have laid a largish bet that nobody would be able to guess her identity before they unmasked. It would be very unsporting to spoil her game.

In any case, there were other, far more important things on his mind. No matter how often Tiger reminded scandalmongers and mischief-makers that his guardians could just as easily have smothered, drowned, or murdered him in a dozen different ways while he slept, swam, rode, drove, or flew (instead of nurturing him so lovingly for nearly 19 years), Nutty's insidious hints and revelations had created several dilemmas for Sir Pratab and Princess Diamond. It was imperative that their nephew remarry if they wanted to escape the stigma of stealing his throne for their own son. But it was also essential for him to forge a matrimonial alliance with someone whose offspring would be acceptable to Fateypur's hereditary chiefs and nobles. They could see that Tiger was infatuated with Elinor Redverse whom he always singled out for attention at every party and function. But there was also Kitten, who naturally accompanied Tiger and her cousins Arjun and Ratna to beaches, casinos, museums, and cathedrals scattered all over

Provence, to the Grimaldi castle, to the various villas for swimming and tennis, to films and shows, and to all the fashionable restaurants along the coast.

However, although he was rather fond of the fun-loving young Kitten, with her remarkable *joie de vivre* and thirst for knowledge, he could never even obliquely broach the subject of another matrimonial alliance either with his own wife or Maharajah Jai Singh. He knew HH Chattargadh's strongly held ultra-modern views on polygamy, even if they had proved to be totally unrealistic, as Koodsu Rao Saheb's case had shown.

The Aga Khan's sumptuous parties were famous even among the super rich and powerful potentates (including kings and queens still on their thrones) who holidayed every year in the South of France. That August evening, the cliff top gardens of his mansard-roofed Cap d'Antibes mansion had been converted into a dazzling stage set, with all the cypresses, mimosa, palms, pines, and rose-trellised arbours and gazebos lit up with hundreds of tiny fairy lights, glowing with the same incandescent sea green and deep blue hues as the waters of the Mediterranean. Pink fibreglass water lilies bearing scented candles floated in the swimming pool, besides lining all the balustrades and steps where exotic orchids and ferns spilled out of alabaster urns.

The lawns were full of famous people whose true identities were camouflaged by silk masks and sumptuous opera costumes, which had been procured from Paris, Nice, or even from Milan across the hostile Italian border, and rigged up by scores of sempstresses working overtime in all the Riviera resorts and hilltop villages.

Accordionists and guitarists spelt out the full orchestra accompanied by singers, who sang arias from Bizet's *Carmen*, Wagner's *Tristan and Isolde*, Verdi's *Falstaff*, Rossini's *Barber of Seville*, and Mozart's *Don Giovanni* while guests disguised as characters from these well-known operas joined the dancers around the marble-skirted swimming pool. Faultlessly attentive French waiters served the finest wines, chilled champagne, and bite-sized canapes that wouldn't smear the masks when eaten. As the party progressed, couples and family groups arriving together agreed that half the fun of that night's Grand Opera at the Aga Khan's was in guessing correctly the identities of their fellow guests. The extra large Falstaff was obviously the King of Egypt. Her Majesty, Queen Frederica of Greece, had come dressed as Electra. Queen Olga guessed that the Redverses had turned up as Hansel and Gretel only because she had told Reverse Gear not to wear shorts! There was a fierce-looking Boris Goudunov, a scantily clad Salome, all the Merry Wives of Windsor, a William Tell, and even brown boot-polish, coated Porgy and Bess. One enterprising soul was disguised as the Thieving Magpie. The dashing Don Giovanni, with his seductive, mellifluous voice and assured manner, had already danced several times with Madame Butterfly. He could only be the extremely popular young Maharajah Tiger Fateypur. Many of the masked guests laughed when they saw a diabolically lurid-looking Mephistopheles chasing the dainty Madame Butterfly round and round one of the foaming fountains flanking the pool. By the time the orchestra struck up Puccini's famous Love Duet, the Japanese Madame Butterfly and the Devil had both vanished.

It was only minutes before they were to unmask at midnight, before the sumptuous sit-down banquet (about to be served on scores of round tables scattered around the deep, colonnaded corridors circling the entire ground floor), that Tiger finally got Madame Butterfly out of the Devil's clutches. The Thieving Magpie, who was none other than Nutty, immediately started rounding up the witnesses he had promised his nephew.

As Tiger led the beautifully coiffured, kimonoed figure wearing the traditional white Japanese socks and sandals away from the others, he caught heady whiffs of Guerlain's oriental *Djedi* perfume, which Elinor always wore. Drawing the still masked lady down besides him on a secluded marble bench facing the sea, HH Fateypur began in his most persuasive manner. 'At times I feel that we hardly speak the same language, sweetheart.'

Putting a silken scarf to her lips, the lady murmured, 'I often get the same feeling myself, Your Highness.'

The Maharajah removed his own mask, and kissed the palm of her gloved hand with great gallantry. 'Three days ago, I made you a promise. Don't look round—but now I'm asking you to be my wife and Maharani of Fateypur before witnesses from both our families. Please say Yes, Darling.'

'Really, Your Highness, I'm only too happy to say Yes!' declared Kitten, unmasking herself.

And before the absolutely flabbergasted Tiger could react, his uncle Nutty—seconded by the Rao Saheb of Koodsu—had thrust a great big coconut into his hand.

And thus, under the watchful eyes of his other uncle, Sir Pratab, their Resident, Lady Dorothy and their host, the Aga Khan, the alliance between Princess Kitten and HH Tyger Fateypur was irrevocably sealed. Ratna hugged Kitten, just as Elinor Redverse, also unmasked, came forward with a beaming smile to congratulate Tiger.

Only Princess Diamond stood apart, wondering how she would explain and justify this engagement (into which Kitten had so obviously trapped Tiger, not only with Nutty's connivance, but with the wholehearted support of their Crown Agent) to her elder brother when they got home.

Paid Back in His Own Coin 9

Arjun clung tightly to anything that was handy as an obviously angry but tight-lipped Tiger drove his open-top Bugatti at a furious pace through the sleepy settlement beneath the Aga Khan's villa. He drove at breakneck speed along the craggy, winding coastline, disregarding dangerous hairpin bends and leaving all the other departing cars far behind. All the cliff-top villages and tiled monasteries, surrounded by vineyards, pines, olive groves, and fragrant lavender fields, whizzed past, blending into a mélange which also included the foaming sea and several boats visible in the first flush of dawn.

'Please, Tiger Baapji,' pleaded Arjun, recalling the alarming accident statistics for this stretch of road as they zipped through an ancient Roman arch.

But his cousin refused to slow down even after reaching Golfe-Juan, where the fashionable Boulevard de la Croisette took a sharp turn towards the small harbour of Cannes directly below. August was the busiest month of the year for the entire Riviera, and business began very early in all the little resorts. Cafes were opening up. Flower sellers, vegetable vendors, and fishmongers were setting up their stalls in the cobbled market place. A farmer's lad setting down cans of milk, exchanged cheerful *bonjours* with a whistling newspaper boy slinging out rolled-up magazines and dailies as he cycled deftly from door to door. He turned to gawk at the two strangely costumed strangers in the beautiful, big convertible car. Someone's Siamese cat crossed the road. With commendable presence of mind, the superstitious young Maharajah immediately swerved to avoid 'that damned unlucky thing' cutting across his path. But the road being extremely narrow, there was precious little space for him to manoeuvre his huge car. He knocked over a milk can with his right bumper.

As the cat leapt towards the puddling milk, Tiger cursed aloud, breaking his self-imposed vow of silence. 'That's *two* bad omens in one morning, even before this damn day has begun!'

'Really, Your Highness, how can you blame cats and spilt milk for your shockingly rash driving?' expostulated Arjun.

Instead of going straight to their hotel for a spot of badly needed shut-eye after an utterly exhausting party and a thoroughly maddening drive, Tiger turned the Bugatti towards the beach. They sat in the low-slung open car, watching the waves pounding the shore and the jutting reddish rocks. It was high tide, and the last few stars were slowly disappearing. The first few birds of the morning began adding their varying notes to the roaring sea song.

The prospect of enduring any more silent hostility made Arjun touch his cousin with a tentative smile. 'Why are you behaving like a wounded tiger?'

'Because I've been trapped!' cried the Maharajah. Steepling his hands, his inseparable companion cocked a sceptical eyebrow.

'You were just doing your duty. And the whole family is so relieved and delighted at the way you stage-managed everything . . . .'

'*I* stage-managed everything? Arjun, have you lost your wits?' demanded Tiger.

Rebuffed, Arjun still continued valiantly. 'It doesn't matter who actually arranged this thing. But we should all be celebrating your engagement, Hukum.'

Turning fiercely on his almost equally handsome cousin-cum-heir, Tiger said through clenched teeth: 'Celebrating? When your blasted sister Kitten is the last girl on earth I want to marry?'

When a triumphant Kitten had revealed her identity, Arjun had also been completely flabbergasted. He too had expected to find an entirely different girl under Madame Butterfly's inscrutable Japanese mask and wig. 'That's what I always thought! So what made you propose to Kitten— and in public, of all places?'

'I was *not* proposing to her!' cried Tiger, tearing off his Don Giovanni ruff and velvet cloak.

'You weren't?' wondered Arjun, his brain assaulted by hideous theories as he tried to digest this statement from his normally truthful relation. 'But apart from me, several extremely influential people, including my parents and the British Resident, heard you.'

The exasperated Maharajah swore. 'You fool, can't you see, I was actually proposing to his niece Elinor. She wouldn't consider any other proposition, except marriage.'

Choking back the sudden spurt of laughter (which would have only enraged his liege lord and older sibling further), Arjun said that he must be joking.

'On the contrary, it is Kitten who has played a damn silly childish joke on me after forcing everyone into taking her to this party togged out as the Devil in black ballet tights! And, don't ask me why Elinor, who is normally so prim and proper, agreed to swap costumes with your mad sister. But you can tell Miss Sticking Plaster that the joke is over.'

Resisting the impulse to say 'Better the Devil you know . . . .' Arjun opted for the dignified reproach. 'Really, Your Highness, must I remind you that you begged the

Chattargadh Princess to marry you in front of witnesses summoned by some busybody. And, you also promised her more rights and privileges than those enjoyed by my respected sister-in-law still recuperating in Switzerland. You also accepted the traditional coconut from *two* of her kinsmen: Maharajah Nut-Bolt Singhji of Pisshengunj, representative of the Rathor ruling house, and Koodsu Rao Saab, representing the Chiefs of Chattargadh State, thus sealing the matrimonial alliance!'

Tiger had nothing to say to this. Convinced that Nutty Uncle had masterminded the whole thing for his own convoluted reasons—in cahoots, of course, with both the girls—Arjun turned his lean, laughing face and looked Tiger right in the eye. '*Raghu kul reeti sada chali ayi, pran jayi par vachan na jayi.* Have you forgotten how many blood feuds and vendettas have resulted from rejected coconuts? And how the kingdoms of Kanauj and Delhi were destroyed by the arrogance of Princess Sanyogita's father, Jai Chand, when he refused to accept Prithviraj Chauhan as his son-in-law even after their famous elopement and love marriage?'

'But dash it, can't you see, she's the wrong girl?' groaned Tiger, recoiling from the fate in store for him.

'Really, Your Highness, *I* know she's the wrong girl. *You* know she's the wrong girl. But unfortunately my silly sister Kitten thinks she's the right girl for you!'

Tiger lost no time in telephoning the Resident and Lady Dorothy and immediately inviting them to lunch at the Colombe d'Or, the celebrated seafood restaurant where even the rich and famous had to book tables in advance at the height of the season. Apart from its enchanting Marc Chagall ceiling frescoes, the restaurant and bar were decorated with paintings and etchings by Van Gogh, Picasso, Utrillo, Matisse, Braque, Boudin, and Bonnard.

All the round tables, draped in rose silk tablecloths topped with delicate lace, had bowls of fresh flowers, hand-painted Sèvres china, and vermeil flatware. Maîtres d'hôtel in immaculate black tails laid napkins across their laps, while the sommelier greeted the Maharajah with a deferential bow before discussing wines to complement the food selected from the glossy, tasselled menu. As they sipped the ice cold Mercier Brut Rose from Rosenthal champagne flutes, while watching the steady stream of fashionable regulars (like Colette and King Farouk, cosmopolitan beauties escorted by ageing tycoons, and dedicated gourmets for whom eating there was very serious business indeed), the British couple and the Indian Maharajah, inevitably, compared notes on the Aga Khan's party.

Savouring the unusual combination of asparagus and artichoke with the Monaco rockfish gallette which had followed the usual *pâté de foie gras,* plus the lemon and egg-garnished caviar starters, Lady Dorothy teased Tiger. 'Really, Your Highness, your perfectly plotted master stroke has left us all speechless!'

'I beg your pardon, Lady Dorothy?' protested Tiger, rather surprised by her reaction.

'I'm referring, of course, to your incredibly romantic public proposal to the princess of your choice,' she continued blithely, having learnt to take a Maharajah's three or four wives in her stride after her husband's longish stints as Resident to the Kings of Bhutan and Sikkim. Her short, puff-sleeved lime green linen jacket and gathered skirt enhanced her burnished auburn hair and hazel-eyed fair face, dotted with freckles which her light make-up couldn't hide.

His normally cool, canny blue eyes twinkling, Redverse drew the Maharajah of Fateypur's attention to a stack of newspapers and tabloids on a nearby wrought-iron stand. 'Every newspaper has gone to town on your carefully concealed romance, old boy. At that time it seemed a trifle dramatic, if I may say so. But upon calm reflection, I can see the wisdom of what initially appeared to be a rather impulsive move on your part.'

'Reverse Gear, you've got to help me sort this thing out before it gets completely out of hand,' began Tiger as soon as the saffron and fennel-flavoured fricassee of prawns had been served.

'At your service, Tiger,' responded Redverse, relishing the truffled potatoes accompanying this Provencale speciality. 'But I doubt that anyone can sell Maharajah Jai Singh the idea of his one and only daughter becoming anyone's second wife.'

'Exactly!' continued Tiger. 'May I count on you as Resident to both our states, to tilt the balance in my favour?'

While the young Maharajah, dressed in a pristine white open-collar shirt tucked into sharply creased white trousers, sat with a brooding expression in his marvellously long-lashed almond eyes, Lady Dorothy watched the packed sandy beach visible from the etched window directly opposite. Bare-bottomed girls and women clad in skimpy bikinis or swimsuits lay about on towels, acquiring suntans. Men in striped bathrobes and women in strappy sundresses lounged with books or newspapers on the wheeled orange deck chairs, where hotel attendants served them iced drinks under fringed beach parasols. Children splashed about in the luminous deep blue sea, running after bright beach balls, licking ice-cream cones and fluffy pink cotton candy, completing sandcastles before their elders dragged them away for unwanted food and boring afternoon naps. Contemplating the magnificent view of the bustling, well-ordered harbour and beautiful bay extending right up to the Isles of Larins, Dorothy's mind turned to the sea voyage which would take her and Gerry back to chaotic India via the Suez in a matter of days.

Meanwhile, Europe was hurtling towards chaos of a different kind if the buzzwords coming from their Chanceries in Germany, Austria, Poland, Hungary, and Belgium were to be believed. But, like all Britons, she was confident that not even the Nazis would dare disrupt normal life in Great Britain. She had concluded that her sons would be safe enough in their prep school after their summer holidays, which were to be split equally between their two grandmothers—Lady Frazer up in Scotland, and the Dowager Viscountess Redverse down here on the Riviera.

Having chosen a *crème brûlée aux zest d'orange* from the temptingly laden dessert trolley, Dorothy found her husband and Tiger still talking at cross purposes as they opted for cheese and coffee. Exceedingly relieved by Tiger's astonishing public proposal and consequent engagement to the Chattargadh Princess (which had certainly put an end to his extremely unwelcome advances towards his niece Elinor), Redverse realised that Tiger was smart enough to know that he would need allies to deal with his future father-in-law.

No one could be more obdurate on points of principle than Maharajah Jai Singh.

'I'll do my best, Tiger. But you've got to remember that HH Chattargadh won't like losing face. As you know, he passed a law forbidding polygamy in his State way back in 1924, when he inherited the kingdom from his father who, I'm told, kept a string of concubines in addition to having two wives. And then, there were all those step-grandmothers making young Maharajah Jai Singh's life miserable, until he settled them all in Mount Abu, in a palace overlooking the Nakkhi Lake.'

Tiger's hopes of getting out of marrying that infuriating brat Kitten began rising as he also remembered HH Chattargadh's reasons for his deep-rooted aversion to polygamy. 'Oh, yes. And quite rightly so. Don't you recall the *tamasha* over Koodsu Rao Saheb's exile for flouting this ban, and remarrying for the sake of begetting heirs?'

The reference made the Resident and his lady recall all
the hold-ups and protocol problems—including the hilarious
pig-sticking business during the Prince of Wales's visit to
Chattargadh—resulting from the differences of opinion
between the two Rathor rulers over progress versus tradition.

'Talking of tradition, wasn't it providential that your
Nutty uncle, HH Pisshengunj, had a coconut handy to seal
the matrimonial alliance between your two families? But
then, I suppose, guests can procure virtually anything they
need at the Aga Khan's. I also have it on excellent authority
that, according to time-honoured Rajput custom, now there
can be no real hurdles to your marriage with Kitten,'
reflected Redverse.

Once again, Tiger Fatehpur had nothing to say.

'Even if it *is* your second marriage, as an independent
ruling Prince, you are not bound by the laws of other
Indian states. And though the Princess herself is subject to
her father's legislation—which has a built-in lacuna because
it omits the word "bigamy" and focuses only on male
polygamy, ha, ha—it will clearly be her one and only
marriage. So, strictly speaking, although His Majesty's
Government prefers that its Agents remain detached, in this
particular situation, it would be quite appropriate for me to
lend you some support,' continued the Resident.

'Mind you, I don't condone polygamy. But in certain
circumstances, one has to be flexible,' added Lady Dorothy
broad-mindedly.

'Specially in India,' concluded Gerald.

'Quite right. What I'm trying to say is—how shall I put
it . . . .?' continued Lady Dorothy.

But her husband cut her short.

'Really, Your Highness, we old India hands know the
score. Marriage for Maharajahs is largely a matter of ensuring
the succession, exactly like for the British monarchy. And
aristocracy,' the Resident assured the Maharajah.

'Let's drink to that,' smiled Lady Dorothy, raising the small sweet Sauternes goblet to toast their young host.

Tiger's hopes of help and sympathy from the British Resident and his wife in this whole unholy mess were completely shattered as he saw them clinking their glasses.

Even though every traditional courtesy had been punctiliously extended to her by everybody as the Maharajah's married sister on a brief visit to her ancestral home, the battle with her formidable brother that Princess Diamond had anticipated was on in full swing. She had realised that it was she who would have to restore calm in the family, and also discuss the hundred-and-one details involved in this unforeseen alliance into which she had been dragged, willy nilly, as the closest relative on *both* sides.

Still feeling euphoric, Kitten was rapidly re-adapting to the desert heat and palace protocol after the blissfully cool and carefree three months in Europe. Four ceiling fans whirred overhead, and everyone was compelled to speak much louder than usual to be heard above the noisy desert cooler throwing a steady stream of *khus*-laden air into her mother's drawing room. She was confident of handling her father's unarticulated yet apparent displeasure regarding her recent betrothal.

Diamond noticed that Maharani Padmini was being even more deferential than usual as she offered her the enamelled cigarette box, once the serving maids had removed the tea trays. Robin immediately brought out his crested Cartier lighter, but himself refrained from smoking out of deference to his parents and aunt. Although Uncle Kishen had also been summoned to this family conclave, he had, for once, remained tactfully aloof, refusing to get involved. He had taken his thoroughly embarrassed other uncle, Sir Pratab, off for a long ride. Having heard the truth regarding the entire affair in which Kitten had been aided and abetted by an astonishing number of people who should have known better, Robin had also decided to say as little as possible. For no matter what his father said, the engagement between his sister and Tiger Fateypur was already a *fait accompli*. And knowing Kitten, who had come back flashing that awfully ostentatious sapphire ring in addition to that dreadful tiger-claw pendant she always seemed to be wearing, Robin was convinced that the marriage would be solemnised exactly according to her lifelong plan.

'My dear Sister, no one's blaming you. We all know that Tiger needs a second wife. Good luck to him, but do we really want our daughter to make such a shocking misalliance?' Maharajah Jai Singh asked.

'Then write and tell him so. But please don't drag me into this tussle. And before you say another word about divided loyalties, Bhai, may I remind you that if Kitten is dearer to me than the daughter I've never had, Tiger is dearer to me than my own son.'

'What a mess,' continued Jai Singh. 'But that's what happens when young people forget their own traditions, and become modern.'

'But Papa,' exclaimed his irrepressible daughter. 'I always thought that you were in favour of modernisation!'

'In moderation.'

'Really, Your Highness, then you'll be very pleased to hear that the correct traditional procedure was followed for securing this extremely advantageous *second* matrimonial alliance between a Chattargadh Princess and a Fateypur Prince. Your dear Nutty relation, the Maharajah of Pisshengunj, acted *in loco parentis*!' laughed Padmini, determined to strike a positive and happy note. '*Hajoor*, if Kitten doesn't mind being Tiger Baapji's second wife, I don't see why we should place hurdles in their path.'

It was really very difficult for Maharajah Jai Singh to convince his wife, who hadn't grown up in a turbulent household seething with the intrigues and demands of four grandmothers, a stepmother, and several rapacious young concubines. But it was his duty to extricate his spirited daughter from this disastrous folly. 'Kitten, haven't you always thanked God for not making you a second son?' When she nodded her head, Maharajah Jai Singh continued: 'Believe me, being a second wife is much worse.'

But Kitten didn't want to be extricated from a situation she had so avidly sought, and worked so hard to create. 'This is my destiny, Hukum,' she said, her face deadpan.

Amused by his iron-willed sister's demure, soft-spoken response, Robin heaved a theatrical sigh. 'Diamond Aunty, d'you think we could persuade Tiger to change his mind?'

'Out of the question!' said his outraged aunt.

'Have you gone mad, Robin? No Rajput worth the name—least of all a Maharajah—can back out of a marriage after actually proposing to the girl himself. And that too in front of witnesses, and after disregarding all the correct customary procedures—like waiting for a third party to make the initial approach, matching horoscopes, etc., etc. On top of that, Tiger even accepted the *coconut*! Don't you know that, among us Rajputs, that is as binding as the sacred wedding ceremony itself?'

'Really, Your Highness,' grinned Robin. 'I thought you didn't want this match.'

His father said that he was astute enough to know that no good could come of any scheme aided and abetted by Nutty. He reminded Robin of all the ugly hoaxes and tricks the Pisshengunj Maharajah had played on his Chattargadh relations over the years, including those false cables sent to him in London with the connivance of bribed British telephone operators. His gut instinct warned him that Kitten had been misled and ensnared by that loco chap for some nefarious purpose of his own. And, he was simply doing his duty as a parent by warning her that she could

still call the whole thing off even if it upset Tiger. She
would apologise to him for the childish trick she had played
on him with their Nutty Uncle's ridiculous connivance, and
get out of marrying him. Young Tiger was far too sporting
and good natured to hold grudges against any one. Besides,
there was no shortage of well-born girls whose parents
would be only too willing to enter into a matrimonial
alliance with a state like Fateypur.

But his daughter would hear none of it.

'Sorry, Father. You see, I have given my word of honour
to Fateypur Durbar. *Raghu kul reeti sada chali ayi, pran
jayi par vachan na jayi!*'

So lavish were the dowry, ceremonies, and celebrations
organised for Princess Kitten's wedding to the exceedingly
wealthy and good-looking Maharajah of Fateypur that even the
Nazi propaganda machinery took time off to focus international
attention on Chattargadh. BBC broadcasts gave details of
everything, including the list of invitees on both sides.

The night before the wedding, several famous
courtesans, imported from Benaras and Lucknow, took
turns at entertaining Maharajah Jai Singh's guests. There
were, in addition, lavishly ornamented local dancing girls in
their flaring *ghaghras* and tinselled veils performing ritual
Rajasthani folk dances to traditional wedding songs sung by
fiesty female singers seated on carpets in the Palace
courtyard. Gifted male musicians accompanied them on
elongated drums, the sarangi, sitar, *tanpura*, and tabla. The
grand marble courtyard, surrounded by colonnaded
verandahs, resounded with the sound of music, laughter,
cheerful voices, tinkling anklet bells and bangles, all of
which rose to the latticed sandstone *jharokhas* (windows)
through which all the maharanis, princesses, their guests,
and maids watched the revelry below. The moonlit
November night was cool enough for the royal ladies to

enjoy dressing in heavy, gold-embroidered satin and brocade costumes and family jewels, without being forced to spoil the whole effect of their ensembles by being covered over by warm Kashmiri shawls.

The jewelled swords and turbans of all the maharajahs, princes, and aristocrats made a colourful splash in the glow cast by several tall Bohemian glass pedestal lamps with tinkling, long crystal lustres. The Europeans invited to this function, including the Resident, Colonel CP, and Baron Tikemoffsky, were distinguished by their faultless white jackets, bow ties, and decorations. All the Chattargadh chiefs and ADCs were busy making sure that the Palace butlers and orange turbaned retainers kept the trays of drinks, kebabs, nuts, and other snacks circulating. In addition to the two professional photographers employed by the Maharajahs of Chattargadh and Fateypur, Colonel Claude-Poole was also busy snapping pictures for the features commissioned by *Life* magazine, and the *London Observer*.

While the dancing and merrymaking continued, Maharajah Jai Singh, his father-in-law Maharawal Bakhat Singh, his brother-in-law Sir Pratab, his cousin R.K. Kishen, son Robin, and grandson Pat took turns waving silver coins over the bridegroom's pink turbaned head (to ward off the evil eye) and presenting them courteously to the dancers and singers. Nutty Pisshengunj also stood up, fanning a stack of hundred rupee notes around his nephew, and tossing them into the veil of the prettiest dancing girl. She withdrew, thanking him profusely with folded palms.

Resuming his seat on Jai Singh's left, the Pisshengunj Maharajah preened himself as he sat swinging a foot—shod in the most extravagantly jewelled gold-mesh slippers especially devised for him—to the music. Craving the attention denied him, Nutty leaned closer to the head of his clan. 'Really, Your Highness, haven't you noticed something special about me today?'

But having kept abreast with the Pisshengunj Maharajah's kinky ideas and utterances by his well-placed spies, Jai Singh pretended total ignorance just to tease him. The story of how his order for a pair of diamond-studded *mochris* (up-curled traditional Indian slippers) had been rejected by the Bombay, Delhi, and Calcutta-based Hamiltons (with the terse response that they were jewellers to Viceroys, not cobblers to Princes), was known to most of the family and friends present.

Still determined on one-upmanship, the Maharajah of Pisshengunj pursed his petulant pink mouth. 'But Bhai, its not enough to say that I'm ALWAYS extraordinary! You must look again.'

Jai Singh gave a puzzled shrug after casting another careful glance over his relation. 'I'm completely foxed. Mr Redverse, perhaps you can guess what HH Pisshengunj means?'

Entering into the spirit of horseplay which seemed de rigueur during every royal Rajput wedding, the Resident set down his whisky glass, and studied Nutty from head to toe. 'Uhhmm . . . Let's see . . . Really, Your Highness, pardon me for mentioning the obvious, but don't you think the splendid effect of Maharajah Pisshengunj's wedding finery is somewhat marred by those dusty slippers?'

'Some people can't tell the difference between diamonds and dust!' scoffed Nutty.

The bride's relations, including Arjun, laughed. Jai Singh solicitously requested his ADC, Thakur Ganpat Singh, to summon a *poshaki* (valet) immediately to clean Pisshengunj Durbar's fancy footwear.

But, before the ADC could react, Robin came and stood deferentially before Nutty. 'Really, Your Highness, why should my favourite uncle look scruffy, when I'm here to serve him? *Ateethi Devo Bhava!*' With a lightning swift, fluid gesture of his athletic polo player's body, Robin removed the diamond-encrusted slippers from the feet of the astounded guest.

Loud spurts of laughter from everyone collected in the courtyard, and all the ladies watching from the upstairs *zenana* windows applauded Robin's actions as he raised the Pisshengunj Maharajah's footwear to his forehead in an obvious parody of Prince Bharat's worshipful action immortalised in the *Ramayana*.

Only Nutty was not amused. Burning with indignation at having the tables turned on him by his presumptuous heir presumptive, and unable to snatch his valuable shoes back without an unseemly public scuffle, Nutty sat fuming. 'Robin, I know you're dying to step into my shoes, but you can't have *this* particular pair.'

'Nutty Uncle, what difference does it make who wears them today, as long as your priceless shoes stay in the family?'

The next day, the Resident dawdled over his restorative black coffee and yoghurt breakfast. The boisterous midnight banquet at the Palace with too many drinks, overspiced Rajasthani kebabs, venison, partridges, rich *pooris,* pulav, and sweetmeats had not suited his system and given him a bilious attack. Suddenly, he heard a car drive into the Residency. Tossing down his napkin, Redverse strolled across the plant-filled verandah. He wondered what had brought Robin and CP here at this eleventh hour, when everybody had their hands full, trying to cope with the demands of various wedding guests and all the prescribed ceremonies, not to mention the bridegroom's procession to the Fort which involved much protocol and precise, astrologically auspicious timing.

'Mr Redverse, you've got to come with us immediately!' urged Robin.

'My dear Prince, Dorothy and I wouldn't miss your sister's wedding for anything. But what's the hurry?'

'If you don't hurry up and get cracking, Reverse Gear, there might be *no* wedding,' said his friend CP.

The Chattargadh heir-apparent cast the Resident a look of such uncharacteristic entreaty as he endorsed this urgent need for haste, that the Englishman, still in his shirtsleeves, smelt a rat. 'Now wait a minute, Robin. If this is another of your famous practical jokes . . . .'

'Would I joke about a thing like this? Our family has been intolerably insulted and humiliated by His Nutty Highness, and there's bound to be bloodshed if things are not put right immediately,' swore Robin.

'Then you must cajole the Maharajah of Pisshengunj out of the sulks by immediately restoring his diamond-studded, gold-mesh slippers!' said the Resident.

Robin told Redverse that this latest development had nothing to do with anything he might have pinched the previous night. No one could make insinuations about their *honour*, and attempt to scuttle the wedding by planting such ugly rumours. The whole world respected his father's integrity. Even notoriously tight-fisted German bankers loaned him millions of pounds just on his verbal guarantee!

More puzzled and concerned than he cared to reveal, the British Resident raised a hand to his firm, bony jaw. 'Hmm. Will one of you please tell me exactly what's going on?'

Colonel CP pushed his hat back ruefully, revealing his red corkscrew curls. 'The Palace was like a madhouse when we left to fetch you, with hot heads on both sides pulling out their swords, and the Maharajah's father-in-law, Maharawal Bakhat Singh, ordering me to surround the place with the entire State army if necessary, to prevent the bridegroom and the *barat* (wedding party) from disappearing without the bride!'

Her hair still damp from a late, leisurely bath, Lady Dorothy joined the three men, looking conspicuously

chagrined and solemn, standing in the Residency verandah.
'Hello, folks. Thought I heard some familiar voices. Would
anybody care for some fresh lime juice, coffee, or tea?'

'Please, Dorothy. Not now.'

'Why, Gerry! Is anything the matter?' asked his wife.

'That's just what I'm trying to find out.'

The Resident's lady suggested that it might be more
appropriate if they all sat down while they got to the
bottom of it all. But Robin said that their hostess must
forgive them, because they had to get back immediately to
the Palace with the Resident to avert absolute disaster.

'It's a damned lie! How dare HH Pisshengunj accuse us
of such an unthinkable fraud?' fumed Robin, directing a
fierce glance at Redverse.

'Please calm down, Prince. CP, can you tell me exactly
what happened to make the doggone Maharajah unleash
this latest fiasco?'

'Aided and abetted by his sycophantic brother-in-law,
HH Pisshengunj has spread a rumour that this wedding is
nothing but a hoax, and that HH Chattargadh is palming
off a look-alike connection (one of the old Maharajah's
granddaughters from his Muslim concubine, to be precise)
on Tiger, instead of the true Princess,' revealed Colonel
CP.

'Oh no!' cried Lady Dorothy. 'Our Maharajah would
never do anything like that. But surely Kitten herself can
quell this rumour?'

'You forget, Lady Dorothy, that my sister has to remain
in complete seclusion in the *zenana* until the wedding is
over once the *haldi* and *henna* ceremonies begin. She's not
allowed to break the traditional taboos even if Uncle Nutty
convinces the bridegroom and his relations to call off the
wedding on some absolutely false, flimsy pretext.'

It was abundantly clear to Gerald Redverse that Nutty
Pisshengunj and his brother-in-law had devised a clever trap

for humiliating Maharajah Jai Singh, and for punishing
Kitten who had made a hobby out of teasing, baiting, and
deflating them. They were trying to settle old scores with a
vengeance by disgracing the entire State, *and* destroying
Kitten's future. No one would marry a Rajput princess so
scandalously rejected by her bridegroom's family just hours
before the ceremony.

Lady Dorothy was also very concerned about Kitten's
happiness. Apart from her great fondness for the
refreshingly sporting and bright young princess, she had
been greatly entertained and impressed by Kitten's
persistent pursuit of an indifferent Tiger whom as everyone
knew, she had adored almost from birth. But the much
older playboy-Maharajah had agreed to marry her purely
for dynastic reasons. Even he seemed to have finally
accepted that his first wife Maharani Yasho Rajya Laxmi
could no longer hope to provide heirs for Fateypur.

A last minute cancellation would break Kitten's heart.

'We can't let them get away with this, Gerry.'

'Of course not,' said the Resident.

The Palace courtyard, which had resounded with so
much music, laughter, and merrymaking only a few hours
ago, had become an arena for disgruntled parties from both
sides to eye each other suspiciously, all the while weighing
the pros and cons of the story which had originated, as
they well knew, from no less a person than the Pisshengunj
Maharajah. The latter had offered his sister's son the
traditional coconut even in a foreign country like France
for the sake of his kinswoman Princess Kitten, who would
have inherited his kingdom automatically had she been the
second son of Maharajah Jai Singhji of Chattargadh.

Sir Pratab and Arjun were the only two people trying to
reason with Nutty. Convinced that Tiger's maternal uncle
was at the bottom of this whole nonsensical business, his
paternal uncle told him in the politest terms not to

embarrass everybody by giving credence to baseless gossip. Any attempt to obstruct the marriage between the Chattargadh Princess and HH Fateypur would have disastrous consequences.

The Resident could see that Maharawal Bakhat Singh was bristling with hurt pride and anger at the ugly slurs cast on his daughter and son-in-law, who was worth more than all the other 17 (already present) Maharajahs put together as far as chivalry, honour, generosity, and other Rajput traits were concerned. Flourishing his gem-embossed, gold-hilted sword, the fiercely bearded old Dudu ruler said: 'Rejdunt Saab, I am told Maharajah Pisshengunj chop my head up, make football, if bride switched-dhwitched from Princess Kitten only. Bloody fool think I lie for my granddaughter even? Now I chop his bloody head, dead!'

Getting the gist of this involved speech, Redverse responded firmly with a tactful bow. 'Your Highness, I'm here to ensure that there's no bloodshed.'

'And the only way you can do this is by telling Tiger's people to get on with the wedding,' said Maharajah Jai Singh.

Determined to bulldoze their way through this incredible situation, the British Resident and the Military Secretary strode up to Koodsu Rao Saheb, who stood whispering and confiding his own opinions to several Fateypur chiefs' glaring balefully at Maharajah Jai Singh. Greetings were exchanged briefly. 'Rao Saheb, as a close connection of everybody involved, this is the perfect opportunity for you to play a statesman-like role. You can convince HH Pisshengunj that there's no truth in this ugly rumour about the bride being someone other than Princess Kitten,' said the Resident.

The Chattargadh chieftain shrugged his shoulders with a positively gloating smirk. How time and destiny had turned the tables! Koodsu Rao Saheb remembered how shabbily this very same Resident had treated him just a year ago when he had gone to plead for the reinstatement of his *jagir* confiscated by Maharajah Jai Singh after he had been exiled for committing polygamy/bigamy—or whatever it was! And now, he wanted his own beloved daughter to do exactly the same with the help of everybody, including the British Government!

'Sorry, Rejdunt Saab. My position is too humble and delicate for intervening in the personal affairs of *three* princely families. So, I'm remaining non-aligned!'

The Resident played his trump card later, much after he had listened to some more of the Pisshengunj Maharajah's awful piffle. 'Really, Your Highness, you have my word that Lady Dorothy will stay glued to the Princess throughout the *zenana* ceremonies and the actual wedding. And although HH Chattargadh disapproves of polygamy *and* bigamy, he wouldn't ruin his daughter's life. Everyone knows how utterly she loves your nephew, Tiger.'

Buttonholing Arjun, Colonel Claude-Poole said: 'Dash it, Arjun. Talk to your cousin. He can't let this disgusting medieval melodrama continue.'

'Expect no help from Brother Tiger. He'll be only too glad to get out of this weird marriage,' sighed the Bhati Prince. Although Tiger Baapji had fallen disastrously into Kitten's complicated charade, he had begun hoping for a sudden reprieve from his fate. 'He doesn't want to be tied for life to that unpredictable, pig-headed Rathor princess, whom we have both been brought up to indulge or ignore like any other irritating younger sister!'

'Indeed!' said the tight-lipped soldier, fixing Arjun with a baleful glance. 'In that case, would you mind enlightening me as to *why* he proposed to our Princess in the first place.'

Family loyalty compelled Prince Arjun to defend Tiger.

'But that's just the point. He didn't. He thought he was proposing to someone else. But she turned out to be the wrong girl.'

Colonel CP couldn't believe what he was hearing. 'Honestly, Arjun, now don't *you* start another silly story.'

'You don't have to believe me, but if the Resident's daft niece, Elinor, hadn't changed places with Kitten, none of this would have happened!'

The Englishman walked off in great indignation. He had had many shocks and surprises during his tenure among these mad Rajputs, but this one really took the cake! Mistaking black-haired, black-eyed Kitten for an English girl, indeed!

At that moment, Reverse Gear wanted a word alone with him, away from all the hypersensitive Maharajahs and their intrigue-ridden retinues. 'Did you tell His Nutty Highness that the Viceroy won't like this *tamasha* one bit, because it's sure to lead to fresh feuds and bad blood between God knows how many princely states?'

'I did. But the Pisshengunj Maharajah retorted that this was a purely personal, family affair between blood relations, in which the British Government wouldn't interfere if they had the least bit of respect for Queen Victoria!'

'Ah, yes. That proclamation. But you and I know this is nothing of the kind. This is pure vendetta about to turn into a blood bath. And who will face the music, when the story reaches His Majesty's Government? You and I, Reverse Gear, the poor sods who happened to be here on the spot.'

Struck with a sudden thought, Redverse clutched his friend's arm. 'Music? Did you say music, CP old chap? You've just given me an idea. Where's the nearest telephone?'

It wasn't long before Reverend Mother Angelus floated through all the assembled arguing maharajahs, chiefs, and other guests, including several influential Europeans. A good deal baffled, Maharajah Jai Singh went forward to welcome the Mother Superior who had educated Kitten from Kindergarten to Senior Cambridge. But she strode straight towards Nutty, with only a polite inclination of her head to Kitten's father.

'Really, Your Highness. What's all this nonsense I hear about the bride not being the true Princess?'

Nutty immediately began shaking his head from side to side in protest. 'I didn't say any such thing, Mother Angelus. If you must blame anybody, you must take my brother Maharajah Jai Singh to task. He has no way of proving that the girl he's bent upon forcing my nephew Tiger to marry is his own daughter!'

Bestowing a scathing glance on the Pisshengunj Maharajah, the headmistress spoke with calm authority. 'Come along with me. We are going to bury this absurd rumour once and for all. For the proof of the pudding lies in the eating. And you yourself must testify that the girl marrying HH Fateypur is none other than Princess Kitten.'

'Certainly, Mother Angelus. But where's the guarantee that there won't be further foul play once you and I are out of the *zenana*?'

'Really, Your Highness, if you suspect me of complicity in any foul play, then I'd better close down our convent in Pisshengunj,' said the aristocratic Irish nun, with icy politeness.

'What!' cried Nutty. 'And stop my music lessons?'

'I'm afraid so, Your Highness.'

'No, never. I won't let you do that, not for anything in the world.'

'Then come along, like a good chap, and identify the bride. And the rest of you get on with the wedding procession, and so on.'

The full horror of what their Nutty Uncle had almost achieved struck Kitten as she joined the Mother Superior on the long piano stool after allowing him to select the music they would play in order to silence all speculations about her true identity. Although seething with rage, and determined to make HH Pisshengunj pay a heavy price for his disloyal perfidy, she chose, for the moment, to behave with unusual restraint. The Maharajah of Pisshengunj had opened the score for Bach's Allegro from the Brandenburg Concerto No. 5. He had also insisted on turning the pages himself.

As if that would frighten her into muffing a piece she could play by ear! Mother Angelus indicated that she take the treble, which involved more finger work. This would convince even the most sceptical acquaintance that she was indeed the Chattargadh Princess, and not one of her grandfather's illegitimate descendants.

Maharani Padmini's drawing-room and annexe were crowded with several witnesses, including the Resident and Lady Dorothy, Ratna, her mother and aunts, and Robin's wife Wendy. Princess Diamond chain smoked throughout the piano recital, glaring balefully at Nutty Pisshengunj, who was bent upon causing trouble for no rhyme or reason. This was the first time a male foreigner—not counting the Prince of Wales, who was family—had crossed the *zenana dyodhi*. But then, this was also the first time anyone had trampled on their family honour.

The Resident's wife led the applause when the romantic piece, originally composed for the harpsichord, came to an end.

'Are you satisfied, Nutty?' demanded Jai Singh.

'Of course, Bhai. Even a carbon copy couldn't go dueting with Mother Angelus. That's my niece Kitten, alright,' admitted Nutty, flushing slightly.

'Really, Your Highness, I'm sure everyone downstairs will be happy to hear your announcement,' said the Resident, rising.

Maharajah Jai Singh thanked Mother Angelus for preventing disaster, and called for some sherry. Instead of apologising for virtually having ruined Kitten's life by succumbing to baseless gossip, Nutty began finding excuses for his unpardonable behaviour. 'This whole unfortunate misunderstanding has been caused by Kitten's unlucky stars. But all is well that ends well; so I'm off now to bathe and dress for the wedding procession.'

Settling her slippery saffron veil over her right shoulder, Kitten rose from the piano to confront Nutty. 'Please don't bother, Nutty Uncle. Let's just cancel the whole thing, because what's the use of fighting malevolent stars?'

There was an upsurge of alarmed reaction from all the queens and princesses, decked out in sumptuous costumes and jewellery. The most serious came from her apprehensive mother who knew her impulsive, headstrong daughter only too well.

But Gerald Redverse caught the naughty little wink she gave him.

'What nonsense!' cried Jai Singh, wondering what had got into their daughter, who had so far insisted on going through with this undesirable marriage to that famous philanderer Tiger, who already had a wife.

Princess Diamond ground out her cigarette and marched up to confront her niece. 'Kitten, you can't insult Tiger like this, by calling off the wedding at the last minute!'

Mother Angelus sighed, dismayed. 'Dear Lord, after all that spade work . . . .'

'Now look here, Kitten,' began Ratna. 'You can't do this to all of us, after everything we've done to make sure you can marry the man of your choice!'

Kitten faced them unwaveringly. 'I'm really sorry to cause so much trouble and expense. But nobody can fight Destiny,' she sighed. 'Perhaps I'm only destined to be a burning bride, like the Khilji Sultan's daughter who dreamt of marrying Prince Biram Deo of Jalor.'

Thoroughly alarmed—for with Kitten in one of her

awfully stubborn moods, one never knew—the Maharajah of Pisshengunj protested. 'But don't you know that the British Government takes a very dim view of things like *sati* and *thuggee*?'

'They even go so far as to depose and exile Maharajahs who participate in—or precipitate—such things,' announced the Resident ominously.

Interpreting this as a warning from the Paramount Power, Maharajah Natwar Singh of Pisshengunj clasped his hands together, looking apoplectic, and struck his forehead. '*Hey Bhagwan!* Kitten Baisa will ruin me, when I have always been her fondest relative and most helpful *loco parent*.'

Maharajah Jai Singh's discomfiture also increased with every passing moment. 'Kitten, please be reasonable. This is hardly the time for obsolete Rajput rituals. You can't throw away your life for nothing! You have our word that the wedding ceremony will take place, as planned.'

'Is this what we taught you at the Convent, my child?' began the Mother Superior. 'HH Pisshengunj is bending over backwards to make amends for all the anguish he's caused. Surely you can show that generosity of spirit for which your clan is famous . . . .'

But at this point, Kitten interposed in a palpitating, grave voice. 'You're forgetting the jinx Uncle Nutty sees in my stars, Reverend Mother.'

'I know ways and means for getting around unlucky planetary configurations, and pacifying each and every bad star!' swore Nutty.

Maharani Padmini cast him an unblinking glance. 'But the sort of complicated *Jantar Mantar* you usually suggest takes too much time, Laljisa.'

'Nonsense,' the Mother Superior remonstrated. 'All we need to settle this entire uncalled-for confusion is a little Christian charity, Kitten.'

'I'm more than willing to repay my debt to parents and

teachers by showing simple charity, Mother. But there isn't enough gold in the entire Chattargadh state to do what our astrologer wants us to do in this particular case, you know.'

'What *does* your Raj Purohit suggest?' demanded Nutty.

Casting down her large, luminous eyes, Kitten replied: 'He wants me weighed against gold coins while he performs some complicated *tantric havan*; and then he wants me to distribute every single coin to the poor and needy *before* I enter the wedding *mandap*.'

The angry, rueful look vanished from Maharajah Jai Singh's face as he listened to his daughter. However, his wife, sister, and all the other ladies present were still considerably agitated by Kitten's threatened self-immolation.

The Resident shook his head sadly, and spoke in the most dejected tone he could muster under the circumstances. 'Really, Your Highness, it's such a great pity that your State cannot bear this burden even for the sake of HH Pisshengunj. But surely a loan can be arranged with a few phone calls?'

Kitten glanced at her wrist watch and heaved a dramatic sigh. 'There's no *time*, Mr Redverse. Therefore, there's no alternative except a dignified death for me; and dethronement for poor Uncle Nutty—the catalyst for my heroic gesture. But all these things don't matter a bit to people like us, who believe in rebirth and reincarnation.'

Thoroughly dismayed, Nutty swore unhesitatingly. 'Resident Saab, Chattargadh may have emptied its treasury chasing canals and other unnecessary things, but its sister state Pisshengunj has enough credit rating to outweigh Princess Kitten three times over!'

With a beaming smile, Kitten promised: 'But I'll pay you back in your own coin, Uncle Nutty!'

At last, as twilight fell, kettledrums, cymbals, horns, and conch shells resounded. Ancient standards fluttered. Tiger's own high priests and *charan bhaats* sang Sanskrit chants and invoked the gods and goddesses of good fortune, smashing coconuts and lighting ritual lamps and incense at the right moment. Magnificently caparisoned and painted elephants, with golden *howdahs* and ADCs perched behind whisking yak tails, carried the bridegroom and his two uncles, Sir Pratab Singhji of Fateypur and Nutty Pisshengunj to Chattargadh's ancient fort for the ceremony. Several senior chiefs and *sardars* walked ahead, dressed in festive robes with brocade cummerbunds. In front of them were scores of brightly costumed and ornamented dancing girls twirling, clapping, and undulating to the brash bridal folk tunes being belted out by Chattargadh's brass and bagpipe bands, marching alongside. The clatter of more than four hundred hooves filled the air as the bridegroom's kinsmen rode jauntily in procession, wearing splendid turbans with jewelled aigrettes and sword-belts. They were escorting the brocade and Basra-pearl draped golden palanquin in which every Fateypur prince's bride was carried away after the ceremony.

The Palace, the Fort, all the temples, and major public buildings were beautifully illuminated with coloured lights for the wedding. And, nearly every dwelling in the city was lit with earthen lamps or tiny electric bulbs (as though it was Diwali) showing solidarity with their esteemed ruling house on this joyous occasion. Public opinion was solidly on the side of their beloved younger princess, who was finally marrying the amazingly rich and handsome Maharajah often seen since the time he was a lively little boy visiting Chattargadh with his foster mother, their senior princess, Diamond Baisa.

Everyone who could manage to do so, had converged on the Fort with all their children, or taken up positions along the barat's route. The streets on both sides were hung with auspicious mango leaf and marigold garlands. From every rooftop, window, and balcony, the popular and well-known young Maharajah of Fateypur was showered with flowers, grains of rice, greetings, and good wishes by the people of Chattargadh. Laughing women clad in bright-hued veils burst into ribald song as soon as Tiger's elephant drew near.

This grand wedding procession paused at the Fort's main gate to allow the bridegroom to touch the ceremonial *Toran* with his jewelled sword. The chanting of traditional mantras by the Raj Purohits was drowned by the flurry of kettledrums, and the plaintive wail of several *shehnais* signalling the end of childhood for Princess Kitten.

Camel-mounted musketeers, lancers on horseback, and soldiers in gala uniforms stood evenly spaced around and inside the Fort to control the celebrating crowd from swamping the procession. But numerous children had clambered on to all the heavy cannons lining the moat. Hundreds of enterprising youths and yokels were perched on the ancient trees growing out of its sturdy walls.

From the Fort's ramparts, groups of aristocratic ladies who observed purdah, and lots of little girls dressed in colourful costumes, watched the bridegroom's procession entering the great unpaved Chattar Mahal courtyard already full of a motley crowd of men, women, and children from the underprivileged classes. These included all the beggars and mendicant priests, who made a living by going from wedding to wedding throughout Rajputana.

The bards and musicians sitting on striped dhurries on the marble terrace adjoining the courtyard, began eulogising the Rathor and Bhati clans loudly as soon as Tiger appeared, his face partially obscured by the tassels of rubies and pearls dangling from the hereditary traditional *Sarpech* worn by every Fateypur Maharajah since the sixth century.

Maharajah Jai Singh, his son Robin, his grandson Pat, his nephew Arjun, cousin Kishen, father-in-law Maharawal Bakhat Singh, and close relations like the Mysore

Maharajah, all stood on the terrace steps. They looked
resplendent in their full ceremonial regalia of diamond-
buttoned brocade and Khinkhab *achkans*, feathered and
jewelled turbans, swords, priceless emerald, ruby, and pearl
necklaces. Tinselled flower garlands and rosewater flagons
were ready in their hands to receive their counterparts from
the bridegroom's family. Chattargadh's hereditary Chiefs
(including Koodsu Rao Saheb); the British Resident (the
one really responsible for ensuring that the wedding actually
took place); the Maharajah's camera-wielding Military
Secretary; and several European guests (especially the Agent
to the Governor-General of Rajputana); and foreign state
officials stood slightly behind them, watching the *mahavats*
manoeuvring their elephants through the crowds. Next to
the Chiefs stood the State's exceedingly wealthy Marwari
Seth-Sahukars (merchant princes), who had already bestowed
the customary lavish gifts on their princess after receiving
the Maharajah's personal invitation.

All the ruling princes attending the Chattargadh
Princess's wedding to the Maharajah of Fateypur sat on
comfortable velvet-upholstered, silver gilt armchairs with
matching footstools, flanked by hereditary *chawari* and *mor
chari* bearers. They agreed that both the weather and the
hospitality were perfect, and that everybody could have a
right royal, rowdy time once the sacred wedding ceremony
passed off without another hitch. Chattargadh's well-trained
butlers and turbaned retainers circulated among them with
silver salvers loaded with drinks and nuts. All the ADCs
stood in watchful groups, ever mindful of the needs of their
respective Maharajahs. Everyone was in their Durbar dress
and heirloom jewellery, befitting the occasion.

As soon as the hullabaloo of *naggaras*, *dholis*, and
damamis singing the happiest wedding songs announced
the *barat's* arrival, the small sandstone balcony overhanging
the huge, iron-spiked arched gateway into the Fort's main

courtyard was filled with beautifully robed and jewelled queens and princesses.

Kitten was easily distinguishable by her sumptuous gold and pearl-embroidered scarlet wedding outfit and gorgeous jewellery. It had, as was the custom, been sent by the groom's family, because unwed Rajput girls were expected to dress very simply and behave modestly. Crimson-coloured ivory bangles covered her arms from wrist to elbow. Tasselled diamond amulets flashed on her upper arms. Beautifully wrought ruby and diamond head ornaments and earrings sparkled in the bright light. The great teardrop pearls of her nosering and heavy breastplate-type bridal diamond-and-gold necklace quivered as Kitten stood there surrounded by her aunts and cousins. Her face was unveiled, and her teeth actually gleamed as she laughed outright.

'Now, everybody! Here comes Uncle Nutty. Let's give it back to him in his own coin!'

The moment Maharajah Natwar Singhji of Pisshengunj began climbing off his kneeling elephant, Kitten, Ratna, Princess Diamond, Princess Sita, the Mysore princesses—and even Lady Dorothy and Mother Angelus—began pelting him with fistfuls of gold coins.

The princesses giggled harder as Nutty turned towards them in stunned fury, crying, 'Stop! What are you doing?'

Fortunately for them, Maharani Padmini—the only person who could quell Kitten in one of her wicked, vengeful moods—was far too preoccupied with her ceremonial duties to be anywhere around. She had already gone, attended by seven happily married Rathor kinswomen, to stand ready with the customary mother-in-law's *aarti* to welcome Tiger at the threshold of the old apartments from where every Chattargadh princess had been given in marriage by her guardians since the 15th century.

Sudden pandemonium erupted in the courtyard below,

as all the children, dancing girls, musicians, beggars, and priests realised that their Princess and her family were tossing *real* gold coins to them. With high-pitched shrieks of excitement and joy, the out-of-control crowd of hereditary largesse-pickers converged on the Pisshengunj Maharajah, laughing and shoving each other good-naturedly as they scrambled to grab the gold before anybody else took away their share. The outnumbered soldiers and lancers failed to restore any semblance of decorum as Kitten and her cohorts kept on targeting Nutty with every coin he had contributed for her ritual weighing.

Those too well born to spread their hands for baksheesh turned their heads and craned their necks to gawk at this unseemly scramble taking place around HH Pisshengunj, who had lost his turban in the melée. Soon, they too began laughing and sniggering as they slowly understood the famous joke played on him by the royal ladies.

Even the aristocrats and Maharajahs couldn't help bursting into laughter as they watched Kitten, relishing every direct hit and laughing uproariously. She was quite unlike any royal bride they'd ever seen!

Tiger was far too well bred to turn around, or look back over his shoulder, to see what the commotion was about. But it was obvious that all courtly decorum had fled from the occasion. The minstrels and musicians had paused mid-song, and launched into a rollicking ditty they kept improvising as they sang on. It was full of unmistakable references to their quick-witted and courageous princess for taking such a delightful and swift revenge on Pisshengunj Durbar. He should have known better than to cross swords with a true Rathor!

Even Maharajah Jai Singh was undismayed. He was only too aware of the ludicrous figure cut by Nutty in his dishevelled finery being jostled and pushed around by beggars he was trying to fend off with his sword. Managing to control the chuckles that overcame him, HH Chattargadh said to his Resident: 'So that's what she meant by paying him back in his own coin!'

'And jolly good too. But we don't want His Nutty Highness trampled to death, do we?' responded Redverse.

'He richly deserves it though,' added Colonel CP.

'Some other time,' Raj Kumar Kishen grinned. 'It wouldn't be considered auspicious on our Princess' wedding day, you know.'

Those standing close enough to hear this remark, including Sir Pratab and Arjun, laughed.

Adjusting their feathered high hats, the British Resident and Military Secretary marched off purposefully to rescue His Nutty Highness while Maharajah Jai Singh began performing the ceremony of welcome for his son-in-law Tiger.

The Jinxed Bride 10

Every single ceremony safely over without any more of his relatives battered by his bakseesh-bestowing bride, Tiger Fateypur reclined with his feet up on a luxurious down-cushioned sofa. He had shed all his heavy jewellery, turban, sword, and other unnecessary stuff, including his buttoned-up-brocade *achkan*. The king-sized ivory-inlaid bed had been lavishly adorned with fragrant jasmine and rose garlands, even though marriages between aristocratic couples such as himself and Kitten were consummated only after several complicated ceremonies, and during the right planetary conjunctions.

Revelling in the privacy regained after being on public display and carrying loads of regal wedding paraphernalia for nearly four days, Tiger blew a cloud of cigarette smoke. His gaze was fixed on the apartment's beautifully carved sandlewood ceiling.

'Arjun, can you fix me a drink now that we're finally alone?'

'Certainly, Tiger Baapji. Hot milk, or cold water?' asked his solicitous cousin, standing before an old-fashioned, ormolu-ornamented commode on which thermos flasks, crystal glasses, fruit and nut bowls were arranged on silver-gilt salvers.

HH Fateypur hurled his gold-braided wedding garland at the prince. 'Stop clowning like your maternal relations!'

Deftly catching the garland with one hand, Arjun pointed
to the uncorked flasks with a flourish. 'Really, Your Highness!
D'you want to spill all this milk, and invite bad luck on
your wedding day?' He poured and sipped a glass of milk.
'Ahh . . . this has got sleep-inducing Ovaltine, y'know. Not
the usual saffron-almond-musk concoction served to chaps
in your position!'

Waving the glass away, Tiger mused: 'I still can't figure
out if it was accidental. Or deliberate . . . .'

'What are you talking about?' demanded the Prince, sitting
down on an armchair facing his Maharajah.

'That shower of gold.'

'Oh, you mean when Zeus came down on Diana from
heaven—or rather, Mount Olympus?'

'My dear Arjun, you've certainly got a good memory,
but I'm not discussing Greek mythology at the moment—
just Rajput mentality,' he said, looking down his aristocratic
aquiline nose.

'Ha-ha-ha-ha!' laughed his cousin. 'Really, Your Highness,
if you want to live in peace now that you're a twice-wed
man, please remember that dear Kitten believes in good,
old-fashioned, instant, Rajput-style revenge!'

'Spoilt brat,' said the Maharajah, clicking his tongue. 'I
don't look forward to acting as a buffer between your crazy
sister and my Nutty Uncle . . . .'

A polite knock stopped him from saying another word
about the princess. Instead, he asked Arjun to get rid of
whoever it was outside. Didn't they realise how late it was?

However, disregarding his young nephew, Raj Kumar
Kishen strode in. He had come to implement his *own*
Maharajah's instructions regarding meticulous attention being
paid to Tiger's slightest whim. HH Fateypur was not just
another visiting Maharajah. He was now their son-in-law, with
virtually limitless claims on their hospitality and resources.

Tiger instantly sprang up, courteously assuring the elderly

Chattargadh prince that all the *bandobast* was absolutely first rate, and they didn't really need anything.

'Well, if you insist, Uncle Kishen, we could certainly do with a couple of White Ladies before going to sleep.'

Completely flabbergasted by this unexpected demand, R.K. Kishen held a hurried confab with HH Chattargadh's most trustworthy ADCs, Zorji and Thakur Ganpat Singh. They too expressed their surprise and shock at this latest twist to the already excruciatingly taxing and humiliating day in which they hadn't known till long past midday whether their Princess's wedding would actually take place. And now, this.

'You must be joking, Raj Kumarsa. Even Fateypur Durbar couldn't have asked you for a couple of White Ladies on his wedding day . . . because you're just like his own father-in-law!' protested Zorji.

'Come on, Zorji. Tiger's not going to change his spots just because he's married to Kitten Baisa now. And you heard Baapji's orders.'

Thakur Ganpat Singh sighed. 'For the Princess's sake, we have to keep him happy at all cost. Particularly after this morning's fiasco.'

'You've said it,' agreed the Chattargadh Dewan. 'But where are we going to find the type of White Lady Tiger prefers in a small place like Chattargadh, and at this time of night?'

'Simple. I'll ask the Rejdunt, or Colonel CP,' said Zorji.

'Over my dead body!' cried the prince. 'This is a private Palace *mamla* (matter), not something for the Residency and all our European guests to laugh about.'

Ganpat Singh made a pacifying gesture. 'Raj Kumarsa, Fateypur Durbar is really a very easy-going, good-natured prince. Why don't we just inform him that we are unable to fulfil his wishes due to circumstances beyond our control?'

R.K. Kishen nodded. 'All right, Gadbad Singhji. You be the informer.'

The ADC soon returned in high dudgeon. His

companions sat awaiting further developments on the marble benches placed in the verandah overlooking the lily pond. 'I'm not ready to stand such humiliation ever again, Raj Kumarsa! What sort of State does Fateypur Durbar think we are?' he said angrily.

'Don't get so worked up over nothing, Gadbad Singhji. There is always a lot of leg pulling, and jokes between both sides during any Rajput wedding, as you well know,' said R.K. Kishen.

'Yes, Hukum. But you too will be shocked to hear what Fateypur Durbar said. He thinks we should look in the Palace *cellars* for White Ladies! As if our Maharajah would leave anybody alive if they dared to hide any such stuff there. Such things have never happened in any decent Rathor State in our entire 1400-year-old history!' he retorted hotly.

'This is getting serious, Raj Kumarsa,' Zorji said in a subdued tone.

Kishen Singh's apprehensions regarding Kitten's future increased as he recalled how stubbornly she had dismissed all their advice about not demoting herself to the position of a mere second wife. And that too of a renowned ladies' man like Tiger. Now her family members could only hope and pray that she would quickly have a son. Then everybody in Fateypur would be compelled to treat her with the respect and consideration due to the mother of the heir to the kingdom.

The Rathor prince rubbed his eyes. 'If we were sitting in Bombay, Delhi, Calcutta, Bangalore, or Ooty at this moment, one phone call would have flooded the palace with White Ladies.'

'Raj Kumarsa, I still feel that the Rejdunt will help, especially now that Baapji has made him a *pagri-bandh* brother (blood brother by exchanging turbans),' reiterated Zorji.

'Oh no, Thakur Saab. We must keep the British out of this because it's an extremely delicate, personal matter. Ganpat

Singhji, why don't you grab the first car, rush to Khanpur Cantonment, and bring back some White Ladies as fast as you can, and no matter what it costs. In the mean time, I will apologise to Tiger for the delay.'

Colonel Claude-Poole was just in time to prevent the ADC from commandeering the Palace car assigned to take him home. He had just escorted the Rajputana AGG and other bigwigs attending Kitten's wedding bash to the Maharajah's recently constructed European-style guest house, surrounded by sturdy shade trees beyond the Croquet Lawn. 'Wait a minute, Thakur Saheb. You can't pinch the car I've just managed to order from the motor garage!'

'Sorry, Kernull Saab. But Raj Kumar Kishen Singhji has just instructed me to grab the *first* car, and drive non-stop to Khanpur Cantt.'

The British officer was frankly puzzled. 'What on earth for? It's nearly two o'clock in the morning. And surely you deserve some rest, after all the running around you've been doing for the *bandobast* since the day before yesterday?'

'A Maharajah's ADC is never off duty . . .' said Ganpat Singh with a characteristic shrug of the shoulder as he opened the front door.

Knowing from past experience that there was no reasoning with any of these Indian chaps once they started rationalising their often odd behaviour, Colonel CP conceded defeat, merely requesting the ADC to drop him off at his bungalow. However, curiosity compelled him to ask why Ganpat Singhji was dashing off to Khanpur, a British cantonment located nearly 43 miles north-west towards Punjab in the middle of the night.

'To fetch a couple of White Ladies for our son-in-law, HH Fateypur.'

'Driver, stop!' cried CP, chuckling merrily as the full force of this ridiculous revelation hit him. 'You don't have to go traipsing off to some cantonment even if you have to oblige

Maharajah Tiger Fateypur! Just ring up the Residency if the Palace has run out of stock.'

'Certainly not,' snapped the ADC. The uniformed Palace driver kept the car stationary but the engine running until Thakur Saab and Kernull Saab decided what to do. 'We can't insult the Rejdunt by making him procurer for the Palace. That idiot Zorji suggested the same thing! And now, you too.'

'Oh, Gar-bar Singhji, Gar-bar Singhji!' exclaimed the Englishman, laughing uproariously. 'I say, let's go and check out the Palace cellars first before calling up anybody.'

A few minutes later, Tiger and Arjun were gleefully quaffing cocktails as their good Samaritan, Colonel Claude-Poole, regaled them with this latest evidence of Rajput madness. Undecanted bottles of vermouth, Martini, vodka, and white wine stood on the ivory-inlaid table between them, with buckets of ice, and crested cocktail shakers.

'My reputation, CP, my reputation!' cried Tiger, shuddering melodramatically.

'Would have been mud, my dear chap, if I hadn't caught our good old Faulty Tiger Gar-bar Singh in the nick of time. You and your White Ladies!'

Levity got the better of the three young men enjoying the perfectly concocted White Ladies, a real passion with the Fateypur Maharajah, in addition to pink champagne. 'I can't understand why your illustrious uncle surrounds himself with rustics who don't know the difference between a drink and a dame!' said Tiger, his eyes twinkling merrily.

'Because they are a darned sight better than the intriguing rascals surrounding *your* Nutty Uncle!' retorted Arjun.

Two days of tedious train travel even in his sumptuously appointed royal saloon was not something Tiger willingly subjected himself to, especially after he had attained his majority and been invested with full ruling powers by the British Government. But his foster parents, Sir Pratab and

Princess Diamond, had prevailed upon him against flying in and out of Chattargadh for his own wedding because of the hundred and one ceremonies and superstitions involved. He had agreed, finally, to go by road. Fortunately, the road journey between his coastal state (which stood on the Indian peninsula's western-most tip bordering Saurashtra and Rajputana) and Chattargadh (due north-east at a distance of about 500 miles) could easily be accomplished in a matter of hours, provided the roads were in good condition. And in Rajputana, just as in Saurashtra, the rulers saw to it that these were properly maintained, except when sandstorms, typhoons, floods, or other acts of God worked to spoil them.

That was how Princess Kitten, now the junior Maharani of Fateypur, found herself travelling to her new home in great style. A cavalcade of roomy Rolls Royces and Bentleys transported her and all immediate family members and personal attendants. The rest of the *barat* travelled in the special train chugging its way to the same destination via the circuitous metre-gauge tracks which would take them first to Jodhpur, Abu Road, and then all the way down to Palanpur, before halting finally at Fateypur.

For a bride venturing into an awesomely new environment where her beloved bridegroom already had a Senior Maharani who would always take precedence over her, Kitten appeared to be ecstatically happy and cheerful. She even had an unseemly giggling fit when her cousin-cum-sister-in-law regaled her with a second-hand version of the previous night's White Ladies incident, which had been prevented from becoming another infamous Chattargadh hospitality fiasco which the other States could enjoy sniggering about if they got to know, by Colonel CP's timely intervention.

Finger to lip, Ratna shushed her. Uncle Kishen and Thakur Ganpat Singhji, doing escort and driver duty on this occasion, were bound to overhear them even through the glass partition that separated them. Kitten, who often fought a losing battle between her inborn tendency for levity and a carefully cultivated propriety, was not in the least offended by this reprimand from her impeccably well-behaved relative. Both the princesses riding in the lavishly decorated Rolls wore beautiful new *zardosi* embroidered *lehnga-dupattas*. One was in salmon, the other in shocking pink, and had been chosen from their respective bridal trousseaus. They were offset by truly magnificent heirloom jewellery from the Fateypur ruler's collection. In addition to their car's tinted glass windows, they were completely screened off from all curious eyes by thick strands of pearls hung inside the windows, and elaborate flower garlands draping the entire Rolls on the outside.

They also obstructed Kitten's view of the unknown but new countryside, so different from the desert States she had travelled through so far.

'Ratna, don't you wish we'd gone all the way to Fateypur by train? Then we could have moved about a bit and chatted with our husbands and brothers, instead of sitting here cooped up in the back seat of this stuffy, slow-moving car, worrying about people overhearing our conversation. This purdah business is too suffocating!'

'Kitten, will you please stop grumbling. You'll have to make lots of adjustments in your new position. And the sooner you start behaving like a mature married lady, the better it will be for the entire family.'

'I can't suddenly start behaving like you, even if I want to,' said Kitten disconcertingly.

Ratna turned around to give her cousin a teasing smile. 'We all know that leopards don't change their spots. I only meant that you'll have to toe the line and at least conform to the norms laid down for newly married Maharanis. Until, that is, you've established your hold over Tiger Baapji . . . .'

'I wonder how long that will take.' said Kitten pensively, gazing at a noisy nomadic encampment besides a pond full of buffaloes bathing amidst water lilies.

'Well, that will depend largely upon you and your Kismet!' replied Ratna with a roguish expression.

'You silly thing,' scoffed Kitten, playfully thumping her with one of the velvet cushions provided for their comfort. 'I was asking you how long will it take before we reach Fateypur?'

Ratna gave her a look, and glanced at her diamond-encrusted wrist watch. 'Hmm . . . It's a quarter to seven now, and we've already passed Jhabua where we stopped for tea. So we should be home in another hour or so.'

'Isn't there some shooting lodge or inspection bungalow where we could stop?' asked Kitten.

'I'm afraid not, because its so close to the city. But we'll ask Uncle Kishen to stop our car near some bushes.'

Discomfort overcoming all refinement-induced embarrassment, Kitten was forced to slide open the curtained glass partition ensuring their privacy. 'Uncle Kishen, I'd like to go around the corner.'

'My dear niece, you must be joking! Why should you go around corners when Fateypur has such nice, broad roads?' demanded Raj Kumar Kishen Singh over his shoulder.

Amused—and somewhat stumped—by his inability to comprehend a politely worded request for catering to basic needs, Kitten clutched her sides in spurts of laughter. So far, her governess and nannies had always taken care of all this with commendably quiet efficiency, and without the appalling indecency of involving male family members, or ADCs. Ratna also succumbed to giggles, with much clinking of bangles and jangling of jewellery.

'Do something to make them stop the car!' cried Kitten. Saying that it was even more embarrassing for her to approach their thick-headed escort with such a delicate request, Ratna leaned forward, clearing her throat.

'Uhh-hum, Uncle Kishen, could you please stop the car for five minutes? We want to spend a penny.'

'In the middle of this jungle?' responded the Chattargadh

prince with a jovial chuckle. 'And in any case, as long as I'm with you, do you think I'll allow you children to spend your *own* money on anything, even if you're married into one of the richest states of India?'

The two cousins couldn't help hugging each other, and rocking to and fro in helpless mirth at this priceless response. However, this only increased Kitten's discomfiture, especially when she thought of all the lengthy ceremonial welcome rites she would have to endure *after* the long palanquin ride through the city streets before she gained any privacy. As the Queen of England had said, 'one must go whenever one can, because who knows for how long one won't be able to, y'know!'

'Uncle Kishen, kindly stop the car immediately. I have to powder my nose,' announced the newly wed Maharani imperiously.

The exasperated elder, teased once too often by this girl, heaved an exaggerated sigh. 'Don't you realise that you'll be in purdah all the time, Kitten? So, nobody's going to really see *your* face. Why waste time on make-up shake-up? I can already see the great glow of lights over Fateypur, where all your new relations and subjects are waiting to welcome you.'

This sent Ratna off into another helpless giggling fit. However, by now, Kitten was only aware of her continuing ordeal. She groaned loudly. Tossing aside all well-bred restraint, she ordered: 'Thakur Ganpat Singhji, stop this car *now*. We have to go to the jungle!'

The ADC immediately braked. Holding the door open solicitously for his descending niece, Raj Kumar Kishen Singh said with an impatient click of his tongue; 'Why didn't you say so in the first place, instead of beating about the bush?'

Since she had already spent too much time gazing out at the enticing, unfamiliar sea swirling right up to the palm-fringed beach beneath her windows, Kitten realised that she would have to rush through her bath. She had slept late, lulled by the soothing sound of the waves which reminded her of her marvellous Riviera holiday and her dreams of somehow marrying Maharajah Tiger Fateypur. They had materialised, once she had got him to propose. But now that the wedding ceremonies were over, she was thankful that she would no longer be subjected to those great gooey globs of almondy turmeric paste being slathered all over her body, morning and evening, for seven days, by seven beaming aunts and cousins, all in the name of bride beautification.

Half an hour later, she sat radiant faced, with every pore in her powdered and perfumed body tingling with anticipation as the senior-most married maid who was part of her dowry, dried her hair expertly with warmed towels.

Kitten was actually looking forward to shedding her old identity as an individualistic and self-centred unmarried princess, and taking on the richly rewarding role of her husband's indispensable alter ego. She had begun doing so since the day she had been joyfully received into the family fold by the Fateypur Maharajah's Bhati *kabila* (extended family), and *bhayat* (blood brotherhood), after the worship of their family deities at the Fort and the port, were over.

A soft knock on the door put on end to any further fantasies. She was in the process of draping her scarlet wedding veil to her satisfaction. She did not want it to obscure the awesome, two-ton diamond-encrusted bridal necklace. Jamna Bai gave the heavy, flared *lehnga*—loaded with gold thread, sequins and pearl embroidery—a final tug. So busy was she in arranging her veil that she hardly heard the faint tinkling of glass bangles, the jewelled anklets, and the politely articulated request. Before she knew it, Maharani Yasho Rajya Laxmi had floated into her husband's brand new second wife's apartment.

She had done so at a most awkward time. And without any prior warning.

Diminutive, unbelievably dainty, and porcelain-pretty, the Nepali princess (who had been married to Tiger for almost seven years) made herself at home on the large chaise-longue piled with tasselled silk cushions. 'I'll have my bed tea with Princess Kitten. Or should I say, the younger Maharani Saab?'

Kitten's personal maid, dressed in a festive *zari*-work *bandhni* outfit, went off with folded palms to carry out this command. After giving the braided and appliqued taffeta bedcover on the huge, art-nouveau-style bed a final pat, her childhood nurse, Jamna Bai, also retreated.

There couldn't have been a greater contrast between the ethereal, soft-spoken, and gracious older Maharani wearing an elegantly seductive Parisian chiffon-and-lace negligee and nightgown, and the formally costumed and jewelled younger girl, still very much a stranger to this place. For the first time in her life, Kitten found herself at a disadvantage, for she was totally unfamiliar with Fateypur's palace protocol and customs. Since too many kingdoms and fiefdoms often got gobbled up by solicitous fathers (and brothers), visiting daughters (and sisters) with minor sons and heirs, there was a very strong taboo against such visits among Rajput royal families. It was thus that, even though her aunt Diamond had been living in Fateypur for ages, Kitten had never visited it before her wedding.

As they sipped tea from the fragile and translucent rose-patterned bone china cups, the senior Maharani graciously asked Kitten to help herself to the delicious assortment of British biscuits on the table between them.

'I hope you don't mind this informality, my dear. Usually, one doesn't dream of stepping beyond one's apartment in a dressing gown. But HH is still fast asleep, you know. And I simply didn't have the heart to disturb him. But duty prompted me to make sure you've been made comfortable in this unfamiliar new place!'

Doing her best to appear unflustered by this clever

hammer-blow to her emotions and aspirations, Kitten merely murmured a few courteous words of thanks.

The Senior Maharani's slanting topaz eyes appeared even more feline in her high-cheekboned face which was framed by tousled ebony curls cut just above her tiny waist. 'Darling, you don't have to be so formal with me, you know, now that we're *both* married to the same man!'

Blushing a brick red, Kitten made a brave attempt to explain the inexplicable. But Tiger's first wife floored her by revealing that she knew all about how *Hajoor* had proposed to Kitten under the illusion that he was, finally, about to get hold of a British bride!

'There's no need whatsoever for either of us to feel awkward, Kitten. Multiple marriages are the custom rather than the exception in families like ours. I myself grew up in a bustling, happy home, with four mothers, and *nine* grandmothers, each one of them a character in her own right! Think of all the fun we can have together, going for picnics, sailing and swimming in some of our lovely little lagoons during the summer; or else playing cards or mah-jong; and even tennis doubles with Diamond Aunty and Ratna, *without* waiting for HH or Arjun to join us.'

Entering into this civilised spirit of camaraderie displayed by the exceedingly refined and well-bred Nepali princess, Kitten confessed: 'At home, Ratna and I often got the Resident and his wife, or Colonel CP and one of the ADCs to give us a proper game if family members were not free.'

'Uhh-humm,' said the Senior Maharani, pouring herself a second cup of the fragrant Chinese jasmine tea. It was sent to her regularly via Kathmandu. She took it twice a day with only lemon and honey which kept her skin and system toned. 'Isn't it too bad, Darling, that Maharanis can't do so many of the perfectly innocent things unmarried princesses can?'

'But I've always had the impression that Tiger Baapji is even more progressive than my own father.'

Maharani Yasho Rajya Laxmi gazed at Kitten with a coy half-smile, only slightly raising her delicate, wing-tipped eyebrows. 'That's what you think! Just wait till you get to know him a wee bit.'

'Well actually, I've known him since the day I was born!' retorted Kitten.

'But you've never been what I would call really *intimate* with him, Princess,' teased the first wife, walking gracefully towards the door. The Palace tower clock had started chiming eleven. As the door shut behind her, she left behind an incredulous Kitten who was now wondering how she was going to achieve the great transition which had seemed so easy and natural only an hour ago.

Baffled but unbeaten, Kitten tackled this task by settling down in her new home *before* she began the slightly more difficult one of securing her bridegroom's undivided attention. Since hers was a hyperactive mind encased in a hyperactive body currently caged by conventions pertaining to royal Rajput brides, she began by exploring Tiger's home turf under the aegis of her uncle and aunt. They were clearly keen to hurry things along by building a bridge between the newly-weds. The raison d'être for this muddled marriage could so easily be defeated by their nephew flying off— perhaps never to return—to fight in a war which was really none of anybody's business in India.

With so many celebrations and ceremonies to keep her busy and entertained following her arrival in Fateypur, Kitten had very little time for private reflection about her bridegroom's peculiar behaviour. For, Tiger was continuing to treat her exactly like a close relative on an extended visit to his State. He made all the appropriate arrangements for her comfort, including a monthly allowance running into quite a few lakhs out of his own Privy Purse. She was entitled to this according to the legal settlements incorporated in their nuptial agreement. He also turned up punctiliously twice a day in her apartments to make good-natured enquiries about her welfare, always encouraging her to read and ride just as much as she used to before they were married.

Standing on the westernmost tip of the Indian peninsula which jutted out into the sea beyond the Rukmini delta, Fateypur was not hemmed in like the other Saurashtra States. One of the legendary nine 'Nau-Kot Bhati' States founded by the descendents of Shri Krishna—that most endearingly human, profoundly philosophic and irresistibly amorous of all Indian deities—Fateypur had a distinguished 3,000-year-old history which Kitten found engrossing. The track leading to the actual spot where Krishna's wedding to Rukmini was solemnised with Vedic rites before he installed her as his chief Queen at Dwarka, was lined with stone carvings depicting scenes from the *Bhagawat Purana*, the *Mahabharata*, and verses from the *Gita*.

Blessed by the goddess Laxmi in her Rukmini *avatar* (incarnation), Fateypur was a region enriched by fertile cotton fields, groundnut and banana plantations, and good grazing land along the delta named after her. Kitten found that this lotus-eyed daughter of the Sea, also renowned as Laxmi, the goddess of wealth, had also blessed Fateypur with inexhaustible pearl fisheries, beautiful coral formations, mangrove forests, and abundant sea fish. At least its non-Brahminical population could feed off the latter in the worst of times!

An impregnable harbour dominated by twin forts made Fateypur a secure refuge for fugitives fleeing persecution from nearby countries. It wasn't surprising that during its three millennium-long existence, this entrepôt acquired the greatest number of immigrant communities to be found anywhere on the Indian subcontinent, after Bombay and Calcutta. That all the refugee Parsis, Jews, Syrian Christians, Shia Persians, Ishmailis, Ethiopians, Arabs, Anglo-Indians, and Eurasians found not only security but an astounding degree of prosperity, spoke volumes for the astute and fair-minded rulers who had accommodated them over the centuries.

Fascinated by her new home's history, Kitten discovered that seafarers like Herodotus, Ptolomy, Pliny, Ibn Batuta, Ibn Senna, Vasco da Gama, Tavernier, and even Admiral Yamamoto—before the Japanese invaded Britain's Far East colonies—had not only cast anchor in Fateypur's fjord-like harbour, but also kept copious records of their dealings with its shrewd natives. Even without reading between the lines, she could tell that all these famous travellers sounded downright envious of the local people's flair for maritime and mercantile activities. She, in fact, saw no harm in people making trade and the acquisition of wealth, their main preoccupation.

Even the Mughals, it appeared, had appreciated Fateypur's commercial clout by exempting its rulers from tribute *and* matrimonial alliances, because their navy helped control Arab and European piracy on the western coast. The Fateypur kings also considered it their sacred duty to grant free passage to *all* Haj pilgrims setting out for Mecca from their port.

Besides becoming an unrivalled diamond and gem-cutting centre (and pearl mart) long before the Mughal era, Fateypur had always been a bustling sea port. Kitten found that more than one thousand registered ships had been trading out of Fateypur since 1820. Harbour dues yielded more and more millions every year; and its renowned hereditary traders, especially the Aga Khan and his Ishmaili followers, had establishments in all the major ports of Asia, Africa, and Europe.

Kitten also discovered how dependence on the sea had given Fateypur an early entrée into the modern world of industrialised Europe. Much in the style of Peter the Great, Fateypur's mid-eighteenth century Bhati ruler had sent his restless younger brother Dalpat Rai to Europe in a French merchant vessel to prevent him from plaguing everyone with his pranks. There, the insatiably inquisitive and brilliant young prince had mastered a whole range of useful industrial skills—clock-making, glass-blowing, tile making, better textile-weaving and dyeing, foundry work, and the enamel inlay work in which French jewellers excelled.

That is how, by the end of the 18th century, Fateypur hummed with the latest skills imported from Europe, in addition to its age-old sea-faring, pearl-fishing, gem-cutting, textile-printing, and zari-embroidering industries. Fateypur's iron foundries manufactured cannon for the Maratha and Sikh wars. Its harbour-front workshops turned out excellent European style clocks and watches which could hardly be distinguished from their Swiss originals. Delft, Meissen, and Chinese tiles were deftly duplicated. Its Fabergé-inspired enamelled gold and silver jewellery and decorative objects soon became quite the rage with foreign memsahebs, and upper caste Indian ladies, quick to copy fashionable trends.

Tiger was not the first Francophile to rule Fateypur. His grandfather, Maharajah Sher Singh, had strengthened the French connection to such an extent during his 53-year-long reign, and fought so valiantly during the First World War, that he was awarded the Grand Cross of the Legion d'honneur besides a British Field Marshal's baton. He was also invited to sign the Treaty of Versailles as a representative of India and its ruling Princes.

Kitten was not the first newcomer from Chattargadh to be bowled over by Maharajah Sher Singh's exotic version of Fontainbleau by the Arabian Sea. Lapis lazuli columns imported from Italy enhanced the Durbar Hall and drawing rooms where the carpets were all Aubusson, Savonnaire, or Axeminster. Louis Quatorze furniture imported from France mingled with Empire-style tables and jardinières. Wheel-shaped chandeliers, festooned with crystal balls and prisms (which tinkled in the faintest sea breeze) provided the perfect nautical touch. Glass vitrines filled with exquisite amber, amethyst, rose quartz, and imperial jade figurines stood beneath original oil paintings and portraits of Fateypur's four most recent Maharajahs. Gobelin tapestries, gilded mirrors, enamelled ormolu vases and clocks, Sévres porcelain vases bearing portraits of Maharajah Sher Singh and Tiger's father, Maharajah Maan Singh, were arranged in the various meticulously maintained apartments scented with pot-pourri, fresh flowers, sandlewood sticks, and heavenly camphor cubes tucked into every sofa and drawer to protect them against insects and moths.

White Burmese peacocks outnumbered the brighter-plumaged Indian birds roaming the extensive grounds surrounding the mansard-roofed Palace, which included a largish lily-and-lotus-strewn lake that doubled as a bird sanctuary attracting rosy pelicans, cranes, and pink flamingoes. Two European-style guest houses, and a hillock on which stood the ancient family shrine to Shri Krishna added to the park's charm. Beside the tennis and squash courts, and an enormous indoor swimming pool, there was an excellent polo field adjoining the formal garden strewn with marble fountains, parapets, statues, and benches in the French style.

Kitten was accustomed to joining, not watching passively from a safe distance, while others displayed their horsemanship. But Tiger, Arjun, and Sir Pratab were practising tent-pegging before they took off for Calcutta, where they participated in various horse shows, in addition to playing polo throughout the season. So she sat restless astride the most manageable mare they could find her. The senior *risaldar* in charge of the Maharajah's stables raised the red flag every time one of the three Bhati princes, who came galloping up the sandy side track, actually picked a peg clean off the ground with his lance. Turbaned *sowars* in Fateypur livery quickly replaced each wooden peg, loudly keeping count of the points scored by each of them.

When Tiger failed to pick two pegs in succession, Kitten simply held her hand out for the lance belonging to the ADC, Phool Singh. 'May I, Kanwar Saab?'

A bit doubtful, but too well bred to argue with princesses, the young man said, 'Certainly, Your Highness. But can you?'

The Junior Maharani merely grinned, having no time to enlighten him about her pig-sticking past. Collecting her 'more Arab than Kathiawari black' with a practised left hand even as she levelled the lance with the right, Kitten merely touched boot heels to flanks with the lightest rein signal, thigh pressure, and a confidently crooned command. All the experienced riders watched anxiously. In the twinkling of an eye, she had the horse (derisively nicknamed Palanquin) galloping in perfect stride, its ears cocked and neck elongated to balance the feather-light rider leaning dangerously forward, with the lance point dipping down at the precise moment. Kitten's unerring eye, aided with the galloping mare's perfect momentum, helped her pluck the peg clean off the ground.

Her husband, Maharajah Tiger Fateypur, gave her a jaunty salute and a smiling 'Well done!' when she finished her tent-pegging round with a perfect score.

But her cousin Arjun, cantering up to her on his foam-flecked grey gelding, ticked her off in no uncertain terms for butting in 'as usual,' and obstructing her elders.

And although Sir Pratab, the senior-most family member present, did not want to stoop to chiding his niece-cum-daughter-in-law in front of sundry relations *and* retainers, he couldn't help wishing that Kitten would spend less time perfecting her horsemanship and more on ensuring the succession.

Instead of excusing herself gracefully and retiring upstairs to her own apartment like her aunt and Ratna, (who also rode quite often), Kitten automatically joined the princes for tea in the Maharajah's study, exactly as she used to do back home in Chattargadh.

A brisk sea breeze blew in through the open windows of the pleasant book-lined room which bore the unmistakable imprint of Maharajah Tiger Fateypur's admirably macho personality, pastimes, and history. A large family tree containing miniature ivory portraits of every Fateypur Maharajah, including Tiger, occupied the place of honour facing his desk. Above this painting hung the jewelled and enamelled family crest of the flute-playing cowherd, Krishna (dancing on the hooded snake Seshnag over the sea waves) and the family motto: 'Oceans and overlords observe self-restraint.'

A unique Baccarat boat with gilded crystal sails and gambolling gold cherubim dominated a four-foot-long, lapis lazuli-topped table simulating the sea. Crested silver frames containing autographed photographs of his father, uncle, the entire British Royal Family, Maharajah Jai Singh, his Nutty Pisshengunj uncle, and some of Tiger's favourite group shots with various friends and relations stood next to model aeroplanes, polo and racing trophies on shelves lining the walls.

The welcome winter sun sent sunbeam shafts to strike iridescent rainbows off the enormous icy blue diamond standing on his meticulously arranged writing desk. Weighing a trifle more than any of the world's better-known big diamonds, this priceless heirloom was reputedly bequeathed to Fateypur's first Bhati king by his legendary ancestor, Lord Krishna. Handed over from father to son, it was firmly believed by everyone in Fateypur to be a potent talisman— the *perfect* conductor of Cosmic energy.

The extremely superstitious young Maharajah Tiger certainly believed so.

HH Fateypur urged his uncle to extend their stay in Delhi for the purpose of conferring with the Viceroy, and the nationalist leaders, who were bent upon preventing all the Indian Maharajahs from performing their proper warrior dharma/karma, when so many battles were being fought in theatres as various as Russia and China. Sir Pratab reiterated

that there was no need for Tiger to be in such a tearing
hurry to fly off anywhere. They were going to be very busy
for the next month playing polo in Calcutta with the
American, Irish, Spanish, and Brazilian teams. This was so
even though the Australian riders had cancelled at the last
minute and the Argentine team had been rudely warned off
by the IBPA (Indo-British Polo Association) *and* the Turf
Club for being suspected Nazi collaborators.

Arjun accepted another cup of tea from Kitten, thanked
her, and began adding his own entreaties to Tiger's. 'Don't
you think we're obliged to uphold the family tradition,
Hukum? It's all right for those non-violent Congress *wallahs*
to remain nonaligned. But *our* grandfather was fighting and
winning a world war when he was well past 70!'

'Your grandfather left behind *two* sons . . . And *two*
grandsons to look after his State,' said Sir Pratab, after a
pregnant pause.

Kitten immediately stood up, ready to leave the room
before he made any more pointed remarks. The men all
stood up also. Gesturing towards the stack of brand new
books arranged on HH's desk, Kitten asked politely: 'Tiger
Baapji, may I borrow one or two of those Agatha Christie
and Wodehouse novels? And that Hemingway that's said to
be a realistic portrait of the Spanish civil war?'

'Certainly, Kitten,' said Tiger, smiling generously. 'Take
anything you like.'

'Anything?' queried his bride, looking extremely young
and impish in her muddy boots and breeches.

'Of course,' he responded automatically, still the perfect
host. Kitten calmly collected some books.

And the Maharajah's heirloom diamond paperweight.

But Tiger saw at once what she had done.

Before she could waltz out of his study, parodying a
pauper's heartfelt thanks, Tiger protested: 'But dash it, Kitten!
I didn't mean you could take my lucky stone!'

Not long after, Princess Diamond sent her daughter-in-law Ratna to summon Kitten, and gave her a royal scolding. Never before had her aunt spoken so sharply to her.

Tilting her determined chin, Kitten explained that no matter what *anybody* said, Tiger Baapji had *given* her the diamond. 'Before witnesses, too. So he can't backtrack now, and go around maligning me by saying that I pinched it!'

'You and your witnesses, Kitten!' said Princess Diamond in exasperation. 'Can't you see that you've gone and created exactly the kind of situation which makes everybody so uncomfortable? And quite unnecessarily. Don't you know that you're married to one of the most superstitious men probably in the whole *world*? If anything goes wrong from now on, Tiger will blame you, because you took the magic diamond given to Rao Fatey Singh by their ancestor, Shri Krishna?'

'That calls for far too much suspended disbelief, Aunty!' scoffed her niece, tossing her sari-draped head. 'Because we both know that Lord Krishna lived at least 2000 years before that Bhati bandit crowned himself King of Fateypur.'

Loth as usual to bring up delicate intimate matters, Princess Diamond had an excellent inkling about Kitten's motives for carrying on like this. But, as long as Kitten kept on behaving like an aggressive little attention-seeking child, Tiger would continue to treat her like one. She also knew that neither was it easy for her nephew to bring about a complete change in his attitude towards Kitten. He had been brought up to consider her exactly like a sister, as had Robin and Arjun. Therefore, it was imperative that Kitten become more appealing, more feminine, more ladylike.

Referring to the decorum expected of newly-wed Fateypur Maharanis, Princess Diamond urged her niece: 'You could try emulating Yasho.'

'What! Go barging into other people's bedrooms, boasting of my sex life? No thanks!' snapped Kitten, sending her aunt and Ratna into paroxysms of loud, unladylike laughter.

Heir(ring) On . . .   11

'It isn't just the stone. It's the stars too,' fumed Kitten, as she stood in her cousin's bedroom, swamped by another well-meant avalanche of advice from Ratna. Down below, members of the Ooty Hunt, gathered in the grounds of Fateypur House, were trying to keep their horses from chomping all the flowers and shrubs. The hounds contributed to the merry mayhem by barking and whining, eager for their run.

Looking absolutely adorable in a pukka black hunting jacket over a colourful silk scarf held in place by a jewelled pin, and white whipcord breeches tucked into knee-high riding boots, Kitten had charged upstairs impatiently to hurry Ratna along. Everybody liked to see her exceedingly popular relative participating in all the Ooty events. But when she caught her cousin still sitting, draped in a cosy shawl over her quilted satin dressing gown, consuming a huge breakfast of grilled sausages with tomatoes, eggs, and pan-fried mashed potatoes, plus lots of buttered toast, Kitten put two and two together.

'Oh boy! So you've done it at last!' cried Kitten in delight, giving her a warm-hearted smile.

'And so should you,' began Ratna. 'It's over six months since you've been married to Tiger Baapji. And nobody's been cramping your private life since my senior sister-in-law buzzed off to her father's place in Nepal from Calcutta, right after we finished celebrating Christmas, New Year, and all those polo victories. If you too could stay at home peacefully like me, instead of galloping all over the countryside, and just *allowed* Mother Nature to work her magic . . . .'

For a change, Kitten simply stood there, listening to Ratna going on and on. She did not say anything, however. There were some things one simply didn't share even with one's closest friends and relations. Kitten had no intention of becoming the butt of rude jokes and mocking laughter in princely circles by revealing how matters really stood between herself and her husband to anybody. Ever.

The traditional opening meet of the Ooty foxhounds was invariably held at Fernhill Palace under the aegis of the Mysore Maharajah come November's dry weather. But they always had a couple of lawn meets earlier at Fateypur House where they came up during summer with scores of horses and riders, and an equal number of followers. Although there were no foxes in the Nilgiris, and the lurchers (fox hounds) were only trained to run jackals to earth, the horsy set which congregated at Ooty year after year—the British officers, boxwallahs, planters, and memsahebs who had no illusions about cracking county circles or owning boxes in hunt-country back home—could enjoy a day in the field, rubbing shoulders with Indian royalty while riding over countryside more akin to the Cotswold hills and Sussex downs than any other place in the subcontinent.

The moment Princess Kitten was safely in the saddle and the saddle cup drunk, imperceptible signals were exchanged between the Master of the Hunt, Brigadier Roberts, and the Master of Hounds. The hunting call was blown, and the field set off. Bonhomie was rife among the scarlet and black-coated gentlemen and ladies as their horses fast-trotted or cantered off behind the hounds towards the undulating hills. Weather-beaten faces beamed beneath sola topees, and regulation riding hats. The Maharajahs of Fateypur, Chattargadh, Pisshengunj, Sir Pratab, and several other Rajput princes could be distinguished by their crisp pink turbans. Born riders, they sat their horses with effortless grace, their backs straight, their shoulders perfectly relaxed. They controlled and guided their mounts through the lightest mouth contact, seat pressure, and the shifting of weight. Tiger and Arjun cut dashing figures as they spurred their horses on, keeping well ahead of Nutty Pisshengunj and his brother-in-law, Koodsu Rao Saheb.

Kitten followed. She was riding her striking bay mare with white foreleg stockings and head star. All her cares—and the injustice of her best friend's words—were forgotten as the field opened out. As her horse got into full stride, she found herself enjoying the marvellously exhilarating experience of riding neck to neck once more with her father. The Resident and Colonel CP, mounted on stable mates used to hacking and hunting together, followed close on their heels through the flying turf clods. Of course, Maharajah Jai Singh drew the line at hacking his polo ponies. In this he was like all the other serious players she knew. And, in her opinion, nobody—not even Tiger Baapji—could ride like her father. For the Rathors were born to the saddle more than any other clan.

Trained to hunt with the Quorn and Warwickshire from childhood, Redverse found himself concurring with CP that, after all the hullabaloo, the Ooty version of blue-blooded British fox-hunting was frightfully overrated and tame. 'Give me pig-sticking any day,' thought the Englishman, keeping his spirited chestnut well in hand as they thundered over the gently rolling green downs dotted with wild flowers, cattle, and sheep. Here there were no fences to jump, gates to shut, or farmers to be cajoled and pacified. Soon the hounds gave tongue, and turned to follow the scent through a tall bracken-choked grove of cypress, rhododendrons, and palms towards the second point at Wenlock.

Away from the field, Tiger watched intently as the huntsmen drew the jackal from covert to covert. When the baying hounds had gone away, he took his own line over the eucalyptus forest and the huge Nilgiri rocks looming out of the morning mist. Unable to face the wanton savaging of a helpless animal by other bloodthirsty beasts even as so-called ladies and gentlemen who relished the spectacle in the name of good sport, the Maharajah of Fateypur always made it a point to lose his way long before the kill. Apart from his ingrained aversion to any shooting or hunting (except for the pot, or for public protection against man-eaters and other marauders), Tiger had discovered years ago that hunt meets in Ooty provided him with the perfect opportunity to pursue other game. His curious (or censorious) friends and relations were much too absorbed in sticking to the scent, to not committing the unforgivable crime of riding over hounds, and to not obstructing the chief Whipper-In, to pay his absence too much attention.

Instead, this irresistibly good-looking, virile, and suave young Maharajah had long ago discovered the more amorously inclined of the attractive younger plantation ladies, who were less shy and quick to seize the initiative. They always informed HH Fateypur that he would be welcomed with open arms if he cared to drop in for potluck when the next meet was well under way.

The significance of Ratna's absence from the hunt had not been lost on any of her relatives and well-wishers, for this unfailingly courteous, modest, and good-natured princess was a universal favourite. It was generally acknowledged that she handled her horses very well, and took as much delight in the freedom and informality offered by a day out with

the Ooty Hunt as her more intrepid mother-in-law, Princess
Diamond, and her inseparable cousin/companion-cum-sister-
in-law, Princess Kitten.

The mud-spattered, slightly dishevelled and flushed
Maharajah of Pisshengunj was more chagrined than pleased
by this latest development in his nephew's family. As they
rode back after a thoroughly satisfying day in the saddle,
Nutty told Koodsu Rao Saheb that this fresh equation had
created a new twist to the whole scenario. And he would
have to take it into account before he chalked out his next
move.

Patting the neck of his sweating and heaving horse
before dismounting, the robust and equally well-exercised
Rao Saheb considered the Maharajah's words. '*Hajoor*, I
hope you understand the long-term implications of this
good news.'

Once indoors, respectful retainers pulled off their muddy
riding boots while they settled themselves into deep sofas
flanking the freshly lit, fragrant eucalyptus and juniper wood
fire. The head butler ceremoniously served them some
excellent brandy. The moment they were alone, Nutty
began berating his brother-in-law. 'How many times have I
told you not to take me for a fool, Rao Saab! I'm perfectly
aware that if anything happens to my nephew Tiger before
his useless wives give him at least *one* son, then Fateypur's
3,000-year-old throne will automatically pass on to those
vultures standing next in line—like Arjun. Or his son.'

'Daughter's son, or sister's son,' mused Rao Saheb,
between sips of brandy. 'Either way, we lose. And apart
from making sure that we teach Princess Kitten the real
meaning of "tit for tat," plus "getting paid back in your
own coin" as she's so fond of teasing Your Highness, you
gave your solemn oath to help me avenge all the insults
and injuries her father, Maharajah Jai Singh, has inflicted on

me—a Pillar of his State. Only because I also big-me'd for begetting heirs, exactly like his own daughter!'

'My dear Rao Saab, we both have several scores to settle with His Progressive Highness. Therefore, my nephew's throne won't be allowed to pass to Maharajah Jai Singhji's grandson *or* grandnephew as long as there's breath in my body. But I wasn't prepared for this sudden coup d'état by Ratna Baisa!'

Swirling the deep amber Armagnac around the snifter after a reviving draught, the Maharajah of Pisshengunj recapitulated his entire game plan, which had gone off without a hitch until this point. But he wasn't about to admit defeat just because Mother Nature had also decided to take a hand in Fateypur's affairs. Nutty forced his brother-in-law to agree that even though the first step hadn't been easy, everything else had followed exactly as he had predicted once he had persuaded Tiger to walk into the trap baited with Elinor Redverse, and then right into Kitten's clutches. Step Two had misfired because both the Resident and the ecclesiastic long arm of the British empire in the form of his piano teacher, Mother Angelus, had interfered in the most deplorable fashion. They should, really, have had the decency to let the three princely families sort out their own affairs according to long standing Rajput customs and treaty rights.

Reminding Koodsu Rao Saheb that he still controlled his superstitious nephew's karma through sufficiently horrific and mystifying horoscope readings, Nutty felt that it was high time they played their trump card. Rao Saheb warned that it would be more appropriate to summon Fateypur's High Priest-cum-court astrologer to Pisshengunj House instead of meeting him even accidentally on purpose in public—one never knew *who* might be watching with this war on and all that talk about spies and fifth column *wallahs*.

However, Nutty gave him a scoffing glance from his large, protruding eyes. 'Use your common sense, Rao Saab. Even palace walls have too many ears—the Resident's ears, Viceroy's ears, HH Chattargadh's ears. And among these I'm forced to include *your* own sister, who's no longer satisfied with just taking undue interest in Kitten's clothes, and sayings and doings. She has even begun to exhibit a deplorably partisan attitude to *this* devil incarnate!'

'That's but natural, Hukum,' Koodsu Rao Saheb replied with a gold-capped smile. 'It's human nature to feel terribly flattered when your Maharajah's daughter suddenly turns into your daughter-in-law or niece, and the protocol tables get turned. And we've all seen how meticulously Kitten Baisa observes all the traditional courtesies whenever she meets my younger sister, Neeru Baa, even though we only rank as aristocrats in the Rajput hierarchy. Only you all, and the two Senior Pisshengunj Maharani Saabs, are real royalty.'

'Nobody says that Kitten wasn't well brought up. She is just badly behaved. So, her karma's bound to catch up with her. And sooner rather than later, if the Gods are listening to all my heartfelt, humble prayers. And if my *tantric Siddhis* are developing along the right lines.'

Not normally a man who offended Maharajahs even inadvertently, the Koodsu chief could not refrain from mentioning his reluctance to be seen in public with HH Fateypur's High Priest. He didn't want the finger of suspicion falling on them, which it surely would if anybody from Chattargadh, not to mention Sir Pratab—or even Arjun—ran across them sitting down with horoscopes they had no business misinterpreting in a small place like Ooty. After all, it was just an overgrown English village, with nowhere to hide one's guilty conscience. Even if he was too high and mighty to pay any attention to all that wicked gossip going on in the Club, the Savoy Hotel, and the

Governor's garden parties, HH knew that Ooty was a place where every busybody knew everyone else's business.

'We might look suspicious if we were caught sitting in some hotel-shotel with a saffron-clad vegetarian brahmin Maharaj, who has no business going anywhere where even the tea is bound to be polluted with foul, fishy hands and spoons, Rao Saab. But nobody suspects open-air brain-picking, better known as skulduggery, in all those Sour-luck Oms and Perry Mash-on books,' insisted Nutty.

'But supposing our new plan also fails?' mused the Koodsu chief.

'The trouble with you Chattargadh chaps is that you don't understand the psychology of the individual, who, in this case, happens to be my favourite nephew, Tiger, who was asking for White Ladies even on his wedding night!'

Koodsu Rao Saheb wondered if his brother-in-law had anybody in mind. The Maharajah assured him that although he hadn't given the matter much thought until *then*, some suitable candidates were bound to turn up. 'As Our Lord Jesus Christ says: "Ask, and you shall receive."'

Soon, the modalities for continuing to throw mud in his nephew Tiger's eyes through some more horoscopic mish-mash had been worked out in minute detail. These included how to avoid every conceivable pitfall in the consummation of conjugal rights as well as how to avoid detection by any of the hostile agencies overly active against himself and his nephew's best interests.

All this was difficult but exciting business. Nutty was *only* about an hour late for his top secret appointment. This was entirely due to the unavoidable delay caused by his ADC's inability to follow clear-cut instructions in the absence of his dependable Dewan. Baron Tikemoffsky had gone off, as usual, for his annual leave with his reunited wife—that fancy fraudulent Russian Tarot-card reader who had somehow managed to escape alive from Shanghai—to

Singapore, of all places! The Baron couldn't even be summoned by telegram or trunk calls. In the absence of such communication, he was no help at all. Neither was he going to be able to fetch his frustrated Maharajah the *right* dog collars for taking a simple stroll in the Botanical Gardens.

'NOT the diamond and emerald Cartier chokers, Thakur Saab. We usually wear those only for formal occasions,' explained the exasperated Maharajah of Pisshengunj.

Thakur Kalu Singh rushed off to the basement strong room where all the valuable jewellery was deposited daily for safe keeping. He returned speedily to the drawing room clutching two different, flat, gold-embossed leather cases, to where HH was waiting impatiently with the lucky pair of dogs the world would be privileged to see him airing that day in the park.

Nutty drew a deep, exasperated breath and pursed his well-moulded House-of-Marwar mouth when he saw what the ADC had brought. 'Are you colour blind? I'm saying sapphires, and every time you keep bringing me green stones! I'm getting *blue* in the face, having to beg my own ADCs to perform a simple errand. But no! Thakur Saab doesn't condescend to understand!'

Equally anxious to reach their carefully chosen rendezvous before the place got crowded, and understanding that the nervous astrologer priest might disappear from the scene fearing a no-show or detection, Koodsu Rao Saheb persuaded his brother-in-law to let *him* go down into the *Toshakhana*, and bring whatever Durbar demanded.

'I'll be extremely grateful, Rao Saab, if you would kindly fetch me the Boodle-Poodle collars—the plain gold ones, with those single sapphire pendants just right for a casual afternoon walk—even though you are our guest, and its against our dharma to ask you to run errands.'

Famous for his precision regarding points of protocol,

the Maharajah of Pisshengunj had sent another ADC ahead to warn the Horticulture Director of his impending visit to the famous Botanical Gardens accompanied by his pink poodles, Clair de lune and Fleur de lis. Therefore, no one was surprised to see two swarthy park sweepers in proper uniform and caps, armed with poop-picking shovels and brooms, following Nutty's party all over the 54 acres of sloping lawns interspersed with shady bowers, fountains, flower beds, fern houses, and orchidariums. They took good care to nip behind one of the larger cedars or monkey puzzles favoured by empire builders whenever the Maharajah condescended to nod, or glance over his shoulder at some acquaintance, or bent down to adjust the pretty little custom-made, crocodile skin booties worn by his beautifully groomed French poodles.

The high level of humidity plus the altitude of the Nilgiris, had permitted a succession of horticulturally inclined British expatriates to experiment with plants transplanted from Europe and the Southern hemisphere, particularly New Zealand. Eye-catching tulip trees smothered with scarlet flowers stood silhouetted against the dramatic hillock, boasting Italian-style grottos and staircases. The balustraded terrace adjoining the wisteria-draped bandstand was scattered with stone seats, satyrs, nymphs, horses, and hounds in the approved English manner.

Drifts of lavender, lobelia, silvery begonias, and multicoloured impatiens spilled over the flagstoned path that Nutty trod towards the carefully selected, inconspicuous arbour which was virtually curtained off by trellised roses and mossy hanging baskets displaying glorious blue Vandas, Dendrobium, Cattleya, and Paphiopendilum orchids in full bloom. He looked forward to sitting down comfortably on the cushioned folding chairs (sent ahead from Pisshengunj House) as he talked things over with and issued crucial instructions to the one man Tiger was inclined to consult and trust. He wouldn't be caught dead squatting down on those horrible *public* benches, like his pretending-to-be egalitarian Chattargadh relations! One never knew what germs one could pick up.

Thoroughly riled because his brand new pair of Hush Puppies were pinching feet more used to staying safely off the ground in stirrups or on sofas, His Nutty Highness also cursed the cussed British practice of taking long walks at awkward times, especially in the middle of the afternoon when sensible people everywhere else in the world (and not just 'lazy Indians') wisely took rejuvenating naps after lunch. Now, owing to his ADC's failure to follow his simple instructions, he was caught in this crowd of gawking foreigners who had nothing better to do except to go around invading a park he had so carefully chosen for this perfectly innocent-looking public meeting with the Fateypur High Priest. Didn't the worst busybodies in Ooty ever eat lunch?

Urging Koodsu Rao Saheb to ensure their privacy, the Pisshengunj Maharajah settled down to do business with Tiger's rapacious astrologer. The latter's demands had skyrocketed because of *his* Maharajah's irrevocable decision to go around flying aeroplanes in the unsafest part of the world in the midst of a war between two white races (which had nothing to do with *Sanatan Aryan Dharma*). This had exacerbated an already serious situation. But it wasn't worth haggling. Once they had unrolled the horoscope to be scrutinised on the folding picnic table also brought from Pisshengunj House, the priest painstakingly reiterated what he had already pointed out *months* ago to Pisshengunj Durbar—that the lord of Princess Kitten's sign was the Sun, denoting universal energy.

'The Chattargadh Princess was born in Leo ascendant *plus* Leo *navamsa*, which makes the ascendant *varagottam*. And as *Annadata* knows, whenever a planet or *lagna* becomes *varagottam*, it gives the native tremendous energy, courage, aggression, and mental balance—in other words, the Raj Yog of a Chakravarti Samrat, not just the qualities of a great Rajput king or queen. *Hajoor* must please mark my words. Added to this is the Gaj Kesari Yog, signifying wealth with power according to the harmonious alignment of *these* planets. And on top of this, not only are Jupiter and Venus involved in a mutual aspect, making her extremely intelligent and result oriented, but the placement of Mars, Mercury, and Ketu in the 4th house represents great happiness, both in the mother's home *and* in the husband's.'

Coming to a quick decision, Nutty took the bulkier brocade bag out of his blazer pocket, and placed it on the horoscope hand-charted by the most erudite astrologers assembled at Chattargadh at the precise moment of Princess Kitten's birth 18-years ago, on November 24. Before the beaming, conspicuously saffron-clad priest could put back all the valuable gold ornaments so generously presented to him by the Maharajah, they heard a rather familiar voice amiably adjuring Reverse Gear to move a little closer to his wife if he didn't want half his face missing.

Colonel Claude-Poole clicked his camera just in time to catch HH Pisshengunj's startled eyes staring at them.

Shrewdly concluding that it would look even more shady if he pretended to ignore these most unwelcome acquaintances at this particularly inopportune moment—his generous gifts to Tiger's bribed personal adviser were lying in full view of the two interfering Englishmen who had far too much clout with the British government—Nutty decided to act as though he was actually pleased to see them.

But his spirits actually revived when he recognised the other two persons accompanying them, apart from Lady Dorothy. He *had* read all about the Rumanian Crown

Prince, Rudolf, ferrying all those planes to India from France just *hours* ahead of the Nazi occupation. And the Vicereine, Lady Axeminster, had mentioned during the course of a Bombay shopping spree—when he had naturally insisted on picking up the bills—that she was expecting a visit from her close connection, Honey Moneykurl, the American heiress whom surely HH knew well from their days together in London and the Riviera. But Nutty hadn't expected them to turn up together in Ooty, of all places.

Everyone who heard the BBC religiously three times a day like devout Catholics saying the Angelus, knew exactly how and why Prince Rudolf had landed here. But only those who were privy to the inside guff, like Maharajah Tiger Fateypur, knew that this flying ace had been reduced to ferrying the Hurricane Squadron bought up dirt cheap by His Exalted Highness, the Nizam of Hyderabad, for the defence of his *own* realm (this much maligned miser had already gifted one to the RAF), because His Majesty's Government had made it quite clear that they were *not* going to infiltrate His Imperial Highness Prince Rudolf behind enemy lines into Rumania, to activate another Tito-type partisan group—not even if he code-named it DRACULA.

Kitten thought it must have been so disappointing for him to be hindered from reaching Bucharest, when he might have galvanised Transylvania, because he 'DID have the right connections and training, didn't he?'

His hooded light blue eyes twinkling, Prince Rudolf laughed. 'Honestly, Kitten, I doubt the Hapsburg cocktail contains any vampire blood, y'know.'

'I was only talking Napoleon-style nepotism, Prince,' the grinning girl retorted as they proceeded towards the tennis court reserved for them at the Club. While Rudolf wore immaculate shorts and shoes with his Lacoste T-shirt,

Kitten's tennis whites resembled the cricketing outfit de rigueur at Lord's. Showing bare legs was *verboten*. In further concession to tradition, she was also weighed down with ivory bangles, diamond nose pin, rings, earrings, and the compulsory gold anklets worn over her candy striped white socks.

Passers by stopped to watch as Tiger and Kitten took on Honey Moneykurl and the Rumanian Crown Prince in what began as a friendly mixed-doubles game, with the gentlemen feeding easy balls to their female opponents. But very soon, however, this turned into a hard fought set as the foursome's essential play-to-win natures and years of first class pro training took over. The springy, painstakingly maintained tennis lawn was easy on the players' feet as they went into the third set. Honey's short white skirt swung up, displaying a good deal of her shapely thighs as she lunged forward with her racquet, just missing the low ball lobbed over the net. Even her extremely athletic and long-limbed partner couldn't save the last game. Club members murmured, 'Well played!' and clapped as the Maharajah and Maharani of Fateypur wiped their damp palms on monogrammed handkerchiefs before shaking hands with their guests over the net.

After a quick wash to freshen up, and with their damp, dishevelled hair rearranged and brushed back becomingly from faces aglow with healthy exertion, they automatically gravitated towards the group surrounding Kitten's father, which included Gerald Redverse, his wife, and Colonel CP. Motivated by gratitude, and a desire for congenial, competent companions to play polo, tennis, bridge, and billiards with him, HH Chattargadh had insisted on bringing them once again to Ooty as his guests for the summer.

Maharajah Jai Singh and the British officers immediately rose, drawing armchairs forward for the two young ladies.

Two Club bearers, with starched white turbans, red cummerbunds, and long black coats, began serving tea. As the stacks of freshly made salmon paste and cucumber sandwiches disappeared under the onslaught of four hearty young appetites (with Kitten demanding some *more* of the scrumptious strawberry tarts, if you please), the talk turned—inevitably—to the war in Europe.

Now that Chamberlain was finally out and Churchill in, the Indian Maharajahs were keen to commit their armies to the Allied cause, even if the Yanks were holding back. And despite countries like Spain, Portugal, Turkey, and the entire Middle East preferring to remain neutral.

'Can you blame them?' Tiger said, referring to the sell-out after World War I. 'It was Faisal, not Lawrence, who delivered Arabia to the Allies. But some cockeyed war correspondents *and* their Foreign Office connived at slanting the news, and giving all the credit to that Brit.'

The Resident adroitly gave the conversation a lighter tone by asking Honey how they were faring at Hyderabad House, rumoured to have just a 'skeleton staff' to serve them.

Displaying perfectly even white teeth in a joshing smile, Honey retorted that she hadn't had time to count the *khidmatgars* at their disposal. But whenever she and Rudi returned there to bathe, change, and sleep after Ooty's endless polo, cricket, and tennis tournaments, military *bara khana*s, planters' luncheons, picnics, tea parties, dinners, and balls (to which they were chauffeured in one of the Nizam's red-plated and crested Rolls), she always found the whole palace, specially her suite, absolutely spic and span, even though they never *saw* the staff.

Kitten joked that she wouldn't be surprised if the old man had conjured up Alladin's genie to cater to his house guests in absentia.

When Honey and Prince Rudolf had turned up

simultaneously, yet separately in India, they frequently found themselves orbiting Viceregal circles because of their solid connections. In her case, these included several American robber barons; in his, the entire *Almanach de Gotha*. A royal marriage for her remarkably wealthy and good-looking protégé had become an *idée fixe* with Lady Axeminster ever since she had presented Honey at Court last year. Therefore, after helping her sell a cut-rate Corvette to the wealthiest Indian ruler from Hyderabad, the Vicereine had encouraged the girl (plus her tiny entourage) to tag along with Rudolf, who was flying home in a roomy Dakota on behalf of the British Red Cross. The aircraft had been gifted by all the Hyderabad Begums in lieu of active participation in nursing the war-wounded. It was understood that this scion of the Dual monarchy would make a detour via Ooty, because that was where most of his closest friends and acquaintances in India were gathered for the summer.

Tiger was extremely irked by the fact that he couldn't invite either of them to stay because Fateypur House was already full. The four ADCs were reduced to sharing bedrooms. But nobody else could. Or would. Or should, according to his astrologer. The situation would have been even worse if his first wife had also decided to join him in Ooty—which she fortunately disliked, being disinclined towards strenuous outdoor sports so loved by all the other members of the family.

In any case, the property belonged to his aunt, Princess Diamond, even though she was gracious enough to insist that it was Fateypur House, and HIS guests were always welcome. With Arjun and Ratna on the verge of adding new members to the family—besides Kitten—the Maharajah of Fateypur wished he had bought that bungalow beyond Fern Hill much earlier. But now that he had, at least he had killed two birds with one stone. It gave Kitten a place of her own, and it would keep her gainfully occupied playing around with landscaping and redesigning the interiors. Then he would be able to invite people to stay during the Ooty season without consulting anybody else, especially now that those *ism-wallahs* (with their foul bombs and torpedoes) had made it impossible to travel around Europe purely for pleasure.

The Hapsburg Prince was a kindred spirit who refused to be a detached spectator while others fought fascism. Rudolf had been a year ahead of him at Cambridge university. While the Indian Maharajah had focused on astro-physics and astronomy, the European Prince was keener on actual aviation technology. But they both shared a love for flying, in addition to fast cars, fast horses, and exceptionally attractive women. Since Rudolf's family had a major stake in the French aircraft factories manufacturing Hurricanes and other well-known planes, it had been easy for the Prince to surmount prejudice by simply sliding into a test pilot's role. But staying on would have been suicidal under Marshal Petain, a confirmed Nazi collaborator.

Rudolf was as amazed as the American (shipping, mining, railroad, and oil) heiress to learn that there were simply *no* aircraft factory or modern shipbuilding facilities in India, despite 90 years of British rule. Even the locomotive engines pulling every single Indian train, they were told, came from England.

'Yes, but what about repairs and maintenance?' demanded Honey, her mercenary mercantile mind computing costs and overheads.

'We've got Mudd Island and the Calcutta docks for servicing naval vessels and overhauling merchant ships,' Colonel CP replied cheerfully. 'And we simply send the broken bits of railway and aeroplane engines back where they came from to be fixed, thus generating a lot of business which keeps everybody happy. Y'know what I mean.'

Tiger scoffed. 'You British like to maintain that manufacturing anything modern in India is out of the question, because native genius is geared towards handicrafts! But ask anyone who can't afford to have his machinery serviced abroad by the original manufacturers—or get genuine spare parts for his trucks and cars—and they'll vouch for our ingenuity in duplicating anything and everything. In Fateypur, my forefathers built thriving industries largely based on this trait.'

Redverse said that he had just been discussing diversification and investment options with HH Chattargadh before they sat down to tea. Maharajah Jai Singh said that although he concurred with the Resident's views, he personally found urban property, and mass consumption items like tea, coffee, sugar, stone, coal, textiles, and railways—besides camels, cattle, sheep, human resources, and other livestock—more palatable options than the high-yield armaments and other profitable mass destruction means *he* was recommending.

Lady Dorothy joined in the laughter this remark provoked, but added that everybody expected the Princely States to pitch in chivalrously—as usual—now that Britain was carrying on almost single-handedly. The Maharajah of Fateypur finished his second cup of tea, set it down on the table, and said in a deceptively meek voice that he would consult his clairvoyant astrologer immediately about her suggestion, and find out which date was the most auspicious for 'pitching in!'

'*Now* will you believe that clairvoyants control the men who control events in India? In the West, isn't it market forces?' demanded Kitten, swivelling her lithe, lean body towards Honey.

But Honey asked eagerly if the Princess could recommend anybody who could foretell HER future?

Kitten could see that the American girl was enchanted

with the entire exotic package of ancient India where anybody with sufficient funds, particularly Maharajahs, could immediately access esoteric occult knowledge offering guidelines for every single action. They had access to what the Aryans termed Akashic records; the Chinese, Feng Shui; and the Greeks, Delphic Oracles. It was amazing how anybody as up to date and business oriented as Honey was ready to believe the most far-fetched rubbish people fed her via personal anecdotes and popular myths. Kitten had begun distrusting astrologers ever since every famous chap consulted by her family just before her marriage had insisted on predicting that she would have three sons in the *same* year! To think that they not only got away with peddling such silly and utter rot, but also made pots of money by bluffing gullible people.

'Try our Uncle Nutty, who's just approaching your starboard like Moby Dick. He's the master chef of magic mantras, *tantra*, and other odd phenomenon which nobody in their right minds would credit!'

Although he'd never actually bothered to read Machiavelli himself, it had been quoted to him so often by his White Russian Dewan that the Maharajah of Pisshengunj couldn't agree more with its basic tenet: 'Those who desire to win the favour of Princes generally endeavour to do so by offering them *those* things which they themselves prize most, or such as they observe the Prince to delight in most.' Although he had no need whatsoever of fishing for favours from brother princes—or nephews in this specific case—common sense decreed that he kill as many birds as possible with *one* stone, which a benevolent Providence had sent him in the shape of *another* blonde beauty. Luckily, the latter was an independent and vastly wealthy young woman controlling an American business empire, and didn't need anybody's permission to marry anyone she liked. Her

reclusive invalidish grandmother, and indifferent bachelor
uncle, didn't count. Nutty had been quick to catch her
drooling over royalty since their first meeting in London
the previous year. And, it had become clear on the Riviera,
that Honey hankered after a grand alliance which would, at
least, entitle her to be called Princess, if not Grand
Duchess, Queen, or even Maharani!

This time things will go exactly according to my carefully
laid plans, resolved Nutty. No ill-conceived fancy dress balls
or piano duets would be allowed to come to the
outrageous Kitten's assistance!

Walking purposefully to his waiting Rolls after dutifully
admiring the spacious mansion which Tiger had just bought
his bride, the Maharajah of Pisshengunj said that although
he would have loved to also take a look at its famous
terraced gardens and conservatory, things like protocol
prevented him from lingering. He couldn't afford to be
late when the Governor of Madras and Lady Hugging-his-
bottom—Ha-ha-ha!—insisted on his attendance at a
Tambola and Tea party being held in aid of the new
Indigenous Blue Mountain People's Own Ooty Hostel of
which they were patrons. 'But I'm sure Honey would enjoy
exploring Kitten's property rather than accompanying us to
such a dull affair.'

As predicted, Tiger said that they would be following
his uncle. As the car containing HH Pisshengunj and
Koodsu Rao Saheb drove off down the curving pink acacia
and dark green fir-lined avenue to the gate, Tiger led
Honey to his low slung sports car, perfect for a cosy
twosome.

But, no matter how many times he tried, the Maharajah
of Fateypur's meticulously maintained Talbot refused to
start.

'Blast it! This only happens when I don't bring my ADC
or driver.'

Glancing at his plain Patek Phillipe wrist watch, Tiger got out of the car, opened the bonnet, checked the wires and battery, and found that the spark plugs were all clean. Back in the driving seat, he set about starting the car again. He still found it impossible to get a response from the engine, no matter what he tried. An experienced and often reckless driver whose vehicles were always kept in perfect running condition by an efficient, adoring motor garage staff whose lives were dedicated to serving him—just like everybody else he employed—Tiger knit his brows in a puzzled frown, trying to figure out what was wrong.

Honey gave the Maharajah a dazzling smile. She glanced at her high-heeled snakeskin pumps, clutched her matching purse provocatively to her breasts, and said that she wouldn't mind strolling back with him if he just took it easy. Or else, they could just sit there peacefully, enjoying the lovely views after he rang the palace for another car.

'We haven't got a telephone yet. And not even a skeleton staff! Apart from the carpenters, plumbers, and electricians carrying out their final check, there's only old Aasji, who's waiting to shut the gates after we depart. He's slightly deaf, so I'll just run along and ask him to pop over next door to the Mysore palace, and request one of their ADCs to arrange a lift for us.'

As they returned to the unfurnished drawing room which only contained the grand Steinway piano and stool, which had arrived before any of the more essential stuff and staff already dispatched days ago from Bombay and Fateypur, Tiger looked appreciatively at this much-courted American girl who gave off such unmistakable signals.

'I hope you're not too disappointed about missing the Governor's do, and being stuck here with me instead, Honey?'

Miffed with Rudolf for not yet popping the question despite scores of opportunities, and for keeping her on tenterhooks with his incomprehensible neglect, Honey couldn't resist this lethally attractive though twice-married Indian Maharajah. She had found him dishy the very first time she'd set her eyes on him in London the previous year.

Leaning close enough for one perfectly curved magnolia-skinned cheek to brush against his tightly muscled shoulder, she purred: 'Darling, I don't mind being stuck with you for hours!'

This was more than enough to liberate Maharajah Tiger Fateypur from any self-imposed restraint in his dealings with this blonde bombshell. Hadn't she so far been more inclined towards his friend Rudolf? But now it seemed that he had guessed wrong. Drawing the eager girl closer into the arms, he gazed into her light, amber-flecked eyes with his famous seductive smile that nobody could resist. Caressing her artfully made-up face with deft, experienced fingers, Tiger began kissing Honey until she pulled her pleasantly perfumed, curvaceous Mae West body away. 'Really, Your Highness, I've got to breathe, y'know!'

Indulging Honey with complimentary banter, Tiger drew her towards the piano stool with polished ease. Between fondling, nuzzling, and crooning sweet nonsense to each other, they forgot the wide open front door. As time dissolved for the twosome trapped in a heightened frenzy of mounting passion, they also failed to hear a car driving up.

Kitten was the first to spot the hideous snakeskin purse the woman must have dropped without noticing. Females mesmerised by her husband Tiger, seldom noticed anything except him. Under the pretext of untangling a twig from her sari, she retrieved it with a swift movement. Speaking loudly, she called over her shoulder to her companions. 'Bhai, would you kindly blow the horn? That will warn Tiger Baapji that the rescue party is here.'

When Arjun, Ratna, and Prince Rudolf followed Kitten

indoors, they found the Maharajah of Fateypur and his guest talking and tinkering with the piano, sitting innocently side by side. No one would have given their close proximity a second thought if Honey's invariably perfect lipstick and blonde bouffant bob didn't look such a mess.

Nutty was thoroughly disgusted when he discovered that instead of throwing a temper tantrum on finding her husband on the verge of seducing Honey under her own roof, Kitten ignored the incident with a dignity and maturity he didn't find at all praiseworthy. After going to all that trouble with the carburettor—even though it had been Koodsu Rao Saheb, and not himself, who'd got his hands filthy—and that phone call making *sure* Kitten got there in time to stage one of those dreadful *zenana* rows guaranteed to make Tiger dump her once and for all without a single qualm—things had still misfired.

And now, the whole town was buzzing with talk of Kitten's latest hobby, flying. That dolt Prince Rudolf! Instead of getting back to where he belonged—in bombed out Europe—he was teaching this shockingly unconventional girl how to fly an aircraft meant for evacuating war casualties. He was also encouraging her to buy her own Cessna, and get a solo pilot's licence in the shortest span of time by clocking as many hours as possible up in the air, when she really should have been grounded for constantly frustrating her elders.

Little did the Maharajah of Pisshengunj realise that Prince Rudolf was really pursuing his own goals when he undertook Kitten's entertainment. It made for Honey's predictable annoyance. He had prolonged their brief, flying visit into a fortnight's furlough so that she could revel in the great social cachet of Indian Maharajahs, and all the other advantages that came from being aligned to a well-known royal Hapsburg. The Moneykurl heiress had been carefully selected by his family from the pick of American debutantes deluging Europe in search of titles. She owned controlling shares in industries which had already diversified into aircraft production, and were ahead of several others chasing the wartime boom. And although his family fortunes were largely tied up in Austrian and French estates and factories now in Nazi hands, and his father's throne was long lost, he was still a very eligible royal catch. But he was biding his time till he was absolutely certain that she would jump at his proposal. A rejection would not be in keeping with his imperial dignity, however residual, for the Holy Roman Empire and the Dual Monarchy were, as everyone knew, just history.

Convinced that he had found the key to all these ridiculous complications in the wake of the American girl's arrival with the Rumanian Crown Prince, Colonel CP indicated his need for an urgent, private word with Reverse Gear. The house purification ceremony had just ended. While their other guests and family members collected around Tiger and Kitten, admiring their tastefully appointed new home, the two Englishmen and Lady Dorothy hurried outdoors, to the lovely sunlit garden beyond the balustraded terrace on which the impressive slate-roofed mansion stood.

Colonel CP sounded quite indignant. 'I *knew* it! Knew I'd seen that chap somewhere before. Couldn't place him, no matter how hard I tried. Now there he sits like a fat canary. With everyone touching his toes!'

'Cool down, CP. What—or more precisely—whom on earth are you talking about?'

'About putting two and two together the minute I clicked those photographs. Don't you remember?'

'Rather difficult, old chap. Aren't you always taking snapshots?' responded Redverse.

'But you were both *in* them!' continued CP, his reddish

handlebar moustache bristling. 'The prints will make you goggle, I promise. And as luck would have it, the packet I collected from the studio this morning is lying handy in the car which brought us here!'

'Get to the point, CP,' urged Lady Dorothy, aware that it was only a matter of minutes before some curious prince or princess would saunter over to see what was keeping them. They should be circulating, instead of clubbing together and gossiping like this. 'Is this the time or place to discuss our host's latest peccadillo, or our hostess's predicament?'

'Patience, Dorothy. It all adds up. Don't you recall the pictures I took of you all when we showed those new arrivals wreaking such havoc in Ooty, our Botanical Gardens? Didn't it strike you as very strange, that a Maharajah—*any* Maharajah—should be seeking astrological advice from somebody in a *public* park?'

Shrugging his pinstripe-coated shoulders in a dismissive fashion, the Resident said that he was long past considering anything that lot did as strange.

'Indeed?' said CP. 'And what would you say if I told you that the Maharajah in question happens to be His Nutty Highness? And the astrologer, High Priest to HH Fateypur?'

'In that case, they could have met more comfortably at the Pisshengunj palace, or Fateypur House,' Redverse conceded with a nod.

Colonel CP swallowed most of his gin fizz, and said that he knew that Nutty couldn't afford to be seen hobnobbing with Tiger's astrologer because he was really bribing the fellow to subvert his superstitious nephew's marriage to Kitten. Didn't they recall the classic case of Maharajah Madho Singh of Jaipur? He had 53 acknowledged royal bastards, but not a single legitimate child from any of his five maharanis, because several astrologers, numerologists, and clairvoyants had convinced him that he would die the day he had an heir? And since the prevailing wisdom in princely families advocated polygamy as a panacea for almost everything, the Maharajah of Pisshengunj was simply pandering to Tiger's well-known penchant for good-looking white ladies by dangling Honey before him as the NEXT candidate.

'A classic case of conquering the conqueror's women,' sneered Dorothy, tugging down her flared, flower-patterned primrose silk frock to prevent indecent exposure by the increasingly brisk breeze. 'None of this nonsense would be happening if people stuck to their original schedules, instead of hanging on forever.'

The Resident was forced to acknowledge that, indeed, things were delicately poised. There was every indication that Maharajah Tiger Fateypur might be considering a third marriage to 'you know whom!' And Sir Pratab, instead of putting an end to such a crushing blow to his niece Kitten's dignity, was actually promoting the idea. He was suggesting that if the raison d'être for the second alliance was defeated by the Junior Maharani's barrenness, she too would do the gracious thing by consenting to a *more* productive alliance, just like the Senior Maharani.

Lady Dorothy clicked her tongue disapprovingly as she drew her cloche hat down a little more to shade her lightly freckled nose and hazel eyes. But CP said that he wasn't one bit surprised, because one couldn't find a more calculatingly conscientious caretaker in any other princely state. His Midas touch was admired even by the Rothschilds, Rockefellers, and the Aga Khan. 'Can you see Sir Pratab sacrificing the Moneykurl fortune merely out of sentimental regard for any niece by marriage? Particularly when this new alliance would guarantee something every coastal state in India hankers for: a proper shipyard equipped to design and construct not just small fishing boats, tugs, and coastal ferries but ocean-going freighters, racing yachts, and passenger ships. And engines provided by the parent company in the US of A, thus bypassing all British technology transfer restrictions and patent safeguards.'

Even though Residents were advised to steer clear of any involvement in the personal lives of Maharajahs by His Majesty's Government, Redverse realised that he had no alternative except to scupper this deal by immediate intervention. In fact, it was quite called for because British commercial interests, Foreign Office practice, and his own personal inclinations had converged rather happily.

'I suppose Princess Kitten's parents won't add to their loss of face by interfering in anything involving the Fateypur succession. Their own daughter has failed to deliver the goods, so to speak,' said Dorothy as she finished her sherry. She proposed a two-pronged attack. 'First, confront the astrologer right away with your photographic evidence, and put the fear of God in him by swearing you'll have him deported to the Nicobar Islands by the Viceroy for sedition. Second, drop a hint to Honey about the imminent restoration of the Dual Monarchy as soon as this war ends! No ambitious American heiress is going to resist *that* pipe dream. Meanwhile, I shall steer the Hapsburg Prince in the right direction.'

'The Raj to the rescue once more, Reverse Gear,' chuckled the Colonel as they sauntered back towards the Maharajahs, their strategy all chalked out.

Kitten conducted the informal candlelit dinner party a few days later for their tight little circle of friends and relations with great panache, revelling in being mistress of her own home at last, and in not having to defer to her mother or aunt. Her parents had taken Diamond Aunty and Sir Pratab to see the latest Sohrab Modi film starring the singing sensation Saigal and the gorgeous Devika Rani. Since their British house guests had no interest in it, Kitten had happily invited them over. Now that the elders had gone, the brown and white faces around her gleaming glass dining table were more evenly balanced.

Kitten had, finally, realised that although you can take a horse to water, you cannot make it drink. The impetuous young wife had come to the conclusion that it was time to even stop trying, and get on with all the other interesting things she wanted to do in this lifetime. However, nobody was more surprised than Tiger when he heard Kitten's plans about becoming a war correspondent. She announced this just as they had begun eating the flambéed mango mousse. Setting down his dessert spoon, HH Fateypur wondered where she got her crack-brained ideas.

'From you,' continued Kitten, tilting her imperious little nose as she reminded her husband about his own words regarding the conspiracy between the British Foreign Office, the Press Barons, Fleet Street hacks and their power to slant world news. 'And five of the people sitting around this table also heard you. So there, I've got witnesses.'

The Resident's unexpectedly wicked sense of humour manifested itself when he suggested that Princess Kitten would first have to get herself accredited to some major news syndicate, like Reuters or Associated Press before anyone would let her get anywhere near the war zone in Asia, Africa, or Europe.

'Oh, all that can be arranged with one phone call to my buddy Randolph Hearst! *He* isn't controlled by the English Foreign Office, y'know,' murmured Kitten. Her feathery diamond earrings and tiny nose pin flashed as she turned her head from person to person, listening to all the opinions and arguments.

Her cousin Arjun said that he still thought she would be an idiot to do anything so daft as becoming a war correspondent. How could she fancy herself in the Pulitzer prize winner league? She was just a pampered little girl who'd never seen the ugly side of life!

'Some of the best war reporters these days are young women like me,' rejoined Kitten, reminding him of Clare Hollingworth, who had given *The Daily Telegraph* a scoop about the outbreak of World War II after being witness to the German invasion of Poland. And weren't they forgetting Martha Gellhorn, Hemingway's current wife, who wrote the best Spanish Civil War dispatches from their guerrilla bases?

'Editors in America would pick up and syndicate your scoops LIKE THAT!' encouraged Honey, toasting her hostess with champagne.

Kitten had weighed her options before announcing her decision. She wanted to do something completely original, something far removed from her privileged princely world. And what could be better than going off to report a horrendous global conflict? It would certainly make her rise above her own petty problems, and she knew she could get the most brilliant material out, once she went after a story. The sheer danger of flying off to some unknown place, with only a plastic name tag and a paper accreditation card for protection excited the 18-year-old Maharani no end. It would be rather challenging to go out into the world and do something on her own—even if it was just reporting a war and not fighting it—without the aid of her famous father or husband.

The complex, symbiotic relationship between Princess Kitten and outright unorthodoxy was nothing new for Colonel CP. But he also understood the real reason why she had chosen to stage a dignified retreat at this precise point in time. This was a great pity, considering the considerable spadework put in by Reverse Gear and himself on her behalf with Tiger's astrologer. 'Really, Your Highness, there's nothing glamorous about war, although

I'm ready to concede your point that the war zone commands the front page like nothing else.'

'Colonel Claude-Poole's absolutely right, y'know,' Prince Rudolf added chattily, looking down his bony, high-bridged nose at Kitten. 'Much of the time, nothing is happening, and you're just hanging around, waiting for the balloon to go up. But when bombs start dropping, they don't distinguish between combatants and civilians, sweetheart.'

Lady Dorothy forced herself to speak as lightly as possible. 'I say, Princess, it might be loads more fun if you take a crash course in photography before dashing off to cover the war in Europe, y'know. It's the photo journalists who grab all the crack assignments, while mere writers are relegated to recycling military publicity handouts.'

This encouraged Ratna to also prick her exasperating friend's vanity. 'My dear Kitten, which impractical crackpot has told you that you can just land up in some unknown foreign country, without being able to speak a word of their language? And where the only people you might know would be too busy conducting the war. They would have no time to accommodate or entertain you in the style to which you're accustomed. And don't tell me you can rough it out, because we all know how squeamish you really are!'

The Rumanian Crown Prince added fuel to the fire. 'Well actually, Kitten, you belong at Bletchley, helping our experts crack Nazi codes even before they are encrypted!'

While the others laughed, Tiger bit his lower lip to stop himself from saying anything that would compel Miss Sticking Plaster to do the unthinkable, and go off on her own. Years of close observation—and scores of personal encounters, particularly the one leading to this ridiculous marriage—had taught him that once Kitten decided to do something, she would do it. And, she had perfected the art of getting her own way, sweeping aside all opposition with the patent old Rajput non sequitur: '*Raghu kul reeti sada chali ayi, pran jayi par vachan na jayi!*'

Kitten did not allow herself to dart anxious glances at Tiger Baapji as he drew Honey into the drawing room ahead of the others, declaring that they could dance just as well without a band if she came and selected the right records. Instead, she made a great fuss over helping her not-yet-noticeably pregnant cousin Ratna settle down comfortably on the sofa with cushions, a footstool, and the tiniest thimble glass of her preferred Bailey's Irish Cream. As she continued hovering around Ratna, Arjun told her to relax and stop reversing roles.

A sexy Duke Ellington number sounded from the radiogram around which Tiger, Honey, Rudolf, Colonel CP, Lady Dorothy, and Redverse stood, discussing the rival merits of various jazz bands. The dancing began even before the butler had finished serving everyone their choice of liqueurs and coffee.

Beautifully enamelled gem-embossed gold cigar boxes, cigarette cases, and lighters (made in Fateypur) stood on the two glass-topped centre tables, which also held low Kang Hsi bowls of fragrant white flowers.

Even before her marriage into a family of acknowledged collectors and connoisseurs, Kitten had acquired an unerring eye for stylish originality. Besides being all too evident in her extensive wardrobe, this characteristic quality was reflected throughout the palatial mansion which she had renovated, furnished, and decorated in a matter of days to reflect her own taste. She had created an airy and refreshingly different holiday-home ambience. Several art nouveau mirrors reflected the glorious gardens and the distant Blue Mountain vistas during the daytime through the open French windows. Now they were letting the moonlight pour into a room lit only with scented candles. The shining bleached wood floors were spread with timeless

Osagh rugs. The sinuous, curving shapes of all the drawing room sofas and chairs piled with cerulean and apricot cushions invited repose. Huge blue and white Chien Lung porcelain pedestals acted as side tables, and identical Chinoserie vases and fine pots displayed the rarest orchids, ferns, and palms, brought in from the well-stocked conservatory.

However, the unforgettable pair of enormous silver-mounted ivory tusks flanking the door between the drawing and dining rooms; two rare Lalique wall plaques; an equally precious Georges Foquet clock; Galle Cameo glass lamps; three authentic Delacroix, Bertha Morrisot, and Marc Chagall bird paintings; jewel-toned ancestral Rajput miniatures flanking marvellous crayon portraits of Tiger, both his wives Yasho Rajya Laxmi and Kitten, Princess Diamond, and Sir Pratab, executed by Maharani Padmini; the meticulously selected sculptures of Han horses, Bactrian camels, bronze birds; and the life-size silver flamingoes (grouped amidst the frothing ferns screening the marble fireplace), made it clear that this wasn't your average holiday home.

Even though he himself was busy matching Honey's brisk, energetic, and frenzied jiving on the dance floor as soon as the record changed, Tiger did not at all like the way Kitten was conducting an animated conversation with Rudolf as they danced. The latter kept drawing her close enough for their cheeks to touch. He also didn't like the way she had draped her nearly see-through sequinned chiffon sari provocatively around her increasingly feminine body. He didn't know exactly when, but all of a sudden he was forced to concede that the exasperating but reassuringly tomboyish little girl he had known all his life (and who had tricked him into marriage) had begun looking so dashed pretty.

This metamorphosis could have been caused by the

recent addition of a dignified poise to Kitten's original vivaciousness and fantastic intelligence. She had also restyled her thick, unruly hair in an attractive new way so that it framed her face instead of obscuring most of it. She still, however, retained her refreshingly natural look, using only the faintest touch of eyeliner, lip gloss, and powder to enhance her face.

There was only one way Tiger could make sure that practiced philanderers like Rudolf didn't ruin things by enticing his young Kitten to flirt, God forbid, like Honey and all the other glamorous women they both knew so intimately. To the British contingent's barely contained amusement, HH Fateypur lost no time in presenting the American girl whom he had been monopolising all evening, to His Imperial Highness. Handing her over with a devilish smile, he then waltzed off, very gracefully but very deliberately, with his own wife.

Ratna and Arjun were utterly amazed by Tiger Baapji's inexplicable action. Never before had they seen HH Fateypur dance willingly with Kitten. Their eyes met. When her husband quirked one questioning eyebrow, Ratna rolled her eyes upwards with a shrug.

All the twirling around, reversing, glorious glissading, and gliding that followed led them *miles* away from the drawing room, far down the long chandelier-lit hall where they could barely hear the music. For the first time in her life, Kitten found herself some what flustered. The instant the Maharajah waltzed her into his spacious suite, she quickly began to remind him about their duties as hosts. Perfectly drilled in the princely 3Ps—politeness, punctuality, and patience—she suggested that they ought to be getting back. 'Ratna likes to get home early these days, you know.'

'Naturally,' said her husband. 'But hasn't it occurred to you that I too can't be saddled any longer with a barren bride?'

'But virgins are bound to be barren, y'know,' countered Kitten with devastating logic. She was now fully recovered, and seizing her opportunity, had dared to mention the unmentionable.

Tiger looked into her face. He couldn't resist the luminous, long-lashed eyes focused on him in pure bewilderment.

'Oh Kitten, Kitten, you absolute ghastly horror, Kitten!' laughed one of the world's most celebrated lovers, as he hugged her ruthlessly.

Although she had always loved him desperately, and adored the very ground he walked on, Kitten could hardly believe that her husband had, at last, stopped behaving like the proverbial horse who wouldn't drink when led to water!

What followed was so enjoyable that she couldn't resist asking between kisses: 'Really, Your Highness, what were you waiting for all these months?'

'The RIGHT conjunction of stars, plus the full moon, idiot!' retorted Tiger, completely amazed at how alluring he had begun to find his unpredictable bride.

Camels to the Fore   12

Despite the upgraded 19-gun salute, and the first-rate reception accorded him by the new Viceroy, Maharajah Jai Singh knew that, in actual fact, he was dealing with a closed mind the moment he entered the massive reddish-brown monstrosity on Raisina Hill designed as New Delhi's core by Lutyens. And all because the old King had decided to pass on. The Prince of Wales and his Dutch bride had disappeared into the Bermuda Triangle during their honeymoon and he wasn't intimate enough with the new King and Queen to demand intervention. As for their Heiress Presumptive, she was too young to be taken seriously by any war office or viceroy.

But Field Marshal Lord Wavell was too much of a soldier—and an old India hand—to be seduced by HH Chattargadh's gallant offer about leading his State forces to the European theatre. He had already explained why the Chattargadh Camel Corps was not fit for the waterlogged Burma front. Or the assault on Italy, which already included Indian State Force troops. Or for a passage to Egypt even after Reich Marshal Rommel pulled out of North Africa.

'Waging war for a just cause is our dharma as you are well aware because of your familiarity with the *Gita* and other Indian guidebooks. Surely HM's Government doesn't want to deny us our birthright!'

'Of course not, Your Highness. This is January 1944, and we're now in the era of highly mechanised modern warfare which calls for a bit more than your clan's splendid chivalry and valour,' said the Viceroy. 'All the Indian princes serving on various fronts today belong to regular infantry, artillery, armoured, or engineer regiments; or to the Raaf, like your son and son-in-law. But despite all our set-backs, and our need for more manpower, we've kept all the unmechanised cavalry units in India.'

'The Allies can't expect victory until they CROSS the Maginot Line and attack Germany, y'know,' observed the Maharajah.

'Really, Your Highness, there's nothing we'd like more. But right now, we don't even have a bridgehead in Europe,' clarified Field Marshal Lord Wavell.

'Precisely. Because those chaps planning Imperial Ops have such narrow visions.'

The Maharajah's Military Secretary and the Viceroy's GQ exchanged dazed glances as they listened to HH Chattargadh's supposedly 'fresh approach' advocating the use of mobility and fire-power; plus the invaluable element of surprise in getting into Paris, Berlin, Belgium, or wherever else they pleased, through the south of France.

Lord Wavell had no intention of giving the Nazi propaganda machinery a true coup by rushing some Camel Corps off on a wild goose chase to France, or allowing the American press to accuse him of retaining a Charge-of-the-Light-Brigade mentality. 'Regretfully, Your Highness, the Allied cause must continue to suffer because we are not in a position to implement your scheme due to logistical constraints.'

The turbaned Maharajah, wearing a British Lieutenant General's insignia, looked the Viceroy, who outranked him, right in the eye. 'My dear chap, do I detect a racist bias in your refusal to let my Rajputs blitzkrieg through German defences in the Maritime Alps?'

Appalled at such a direct accusation, this most favourably disposed of all the white sahebs ruling India, protested. 'Really, Your Highness, that's preposterous. We've got to keep you in India because the Chattargadh Camel Corps is far more useful to the Allied war effort in its natural environment, which is sand, not snow.'

'Nonsense. If Hannibal could get his elephants across the Alps, d'you think anything can stop my Camel Corps?'

'But times have changed, Sir. If the Wehrmacht don't get you, the Luftwaffe will,' reasoned the Viceroy.

The Maharajah of Pisshengunj got to hear every little detail of this fiasco even before HH Chattargadh's cavalcade left Viceregal Lodge. This was because he always kept several palms well greased for keeping their ears to the ground throughout the British Raj.

'Our scriptures say that serving others is the highest form of dharma,' began Nutty, addressing his devoted Dewan and his brother-in-law as they strolled up and down the broad lawns of his own New Delhi residence near India Gate. 'Put yourselves in my beloved brother's place, and feel how he must be smarting under the insult of being denied the warrior's vocation of finding glory on some European battlefield, unconcerned about death!'

'Nevertheless, we have it on excellent authority that the Viceroy—who's also Asia's Supreme Allied Commander—has even denied HH Chattargadh a stint nearer home in the Middle East, or even North Africa, by making it quite clear that they've already got plenty of local camel *wallahs* in those parts for scouting, patrolling, guard mounting, and *dak*-delivery duties. Which is, really, all they're fit for!' chuckled Baron Tikemoffsky.

Koodsu Rao Saheb stroked his grey moustache, pondering over his feudal lord's plight. 'I don't think that Chattargadh Durbar is going to swallow such an insult without turning the tables on this Viceroy, who is going around dressed like a Field Marshal.'

'Exactly,' cried Nutty. 'And it's our duty to help him show these foreigners that though times have changed, and the world has moved beyond elephantry, cavalry, and camelry towards modern weapon systems, the Rajput fighting spirit is not yet redundant.'

'Chivalry and valour will always count,' agreed Tikky.

Koodsu Rao Saheb ticked off the various battle honours won by their Camel Corps in places as far flung as China, Mesopotamia, and New Zealand.

HH Pisshengunj remarked that this impressive list removed the last lingering doubts from his mind about helping Maharajah Jai Singh. It was so simple really, that he wondered why he hadn't thought about it earlier. 'But there have to be no snags this time,' Nutty warned his henchmen.

The latter couldn't stop laughing when he revealed his plan. Koodsu Rao Saheb said that it was even better than the time his sister's husband had kept the Chattargadh Maharajah going round and round in his special train, circling Pisshengunj for one whole night, and annoying the old viceroy, Lord Axe, for failing to keep his appointment in the capital.

'Now Tikky, all you have to do is to see that a cable is sent immediately to HH Chattargadh from London, with the necessary instructions. I take it you have the right contacts at the War Office?'

'Indeed, Your Highness. Would you prefer activating a Red mole or a White one?' inquired the Russian baron.

'Who cares about colour-shulur? As long as he's willing to do his bit for our side by helping us reinforce the Allied forces in Europe,' stressed Nutty.

As the Maharajah paused to admire his dogs being paraded round the garden's rectangular reflecting pool, Baron Tikemoffsky addressed him again. 'Just one more little thing, Your Highness. The cat will be out of the bag the minute HH Chattargadh starts harassing the British naval authorities for ships to transport his troops.'

'Don't bother me with these minor details, Tikky. Surely you can take care of small things like that, plus providing a convoy of proper battleships for my esteemed brother?'

Koodsu Rao Saheb suggested that the Dewan could contact the firm Pisshengunj Durbar used for ferrying his polo ponies to England every summer. Delighted with this suggestion, Nutty immediately sanctioned outright purchase of four such ships.

'Camels are bound to need more leg room, y'know. In for a penny, in for a pound, I always say. Besides, a ship's captain can't question his owner's orders, regardless of race!'

Nutty relished the delightful possibilities concealed behind his ingeniously charitable idea. If Maharajah Jai Singh sailed off without hindrance, he ran the risk of being attacked and sunk by every enemy, including bad weather. If the British port authorities caught him red-handed for disobeying their Supreme Commander's orders, he could be court-martialled, or even deposed for endangering the lives of so many helpless animals, usually dearer to the English heart than native sepoys. If he did manage to land in France with his celebrated Camel Corps, the Gestapo would arrest him in minutes.

And, there was no way you could camouflage 400-odd camels ridden by Indians in flaming orange turbans. Even on the Riviera!

Colonel Claude-Poole was eternally grateful to the Powers Above, when they reached the Riviera without encountering

anything more deadly than the frightful lectures on European
military history given by Maharajah Jai Singh.

Throughout the tense sea voyage from Karachi to the
Mediterranean through the hotly contested Suez canal, he
had harped on the fact that Hannibal, Julius Caesar,
Augustus, Napoleon, and Messina had used the ports of
Nice, Marseilles, and St. Raphael for various campaigns and
conquests. So, why couldn't they do the same? According
to HH Chattergadh, in 13 B.C., the ancient Celtic village
of Cemenclum was the Roman Headquarters for the
Maritime Alps area. A Ligurian legion stationed there had
protected the Via Julia Augusta between Rome and Spain.
Everybody knew about the aqueducts, baths, villas, theatres,
and triumphal arches to be seen along the Côte d'Azur.
But this Maharajah also knew that when Napoleon paraded
the plundered art works of Egypt and Italy in Paris, they
were accompanied by lions, ostriches, and CAMELS!

After what seemed like eternity, the entire Chattargadh
Camel Corps disembarked near St. Raphael, a private pier
where entire fleets of ocean liners could dock, their officers
and JCOs thanking their lucky stars for a dark, moonless
night. But even before the last soldier went ashore, clinging
to the tail of his sure-footed mount, the Free French came
calling, lugging cases of lukewarm wine.

Their cell had been on the lookout for some American
agents they had orders to help and hide, when they had
suddenly found their secret rendezvous swarming with
strange beasts and turbaned men.

'So much for military intelligence!' their leader scoffed
in tolerable English. 'I suppose they didn't want to alarm
us by giving us the true picture . . . .'

'Misunderstandings and rumours are bound to arise
during wartime, when half the Allies can hardly stand each
other, let alone speak the other chap's lingo, y'know,' Jai
Singh said chattily in the excellent French acquired from

years of holidaying in Europe, and which was a real bonus the Maharajah wasn't about to throw away by confessing that they were not exactly the agents he was expecting. Once the veteran Resistance organiser was assured that far from expecting him to conceal so many of them in these caves which could turn into a deadly trap if anything betrayed their presence, all that his Indian allies wanted was a proper briefing about enemy deployment—a guide if they could spare one, and any snags they might encounter en route to Paris, he was only too happy to oblige.

The Maharajah and his Military Secretary were relieved to hear that the Germans had withdrawn most of their heavy artillery from this sector. Or had been spiked by the local Maquis. But there was still considerable danger from enemy planes, Nazi patrols, and ambush parties. And, of course, Vichy French informers whom they would activate the moment they sought fresh food for so many persons.

The Maharajah said that they'd come very well equipped with dry rations to see them through the six-day march on Paris. And his 100-miles-a-day camels, who knew how to live off the thorniest desert, could be trusted to fend for themselves in the fertile French countryside.

Burrowing through these caves, which also had openings on the other side of these Provincial hills, Jai Singh wanted to follow the Rhone till it became the Soane, turning northwest from Lyon towards Paris.

'There will be no other regiments in support?' the flabbergasted French commander pointedly asked the one and only sane-seeming British officer.

'Who needs them!' It was bound to be a debacle, but there was no retreating now. What the hell, thought Colonel CP. In for a penny, in for a pound.

The atmosphere of the Croydon mess from which 'Gentlemen Volunteers' like Maharajah Tiger Fateypur operated, was even wilder than that of other RAF units, including the notorious 351st Bombardment Squadron at Thrope Abbots, to which his brother-in-law Robin belonged. But these fighter pilots all had the same cynical approach to anything that smacked of leg pulling.

Therefore, when Wing Commander Crown Prince Rudolf strode in that night after a hush-hush sortie with his goggles pushed up above an unsmiling face, still encased in the hideous leather flying helmet with built-in earphones, swearing that he'd seen the most incredible sight of all times today, nobody took him seriously.

Until someone suggested over the constant din of a scratchy record, hurled oaths and darts, thumped beer mugs, a loud telephone conversation at one end of the bar, and the roar of Hurricanes heading towards the Channel, that perhaps His Imperial Highness was hallucinating more than usual today.

'Care to share it, as the shrinks say?' Tiger too teased his friend.

Irritable and still on edge, Rudolf took the proffered seat and cigarette. 'It was one of those air-dropping sorties over southern France,' he began. 'The cloud bank was thicker than I had expected. The wind had been rising steadily. And you know how difficult it is to keep vital supplies from falling into the wrong hands even from Harriers which can touch down in the roughest fields . . . When, what do I see, with one eye peeled to spot any Huns patrolling this airspace? Camels! Hundreds upon hundreds of camels, carrying riders wearing WHITE. It could not be a circus, because we know that those nasty Nazis have driven them underground. And it was too persistent to be a mere mirage, you know. But I say, Tiger, hallucinating while flying behind enemy lines in the Maritime Alps could prove quite sticky . . . .'

His shoulders shaking with spontaneous bouts of

laughter, Tiger told the Prince to stop worrying. 'My dear Rudolf, that was no hallucination or mirage. Only my father-in-law, Maharajah Jai Singh, giving his Camel Corps a taste of action before the war's over!'

'Good Lord, I thought the Nutty Maharajah was your uncle; and your father-in-law the sound egg?'

'The Hun front line stretches all across the Maritime Alps, right? My father-in-law has a theory that if Hannibal could deliver his firepower to the gates of Rome over those mountains, using African elephants, he can jolly well do the same thing in the opposite direction, with Indian camels!'

But instead of bringing the Hapsburg Prince some much-needed relief, this information only increased his consternation. There was only one thing they could do, he told Tiger. Give HH Chattargadh a sporting chance by warning him to steer clear of the Panzers controlling THAT strategic route.

After sighting the Panzers concealed in a valley surrounded by high hills covered with Alpine forests, Maharajah Tiger Fateypur banked left at 8000 feet, peeling off from his Spitfire squadron even though it was against regulations. Observing complete radio silence, with his gun buttons set to fire, and neck swivelling for that first tiny glint of metal which meant an enemy aircraft, he also kept a watchful eye on ground zero, marked out on the navigation map by his friend Rudolf.

He too was struck by the sheer absurdity of the magnificent, mad spectacle of 460 camel-mounted Rajputs riding confidently behind their trusted Maharajah and his Military Secretary, straight towards a dreaded German Panzer regiment! Slanting sun rays lit up the golden aigrettes worn by all those warriors resplendent in saffron turbans over pure white uniforms. So much for the wartime principle of camouflage, thought the fighter pilot. They undoubtedly LOOKED splendid, but surely Uncle Jai could have increased their safety by at least putting his chaps in khakhi or OG even if he had planned to traipse through this mountain region, because there was no likelihood of their merging into any snowscape in early June at this altitude! Fortunately, no Meserschmitts had spotted them yet, because they kept to the umbrella-like tree cover between two streams. But there was the Hun dead ahead . . . .

They were still roughly 22 miles from the tanks. So there was time to drop them a friendly warning, although Tiger very much doubted that his father-in-law would change his original strategy. There were no high tension wires directly below in the rough hilly terrain. But plenty of tall trees. Yet he knew that it was crucial to get someone's attention. Grasping the control stick with his gloved right hand, Tiger waggled his wings, plunged down to tree level and began circling the Camel Corps stretched out all over the forest below in the hope that they would spot his RAF markings. His barograph needle marked 430 feet when he pulled his plane's nose up once more.

Most of the soldiers grew alarmed at the pilot's antics as they peered skywards, muttering suppressed curses while trying to control their spooked and restive camels. Maharajah Jai Singh wondered why the silly ass in that Spitfire was showing off like the schoolboy he probably was by performing dangerous aerobatic feats at this ludicrously low height, instead of getting on with his mission. And leaving his Camel Corps to get on with their own.

Well aware that an enemy aircraft would have strafed them by now, Colonel CP scanned the sky with his field glasses. 'Thank heavens somebody up there woke up to the fact that we need air cover,' he said to the Maharajah.

'Indeed, Colonel CP? I, on the other hand, consider

this uncalled-for intervention by the Raaf nothing short of sabotage.'

'Really, Your Highness, without air support, the Chattargadh Camel Corps has less chance of survival in enemy territory than a snowball in Hell!'

'Use your common sense, CP. Those planes will alert every enemy unit around us, and ruin our chances of surprising them.'

'I should think our ceremonial wardrums and flaming orange turbans are already doing a marvellous job of advertising our presence.'

'Uff-oh, you Englishmen will never understand our ancient Indian logic. The sound of kettledrums creates a scientific chain reaction, energising both soldiers and camels, plus striking terror in the enemy's heart, y'know.'

'That was true in medieval times, Your Highness. But modern warfare is quite another kettle of fish.'

'Quite right,' conceded the Maharajah. 'Will you kindly radio Raaf headquarters, and tell them to call off those chaps before they tip off the enemy, and bring the Luftwaffe down on us.'

'Really, Your Highness, we have managed to get this far by maintaining strict radio silence. But the minute I try to raise Raaf HQ, the fat will be in the fire.'

'Which might be sooner than you think, if those flying fools succeed in stampeding our camels,' Jai Singh said as the Spitfire swooped down once more.

The quick-witted Maharajah of Fateypur had speedily resolved the dilemma of dropping an unmistakable warning to his countrymen about their danger. He had scrawled a brief, explicit message on one of the maps from his flying suit's zipped leg pocket after circling the spot; wrapped it round his crested gold lighter; and placed the packet safely inside the ingeniously constructed self-inflating Mae West (rubber dinghy) provided to all Allied pilots along with parachutes after Dunkirk, in case they were shot down over the sea.

The moment Maharajah Jai Singh read the retrieved message bearing his son-in-law's unmistakable seal and signature, he smiled ruefully as he pocketed the cigarette lighter, and tucked the Mae West into his saddle bag. 'What a foolish thing to do. But that's Tiger Fateypur for you. No thought about his own safety or survival, if he is shot down into the cold North Sea.

Colonel Claude-Poole's sense of futility increased with every mile covered. The Rajputs treated war exactly like another blood sport, a spot of adventure to break the monotony of daily existence. But war today—not just in Europe, anywhere in the world—was a matter of machines more than valour.

He listened aghast to the Maharajah's cheerful pronouncement of further battle plans, controlling himself with great difficulty. Having won the point about observing radio silence, he was not about to make the blunder of disagreeing with HH, because that only drove this typical Rathor prince to do the impossible. Like airdropping elephants on the palace roof just for the sake of forcing him to instal some silly chandeliers! But this was serious. Really serious. The worst that could have happened then was a collapsing roof, for which no one could have blamed the Maharajah's architect. But as Military Secretary, he wouldn't get off so lightly, or escape all blame merely by pleading that he was obeying orders like a good soldier if the Chattargadh Camel Corps were decimated by enemy tanks. Or worse still, captured by the Nazis. Who didn't have enough food for their own troops, let alone anyone else they might have agreed to feed at some silly Geneva Convention.

The British officer's anxiety increased with every passing mile, but he was determined not to show it, lest the men got demoralised. He had no illusions about this Maharajah listening to reason. Extraordinarily courageous, competent and resourceful, Maharajah Jai Singh was not the man to order a retreat even if they were surrounded by tanks. SPECIALLY if they were surrounded by tanks.

A German dispatch rider roared off on his heavy black motorcycle from the Panzer regiment cleverly concealed in a ravine formed by some rock outcrops in the low, wooded valley sloping down to a small lake near Crest. Its noxious fumes mingled with the smells and smoke rising from the field mess tent, outside which several soldiers clad in grey uniforms were lined up with plates and mugs to receive their spartan evening meal. By June 1944, even the resourceful Nazis with all their terror tactics and collaborators were finding it difficult, if not impossible, to extract and extort the last ounce of food and drink from the stripped French farms and vineyards. But they were still better off here than they had been in the desert, when the Afrika Corps was pushed back to Tunis after El Alamein.

Two freckle-faced replacements for the considerably diminished 39th Panzer Regiment stood debating their chances of cadging a ride to the nearest town with some lively girls and a cinema, since they had got a few precious hours off tomorrow. An older, scar-faced gunner named Spitz sat smoking, perched atop a conveniently flat boulder on a hillock facing the mountains. Though this Southern air didn't have the refreshing crystalline quality of his Tyrolean homeland, he found this quiet twilight break between endlessly monotonous military chores, and officers promoting disinformation, good for clearing the cobwebs.

Spitz's eye caught a sudden flash of something so familiar from his years in Africa, that he sat up with a jolt. His eyes goggled in disbelief as he continued to see a sufficiently distinct mirage shimmering against the mountains. Could it be a projection of his own mind, like the famous Swiss echo, he wondered? . . . . But it was a prodigiously PERSISTENT mirage. The soldier knew his duty.

The duty-Sergeant grunted at the reprehensible suggestion put forward by somebody who would soon be digging latrine pits for the duration of this war. The fool thought he was seeing camels, was he? Thought he was outside the Berlin zoo, or anticipating an evening at the Circus, he demanded with heavy sarcasm.

Captain von Knips overheard this while checking his squadron before going down to the officers' lakeside mess for his own dinner. Since Spitz was one of his own reliable troopers, even though he wasn't a real German, Captain von Knips asked what was wrong.

'Look, Herr Captain! Camels along those hills, to your right . . . . Just there, Sir.' But by the time von Knips turned to peer in the direction pointed out by the emphatic Austrian, shaded his eyes, and swivelled them to scan the horizon, the camels were hidden from view. 'Where? I do not see a thing.'

'But Sir, they are THERE. I saw humps, and a flash of colour . . . .' Spitz continued with staunch conviction.

Some of the soldiers who stood around, laughed; someone made a ribald joke about 'Humps!'; and two of the heavily armed sentries patrolling the German camp emphatically denied having seen anything out there, apart from the usual errand boy cycling past or peasants driving farm wagons along the dirt track connecting nearby villages.

'There is nothing out there except Spitz's imagination running wild, Herr Captain!' The Sergeant swore, standing stiffly to attention.

'I swear by the Fuhrer . . . .' began the gunner.

'Don't you DARE take the Fuhrer's name in vain!' one of the sentries said menacingly.

Face flushed with the frustration and desperation of a man who knows he is speaking the truth, the gunner cried: 'All right. May I have the Captain's permission to swear by the Saints, sweet Jesus, and my blessed Mother that I am telling the truth? There are camels . . . enemy camels . . . out there.'

The Captain looked at his watch, and sighed. Their CO was a stickler for punctuality, and it was already two minutes past seven. But Gunner Spitz would not let go of his strange fixation after so many comrades had called him a liar.

'Sir, you will soon know who is the liar if you send out a patrol or recce party . . . .'

'Spitz, are you telling me how to run my squadron? Or are you having trouble with your eyes?'

The miserable soldier said that his officer was forcing him to turn a blind eye on the enemy. Determined to settle this row before someone distorted it into a rumour-mongering offence carrying the Wehrmacht's wartime death penalty, Captain von Knips sent a soldier off to fetch his field glasses; and another with an apologetic message to the officers' Mess.

From a tree-top lookout tower, von Knips scanned the whole southern range of mountains, focusing his night vision-equipped Hessalbled binoculars. There was no denying it. There WAS some odd phenomenon circling the area far to the southwest. He could no longer claim that gunner Spitz's bizarre claim could not be substantiated by the evidence of his own eyes! For a queer mass of oddly shaped orange, white and brown substance streaked the horizon at tree level, vanishing and reappearing rapidly even as the normally pragmatic Prussian officer tried to figure out what it could actually be.

He gave the Sergeant and camp guards standing at his elbow the opportunity to see for themselves. Afrika Corps veterans, one by one, all three stood open-mouthed, gaping at the hallucinatory pageant of hundreds of camels, which simply refused to melt away into the evening haze surrounding those European hills after sunset.

A hush fell round the dining table when Colonel Braun leaned back in his chair, raking his Squadron Commander's face with disgusted eyes. 'Death and damnation, von Knips! I have heard enough about camels advancing against us from common soldiers. Now my officers start hallucinating.'

'Believe me, Sir, I was as sceptical as you until I decided to see for myself . . . .'

'That will do. This might be my first stint of duty outside the Fatherland, but I have trained enough Panzer officers and troops to know what they can and cannot see, smack in the heart of Europe. Unfortunately, we know that everyone in Reich Marshal Rommel's Afrika Corps was exposed to camels and sunstroke. But that's no excuse for cracking up when Germany needs every fighting man, Captain.'

Von Knips forced himself to speak in a civilised, rational manner. 'Indeed, Sir, I am not prone to hallucinating; and nor are my men. I swear by the Fuhrer that we ALL saw those camels.'

This evoked sceptical smiles, grunts, and scoffing comments from the six Nazi officers left in charge of the considerably decimated tank regiment. They began to guffaw loudly even before their CO finished his next sentence. 'Use your common sense, Captain von Knips. Even the Brits would not be stupid enough to send some silly camel corps against a crack Panzer unit.'

'Sir, I am only asking for a reconnaissance patrol. The Allies might have developed a secret weapons system, for all we know.'

'Which now you see, and now you don't. Is that it?' the broad-browed Colonel demanded. His second-in-command added that it sounded suspiciously like some Greek Trojan horse tale. But neither their usual informers, nor the Gestapo had alerted them about any exotic beasts abroad; so he presumed that all was well despite this modern Cassandra called von Knips.

The humour-loving Quartermaster who was a peacetime history teacher, studied his fellow officers through steel-rimmed spectacles. 'Surely, gentlemen, you have all heard of Hannibal's exemplary military feats?'

Snorting derisively, Colonel Braun snapped: 'Yes, we know all about Hannibal and his elephants. And don't let me hear anyone even MENTION the Magi who converged on Bethlehem riding camels from India, China, and North Africa!'

The medical officer advised everyone to have another glass of the excellent Chateau Lacoste they had found en route, instead of indulging in a futile argument which could be settled by the CO taking a look at the countryside, just to be on the safe side. After dinner, of course. They weren't barbarians.

But during the 40 minutes between this decision and its implementation, no matter how hard Colonel Braun tried to focus his binoculars on something alien out there from the ridge behind which he had so cunningly positioned his tanks, he couldn't discover hide or hair of anything remotely resembling a camel. Horse. Or cow.

His orders to the medical officer were brief and explicit. Keen to conserve those precious tranquillisers for those dreadful burn cases and other equally horrendous casualties, which were inevitable whenever tanks went into action, the German doctor demurred. But not for long, when he was given a direct order by the Colonel, who needed every soldier alert at his station tomorrow, because of the alarming news from Paris and Marseilles that the Allies were about to land on *both* the French coasts.

Fortunately for the Chattargadh Camel Corps, they had become invisible as soon as they rode down a defile, which ended in a tree, choked hollow completely screened by thick oaks and rowans. They could not be spotted even through powerful binoculars, because the German colonel had been scanning the higher hills opposite his camp, in the belief that something as obvious as a camel cavalcade would automatically be exposed against the skyline, which was still tinged with brightness during this long summer twilight.

As they were riding downhill through the tall fir trees with the French guide who had brought them so far without mishap, Maharajah Jai Singh had realised that they were indeed just a few miles away from several German tanks positioned in a rough circle where two tracks, a lake, and stream converged. So Tiger was right. But it was too late to outflank them now. So he had no choice except to order a night halt with a dry camp, no fires, no smoking, and absolute silence to be observed by everybody as they sheltered behind their resting camels. And a full frontal assault after encircling the Panzers at first light. For the crucial element of surprise was still in their favour.

Absolutely composed and determined, Maharajah Jai Singh led his men into battle next day as soon as dawn streaked the sky. He was flanked by two camel-mounted standard bearers carrying Chattargadh's crimson-and-saffron banner, and the Union Jack. Behind them, four buglers blew a fanfare; trumpeters sounded the attack; and drummers began beating a resounding tattoo. The disciplined ranks of Rajput soldiers and officers in their bright saffron turbans sat confidently on their trusted mounts, holding fully charged machine guns and carbines at the ready. The Maharajah's Military Secretary had already set up the mortars and field guns at strategic spots overlooking the enemy camp. Colonel Claude-Poole looked down upon the awesome iron monsters with their deadly turrets and crushing caterpillar tracks, and wondered how many of the soldiers dragged here on this mad adventure would live to tell this tale?

The unearthly din of ululating camels, trumpets, drums, and men shouting battle cries in some strange foreign language shattered the deep, early morning sleep of those few guards, cooks, and officers left undrugged by their CO's wisdom. The valley was swarming with camels. A huge horde of turbaned Indians had really surrounded their tanks! After one look, the Medical Officer plunged back into his tent with an ashen face.

Stunned and somewhat unnerved by that phalanx of camels marching straight towards him when he didn't even have his proper uniform on, let alone a firearm or troops even half awake, Colonel Braun realised that for him and his men at least, the war was over.

Jai Singh gauged the true situation from the demeanour of the German commander standing distraught—surrounded by 13 out of the 40 tanks he controlled intact—in his silent camp. The Indian prince knew EXACTLY what to do with this war booty. Straight away, he would launch a Rajput version of Skorzeny's Trojan Horse Brigade, (American speaking German troops with captured American tanks in American uniforms, wreaked havoc across Allied lines in the Ardennes), which would give them some REAL victories over the Nazis before they reached Paris. So that he needn't feel embarrassed about this ludicrous walk-over among his own kith and kin when the story got out. As was always the case when one was dealing with a leaky War Office. And a gossipy journal-keeping Viceroy.

Maharajah Jai Singh simply raised his empty left hand, and rested his weapon. Their chief's bearing and demeanour communicated his wish to all his clansmen. And they did what was expected of them in this weird situation. To the man, they sat stock still on their 100-miles-a-day mounts, holding their fire.

Up on the knoll where he had positioned their Lewis and Hothkiss field guns, Colonel CP could not believe his eyes. The Chattargadh Camel Corps had captured a whole Panzer regiment without firing a single shot! And if he knew his Maharajah, Jai Singh was going to refuse Britain's highest battle honour—the VC—precisely because of this.

Merger Muddles
13

It soon became evident to Jai Singh, Tiger, Sir Pratab, and Gerald Redverse that realpolitik was totally beyond HH Pisshengunj's perception. Sir Pratab, who came up to Delhi frequently as a member of the Constituent Assembly, had heard several other rulers voicing similar sentiments. But at least his own nephew and brother-in-law knew that significant changes were about to take place. The wisest course for them was to clarify the negotiable and non-negotiable issues with their Resident before that afternoon's crucial Chamber of Princes meeting with the Viceroy. Hopefully, there the modalities for accession and the eventual merger of all the Princely States with independent India could be hammered out without undue loss of face.

The table around which they sat in Maharajah Jai Singh's study in Chattargadh House overlooking the neat tree-lined lawns and lily pools around India Gate, was stacked with treaties and maps. Tapping one of them, Nutty kept harping on the implications of Paramountcy. 'Why should we deal with mere viceroys and politicians, when our treaties are with the British Crown? And under international law, aren't we answerable only to the Paramount Power—who happens to be the King of England, and not his cuckolded cousin, or his wife's bogus Marxist lover?'

Bred to diplomacy, Redverse looked the other way. But Jai Singh said with a restraining hand signal: 'Nutty, don't you realise that the interim government formed by the Indian National Congress *is* the de facto successor to Crown Paramountcy? And that we've got to negotiate with them?'

'You've left out Jinnah and the Muslim League,' countered his cousin.

Without a moment's hesitation, HH Chattargadh retorted, 'Mr Jinnah and his Carte Blanche don't figure in my calculations.'

'But it's our sacred, God-given *duty* to strike a blow for secularism!' Nutty insisted. 'Shouldn't we three, as rulers of contiguous states with a proud tradition of accommodation, coexistence, and cohabitation, put our full weight behind tilting the balance in favour of oppressed minorities, before outsiders like the UN Human Rights Commission and Amnesty International start messing around with our internal affairs?'

Everybody sitting around that table was aware that it was not mere weakness that had made the British succumb to Jinnah's demand (on behalf of India's 76 million Muslim minority) to partition the Indian subcontinent before granting independence. If Pakistan was clearly set to becoming a reality, it was because it suited the entire Western world—including the US and the Soviets—to scuttle the emergence of another Asian superpower besides China, with all ensuing ramifications in global market shares and racial rivalry. And, the formal integration of the 567 Princely States into the two successor states of the British Raj was just another problem to be solved as rapidly as possible. Engrossed with his own future agenda, Prime Minister Nehru had entrusted the merger issue to Sardar Patel (his Deputy PM-cum-Home Minister) and the outstanding official, V.P. Menon (now Constitutional Adviser to the Viceroy). The seasoned lawyer-cum-demagogue, Jinnah, had immediately offered carte blanche to the rulers of all the contiguous states to tempt them into merging with Pakistan.

Instead of denigrating the Congress leaders orbiting round Mahatma Gandhi, Maharajah Jai Singh had kept himself well informed, listened to their impassioned arguments, and even provided secret financial support to patriotic stalwarts like Rajagopalachari, Madan Mohan Malaviya, Maulana Azad, and Sardar Patel. They had often discussed national problems and the inevitable fate of the Princely order if they did not compromise with modern ideas. So many still believed that an obstinate attachment to their sovereignty, their people's loyalty, and their treaties with the British Crown, would be enough to safeguard their future.

Jai Singh tried telling Nutty why the Congress government in New Delhi—which consisted mostly of freedom fighters who were lawyers, academicians, and doctors elected to power by provincial legislatures—had realised that the Princely States would only stall, and not sabotage, full independence if they refused to merge with the secular Indian Union, or held out for Crown Colony status, or acceded to the new, theocratic nation of Pakistan. They would, however, certainly be able to disrupt the whole country because all the roads and railways ran through them. Surface transport could be brought to a standstill, and disastrously effect India's trade, economy, social life, administrative functioning, and political organisation; as well as the post and telegraph systems, and the fledgeling airways. Therefore, the pragmatic Patel had suggested that the Princely States should accede only the same three things that they had already conceded to the British Crown by *sanads* and treaties between 1858 and 1890—defence, foreign affairs, and communications. In return, Sardar Patel promised that the Government Of India would respect their autonomy and titles; grant them privy purses commensurate with their existing revenues; as well as certain constitutional rights. These would include recognition by the President, Parliament and the apex Court of all hereditary Princes with adoption rights; inalienable tax-free ancestral property; diplomatic passports, protocol, and immunity; the right to fly State flags on forts and palaces; and the right to flag cars with red State number plates, among other things.

But the Maharajah of Pisshangunj wasn't ready to give up. 'If all the 567 Princely States stand united, nobody can touch us. Haven't we all got standing armies which have outperformed other Allied units in *two* World Wars? Didn't the Chattargadh Camel Corps capture an entire Nazi Panzer regiment thanks to me and my ships *before* VE day—for which you, Bhai, coolly refused the Victoria Cross just because no shots were fired by either side. You did not care that you were cheating all your kinsmen of all that reflected glory! So why should we meekly sign away everything our ancestors fought so hard to create over a period stretching back nearly fifteen hundred years, if not more?'

'We appreciate your sentiments, Uncle Nutty,' said Tiger. 'But no "sensible" Maharajah believes in the possibility of a third country made up of the Princely States.'

His father-in-law cast him a commiserating glance. 'When you say "sensible," Tiger, you automatically disqualify our Nutty relation.' This sally drew laughter from Sir Pratab, R.K. Kishen, and Tiger. But it made Nutty glare at Jai Singh, while Tikky bristled in his master's defence.

The British Resident could see why several rulers, not just His Nutty Highness, were so loth to surrender their territorial autonomy and ancient hereditary rights to a notoriously socialist interim government led by Jawaharlal Nehru. Therefore, they kept invoking the principle of Crown Paramountcy. However, this was also being used as a bargaining chip and negotiating device to wrest the most favourable terms and constitutional guarantees for themselves and their heirs in exchange for accession and merger with free, democratic India.

'Really,. Your Highness, the wisest course would be to recognise the new forces of history which cannot be tackled by imitating the ostrich.'

'Are you calling me an ostrich, Mr Redverse? Who helped you rule an empire? How can you ungrateful Englishmen allow Paramountcy to lapse?' demanded the Maharajah of Pisshengunj.

The Resident gave a dismissive shrug. 'Simply because we can't afford to keep it going any longer, Your Highness.'

'Ah, the occupational hazards of being a nation of shopkeepers, Reverse Gear!' teased Tiger, twinkling at the Resident and making everybody laugh.

The telephone on Maharajah Jai Singh's desk began ringing. After answering it and listening intently to whoever was on the line, he said 'Not again!' quite sharply, before beckoning Tiger.

The Maharajah of Fateypur cast his eyes up in dismay as he listened to the latest barrage of information about his absconding sons being told him by their frantic mother, Kitten. He tried to reassure her by telling her that they were probably in the stables or the motor garage, and that she should not panic. 'Boys will be boys, y'know . . . No, they haven't come here YET . . . of course I'm going to call up the police! But we'll look rather foolish if they've simply locked themselves into some bathroom, to splash around in the bathtub because they miss the sea . . . .'

'That's it!' Kitten cried into the phone. 'Why didn't I think of it immediately? They've run off to the boating club across the road, and are probably having the time of their lives, scaring the boatmen by appearing and disappearing in rotation, like some evil water spirits. Wait till I get my hands on those little monsters.'

'But they could have gone anywhere in India Gate. To

that children's park with all the slides and swings, like last time? Or, may be they've climbed up to South Block. I wouldn't even rule out Viceregal Lodge,' reasoned Tiger, veteran of a thousand air battles and dog fights. 'So the thing is, we'll get people with binoculars to sweep every inch of ground until we locate them, before you drive them into playing some *more* hide and seek.'

Nutty immediately declared that he would personally supervise the search for his missing grand-nephews by releasing each and every dog he'd brought to Delhi to track and flush them out in a jiffy, if Kitten would kindly let him have their shoes or slippers as soon as his ADCs got to Fateypur House, which was next door.

But Maharajah Jai Singh and Sir Pratab had already gone off to organise search parties, armed with field glasses and telescopes, as Tiger had suggested, even before he put the phone down.

It never failed to amaze him how three little boys could give the slip to four extraordinarily efficient and intelligent women like Kitten, Yasho, Aunt Diamond, and Ratna, plus a host of nannies, tutors, ADCs, bodyguards, and retainers, who all had strict instructions *not* to allow the princes to leave Fateypur House. Too well known in their own State to get much mileage out of their pranks, this was the second time they had given everybody the slip. They had managed to sneak out of their tightly guarded home, which was encircled by a supposedly impenetrable and unscalable 16-feet high wrought-iron railings.

'We've *got* to figure out how those rascals get out, before we can put an end to their excursions,' announced Tiger over the telephone, keeping his apprehensions about their safety to himself. Apart from the daily disturbances, processions, and communal clashes occurring in this ancient historic city, there were frequent newspaper reports of children being abducted by criminal gangs and professional beggars. And kidnapping for ransom couldn't be ruled out even in India, although princely families were still held in esteem in a country seething with sectarian violence.

'You think I haven't been racking my brains over this?' said Kitten. 'But you wouldn't hear of it, when I said that the so-called sacred banyan tree overhanging our railings towards Queensway should be pruned, because it's bound to attract our own children to climb it, besides all those monkeys.'

Grinning ruefully at Redverse after concluding this conversation, Tiger said that he would prefer to forget the more harrowing moments caused by his sons. The Resident remarked that as the father of twins—who weren't even identical—he knew the meaning of the phrase 'Double Trouble'. But with triplets whom even their mother had trouble telling apart, it must be even worse!

Tiger could never forget Kitten's response when the twins the lady doctor prepared them for, had miraculously increased by one.

'There are three of us in this family. And now, there's a son for everyone,' she had said, with a special smile for his first wife.

Now he prayed that someone would find them before they ran into real trouble, and before they drove the entire family mad with their thoughtless behaviour. But before he too strode off to join in the search for his sons, the phone rang again.

Answering the query in the Resident's eyes, the Maharajah of Fateypur said with a relieved smile: 'For once, Nutty Uncle's dogs did the trick. Siddharth, Shivraj, and Surender were flushed out of the very tree Kitten mentioned. They were discovered trying to climb down without getting caught! Now there will be no peace till I have some of it chopped down to prevent future excursions, regardless of the sanctity of bargad trees in our country.'

There had been no opportunity for Redverse and CP to discuss the issues uppermost in their minds until they gathered at the Residency on the afternoon of their return to Chattargadh from Delhi. They had met to put their heads together over the programme for Maharajah Jai Singh's Silver Jubilee celebrations. Everybody who was anybody in the State had agreed that the British Resident and Military Secretary were better qualified than R.K. Kishen or Robin (who had finally found his niche in the fledgling Indian Air Force), to undertake its organisation. Only they could ensure a memorable tribute for their beloved Maharajah on the 25th anniversary of his accession to Chattargadh's throne, make it an enjoyable occasion for everyone who participated in the week-long festivities.

After agreeing on a programme which would include traditional processions, parades, banquets, and public Durbars in addition to a horse show and inter-school sports, the two Englishmen began discussing the unequivocal orders they had both received from the Political Department regarding their role during this crucial period.

A Brigadier in the British army since 1945, Cedric Claude-Poole lit a cigarette after sinking into one of the cushioned cane chairs arranged on the sunny lawn around the tea trolley. One of the Residency bearers had wheeled it out as soon as Lady Dorothy had joined them. She discarded her hat (which hadn't done much over the years to prevent serious freckling and tanning of her extremely sensitive, creamy skin), and the secateurs with which she had been busy clipping some early jasmine and plumbago sprays for her vases. Drawing off her rubber gardening gloves, she began pouring the tea, telling the men to help themselves to the sandwiches and the walnut-topped brownies. The gardeners went off duty after collecting their various tools and cans. The shrill striped squirrels, chirping wagtails, bulbuls, grey tits, brown robins, sparrows, and other small birds which appeared and disappeared with the short desert winter, flocked around the three Britons scrounging for every biscuit, bread, and cake crumb that fell from their fingers.

A feeling of unfairness grew in CP as the Resident outlined the Labour agenda for India. Redverse realised that every Englishman who empathised with this country and its people, would balk at the unseemly haste being shown by London in abandoning the subcontinent to its own leadership and fate. Moreover the parting of ways would be hardest for people like themselves, who had 'gone native,' as so many of their envious colleagues back home often said.

They agreed that Boy Malcolm had proved prophetic. Understanding the realities of long-distance-imperial-power projection better than most British governments since his 18th-century stint as Resident in the Central Provinces, he had predicted that they would be able to keep their Indian empire going only as long as they had naval superiority in Europe.

'But damn it, Reverse Gear, why this deadline? Since when have empires become Fleet Street rags which must hit the streets before sunrise? Why not give chaps like Gandhi and Jinnah another year or two to come to a more pragmatic settlement, instead of splitting the country into three artificial units over religion, when we spent nearly two hundred years unifying it in the first place?'

'Well, CP, there's really nothing WE can do about it. HM's Government has issued clear-cut instructions about withdrawing immediately after the partition and independence of the two separate nations of India and Pakistan. I've been given only one brief: to persuade the three Princely States under my charge to sign the merger pact with either one of our successor states, because they can't possibly become viable administrative units on their own,' said the Resident.

CP's weather-beaten face hardened as he brushed a fly off his teaspoon. 'I know all that, Reverse Gear. But does Lord Wavell's replacement—who's considered the most incompetent, accident-prone bounder in naval circles—have the least inkling of how things really stand in this country? Does he know how reluctant people in Rajputana are about changing the status quo? For them feudalism has always been a two-way street, with the Maharajahs providing a safety net for virtually everyone, including hardened criminals?'

Lady Dorothy was compelled to smile at this, but added that the war had changed things drastically for the British empire. Nobody could expect India to stay stuck in some time warp merely for the convenience of Maharajahs, Military Secretaries, or Residents.

Her husband finished munching a ginger biscuit before he clarified, 'Now look here, old thing. None of us want those Congress*wallahs* to go around saying that the ship of Indian freedom floundered on the rocks of Princely Privilege and Paramountcy, do we.'

Since she had nearly broken her leg when a suddenly spooked horse had dumped her during a cross country ride (confining her to bed for four days), Dorothy had been unable to accompany them to Delhi on this particular trip when so much was happening in the country. She was really keen to hear all the latest news and gossip. 'Gerry, you haven't said a word about the goings-on in the Chamber of Princes.'

Chuckling at some funny memory, he answered: 'You know how they go on, Dorothy—with Maharajah Jai Singh and Nutty both trying to be top dog.'

'But I'm told that Tiger Fateypur emerged as their spokesman,' remarked CP, who had his own cronies among HE's staff officers.

'Tiger's a realist,' Redverse said. 'He assured the Viceroy that the Princes would federate with India, provided their rights of recognition, diplomatic privilege, privy purses and private property were guaranteed.'

'This means we'll have to move on, I suppose,' sighed Dorothy, remembering the nine delightful years they had spent in this desert state.

Gerald Redverse cast his eyes over the sun-warmed sandstone kiosks on which peacocks prepared to perch for the night, as usual. 'Well, they certainly won't be needing British Residents and Military Secretaries here much longer. But there's always the Foreign Office for chaps like us, y'know.'

'Or the tea gardens and coffee plantations scattered round Assam, Bengal, and the Nilgiris, where I'm told the British empire intends to live on!' observed CP, making his companions laugh.

Although Redverse sat enjoying the cool breeze blowing off the river through the Maharajah of Pisshengunj's garden after playing three strenuous sets of tennis with his host, he was definitely not enjoying the daft discussion going on between them. Ignoring the parading dogs (which frequently harassed their handlers by trying to chase every bird and squirrel cutting across their path), and those that growled at each other while pausing to raise their legs over the fern-filled porcelain pisspots arranged along the terrace, lawns, and paved walks, the Resident focused his eyes on Nutty. Though his dark hair was greying at the temples, not a wrinkle showed on the Maharajah's smooth, ruddy skin.

'Really, Your Highness, as the Viceroy explained to you in Delhi, Dominion Status is out of the question for any princely state. The Political Department will automatically close down with the lapse of Paramountcy, and all the Crown Agents will be withdrawn. Right now, we can help you make the best of your bargaining position.'

Perched as usual on the wrought iron garden swing from which he could keep an eye on his dogs and the ever-changing river scene, Nutty hinted at the secret leverage he alone enjoyed as master of a riparian state with a link canal to the Sutlej even as he fondled the cute, cuddly little pair of Shitzus nestled between his hairy thighs. He brushed their muddy paw prints off his otherwise pristine white tennis shorts as he leaned back with a satisfied smirk. He had just finished enumerating some of the precedents created by HM's government in its dealings with kingdoms like Afghanistan, Nepal, Bhutan, and Sikkim.

His Dewan, Baron Tikemoffsky, entering middle age with a slightly corpulent physique, thinning hair, and greying brown beard, harboured no illusions about the rapidly approaching redundance of chaps like himself once the British Raj in India ended. For once, he concurred with his wife that they would be better off in a new country where the ruling Muslim elite favoured white foreigners with good professional credentials. Jinnah's emissaries had already placed half a million pounds in escrow for him with a Swiss bank in order that he ensured Pisshengunj's inclusion in the new Islamic nation, just like Hindu Amarkot.

'But why should the sovereign State of Pisshengunj merge with India, rather than Pakistan, Reverse Gear?'

'Because the devil you know is always better than the devil you don't, Tikky.'

There were two sets of documents on the table before the Maharajah. But the flaxen-haired Englishman was getting a bit fed up with all this posturing. It was crystal clear that HH Pisshengunj had only one choice, like all his brother princes in Rajputana. What kingdoms the size of Kashmir and Hyderabad did, was none of his business.

The Maharajah of Pisshengunj frowned at the two Europeans sitting facing him across the round, glass-topped table. He gave the impression of being caught in a dilemma, which really boiled down to an aversion to those who had done precious little about averting the inexorable march of history. If nothing else, they should at least have stretched the deadline. April was already ending, and the British wanted everything signed, sealed, and delivered to their successors on August 15, as though it was some sacred, sacrosanct day, like Rama Navami or Christmas. Everyone knew that this Viceroy had pulled the date out of his hat like a raffle ticket. Nobody showed any consideration for the personal preference of Maharajahs like himself wanting to spend the summer in England and France, like any normal chap.

But he would show them that a real Rajput ruler simply couldn't be bullied. By anyone.

'Mun-humm, Resident Saab. But the trouble is, you're both foreign agents with your own hidden agenda, playing God knows what geo-strategic games with my poor State. And country. What I really need is some truly selfless advice. Which only my loyal, nonaligned Feng and Shui can give!' Scooping up the dogs playfully nipping and pushing each other in his lap, Nutty placed them on the table where the two documents—the Instrument of Accession, and Jinnah's Carte Blanche—lay open, secured by paperweights.

Quite incredulous, Redverse watched the Shitzus sniff the parchments. One dog sneezed. Then, both turned their shiny wet noses up superciliously. 'Feng sneezed. That's a bad omen!' cried HH Pisshengunj.

The very next moment, Feng and Shui were fighting a turf war over Jinnah's Carte Blanche. As they wagged their tails and tapped this piece of blank paper, Nutty laughed effusively, and patted his dogs. 'Well done, my smart Feng-Shui!'

Tikky nodded and cried 'Bravo,' echoing his master. The British Resident heaved a deep sigh. Pronounced dark circles under his eyes and two deep furrows between his brows marred his usually urbane appearance.

'Really, Your Highness, we can't have this sort of thing,' began Redverse, watching the Russian baron gloat as he uncapped a gold fountain pen, and handed it to the Maharajah with a ceremonious flourish. 'Your state's contiguity and the wishes of its Hindu majority must be taken into account before you fill in that Carte Blanche—which frankly isn't worth much.'

'Mr Redverse, my State *is* contiguous to Pakistan,' began Nutty, prepared to counter each point by holding his fingers up one by one.

'And India,' interjected the Resident.

'And the Indian Independence Act created by the British does not require any consultations between the rulers and their people before deciding on accession and merger with *your* successor states!' continued Nutty. 'Besides which, to clinch this argument, my Astrologer also recommends a Western alliance.'

'If only His Highness Pisshengunj would listen to his brother princes, instead of taking a cue from his dogs!' sighed the Resident, regaling Maharajah Jai Singh and the Viceroy's Constitutional Adviser, V.P. Menon, with stories about his unsuccessful trip to Pisshengunj, and its Nutty Maharajah's latest antics, including his decision to merge with Pakistan because Jinnah had said that every Indian state was a sovereign state.

Despite all the apprehensions raised by the Englishman's words, Jai Singh was quite amused. 'Nutty has never been known to agree with anybody about anything.'

'Really, Your Highness, it's the duty of Maharajah Pisshengunj's blood brothers to show him that he simply can't afford to play geo-strategic games at a time like this, when we've got so many problems on our hands,' said the emissary from New Delhi, wiping beads of sweat off his high-domed, intellectual forehead.

'Mr Menon, if experienced Whitehall pundits and ICS mandarins like Corfield and Reverse Gear leave so many loopholes in the Indian Independence Act, why blame chaps like my Nutty cousin for wanting to hold out for maximum advantages?' responded Jai Singh.

The canny South Indian bureaucrat assured the Maharajah that he had a valid point. 'But negotiations for winding up an existing Order are bound to prove tricky, Your Highness. And the Government of India is banking on you to steer the cousin controlling your upper riparian state in the right direction for reasons I don't need to reiterate.'

Only Maharajah Jai Singh understood that there was more to Nutty's illogical tilt towards Pakistan than mere bargain hunting. First of all, he knew that by creating an international boundary between their closely interconnected states, he would give a hammer blow to Chattargadh's prestige. Secondly, he could easily destroy the desert state's new-found prosperity by damming the CP Canal, and diverting its excess waters in the opposite direction into the Sutlej link canal. Thirdly, by opting out of the Indian Union, the Maharajah of Pisshengunj would be under no traditional family or clan pressure to name Robin or his son Pat heir to his far richer Rathor state. Last but not least, Nutty had been deeply offended when neither Kitten nor his nephew Tiger had been prepared to consider his tentative suggestion about his adopting one of the Fateypur triplets. And this despite the many precedents for an Indian kingdom passing through the female line being already set by two Begums of Bhopal, *and* Shivaji's Maratha descendants in Kohlapur. What rankled most in Nutty's heart was the fact that although his own request was denied, by one of those strange quirks of fate and female biology, Arjun Fateypur—his brother Tiger's heir presumptive until recently—had got Shivraj in adoption after Ratna developed complications due to the breech birth of their second daughter.

But Kitten's animosity towards Nutty precluded a similar civilised arrangement for her last born, Surender.

'Having consigned colonialism, despotism, and hereditary oligarchies to the rubbish bin,' observed the Maharajah, shuffling memos and papers back across the table towards the Englishman, 'we are now entering a great new era of power without responsibility.'

The Resident was silent for a moment or two before responding. 'Really, Your Highness, don't you think that elected representatives who are answerable to the people are compelled to act in a responsible manner? And that's why democracies have an edge over every other form of government.'

'D'you really believe that, Reverse Gear?'

'I'm paid to say so, Your Highness.'

They were both chuckling when Menon leaned forward to interject: 'Your Highness, if we could sort out these last points.'

'Certainly, Mr Menon. Where were we?'

'On the verge of acceding to the Indian Union,' he said, courteously holding out a document for the Maharajah's signature.

Contriving to keep a straight face, Jai Singh demurred with equal courtesy. 'For that, you'll have to go to the Chattargadh Legislative Assembly, Mr Menon, which, unlike your Central Legislative Assembly, has been elected on the principle of free and fair adult franchise every five years, since 1924.'

'Really, Your Highness,' protested the Resident. 'Isn't that rather unnecessary?'

'You know that in this State, we've been meticulous about practising what you chaps preach, Reverse Gear' said the 56-year-old Rathor ruler who along with his splendid sportsman's physique, still retained his penchant for fun.

Perceptive enough to realise early that India was heading for federation, freedom, and parliamentary democracy on the British pattern, and yet retaining the hereditary council of chiefs which had helped govern the state for centuries, Maharajah Jai Singh had introduced an elected municipality and legislature in Chattargadh within two years of ascending his throne in 1922. This was not merely common gossip throughout the country. It was also evident to anybody visiting his State. The modern Chattargadh ruler enjoyed the status of no less then a deity, being literally worshipped by his people, including all the elected legislators and counsellors.

Any one would think that HH did not have anything better to do than amuse himself by giving them all the run around, thought Redverse, as he prepared to address a joint session of the Chattargadh Legislative Assembly in his capacity as the Crown representative. The Government Of India's emissary, Menon, accompanied him. Of course, the Maharajah had, as usual, meticulously refrained from attending. But Redverse could see CP and several other camera-wielding pressmen, including some American and European stringers for Reuters and Associated Press, in the Visitors' Gallery above the large, airy chamber cooled by several ceiling fans.

Chattargadh's Dewan, R.K. Kishen Singh, chaired this formal session. Now considerably aged, Koodsu Rao Saheb and the seven other hereditary chiefs present, clad in pure white summer Jodhpur jackets and trousers, sat on one side of the oval ebony table, directly opposite the State's nine elected legislators, who wore an assortment of dhotis and dark trousers under clean, freshly ironed cotton shirts. However, saffron turbans covered everyone's head, because it was a solemn occasion.

Having come to know all of them rather well in the

years that he had served as Crown agent, the British officer
had a distinct premonition that no matter how eloquently
he advocated the cause of federation with the emerging
Indian republic, the majority would remain staunchly loyal
to a regime whose days were definitely over. He rose to
speak as coherently as he could, telling them that they had
a duty to march with the times.

'Of course, according to the clarification issued by His
Majesty's Government, the Princely States are perfectly
within their rights in refusing to have anything to do with
the Constituent Assembly of India, which is empowered by
the British Parliament to ease the transformation of this
dominion towards a sovereign democratic republic. Each
ruler is entitled to decide for himself whether his State
should federate with India or Pakistan . . . .'

'But that's not what you told His Nutty Highness, Mr
Reverse Gear,' the Chattargadh Dewan interjected, eliciting
knowing grins and chuckles from his companions around
the table.

The Resident kept his low-pitched, patrician voice
neutral. 'If you know that, Raj Kumar Saheb, you also
know that the circumstances in your sister State are quite
different to those prevailing here.'

But R.K. Kishen was always a stickler for sticking to the
point. 'Resident Saab, didn't you tell HH Pisshengunj that
he must take his people's permission before signing any
treaty which will affect their future?'

'Well, yes, but that was in an absolutely different
context . . .' began Redverse.

'What's sauce for that goose is certainly going to be
sauce for this gander!' cried Kishen boisterously in his deep,
laughter-tinged voice. Rising to his feet besides the
Resident, he continued: 'Honourable members of
Chattargadh's Legislative Assembly! According to the
democratic norms preached by the British and the Indian

National Congress, we will now take an open vote. It will make things easier for those busy photo journalists and investigative reporters who have taken the trouble of coming here today, chasing this exclusive story. Those Chiefs and MLAs who favour Chattargadh's accession and merger with Pak-less India, please raise your hands.'

The Resident could see CP grinning and V.P. Menon looking appalled as flash bulbs went off, cameras clicked, and feature writers leaned over the balcony, to memorise and record this democratic turning of tables. Every single person round that table simply folded his hands firmly across his chest, gave the typically negative native Indian shake of the head, and said an emphatic 'No!'

R.K. Kishen's rugged bronzed face creased with a triumphant smile. 'Now, all those gentlemen for retaining the autonomy of our kingdom under our enlightened Maharajah, kindly raise your hands.'

All the chiefs and MLAs spontaneously raised their hands, crying 'Yes!'

The news was flashed instantly to the crowds collected outside the Assembly building. Loud cheers invoking a long life and victory for Maharajah Jai Singh rent the air as enthusiastic citizens flaunted the State's flag. Some drummers led the rejoicing crowds, which got its first taste of people's power as they rushed towards the Fort, where their Maharajah waited.

By August, the political situation outside Rajputana was in such an intolerable mess, with the country hurtling towards Partition and Independence, that Maharajah Jai Singh was compelled to veto all extravagance. He insisted on low-key celebrations to mark the silver jubilee of his accession to the throne, which he would, as he had made clear, voluntarily relinquish on the very date, August 15.

As the Resident had expected all along, after having his

moment of fun on the day of the voting, Maharajah Jai
Singh had signed the Instrument of Accession. He had first
taken care to appease the bewildered loyal legislators and
delegations of citizens (who saw no logic behind the
abolition of their paternalistic Princely State in exchange for
some nebulous new government functioning from distant
Delhi) and then, had done so. Jai Singh had also convinced
his ministers and officials to divert all the donations
received for his jubilee celebrations towards the setting up
of proper refugee camps, colonies, and rehabilitation centres
for the victims of communal carnage, slowly drifting into
Chattargadh from Punjab.

The family members gathered at the palace for this
occasion laughed at the story told by Maharajah Jai Singh
about how R.K. Kishen had buckled down to riot
prevention by banning the sale of items which might offend
Hindu or Muslim sensibilities. These included items such as
pork, beef, jelly, and cheese, without which the various
Europeans and Anglo-Indians serving in Chattargadh found
it hard to survive. The ban also included Bull's-eye sweets—
to which all his grandsons seemed so addicted.

They were still laughing when an ADC brought him a
sealed note.

'Bullshit!' cried Tiger, sharing the intelligence conveyed
in the note with HH Chattargadh.

His father-in-law said that, on reflection, he should have
smelt a rat when, instead of insisting on his usual suite, and
the full formality of a pukka 19-gun salute, Nutty had sent
a last-minute apology saying that he was too ill to travel—
even by air.

And now here was his own wife—Koodsu Rao Saheb's
sister, Neeru Baa—pleading *in writing* that the Chattargadh
family must prevent their exile to Pakistan, because Nutty
had four Dakotas loaded and ready to fly them off the very
next day.

With his usual candour, Robin remarked that it would be good riddance. But Maharani Padmini, Princess Diamond, Sir Pratab, and even Arjun, disagreed.

So did the Resident, hastily summoned to resolve this unexpected crisis. 'If it were any other state, I'd say let Jinnah reap what his Carte Blanches have sown. But in this instance, I tend to agree with Your Highness. For we really can't afford the luxury of allowing HH Pisshengunj to fly off to Pakistan, leaving our own State high and dry, no matter what the tripartite agreement says.'

However, nobody had any practical solutions for what was destined to become a fait accompli. 'Really, Your Highness, we've got to stop him. Perhaps Tiger could fly down to Pisshengunj, and talk some sense into his uncle,' suggested Redverse.

Tiger said, with his usual sang-froid, that although THAT was impossible, he could try kidnapping his Nutty Uncle in the national interest.

'Be realistic,' countered the British official. Kidnapping the Maharajah of Pisshengunj from his own palace wasn't going to be possible in the short time at their disposal.

But Tiger clearly felt that nothing else would prevent his Nutty uncle from flying off to Lahore, and handing his rich riparian state over to Pakistan in exchange for all the benefits enjoyed by his Indian counterparts, plus a permanent seat on its governing council as spokesman for the new nation's Hindu minority. He was also quite capable of internationalising the issue by appealing to the United Nations.

With her well-established, incisive ability to get to the heart of any matter, Maharani Padmini felt that the key to resolving this strategic problem lay in Tiger's hand. She urged her son-in-law to offer HH Pisshengunj a last-minute, face-saving device, by giving his energies a positive direction.

'He's childless, but very good with children and animals, as we all know. You will be performing an invaluable national service by permitting the adoption your maternal uncle has been clamouring for. It will automatically involve accession to India for the sake of finally acquiring an heir. It will also prevent the inclusion of our upper riparian state's largely Hindu population in an Islamic theocratic nation, besides securing our own desert State's prosperity thanks to unchecked water-sharing. As rulers, you and Kitten have a larger duty, which you've got to keep in mind even while indulging in this endless Rajput tit for tat.'

Setting down the glass of iced water which was better than any juice, squash, or sherbet for quenching thirst on this searing hot summer day, Kitten announced that her mother was, as usual, right. She was prepared to concede adoption in the larger public interest, because otherwise Uncle Nutty would create an intolerable situation for lakhs of people.

However, she felt that they were not tackling this problem in a logical way. 'Of course, we can't abduct Uncle Nutty. But, we can make him come to us *like that*,' she said, snapping her fingers.

The playful gleam in his versatile young wife's eyes was not lost on Tiger. 'How?' he demanded, sceptical yet curious.

'Simple,' smiled Kitten. 'First we hijack his dogs.'

Her parents protested; and all her other relatives, except Arjun, scoffed at this suggestion. Recalling her penchant for solving tricky problems, plus getting her own way despite dire predictions and the most overwhelming odds, he asked his elders and the Resident to at least hear Kitten out.

Knowing his daughter too well, especially when she had her imagination unleashed, Maharajah Jai Singh suggested that everybody make themselves comfortable and sit down before they heard what Kitten had to say.

She began by pointing out that since the family seemed to dislike the word 'hijack'—though what she was proposing was just like piracy on the high seas—they'd give it a different name. 'Let's call it a mercy mission. But you'll have to come along with us, Mr Redverse, because His Majesty's writ still runs in this country.'

'Only till midnight tomorrow,' the Resident hastened to clarify.

'Not to worry. That still leaves us plenty of time to take care of everything. It's a good thing that Her Highness Pisshengunj had the sense to state their take-off time, as well as their flight destination. And what could be more natural than Tiger Baapji openly landing up in Pisshengunj to dissuade Nutty Uncle from committing this fatal blunder?'

She went on to suggest that, according to both Chanakya and Machiavelli, it would be the easiest to bribe Nutty Uncle's pilots into surrendering their planes. They could, of course, ask the Crown Representative to serve the pilots with requisition orders: 'For emergency duties, y'know. Hints about impounding their British passports will ensure their cooperation, because even the two Irishmen employed by Uncle Nutty wouldn't want to risk THAT!'

And when her brother Robin, the youngest Air Commodore in India's air force, demanded who would then fly those four hijacked Dakotas all the way home to Chattargadh in the middle of August (when sudden summer sandstorms could make flying in zero visibility dangerous even for the most experienced pilots), the Princess put up her chin.

An acrimonious argument followed. Maharajah Jai Singh's heir refused to have Miss Sticking Plaster tagging along. His sister countered by asking the Prince if he had forgotten how to count.

'FIVE planes have to be flown back here from Pisshengunj.

Nutty Uncle always insists on sitting in the cockpit with his own pilot, Tikky. That's one. Then there's Tiger Baapji. You two brothers, and I, will fly the other three.'

The Resident settled their squabble by recalling firmly how Her Highness Fateypur—meaning Kitten—had won her solo pilot's wings in Crown Prince Rudolf's Dakota, way back in 1940.

'She's certainly capable of flying mercy missions.'

The Maharajah of Pisshengunj was confident that as soon as he reached Lahore, Jinnah or his deputies would immediately dispatch a task force to strengthen the State forces, which consisted largely of clansmen conditioned to obeying his orders. He had already had secret discussions with the Englishman appointed Commander-in-Chief of the Pakistan army regarding this operation. Thus, he was perfectly confident about immediate back-up support, once he crossed this Rubicon. But until New Delhi accepted the fait accompli of his merger with Pakistan, he had decided to stay away from his home. He did not want anyone to indulge in last-minute arm-twisting.

Nutty glanced at his diamond-dialled Swiss wristwatch as his High Priest entered the drawing room, accompanied by another brahmin, carefully carrying a tray containing a largish copper bowl with a cover. Continuing to chant some Sanskrit mantra, the priests turned their faces away. The Maharajah removed the silver lid, and gazed at his own face reflected in the pure mustard oil contained in the deep bowl. Then, he held his hands over the copper bowl, fingers down, so that he could study his nails in the oil. This would ward off all evil before he embarked on his journey.

Kitted out in his flying togs (because piloting his master around was part of his strategy for remaining indispensable), Baron Tikemoffsky approached the Maharajah as soon as the priests withdrew after performing the rite. 'All set for take off, Your Highness,' he announced with a courtly bow.

Putting his shoes on again, Nutty said, 'Good. Have the dogs and Maharanis been sent ahead?'

'Yes, Your Highness.'

'Then let's go.'

However, just as the Maharajah was about to step into his waiting Rolls Royce, one of the Pisshengunj ADCs (waiting deferentially in the portico to see off his ruler), sneezed.

The Maharajah immediately halted in his tracks, murmuring a curse under his breath for this inauspicious sneeze guaranteed to bring bad luck, as everybody knew. But his Dewan, Tikky, urged HH to overlook this insignificant matter. 'Really, Your Highness, we must take off before it gets dark, and overflying is prohibited by the increasingly hostile new nations of India and Pakistan.'

At first, everything seemed normal to the Maharajah of Pisshengunj when he reached the private airfield located on flat ground close to the river. But, as he hurried towards the planes ready and waiting for take-off, his large protruding eyes swept the place for the least sign of anything unusual. He was a trifle nervous, especially after that inconsiderate, ill-mannered chap had sneezed just as he was stepping out of his home for the most significant journey of his life. It was then that Nutty turned to the planes again. He began to count. No matter which way he counted, up or down, top to bottom, this way or that, there were *five* Dakotas on his airfield.

'Tikky, who asked you to buy the fifth plane?' demanded the Maharajah.

Equally puzzled and hastening to deny all responsibility, Tikky demurred: 'Really, Your Highness, there seems to be a slip-up somewhere. But I'll get to the bottom of this once . . .'

'Don't give me any of your usual lame excuses,' said Nutty, cutting his Dewan short. 'As you know, I can very well afford a dozen Dakotas. But I hate being disobeyed in anything.'

Tikky cajoled the Maharajah to board the plane. Once they were safely strapped into their cockpit seats, Tikky gave the ground crew the ready-for-take-off signal. Propellers whirled. One by one, the planes taxied off with a slowly increasing ear-splitting noise and spiralling ground winds which flattened all the adjacent grass, tufts, and trees.

Eager to complete this journey without a single hitch, Tikky set course for Lahore as soon as they were airborne. It would be a short uneventful flight, for he had frequently flown HH Pisshengunj to this Punjabi city for various polo matches, weddings, and other functions. Down below, the setting sun sparkled off the Guptaganga river, and the crazy quilt of rain-washed green fields, mud brick hamlets, and tiny thatch-roofed villages set between ancient temples and newer Sikh shrines. There were no signs yet of the reported carnage and destruction inflicted on this needlessly partitioned land. The Shivalik foothills were only faintly visible to the north against a strangely inflamed sky.

The Maharajah urged Tikky to check if the planes containing all his dogs and his three wives, were flying alongside in tight formation.

However, before Tikky could carry out this command, the Maharajah of Pisshengunj was shocked by the sudden appearance of a Dakota swooping straight across their flight path. 'Tikky, tell those fools to behave. I don't care if we're employing two former flying aces *and* a veteran RAF pilot. This is no time for showing off. I want them to observe proper protocol by staying *behind* me even up in the air!'

Tikky began using the radio, which had been pre-set to an interplane frequency, allowing HH Pisshengunj's flight armada to maintain close radio contact with each other throughout the two-hour flight. 'Hello hello! Royal Mary to all her lambs!'

In an adjacent plane—turning annoying aerobatic capers which grossly violated the Maharajah of Pisshengunj's code of decorum—Maharajah Tiger Fateypur turned to his companion. 'Ready, Reverse Gear? One, two, three . . . .'

A cacophony of male voices—one distinctly aristocratic and very English—cackled over the headsets worn by HH Pisshengunj and his pilot, Tikky. 'Mary had a little dog, little dog, little dog . . . .'

And then followed Kitten's frightfully well-known contralto voice: 'And everywhere that doggy went, doggy went, doggy went, Nutty Uncle was sure to go!'

The Maharajah of Pisshengunj balled his fists as he fumed and sputtered with suppressed fury. Sitting helplessly strapped into place by his seat belt, he was unable to prevent this blatant air piracy. 'Just WAIT till I get my hands on you, Kitten!' he swore over the air waves, realising that no amount of MAYDAY distress signals sent to any ground control tower would get his precious dogs out of Kitten's clutches—especially with the British Raj representative aiding and abetting her.

'Oh my God! How did this catastrophe *happen*?' frowned Tikky, as his plane was boxed in by the four Dakotas hijacked by HH Fateypur's squadron of relations.

'This has happened because some bloody fool sneezed just as I was leaving Pisshengunj,' declared the angry Maharajah.

'Really, Your Highness, we must lodge a strong protest with His Majesty's Government about this gross, unforgivable violation of our treaty rights,' advised his White Russian Dewan.

Tiger made a perfect three-point landing in Chattargadh with Robin, Arjun, and Kitten bringing their own heavy planes down one by one without any hitch. And, even before Nutty's plane had stopped taxiing after touchdown, Maharajah

Jai Singh gave the signal to the grand reception committee laid on for his forced-to-come-visiting brother prince.

Gun salutes boomed the moment HH Pisshengunj set foot on the ladder rolled up to his plane. Chattargadh's brass and bagpipe bands began playing the Rathor rallying song. The Guard of Honour stood ready to present arms. Splendidly accoutred, the Chattargadh Camel Corps and cavalry contingents sat their mounts, ready to escort the three Maharajahs, their Maharanis, the various princes, and the Resident back to the palace for the celebrations.

Ignoring the claims of Maharajah Jai Singh, Maharani Padmini, Princess Diamond, Sir Pratab, and R.K. Kishen, the Maharajah of Pisshengunj fixed his entire attention on the three identical boys standing ready to garland him. Too excited to stand still, Siddharth, Shivraj, and Surender began pelting their grand uncle with questions about his dogs, his planes, and what they would all be doing the next day.

'We'll definitely have lots of fun *after* I've settled a few things with your parents,' promised Nutty, pouncing on Tiger, who stood surrounded protectively by all his aunts. 'You traitor! Just let me get my hands on you.'

Dodging behind Princess Diamond, Tiger crowed: 'Uncle Nutty, you've just incurred *two* lifelong debts to your devoted nephew . . . .'

'For providing you with a regular flying circus of blood relations—plus our Resident—to make sure you can't be hijacked lock, stock and dogs by some wicked foreign agents!' grinned Kitten.

Never one to accept defeat gracefully, Nutty shook a finger belligerently in his niece's face. 'Just you wait, Kitten. One of these days, I'm really going to fix you!'

'Of course, Uncle Nutty. It's a free country. But then, who's going to spare you a grand-nephew for adoption?' countered the Chattargadh Princess, having the last word as usual.

Glossary

Aarti. Ritual lamps for gods, goddesses, newly-weds, honoured guests, elders, warriors and rulers.

Akhand jyot. Eternal flame or lamp.

Angrez. Englishman or woman.

Anta, Annadata. Lord and Master, patriarchal ruler who provides food to his people.

Ateethi Devo Bhava. Guests are Gods.

Avatar. Incarnation of God.

Baapji. Father, elder brother, honoured ruler, prince.

Babalog. Children.

Baisa. Princess, sister, lady.

Bajarang bali ki jai. Victory to mighty Hanuman (Rama's devotee, deified as the Hindu Monkey god).

Bajas. Radiograms, musical instruments.

Bandhgala. High-necked Jodhpuri jacket.

Bargad. Large banyan tree.

Bhai. Brother.

Bilayati. European.

Bindi. Dots worn on forehead by Indian married women and girls.

Chawari. Yak-tail whisk.

Chaprasis. Peons.

Chay-pani inaam. Tip for tea, etc.

Chota maharanisa. Junior maharani.

Chukker. Round of polo.

Dewan. Prime Minister.

Dhoti-kurta. Intricately tied unstitched lower garment, and long shirt traditionally worn by Indian men.

Fargal. Long robe.

Fireng memsahebs. European women.

Gadbad ghotala. Awful mess.

Ganga jal. Holy water from the river Ganges.

Ghor kaliyug. The present wicked 'black' era in human history according to Indian mythology.

Guru Maharaj. Spiritual guide, teacher.

'Hajeer Hai'. 'Present, at your service.'

'Hajoor'. 'Highness, Lord, Sir.'

Haka. Noisy beat in jungles during Indian shikar.

Havan. Vedic fire worship performed at major social and religious functions.

'Idhar aah-woh'. 'Come here.'

Jadoo toona. Black magic.

Jagir. Fiefdom recognised and/or gifted by the Maharajah.

Jagran. All night vigil, with chanting of hymns and prayers.

'Jai Jai Siya Ram'. 'Praised be goddess Sita and god Ram.'

Jawaisa. Brother-in-law, son-in-law.

Jiji. Elder sister, nanny, or nurse in Rajasthan.

'Joh Hukum'. 'Your orders will be obeyed.'

Johar. Literally splendour; actually the Rajput ritual of war unto death for men and women alike, when voluntary self-immolation in ritual fire was performed by all females incapable of bearing arms but determined to preserve their honour from all enemies.

Julam Injustice.

Kaleens. Carpets.

Kathiawari. Recognised breed of mixed Arab and Indian horses bred in India's Kathiawar region.

Keekar. Thorny desert tree.

Khamaghani. Masonic style greetings exchanged only between two Rajputs or addressed to Rajput royalty and aristocracy.

Khamma. Greetings.

Khus. Scented vetiver screens used for cooling rooms in summer.

Lat Sahebs. British Lords.

Machans. Tree-top platforms used for big game shikar.

Maharaj Kumar, Yuvraj. Maharajah's son and heir.

Mahavat. Man who cares for and controls elephants.

Malis. Gardeners.

Marwar. Rajasthan's desert region, specially Jodhpur, Bikaner, Jaisalmer and Badmer.

Marwari. People of the Marwar desert region, specially the business and mercantile class.

Mor chari. Peacock feathers.

Modas. Round, high-backed cane chairs or squat stools.

Natch-gaana. Dancing and singing.

Pan. Green befel leaf chewed throughout India and parts of Asia.

Peel khana. Elephant enclosure.

Phata-fatt. Quickly.

Poshaks. Traditional festive costumes worn by ladies and gentlemen.

'Raghu kul reeti sada chali ayi, pran jayi par vachan na jayi'. The Rajput code which dictates that Rama's descendants honour their word, even if they must sacrifice their lives.

Raj tilak. Coronation.

Rajwara. Royal families.

Rakhris. Jewelled head ornaments worn by Rajasthani women.

Ranbanka Rathor. Historically, the Rathors, more than any other Rajput clan, fought with such magnificent madness that they earned the sobriquet 'Devastating in Battle.'

Rawlas. Queens' Court or palaces.

Rudraksha. Beads made of berries from the Himalayan tree called Rudraksha, dear to the Hindu god Shiva. The berries are believed to have soothing medicinal properties and assist in meditation.

Sarpech. Turban ornament.

Seth-Sahukars. Merchant princes.

Shabash. Well done.

Shastra puja. Ritual weapon worship by the Rajput warrior class.

Shikar khana. Hunting department in princely states.

Sipahis. Soldiers.

Sirayati Sardars. Shareholder chiefs, hereditary Rajput noblemen ruling feudal fiefdoms by right of conquest.

Sisodiyas, Shyanis, Bhatis, Rathors. Different Rajput clans ruling different kingdoms and fiefdoms in Rajasthan and parts of India.

Swadeshi. Indigenous, made in India.

Tamasha. Show, disturbance.

Tantric. Esoteric Indian cult focusing on attainment of spiritual and temporal power through ritual Shakti worship involving mantras, tantras, yoga, etc.

Tikka. Saffron and sandal wood paste or *kumkum* mark on forehead.

Tonga. Horse carriages.

Upachar. Remedy.

Vijay Dashmi, Dussehra. Festival celebrating Lord Rama's victory over King Ravana; it falls in October according to the lunar calendar.

Wallahs. Persons.

Yuvrani. Heir's wife, crown princess.

Zenana. Segregated women's quarters.